## Praise for *Redemption Road*

'There's no easier way to say it: *Redemption Road* is simply great writing.'

Brad Meltzer, #1 *New York Times* Bestselling Author

'Big, bold, and impossible to put down, *Redemption Road* had me from page one. John Hart is a master storyteller.'

Harlan Coben

'Five years have gone by since his fourth novel, 2011's *Iron House* was published, but *Redemption Road* proves the wait was worth it. While Hart's previous mysteries were atmospheric tales enhanced by aspects of the Southern novel, *Redemption Road* is fueled by more of a thriller plot with acute attention to its well-sculpted characters. As the title implies, Hart's novel is about redemption, but also about trust and betrayal, and those emotional roads that most of us never want to travel.'

*Washington Times*

'John Hart writes like a poet, and I couldn't put down this novel, an utterly riveting story of crime and its profound ripple effects on the human psyche. I have long been a fan of John Hart, but in *Redemption Road*, he has topped himself.'

Lisa Scottoline, *New York Times* Bestselling Author of *Corrupted*

'In this stellar crime thriller, Edgar-winner Hart (*Iron House*) explores the human capacity for resilience and trust in the face of heartbreaking betrayal . . . Though Hart employs plot twists effectively, it's his powerful, wo        
readers will remember.'

## ALSO BY JOHN HART

*Iron House*
*The Last Child*
*Down River*
*The King of Lies*

# REDEMPTION ROAD

## JOHN HART

HODDER

First published in Great Britain in 2016 by Hodder & Stoughton
An Hachette UK company

First published in paperback in 2017

1

A CIP catalogue record for this title is available from the British Library

Paperback ISBN 978 1 848 54183 2
eBook ISBN 978 1 848 54539 7

Typeset in Minion Pro 10.75/13.75 pt by Palimpsest Book Production Limited,
Falkirk, Stirlingshire

Printed and bound in Great Britain by Clays Ltd, St Ives plc

Hodder & Stoughton policy is to use papers that are natural,
renewable and recyclable products and made from wood grown in sustainable
forests. The logging and manufacturing processes are expected to conform
to the environmental regulations of the country of origin.

Hodder & Stoughton Ltd
Carmelite House
50 Victoria Embankment
London EC4Y 0DZ

www.hodder.co.uk

*For Norde, Matthew, and Mickey.*
*Good men gone . . .*

# ACKNOWLEDGMENTS

I'd like to thank the following people for their kindness, support, and patience: Sally Richardson, John Sargent, Thomas Dunne, Kate Parkin, Nick Sayers, Jennifer Enderlin, Pete Wolverton, Christian Rohr, and Esther Newberg. As always there are others who mattered so much—family and friends—but the unwavering support of such outstanding publishers, editors, and agents has been more than meaningful.

Few books succeed without the tireless efforts of caring, knowledgeable people, and no one understands that better than a working novelist. In that spirit—and in addition to the industry professionals listed above—I would also like to thank Emma Stein, Jeffery Capshew, Ken Holland, Cathy Turiano, Kenneth J. Silver, Paul Hochman, Jeff Dodes, Tracey Guest, Emi Battaglia, Justin Vellela, Jimmy Iacobelli, and Michael Storrings. I would also like to thank the Macmillan sales force—true professionals, and simply the best.

I'd also like to mention the Honorable James Randolph, who advised me on the law. Any mistakes in that arena are mine alone. I'd also like to thank Markus Wilhelm, who has always been supportive. Inman Majors read an early draft and offered exceptional insight. Special thanks goes to the boys of The Hung Jury—Corban, John, Inman, and Chad—you guys are the best, and I love what we've built.

My wife, as always, was a saint, and my children spectacular. Final thanks, then, to Katie, Saylor, and Sophie. None of this makes sense without you.

*It's a cold and it's a broken halleluja.*

—LEONARD COHEN

# REDEMPTION ROAD

# YESTERDAY

The woman was a rare beauty in that she knew nothing of her perfection. He'd watched her long enough to suspect as much, but only in meeting her had his instinct been proven true. She was modest and shy, and easily swayed. Perhaps she was insecure or not very bright. Maybe she was lonesome or confused about her place in this difficult world.

It didn't matter, really.

She looked right, and that was all about the eyes.

Hers flashed as she came down the sidewalk, the sundress loose around her knees, but not inappropriate. He liked the way the dress shifted, and how neatly she moved her legs and arms. She was pale skinned and quiet. He'd have preferred her hair a little different, but that was okay.

It really was about the eyes.

They had to be clear and deep and unguarded, so he watched carefully to make sure nothing had changed in the few days since they'd agreed to meet. She looked about in an apologetic way, and from a distance he could sense the unhappiness born of bad *boyfriends and a meaningless job. She hoped life would be more. He understood that in a way most men would not.*

*"Hello, Ramona."*

*She shied unabashedly away now that they were so close to each other. Her lashes were dark on the curve of her cheek, her head angled so that he lost sight of her flawless jaw.*

*"I'm glad we decided to do this," he said. "I think it will be an afternoon well spent."*

*"Thank you for making the time." She blushed, the eyes still downcast. "I know you're busy."*

*"The future matters for all of us, life and the living of it, career and family and personal satisfaction. It's important to plan and think things through. There's no need to do it alone, not in a town like this. We know each other here. We help each other. You'll understand that once you live here longer. The people are nice. It's not just me."*

*She nodded, but he understood the deeper feelings. They'd met as if by accident, and she was wondering why she'd opened up so readily and to such a stranger. But that was his gift—his face and his gentle manner, the way they trusted. Some women needed that: the shoulder, the patience. Once they knew his interest was not romantic, it was easy. He was steady and kind. They thought him worldly.*

*"Are you ready, then?" He opened the car door, and for an instant she looked unsettled, her gaze lingering on cigarette burns and torn vinyl. "It's a loaner," he said. "I apologize, but my usual car needed service."*

*She bit her bottom lip, muscles tightening in the back of one smooth calf. Stains marred the dash. The carpet was worn through.*

*She needed a push.*

*"We were supposed to do this tomorrow, remember? Late afternoon? Coffee and a chat?" A smile creased his face. "I would have had the other car if plans had stayed the same. But you needed to change the day. It was kind of last-minute, and we're really doing this for you . . ."*

*He let the words trail off so she'd remember that she'd suggested the meeting and not the other way around. She nodded a final time because it made sense and because she didn't want to look like the kind of person who cared about something as meaningless as a car, not when she was too broke to buy her own. "My mother's coming in from Tennessee in the morning." She glanced back at the apartment building, new lines at the corners of her mouth. "It was unexpected."*

*"Yes."*

*"And she's my mom."*

*"You told me. I know." A little frustration was in his voice, a little impatience. He smiled to take out the sting, though the last thing he wanted was to be reminded of the girl's hillbilly roots in some hillbilly town. "It's my nephew's car," he said. "He's in college."*

*"That explains it, then."*

*She meant the smell and the dirt; but she was laughing now, so he laughed, too. "Kids," he said.*

*"Yeah, right."*

*He made a mock bow and said something about chariots. She laughed, but he was no longer paying attention.*

*She was already in the car.*

*"I enjoy a Sunday." She sat straight as he slid behind the wheel. "The stillness and the quiet. No expectations." She smoothed the skirt and showed the eyes. "Don't you love a Sunday?"*

*"Of course," he said, but couldn't care less. "Did you tell your mother we were meeting?"*

*"Not a chance," the girl said. "There'd be a million questions. She'd say I was needy or irresponsible, that I should have called her instead."*

*"Perhaps you underestimate her."*

*"Not my mother, no."*

*He nodded as if he understood her isolation. The mother was overbearing, the father distant or dead. He turned the key and liked the way she sat—back straight, both hands folded neatly in her lap. "The people who love us tend to see what they want to see, and not what we really are. Your mother should look more closely. I think she'd be pleasantly surprised."*

*The comment made her happy.*

*He pulled away from the curb and talked enough to keep her that way. "What about your friends?" he asked. "The people you work with? Do they know?"*

*"Only that I'm meeting someone today, and that it's personal." She smiled and showed the warm, rich eyes that had drawn him in the first place. "They're very curious."*

*"I'm sure they are," he said; and she smiled a second time.*

*It took a dozen minutes for her to ask the first meaningful question. "Wait a minute. I thought we were having coffee."*

*"I'm taking you somewhere else first."*

*"What do you mean?"*

*"It's a surprise."*

*She craned her neck as the city sank behind them. Fields and woods ran off in either direction. The empty road seemed to take new meaning as her fingers touched her throat, her cheek. "My friends will expect me back."*

*"I thought you didn't tell them."*

*"Did I say that?"*

*He gave her a look, but didn't respond. The sky outside was purple, the sun an orange push through the trees. They were far past the edge of town, an abandoned church settling quietly on a distant hill, its steeple broken as if by the weight of the darkening sky. "I love a ruined church," he said.*

*"What?"*

*"Don't you see it?"*

*He pointed, and she stared at the ancient stone, the twisted cross. "I don't understand."*

*She was worried; trying to convince herself everything was normal. He watched blackbirds settle on the ruins. A few minutes later, she asked him to take her home.*

*"I'm not feeling well."*

*"We're almost there."*

*She was scared now—he could tell—frightened of his words and the church and the strange, flat whistle that hissed between his lips.*

*"You have very expressive eyes," he said. "Has anyone ever told you that?"*

*"I think I'm going to be sick."*

*"You'll be fine."*

*He turned the car onto a gravel road, the world defined by trees and dusk and the heat of her skin. When they passed an open gate in a rusted fence, the girl began to cry. It was quiet, at first, then less so.*

*"Don't be afraid," he said.*

*"Why are you doing this?"*

*"Doing what?"*

*She cried harder, but didn't move. The car rolled out of the trees and into a clearing choked with weeds and old equipment and bits of rusted metal. An empty silo rose, round and streaked, its pinnacle stained pink by the falling sun. At its base a small door gaped, the space beyond it black and still. She stared up at the silo and, when she looked back down, saw handcuffs in his hand.*

*"Put these on."*

*He dropped the cuffs in her lap, and a warm, wet stain spread beneath them. He watched her stare desperately through the windows, looking for people or sunlight or reasons to hope.*

*"Pretend it's not real," he said.*

*She put on the cuffs, the metal clinking like tiny bells. "Why are you doing this?"*

*It was the same question, but he didn't blame her. He turned off the engine and listened to it tick in the stillness. It was hot in the clearing. The car smelled of urine, but he didn't mind. "We were supposed to do this tomorrow." He pushed a stun gun against her ribs and watched her twitch as he pulled the trigger. "I don't need you till then."*

# 1

Gideon Strange opened his eyes to dark and heat and the sound of his father weeping. He held very still, though the sobbing was neither new nor unexpected. His father often ended up in the corner—huddled as if his son's bedroom were the world's last good place—and Gideon thought about asking why, after all these years, his father was still so sad and weak and broken. It would be a simple question, and if his father were any kind of man, he'd probably answer it. But Gideon knew what his father would say and so kept his head on the pillow and watched the dark corner until his father pulled himself up and crossed the room. For long minutes he stood silently, looking down; then he touched Gideon's hair and tried to whisper himself strong, saying, *Please, God, please,* then asking strength from his long-dead wife, so that *Please, God* turned into *Help me, Julia.*

Gideon thought it was pitiful, the helplessness and tears, the shaking, dirty fingers. Holding still was the hardest part, not because his mother was dead and had no answer, but because Gideon knew that if he moved at all, his father might ask if he was awake or sad or equally lost. Then Gideon would have to tell the truth, not that he was any of those things, but that he was more lonesome inside than any boy his age should be. But his father didn't speak again. He ran fingers through his son's hair and stood perfectly still as if whatever strength he sought might magically find him. Gideon knew that would never happen. He'd seen pictures of his father before and had a few dim memories of a man who laughed and smiled and didn't drink most every hour of every day. For years he'd thought that man might return, that it could still happen. But Gideon's father wore his days like a faded suit, an empty man whose only passion rose from thoughts of his long-dead wife. He seemed alive enough then, but what use were flickers or hints?

The man touched his son's hair a final time, then crossed the room and pulled the door shut. Gideon waited a minute before rolling out of bed, fully dressed. He was running on caffeine and adrenaline, trying hard to remember the last time he'd slept or dreamed or thought of anything else besides what it would take to kill a man.

Swallowing hard, he cracked the door, trying to ignore that his arms were skinny-white and his heart was running fast as a rabbit's. He told himself that fourteen years was man enough, and that he didn't need to be any older to pull a trigger. God wanted boys to become men, after all, and Gideon was only doing what his father would do if his father were man enough to do it. That meant killing and dying were part of God's plan, too, and Gideon said as much in the dark of his mind, trying hard to convince the parts of him that shook and sweated and wanted to throw up.

Thirteen years had passed since his mother's murder, then three weeks since Gideon had found his father's small, black gun, and ten more days since he'd figured out a 2:00 a.m. train would carry him to the gray, square prison on the far side of the county. Gideon knew kids who'd hopped trains before. The key, they said, was to run fast and not think on how sharp and heavy those big, shiny wheels truly were. But Gideon worried he'd jump and miss and go under. He had nightmares about it every night, a flash of light and dark, then pain so true he woke with an ache in the bones of his legs. It was an awful image, even awake, so he pushed it down and cracked the door wide enough to see his father slumped in an old brown chair, a pillow squeezed to his chest as he stared at the broken television where Gideon had hidden the gun after he stole it from his father's dresser drawer two nights ago. He realized now that he should have kept the gun in his room, but there was no better hiding place, he'd thought, than the dried-out guts of a busted-up television that hadn't worked since he was five.

But how to get to the gun when his father sat right in front of it?

Gideon should have done it differently, but his thoughts ran crooked sometimes. He didn't mean to be difficult. It just worked out that way, so that even the kind teachers suggested he think more about woodshop and metalworking than about the fancy words in all those great, heavy books. Standing in the dark, he thought maybe those teachers were right, after all, because without the gun he couldn't shoot or protect himself or show God he had the will to do *necessary things*.

After a minute, he closed the door, thinking, *Two o'clock train . . .*

But the clock already said 1:21.

Then 1:30.

Checking the door again, he watched a bottle go up and down until his father slumped and the bottle slipped from his fingers. Gideon waited five more minutes, then crept to the living room and stepped over engine parts and other bottles, tripping once as a car rumbled past and splashed light through a gap in the curtains. When it was dark again, he knelt behind the television, slipped off the back, and pulled out a gun that was black and slick and heavier than he remembered. He cracked the cylinder, checked the bullets.

"Son?"

It was the small voice, the small man. Gideon stood and saw that his father was awake—a man-shaped hole in a stretch of stained upholstery. He seemed uncertain and afraid, and for a moment Gideon wanted to go back under the sheets. He could call everything off; pretend none of this had ever happened.

It would be nice, he thought, not to kill a man. He could put the gun down and go back to bed. But he saw the halo of flowers in his father's hands. They were dry and brittle now, but his mother, on her wedding day, had worn them like a crown in her hair. He looked at them, again—baby's breath and white roses, all of it pale and brittle—then imagined how the room would look if a stranger were looking down from above: the man with dead flowers, the boy with the gun. Gideon wanted to explain the power of that image—to make his father understand that the boy had to do what the father would not. Instead he turned and ran. He heard his name again, but was already through the door, half falling as he leapt off the porch and hit the ground running, the gun warm now in his hand, the impact from hard concrete slamming up his shins as he ran half a block, then ducked through an old man's yard and into thick woods that ran east with the creek, then up a big hill to where chain-link sagged and factories were rusted shut.

He fell against the fence as his father, far behind him, called his name over and over, his voice so loud it broke and cracked and finally failed. For a second, Gideon hesitated, but when a train whistled in the west, he pushed the gun under the fence and scrambled over the top, tearing skin as he did and banging both knees when he landed wrong in the overgrown parking lot on the other side.

The train's whistle blew louder.

*He didn't have to do it.*

*No one had to die.*

But that was the fear talking. His mother was dead, and her killer needed to pay. So he aimed for a gap between the burned-out furniture plant and the place that used to make thread but now had one whole side falling in. It was darker between the buildings, but even with loose bricks under his feet Gideon made it, without falling, to a hole in the fence near the big white oak in the far corner. There was light from a streetlamp and from a few low stars, but it disappeared as he belly-slid under the wire and plunged into a gully on the far side. The dirt was dry and loose going down. He slipped—scrabbling to keep the gun from falling out in the blackness—then splashed through a trickle of water and clambered up the other side to stand breathless in an alley of scrub that spread out from metal tracks that looked white against the dirt.

He bent at the waist, cramping; but the train rounded a bend and blasted light up the hill.

It would have to slow, he thought.

But it didn't.

It hit the hill like the hill was nothing. Three engines and a wall of metal, it blew past as if it could strip the air from his lungs. But more cars came onto the hill every second, and Gideon had a sense of it in the dark, of fifty cars and then another hundred, their weight dragging at the engines until he realized the train had slowed so much he could almost keep up. And that's what he tried to do, running fast as the wheels sparked yellow and built a vacuum that sucked at the bones of his legs. He scrabbled at one car and then another, but the rungs were high and slick.

He risked a glance and saw the last cars racing up behind him, twenty maybe, and then less. If he missed the train, he missed the prison. His fingers stretched, but he fell and smeared skin from his face, then ran and reached and felt a rung in his hand as agony burst in his shoulder and his feet thumped across wooden ties before the car, at last, was a shell around him.

He'd made it. He was on the train that would carry him off to kill a man, and the truth of that pressed down in the dark. It wasn't talk anymore, or waiting or planning.

The sun would rise in four hours.

The bullets would be real bullets.

*But so what?*

He sat in the blackness, determined as hilltops rose and fell and houses between them looked like stars. He thought of sleepless nights and hunger; and when the river glinted beneath him, he looked for the prison, seeing a bright light miles out across the valley floor. It raced closer, so he leaned out when the ground seemed flattest and least rocky. He looked for the strength to jump, but was still on the train as dirt flicked past and the prison sank like a ship in the dark.

He was going to miss it, so he thought of his mother's face instead, then stepped out and fell and hit the ground like a sack of rocks.

When he woke, it was still dark, and though the stars looked dimmer, he had enough light to limp along the tracks until he found a road that led to a cluster of brown buildings he'd seen once from the back of a moving car. He stepped beneath a black-lettered sign that said CONVICTS WELCOME and studied the two-windowed, cinder-block bar on the other side of it. His face was a blur in the glass. There were no people or traffic, and when he turned to look south, he saw how the prison rose up in the distance. He looked at it for long minutes before slipping into the alley beside the bar and putting his back against a Dumpster that smelled like chicken wings and cigarettes and piss. He wanted to feel pleased for making it this far, but the gun looked wrong in his lap. He tried watching the road, but there was nothing to watch, so he closed his eyes and thought of a picnic they'd had when he was very young. The picture taken that day was in a frame on his bedside table at home. He'd worn yellow pants with big buttons and thought he might remember how his father held him high and spun him in a circle. He held on to the idea of that childhood, then imagined what it would feel like to kill the man who took it away.

Hammer back.

Arm straight and steady.

He practiced in his head so he could do it right in person; but even in his mind, the gun shook and was silent. Gideon had imagined the same thing a thousand times on a thousand nights.

*His father was not man enough.*

*He would not be man enough.*

Pressing the barrel against his forehead, he prayed for strength, then walked through it again.

*Hammer back.*

*Arm straight.*

For an hour more he tried to steel himself, then threw up in the dark and hugged his ribs as if all heat in the world had been stolen, too.

# 2

Elizabeth should sleep—she knew as much—but the fatigue was more than physical. The weariness came from dead men and the questions that followed, from thirteen years of cop that looked to end badly. She played the movie in her mind: the missing girl and the basement, the bloody wire, and the *pop, pop* of the first two rounds. She could explain two, maybe even six; but eighteen bullets in two bodies was a tough sell, even with the girl alive. Four days had passed since the shooting, and the life that followed still felt foreign. Yesterday, a family of four stopped her on the sidewalk to thank her for making the world a better place. An hour later, somebody spit on the sleeve of her favorite jacket.

Elizabeth lit a cigarette, thinking about how it all came down to where people stood. To those who had children, she was a hero. A girl was taken and bad men died. To a lot of people, that seemed about right. For those who distrusted the police on principle, Elizabeth was the proof of all that was wrong with authority. Two men died in a violent, brutal manner. Forget that they were pushers and kidnappers and rapists. They'd died with eighteen bullets in them, and that, for some, was inexcusable. They used words such as *torture* and *execution* and *police brutality*. Elizabeth had strong feelings on the matter, but mostly she was just tired. How many days now with no real sleep? How many nightmares when it finally happened? Even though the city was unchanged and the same people inhabited her life, it seemed harder each hour to hold on to the person she'd been. Today was a perfect example. She'd been in the car for seven hours, driving aimlessly across town and into the county, past the police station and her house, out beyond the prison and back. But, what else could she do?

Home was a vacuum.

She couldn't go to work.

Pulling into a dark lot on the dangerous edge of downtown, she turned off the engine and listened to the sounds the city made. Music thumped from a club two blocks away. A fan belt squealed at the corner. Somewhere, there was laughter. After four years in uniform and nine with the gold shield, she knew every nuance of every rhythm. The city was her life, and for a long time she'd loved it. Now it felt . . . *what*?

Was *wrong* the right word? That seemed too harsh.

*Alien,* maybe?

*Unfamiliar?*

She got out of the car and stood in the darkness as a distant streetlight flickered twice, then snapped and died. She made a slow turn, picturing every back alley and crooked street in a ten-block radius. She knew the crack houses and flophouses, the prostitutes and pushers, which street corners were likely to get you shot if you said the wrong thing or rolled up hot. Seven different people had been killed on this busted-up patch of broken city, and that was just in the past three years.

She'd been in darker places a thousand times, but it felt different without the badge. The moral authority mattered, as did the sense of belonging to something larger than oneself. It wasn't fear, but *nakedness* might be a decent word. Elizabeth didn't have boyfriends or lady friends or hobbies. She was a cop. She liked the fight and the chase, the rare, sweet times she helped people who actually meant well. What would remain if she lost it?

*Channing,* she told herself.

*Channing would remain.*

That a girl she barely knew could matter so much was strange. But, she did. When Elizabeth felt dark or lost, she thought of the girl. Same thing when the world pressed in, or when Elizabeth considered the real chance that she could go to prison for what had happened in that cold, damp hole of a basement. Channing was alive, and as damaged as she was, she still had a chance at a full and normal life. A lot of victims couldn't say that. Hell, Elizabeth knew cops that couldn't say it, either.

Grinding out the cigarette, Elizabeth bought a newspaper from a machine beside an empty diner. Back in the car, she spread the paper across the wheel and saw her own face staring back. She looked cold and distant in black and white, but it could be the headline that made her seem so remote.

"Hero Cop or Angel of Death?"

Two paragraphs in, it was pretty clear what the reporter thought. Even though the word *alleged* showed up more than once, so did phrases such as *inexplicable brutality, unwarranted use of force, died in excruciating pain.* After long years of positive press, the local paper, it seemed, had finally turned against her. Not that she could blame them, not with the protests and public outcry, not with the state police involved. The photograph they'd chosen told the tale. Standing on the courthouse steps and peering down, she looked cold and aloof. It was the high cheekbones and deep eyes, the fair skin that looked gray in newsprint.

"Angel of death. Jesus."

Tossing the paper in the backseat, she started the car and worked her way out of the bad parts of town, driving past the marbled courthouse and the fountain at the square, then toward the college, where she slipped like a ghost past coffee shops and bars and loud, laughing kids. After that she was in the gentrified section, moving past condo lofts and art galleries and renovated warehouses turned into brewpubs and day spas and black box theaters. Tourists were on the sidewalks, some hipsters, a few homeless. When she found the four-lane that led past the chain restaurants and the old mall, she drove faster. Traffic was thinner there, the people's movements smaller and more subdued. She tried the radio, but the talk channels were boring and none of the music fit. Turning east, she followed a narrow road through scattered woods and subdivisions with stone-columned entrances. In twenty minutes she was outside the city limits. In another five, she started climbing. When she reached the top of the mountain, she lit another cigarette and stared out at the city, thinking how clean it looked from above. For a moment, she forgot the girl and the basement. There were no screams or blood or smoke, no broken child or irredeemable mistakes. There was light and there was dark. Nothing gray or shadowed. Nothing in between.

Stepping to the edge of the mountain, she looked down and tried to find some reason for hope. No charges had been filed. She wasn't looking at prison.

*Not yet . . .*

Spinning the cigarette into the blackness, she called the girl for the third time in as many days. "Channing, hey, it's me."

"Detective Black?"

"Call me Elizabeth, remember?"

"Yeah, sorry. I was asleep."

"Did I wake you? I'm sorry. My mind these days." Elizabeth pressed the phone against her ear and closed her eyes. "I lose track of time."

"It's okay. I'm taking sleeping pills. My mom, you know."

There was a rustling sound, and Elizabeth pictured the girl sitting up in bed. She was eighteen years old, a doll of a girl with haunted eyes and the kind of memories no child should have. "I was just worried about you." Elizabeth squeezed the phone until her hand ached and the world stopped spinning. "With all that's going on, it helps to know you're okay."

"I sleep mostly. It's only bad when I'm awake."

"I'm so sorry, Channing . . ."

"I didn't tell anybody."

Elizabeth grew suddenly still. Warm air rolled up the mountain, but she felt cold. "That's not why I called, sweetheart. You don't—"

"I did like you asked, Elizabeth. I didn't tell a soul what really happened. I won't. I wouldn't."

"I know, but . . ."

"Does the world go dark for you, sometimes?"

"Are you crying, Channing?"

"It goes a little gray for me."

The voice broke, and Elizabeth could picture the girl's bedroom in her parents' big house across town. Six days ago Channing vanished off a city street. No witnesses. No motive beyond the obvious. Two days after that, Elizabeth led her, blinking, from the basement of an abandoned house. The men who'd taken her were dead—shot eighteen times. Now, here they were: midnight, four days later, and the girl's room was still pink and soft and filled with all the possessions of childhood. If there was a message there, Elizabeth couldn't find it. "I shouldn't have called," she said. "It was selfish of me. Go back to sleep."

The line hissed.

"Channing?"

"They ask what happened, you know. My parents. The counselors. They ask all the time, but all I say is how you killed those men and how you saved me and how I felt joyful when they died."

"It's okay, Channing. You're okay."

"Does that make me a bad person, Elizabeth? That I was joyful? That I think eighteen bullets was not enough?"

"Of course not. They deserved it."

But the girl was still crying. "I see them when I close my eyes. I hear the jokes they told between times. The way they planned to kill me." Her voice broke again, and the break was deeper. "I still feel his teeth on my skin."

"Channing . . ."

"I heard the same things so many times I started to believe

what he said. That I deserved what they were doing to me, that I'd ask to die before they were done, and that I'd beg before they'd finally let me."

Elizabeth's hand went even whiter on the phone. Doctors counted nineteen bite marks, most of them through the skin; but Elizabeth knew from long discussions it was the things they'd said to her that hurt the most, the knowingness and fear, the way they'd tried to break her.

"I would have asked him to kill me," Channing said. "If you hadn't come when you did, I'd have begged him."

"It's over now."

"I don't think it is."

"It is. You're stronger than you think."

Channing grew silent again, and in the silence Elizabeth heard the raggedness of her breath.

"Will you come see me tomorrow?"

"I'll try," Elizabeth said.

"Please."

"I have to talk to the state police tomorrow. If I can make it, I will. If not, then the next day."

"Do you promise?"

"I do," Elizabeth said, though she knew nothing of fixing broken things.

When she got back in the car, Elizabeth still felt disconnected, and like other times in her life where she'd had nowhere to go and nothing to do, she ended up at her father's church, a humble building that rose narrow and pale against the night sky. She parked beneath the high steeple, studied small houses lined like boxes in the dark, and thought for the hundredth time that she could live in a place like this. Poor as it was, people worked and raised families and helped each other. Neighborliness like that seemed rare these days, and she thought a lot of what made this place so special came from her parents. As much as she and her father disagreed on life and the living of it, he was a fine minister. If people wanted a relationship with God, his was a good path. Kindness. Community. He kept the neighborhood going, but none of it worked unless it was done his way.

Elizabeth lost that kind of trust when she was seventeen.

Following a narrow drive, she walked beneath heavy trees and ended at the parsonage where her parents lived. Like the church, it was small and plain and painted a simple white. She didn't expect to find anyone awake, but her mother was sitting at the kitchen table. She had the same cheekbones as Elizabeth, and the same deep eyes, a beautiful woman with gray-streaked hair and skin that was still smooth in spite of long years of hard work. Elizabeth watched for a full minute, hearing dogs, a distant engine, the wail of an infant in some other far house. She'd avoided this place since the shooting.

*Then why am I here?*

Not for her father, she thought. Never that.

*Then why?*

But she knew.

Tapping on the door, Elizabeth waited as fabric whispered behind the screen, and her mother appeared. "Hello, Mom."

"Baby girl." The screen door swung open and her mother stepped onto the porch. Her eyes twinkled in the light, her features full of joy as she opened her arms and hugged her daughter. "You don't call. You don't come by."

She was keeping it light, but Elizabeth squeezed harder. "It's been a bad few days. I'm sorry."

She stood Elizabeth at arm's length and studied her face. "We've left messages, you know. Even your father called."

"I can't talk to Dad."

"It's really that bad?"

"Let's just say I have enough judgment coming my way without the heavenly kind."

It wasn't a joke, but her mother laughed, a good laugh. "Come have a drink." She led Elizabeth inside, put her at a small table, and fussed over ice and a half-empty bottle of Tennessee whiskey. "Do you want to talk about it?"

Elizabeth shook her head. She'd like to be honest with her mother, but had discovered long ago how a single lie could poison even the deepest well. Better to say nothing at all. Better to keep it in.

"Elizabeth?"

"I'm sorry." Elizabeth shook her head again. "I don't mean to be distant. It's just that everything seems so . . . muddled."

"Muddled?"

"Yes."

"Oh, bullshit." Elizabeth opened her mouth, but her mother waved it closed. "You're the most clear-minded person I've ever known. As a child, an adult. You've always seen more clearly than most. You're like your father that way, even though you believe such different things."

Elizabeth peered down the darkened hall. "Is he here?"

"Your father? No. The Turners are having troubles again. Your father's trying to help."

Elizabeth knew the Turners. The wife drank and could get abusive. She'd hurt her husband once, and Elizabeth took the call her last month in uniform. She could close her eyes and picture the narrow house, the woman who wore a pink housecoat and weighed a hundred pounds, at most.

*I want the reverend.*

She had a rolling pin in her hand, swinging at shadows. The husband was down and bloody.

*I won't talk to nobody but the reverend.*

Elizabeth had been ready to do it the hard way, but her father calmed the woman down, and the husband—again—refused to press charges. That was years ago, and the reverend still counseled them. "He never shies, does he?"

"Your father? No."

Elizabeth looked out the window. "Has he talked about the shooting?"

"No, sweetheart. What could he possibly say?"

It was a good question, and Elizabeth knew the answer. He would blame her for the deaths, for being a cop in the first place. He would say she'd broken trust, and that everything bad flowed from that single poor decision: the basement, the dead brothers, her career. "He still can't accept the life I've chosen."

"Of course he can. He's your father, though, and he pines."

"For me?"

"For simpler times, perhaps. For what once was. No man wants to be hated by his own daughter."

"I don't hate him."

"You've not forgiven, either."

Elizabeth accepted the truth of that. She kept her distance, and even when they shared the same room, there was a frost. "How are you two so different?"

"We're really not."

"Laugh lines. Frown lines. Acceptance. Judgment. You're so completely opposite I wonder how you've stayed together for so long. I marvel. I really do."

"You're being unfair to your father."

"Am I?"

"What can I tell you, sweetheart?" Her mother sipped whiskey and smiled. "The heart wants what the heart wants."

"Even after so many years?"

"Well, maybe it's not so much the heart, anymore. He can be difficult, yes, but only because he sees the world so clearly. Good and evil, the one straight path. The older I become, the more comfort I find in that kind of certainty."

"You studied philosophy, for God's sake."

"That was a different life . . ."

"You lived in Paris. You wrote poetry."

Her mother waved off the observation. "I was just a girl, and Paris just a place. You ask why we've stayed together, and in my heart I remember how it felt—the vision and the purpose, the determination every day to make the world better. Life with your father was like standing next to an open fire, just raw force and heat and purpose. He got out of bed driven and ended every day the same. He made me very happy for a lot of years."

"And now?"

She smiled wistfully. "Let's just say that as rigid as he may have grown, my home will always be between your father's walls."

Elizabeth appreciated the simple elegance of such commitment. The preacher. The preacher's wife. She let a moment pass, thinking how it must have been for them: the passion and the cause, the early days and the great, stone church. "It's not like the old place, is it?" She turned back to the window and stared out at rock-lined gardens and brown grass, at the poor, narrow church wrapped in sunbaked clapboards. "I think about it sometimes: the cool and the quiet, the long view from the front steps."

"I thought you hated the old church."

"Not always. And not with such passion."

"Why are you here, sweetheart?" Her mother's reflection appeared in the same pane of glass. "Really?"

Elizabeth sighed, knowing this was the reason she'd come. "Am I a good person?" Her mother started to smile, but Elizabeth stopped her. "I'm serious, Mom. It's like now. It's the middle of the night. Things in my life are troubled and uncertain, and here I am."

"Don't be silly."

"Am I a taker?"

"Elizabeth Frances Black, you've never taken anything in your whole life. Since you were a child I've watched you give, first to your father and the congregation, now to the whole city. How many medals have you won? How many lives have you saved? What's this really about?"

Elizabeth sat again and stared into her drink, both shoulders lifting. "You know how well I shoot."

"Ah. Now, I understand." She took her daughter's hand, and creases gathered at her eyes as she squeezed it once and took the seat across the table. "If you shot those men eighteen times, then you had good reason. Nothing anybody ever says will make me feel different about that."

"You've read the papers?"

"Generalities." She made a dismissive sound. "Distortion."

"Two men are dead. What else is there to say?"

"Baby girl." She refilled Elizabeth's glass and poured more in hers. "That's like using *white* to describe a full moon rising, or *wet* to capture the glory of the oceans. You saved an innocent girl. Everything else pales."

"You know the state police are investigating?"

"I know only that you did what you felt was right, and that if you shot those men eighteen times, there was a good reason for doing so."

"And if the state police disagree?"

"My goodness." Her mother laughed again. "You can't possibly doubt yourself that much. They'll have their little investigation, and they'll clear your name. Surely you see that."

"Nothing seems clear right now. What happened. Why it happened. I haven't really slept."

Her mother sipped, then pointed with a finger. "Are you familiar with the word *inspiration*? The meaning of it? Where it comes from?"

Elizabeth shook her head.

"In the Dark Ages, no one understood the things that made some people special, things like imagination or creativity or vision. People lived and died in the same small village. They had no idea why the sun rose or set or why winter came. They grubbed in the dirt and died young of disease. Every soul in that dark, difficult time faced the same limitations, every soul except a precious few who came rarely to the world and saw things differently, the poets and inventors, the artists and stonemasons. Regular folks didn't understand people like that; they didn't understand how a person could wake up one day and see the world differently. They thought it was a gift from God. Thus, the word *inspiration*. It means 'breathed upon.'"

"I'm no artist. No visionary."

"Yet, you have insights as rare as any poet's gift. You see deeply and understand. You would not have killed those men unless you had to."

"Look, Mom—"

"Inspiration." Her mother drank, and her eyes watered. "Breathed upon by God himself."


Thirty minutes later, Elizabeth drove back into the heart of downtown. The city was of a decent size for North Carolina, with a hundred thousand people inside the limits and twice as many spread across the county. It was still rich in places, but ten years into the downturn the cracks were starting to show. Storefronts were shuttered where none had ever been shuttered before. Broken windows went unfixed, buildings unpainted. She passed a place that used to be her favorite restaurant and saw a group of teenagers arguing on the street corner. There was more of that now, too: anger, discontent. Unemployment was twice the national average, and every year it got harder to pretend the best times weren't in the past. That didn't mean parts of the city weren't beautiful—they were: the old houses and picket fences, the bronze statues that spoke of certainty and war and sacrifice. Pockets of pride remained, but even the most dignified people seemed cautious in expressing it, as if it might be dangerous, somehow, as if it might be best to keep one's head down and wait for clearer skies.

Parking in front of the police station, Elizabeth stared out through the glass. The building was three stories tall and built of the same stone and marble as the courthouse. A Chinese restaurant filled a narrow lot on the side street to her right. The Confederate cemetery was a block farther, and beyond that was the train depot, with the tracks running north to south. When she was a kid, she'd follow those tracks into town, walking with her friends on a Saturday morning to see a movie or watch boys in the park. She couldn't imagine such a thing, now. Kids on the tracks. Loose in the city. Elizabeth rolled down the window, smelled pavement and hot rubber. Lighting a cigarette, she watched the station.

*Thirteen years . . .*

She tried to imagine it gone: the job, the relationships, the sense of purpose. Since she was seventeen, all she'd wanted was to be a cop because cops didn't fear the things normal people feared. Cops were strong. They had authority and purpose. They were the good guys.

Did she still believe that?

Elizabeth closed her eyes, thinking about it. When she opened them, she saw Francis Dyer walking down the wide stairs that stretched across the front of the station. He made a beeline across the street, his face familiar and frustrated and sad. They'd argued a lot since the shooting, but there was no bitterness between them. He was older and soft and genuinely worried for her.

"Hello, Captain. I didn't expect to see you here this late."

He stopped at the open window, studied her face and the car's interior. His eyes moved over cigarette packs and Red Bull cans and a half dozen balled-up newspapers filling the backseat. Eventually, the gaze landed on the cell phone beside her. "I've left six messages."

"I'm sorry. I turned it off."

"Why?"

"Most calls I get are from reporters. Would you prefer I speak to them?"

Her attitude made him angry. Part of it was anxiety, and part was the whole cop-control thing. She was a detective, but suspended, a friend but not close enough to justify the kind of frustration he was feeling. The emotion was in his face, in the pinched eyes and soft lips, in the sudden flush that stained his skin. "What are you doing here, Liz? It's the middle of the night."

She shrugged.

"I've told you about this. Until your case is cleared . . ."

"I wasn't going to come inside."

He waited a few beats, the same angles in his face, same worry in his eyes. "Your follow-up with the state police is tomorrow. You remember that, right?"

"Of course."

"Have you met with your attorney?"

"Yes," she lied. "All set."

"Then, you should be with family or friends, people who love you."

"I was. Dinner with friends."

"Really? What did you eat?" Her mouth opened, and he said, "Forget it. I don't want you to lie to me." He looked across the top of narrow glasses, then up and down the street. "My office. Five minutes."

He walked off and Elizabeth took a minute to pull herself together. When she felt ready, she crossed the street and trotted up the stairs to where double glass doors reflected light from streetlamps and stars. At the desk inside, she forced a smile and made a hands-up gesture to the sergeant behind the bulletproof glass.

"Yeah, yeah," the sergeant said. "Dyer told me to let you through. You look different."

"Different, how?"

He shook his head. "I'm too old for that shit."

"What shit?"

"Women. Opinions."

He hit the buzzer, and the sound followed her into the stairwell and upstairs to the long, open space used by the detective squad. It was nearly empty, most of the desks pooled in shadow. For bittersweet seconds, no one noticed her; then the door clanked shut and a massive cop in a rumpled suit looked up from his desk. "Yo, yo. Black in the house."

"Yo, yo?" Elizabeth stepped into the room.

"What?" He leaned back in his chair. "I can't do street?"

"I'd stick with what you've got."

"And what's that?"

She stopped at his desk. "A mortgage, kids. Thirty extra pounds and a wife of what, nine years?"

"Ten."

"Well, there you go. A loving family, thick arteries, and twenty years to retirement."

"Funny. Thanks for that."

Elizabeth took a sour ball from a glass jar, cocked a hip, and looked down at Charlie Beckett's round face. He was six foot three and running to fat, but she'd seen him throw a two-hundred-pound suspect across the top of a parked car without once touching paint. "Nice hair," he said.

She touched it, felt how short it was, the spiky bangs. "Seriously?"

"Sarcasm, woman. Why did you do that to yourself?"

"Maybe, I wanted something different in the mirror."

"Maybe you should hire somebody that knows what they're doing. When did that happen? I saw you two days ago."

She had vague memories of cutting it: four in the morning and drunk; lights off in the bathroom. She'd been laughing about something, but it was more like crying. "What are you doing here, Charlie? It's after midnight."

"There was a shooting at the college," Beckett said.

"Jesus, not another one."

"No, not like that. Some locals tried to beat the crap out of a freshman kid they thought was gay. Gay or not, it turns out he's a big fan of concealed-carry laws. They chased him into the alley by the barbershop at the edge of campus. Four on one, and he drew down with a .380."

"Did he kill anybody?"

"Shot one through the arm. The others split when it happened. We've got the names, though. We're looking for them."

"Any charges on the student?"

"Four on one. A college kid with no priors." Beckett shook his head. "As far as I'm concerned, it's just paperwork, now."

"There's that, I guess."

"Guess so."

"Listen, I've got to go."

"Yeah, the captain said you were coming in. He didn't look happy."

"He caught me lurking outside."

"You *are* suspended. You remember that, right?"

"Yes."

"And you're not exactly helping your cause."

She knew what he meant. There'd been questions about the basement, and she'd been short on answers. Pressure was mounting. State cops. Attorney general. "Let's talk about something else. How's Carol?"

Beckett leaned back in his chair, shrugged. "Working late."

"Some kind of hair-salon emergency?"

"There are such things, believe it or not. A wedding, I think. Or a divorce party. Deep conditioning tonight. Cut and style in the morning."

"Wow."

"I know. She still wants to set you up, by the way."

"With who, the orthodontist?"

"Dentist."

"Is there a difference?"

"One makes more money, I think."

Elizabeth hooked a finger over her shoulder. "I think he's waiting."

"Listen, Liz." Beckett leaned in, lowered his voice. "I've tried to give you space on the shooting. Right? I've tried to be a partner and a friend and understanding. But state cops are tomorrow—"

"They have my statement. Asking the same questions won't get them different answers."

"They've had four days to look for witnesses, talk to Channing, work the crime scene. They won't ask the same questions. You know that."

She shrugged. "The story's the story."

"It's political, Liz. You get that, right? White cop, black victims . . ."

"They're not victims."

"Look." Beckett studied her face, worried. "They want to nail a cop they think is racist, unstable, or both. As far as they're concerned, that's you. Elections are coming up, and the AG wants an in with the black community. He thinks this is it."

"I don't care about any of that."

"You shot them eighteen times."

"They raped that child for over a day."

"I know, but listen."

"Wired her wrists so tight it cut to the bone."

"Liz—"

"Don't *Liz* me, goddamn it! They told her they were going to smother her when they were done with her, then toss her body in the quarry. They had a plastic bag and duct tape all ready. One of them wanted to screw her while she died. He called it a white-girl rodeo."

"I know all that," Beckett said.

"Then this conversation should not be happening."

"But it is, isn't it? Channing's father is rich and white. The men you shot were poor and black. It's politics. Media. It's already started. You've seen the papers." He held up a thumb and forefinger. "It's this close to going national. People want an indictment."

She knew whom he meant. Politicians. Agitators. Some who thought the system was genuinely corrupt. "I can't talk about this."

"Can you talk to the lawyer?"

"I already have."

"No, you haven't." Beckett leaned back, watching her. "He calls here, looking for you. He says you haven't taken a meeting and won't return his calls. State cops want you for double homicide, and you're screwing around like you didn't empty your magazine into two unarmed men."

"I had a good reason."

"I don't doubt you did, but that's not the issue, is it? Cops go to prison, too. You know that better than most."

His gaze was as pointed as his words. Elizabeth didn't care.

Even after thirteen years. "I'm not going to talk about him, Charlie. Not tonight. Not with you."

"He gets out of prison tomorrow. I assume you see the irony." Beckett crossed his hands behind his head as if challenging her to argue the basic facts.

*Cops go to prison.*

*Sometimes they get out.*

"I'd better go see the captain."

"Liz, wait."

She didn't. She left Beckett and knocked twice before opening the captain's door. Inside, Dyer was sitting behind the desk. Even this late, the suit was crisp, the tie drawn tight. "Are you okay?"

She waved a hand, but couldn't hide the anger and disappointment. "Partners. Opinions."

"Beckett only wants what's best for you. It's all any of us want."

"Then, put me back to work."

"Do you really think that's the right thing for you?"

She looked away because his question hit so close to the mark "The job is what I do best."

"I won't reinstate you until this thing runs its course."

She dropped into a chair. "How much longer will that be?"

"That's not the right question."

Elizabeth stared at her reflection in the window. She'd lost weight. Her hair was a mess. "What is the right question?"

"Seriously?" Dyer lifted both palms. "Do you even remember the last time you ate?"

"That's not relevant."

"How about the last time you slept?"

"Okay. Fine. I'll admit that the past few days have been . . . complicated."

"Complicated? For God's sake, Liz, you have circles under your eyes that look painted on. You're never home, best any of us can tell. You don't answer your phone. You're riding around in that broken-down car."

"It's a '67 Mustang."

"That's barely street legal." Dyer leaned forward, laced his fingers. "These state cops keep asking about you, and it's getting harder and harder to say you're solid. A week ago, I'd have used words like *judiciousness* and *brilliance* and *restraint*. Now I don't know what to say. You've gone edgy and dark and unpredictable. You're drinking too much, smoking for the first time in, what, ten years? You won't talk to the counselor or your colleagues." He made a gesture that took in her ragged hair and pale face. "You look like one of these Goth kids, like a shadow—"

"Can we discuss something else?"

"I think you're lying about what happened in the basement. How's that for something else?"

Elizabeth looked away.

"Your timeline's off, Liz. The state police aren't buying it, and neither am I. The girl is squirrely with details, which makes me think she's lying, too. You're missing an hour. You emptied your weapon."

"If we're finished . . ."

"We're not." Dyer leaned back in his chair, unhappy. "I called your father."

"Ah." A world of meaning was in the sound. "And how is the Reverend Black?"

"He says the cracks in you are so deep God's own light can't find the bottom."

"Yeah, well"—she looked away—"my father has always had a way with words."

"He's a good man, Liz. Let him help you."

"Attending my father's service twice a year doesn't give you the right to discuss my life with him. I don't want him involved, and I don't need help."

"But, you do." Dyer put his forearms on the desk. "That's what's so heartbreaking. You're one of the best cops I've ever seen, but you're a slow-motion train wreck, too. None of us can look away. We want to help you. Let us help you."

"May I have my shield back or not?"

"Get your story straight, Liz. Get it straight or these state cops will eat you alive."

Elizabeth stood. "I know what I'm doing."

Dyer stood, too, and spoke as her hand reached for the door. "You drove by the prison this afternoon."

She stopped with one hand on the knob. When she turned, her voice was cold. He wanted to talk about tomorrow and the prison. Of course, he did. Just like Beckett. Just like every cop out there. "Were you following me?"

"No."

"Who saw me?"

"It doesn't matter. You know my point."

"Let's pretend I can't read minds."

"I don't want you anywhere near Adrian Wall."

"Adrian who?"

"And don't play dumb with me, either. His parole came through. He gets out in the morning."

"I don't know what you mean," she said.

But she did, and both of them knew it.

# 3

It was a paradox of life behind walls, that where any day could end in blood, every morning contrived to start exactly the same. A man woke and, for two beats of his heart, didn't know where he was or what he'd become. Those few seconds were magic, a warm flicker before reality walked across his chest, the black dog of remembrance trailing at its feet. This morning was no different from any other: stillness, at first, then memories of all the things that came with thirteen years in a box. Moments like that were bad enough for most.

For a cop, they were worse.

For a cop like Adrian, they were unbearable.

He sat in the dark of his bunk and touched a face that no longer felt like his own. A finger sank into a nickel-size depression at the corner of his left eye. He traced the fracture line to his nose, then across to where long scars gathered in the hollow of his cheek. They'd healed white, but prison stitches weren't the greatest. If time inside had taught him one thing, though, it's what really mattered in life.

What he'd lost.

What he had left.

Stripping off rough sheets, he did push-ups until his arms shook, then stood in the dark and tried to forget the feel of blackness and quiet and memories scratched through to white. He'd come inside two months after his thirtieth birthday. Now, he was forty-three years old, scarred and broken and remade. Would people even recognize him? Would his wife?

*Thirteen years,* he thought.

"A lifetime."

The voice was so light it barely registered. Adrian caught a flicker of movement from the corner of his eye and found Eli Lawrence in the darkest corner of the cell. He looked small in the dimness beyond the bunk, his eyes dull yellow, his face so dark and seamed it was hard to tell where the old man ended and blackness began.

"He speaks," Adrian said.

The old man blinked as if to say, *These things happen.*

Adrian closed his eyes, too, then turned his back and wrapped his fingers around metal bars so warm they seemed to sweat. He never knew if Eli would speak or not, if the yellow eyes would open or blink or stay closed so long the old man faded into the dimness. Even now, the only noise in the cell was Adrian's breath and the sound his fingers made as they twisted, slick and wet, on the metal. This was his last day inside, and dawn was gathering beyond the bars. Between there and the place he stood, the hall stretched gray and empty; and Adrian wondered if the world outside would feel just as blank. He wasn't the man he'd been and had few illusions about the fact. He'd lost thirty pounds since conviction, his muscles hard and lean as old rope. He'd suffered inside, and while he hated the prisoner's lament—that I'm not responsible, that it was not my fault—Adrian could point at other men and say, *This scar came from him, that broken bone from the other.* Of course, none of that mattered. Even if he screamed from the tower that it was the warden who did this or a guard who did the other, no one would believe him or even care.

Too much damage.

Too many years in the dark.

"You can do this," the old man said.

"I shouldn't be getting out. Not this early."

"You know why."

Adrian's fingers tightened on the metal. Thirteen years was at the bottom end for murder two, but only with good behavior, only if the warden wanted it to happen. "They'll be watching me. You know that."

"Of course they will. We've talked about this."

"I don't know if I can do it."

"I say you can."

The old man's voice wafted from the dark, a touch. Adrian pressed his back into the same damp metal and thought about the man who'd shared his life for so many years. Eli Lawrence had taught him the rules of prison, taught him when to fight and when to bend, that even the worst things end in time. More important, the old man had kept him sane. On the forever days in the forever dark, Eli's voice had held Adrian together. That was true no matter how alone he was or how much he bled. And Eli, it seemed, had evolved to fit the role. After six decades inside, the old man's world had contracted to the exact dimensions of their cell. He acknowledged no one else; spoke to no one else. They were tied so tightly—the old man and the young—that Adrian feared Eli would disappear the moment he left the cell. "I wish I could take you with me."

"We both know I'll never leave this place alive." Eli smiled as if it were a joke, but the words were as true as any truth in prison. Eli Lawrence had earned a life sentence for a robbery homicide, in 1946, in the backcountry of eastern North Carolina. Had the dead man been white, he'd have hung. Instead, he got life times three, and Adrian knew that Eli'd never breathe free air again. Staring into the dark, Adrian wanted to say so many things to the old man. He wanted to thank him and apologize and describe all the things Eli had meant to him over the years, to explain that, as much as he'd already endured, Adrian didn't know if he could make it beyond the walls without Eli to guide him. He started to speak, but stopped as lights flickered beyond the heavy, steel door and a buzzer sounded down the block.

"They're coming," Eli said.

"I'm not ready."

"Of course, you are."

"Not without you, Eli. Not alone."

"Just be still and let me tell you some things people tend to forget once they leave this place."

"I don't care about that."

"I spent a lifetime here, boy. You know how many people have said that to me? 'I can handle it. I know what I'm doing.'"

"I meant no disrespect."

"Of course, you didn't. Now, be still and listen to an old man one more time."

Adrian nodded as metal clanked on metal. He heard distant voices, hard shoes on the concrete floor.

"Money means nothing," Eli said. "You understand what I'm saying? I've seen people pull twenty years in this place, then come back six months later on account of the dollars. In and out, like they don't learn nothing. It's only worth so much, the gold and dollars and shiny bits. It's not worth your life or your joy or a day of your freedom. Sunshine. Fresh air. It's enough." Eli nodded in the gloom. "That being said, you remember what I told you?"

"Yes."

"The waterfall and how the creek splits?"

"I remember."

"I know you think this place has used you up for the outside world, but the scars and busted bones don't matter, same with the fear and the dark, the memories and hate and dreams of revenge. You let that go. All of it. You walk out of this place and you keep walking. Leave this town. Find another."

"And the warden? Should I leave him, too?"

"If he comes after you?"

"If he comes. If he doesn't. What do I do if I see him?"

That was a dangerous question, and for an instant Eli's dull eyes seemed shot with red. "What did I just say about revenge?"

Adrian ground his teeth and didn't have to speak to make the point.

*The warden was different.*

"You let the hate go, boy. You hear me? You're walking early. Maybe that's for a reason, and maybe not. What does it matter if you disappear?" The guards were closer; seconds, now. The old man nodded. "As for what you suffered in this place, all that matters is survival. You understand? There's no sin in survival. Say it."

"No sin."

"And no need to worry on me."

"Eli . . ."

"Now give an old man a hug, and get the hell out."

Eli was nodding, and Adrian felt his throat close. Eli Lawrence was more father than friend, and as Adrian wrapped the man up, he found him so light and hot it was as if coals burned in the hollows of his bones. "Thank you, Eli."

"You walk out proud, boy. Let them see you tall and straight."

Adrian pulled back, looking for a final glimpse of the man's tired and knowing eyes. But Eli faded into the shadows, turned his back, and all but disappeared.

"Go on now."

"Eli?"

"Everything's fine," the old man said, but Adrian's face was wet with tears.

The guards let Adrian step into the corridor, but kept their distance. He was not a large man, but even the guards had heard rumors of what he'd endured, and how he'd done it. The numbers were undeniable: the months in hospital, the staples and stitches, the surgeries and broken bones. Even the warden paid attention to Adrian Wall, and that frightened the guards as much as anything else.

There were stories about the warden, too; but no one pushed for the truth. It was the warden's prison, and he was an unforgiving man. That meant you kept your head down, and your mouth shut. Besides, the stories couldn't be true. That's how the decent guards consoled themselves.

But not all guards were decent.

When Adrian got to processing, he saw three of the worst standing in the corner, hard-faced, flat-eyed men that even now made Adrian hesitate. Their uniforms were creased and spotless, all the leather shined. They lined the wall, and a message was in their arrogance. *We still own you,* it said. *Inside. Outside. Nothing's changed.*

"What are you looking at, prisoner?"

Adrian ignored them and took his cues, instead, from a small man behind a counter topped with steel pillars and chain-link.

"You need to strip." A cardboard box settled on the counter, and clothes unseen for thirteen years came out. "Go on." The clerk flicked a glance at the three guards, then back to Adrian. "It's okay."

Adrian stepped out of prison shoes and stripped off the orange.

"Jesus . . ." The clerk paled at the sight of all the scars.

Adrian acted as if it were okay, but it wasn't. The guards who'd brought him from the cell were silent and still, but the other three were joking about the crooked fingers and the vinyl skin. Adrian knew each of them by name. He knew the sounds of their voices, and which was strongest. He knew which was most sadistic, and which one, even now, was smiling. In spite of that, he kept his back straight. He waited until the whispers stopped, then put on the suit and turned his mind to other things: a dark spot on the counter, a clock behind the chain-link. He buttoned his shirt to the collar, tied his tie as if it were Sunday.

"They're gone."

"What?"

"Those three." The clerk gestured. "They're gone." The clerk's face was narrow, his eyes unusually soft.

"Did I blank out?"

"Just for a few seconds." The clerk looked away, embarrassed. "Like you went away."

Adrian cleared his throat, but guessed the clerk was telling the truth. The world went dark sometimes. Time did strange things. "I'm sorry."

The small man shrugged, and Adrian knew from looking at his face that those particular guards made a lot of lives miserable.

"Let's get you out of here." The clerk pushed a paper across the slick surface. "Sign this." Adrian dashed his name without reading. The clerk thumbed three bills onto the counter. "This is for you."

"Fifty dollars?"

"It's a gift from the state."

Adrian looked at it, thought, *Thirteen years, fifty dollars*. The clerk pushed the bills across the surface, and Adrian folded them into a pocket.

"Do you have any questions?"

Adrian struggled for a minute. Other than Eli Lawrence, he'd not spoken to another soul in a long time. "Is anyone here for me? You know . . . waiting?"

"I'm sorry. I wouldn't know that."

"Do you know where I might find a ride?"

"Cabs aren't allowed at the prison. There's a pay phone down the road at Nathan's. I thought all you people knew that."

"You people?"

"Ex-cons."

Adrian let that sink in. The guard who'd brought him from his cell gestured at an empty hall. "Mr. Wall."

Adrian turned, not sure what he thought about all these strange words.

*Mr. Wall . . .*

*Ex-con . . .*

The guard lifted a hand, indicating a hallway to the left. "This way."

Adrian followed him to a door that cracked bright and split wide. There were still fences and chain-link gates, but the breeze was warm on his cheek as he turned his face from the sun and tried to quantify exactly how it felt different from the one that shone in the yard.

"Prisoner coming out." The guard keyed a radio, then pointed to a place where gates rolled on wheels. "Straight through the gate. The second won't open until the first one closes."

"My wife . . ."

"I don't know anything about your wife."

The guard gave a shove, and Adrian—like that—was outside. He looked for the warden's office and found the right windows three floors up on the east wall. For an instant sunlight gilded the glass, then clouds slid across the sun and Adrian saw him there. He stood as he liked to stand. Hands in his pockets. Shoulders loose. For a moment the stare held between them, and with it enough hate to fill another thirteen years of Adrian's life. He thought the guards would appear, too, but they didn't. It was he and the warden, the slow tick of a dozen seconds before the sun burned through and mirrored the glass again.

*Walk out proud, boy.*

He heard Eli's voice as if he were there.

*Let them see you tall and straight.*

Crossing the parking lot, Adrian stood on the edge of the road and thought maybe his wife would come. He looked once more at the warden's office, then watched one car blow past, then another. He shifted from foot to foot as the sun walked up the sky, and the first hour stretched into three. By the time he started walking, his throat was dry and he'd sweated through his shirt. Staying on the verge, he kept one eye out for cars, and the second on a clutch of buildings dropped like blocks a half mile down the road. By the time he reached them, it was over a hundred degrees. Lots of shimmer coming off the road, lots of pale, white dust. He saw a pay phone next to a self-storage place, a shipping company, and a bar called Nathan's. Everything looked closed but the bar, which had a sign in the window and a rusted-out pickup angled in near the front door. Adrian fisted his hand around the wad of bills in his pocket, then turned the knob and walked inside the bar.

"Uh-oh. Free man walking."

The voice was rough and sure, the tone amused but not in a bad way. Adrian stepped closer to the bar and saw a sixtysomething man in front of rowed bottles and a long mirror. He was tall and wide, grizzled hair pulled back over a leather vest. Adrian limped a little closer and returned the half smile. "How'd you know?"

"Prison skin. Wrinkled suit. Plus I see about a dozen of you every year. You need a cab?"

"Can I get change?"

Adrian held out a bill, and the bartender waved it away. "Don't sweat the pay phone. I've got 'em on speed dial. Take a load off." Adrian sat on a vinyl stool and watched the man dial. "Hi, I need a cab at Nathan's. . . . Yeah, out by the prison." He listened for a moment, then covered the phone and said to Adrian, "Where to?"

Adrian shrugged because he didn't know.

"Just send the cab." The bartender hung up the phone and moved back down the bar. The eyes were gray under heavy lids, the whiskers yellow-white. "How long were you inside?"

"Thirteen years."

"Ouch." The bartender held out a hand. "Nathan Conroy. This is my place."

"Adrian Wall."

"Well, Adrian Wall"—Nathan tilted a glass under the tap, then slid it on the bar—"welcome to the first day of the rest of your life."

Adrian stared at the glass of beer. It was such a simple thing. Moisture on the glass. Cool when he touched it. For an instant, the world seemed to tilt. How could things change so much so fast? Handshakes and smiles and cold beer. He found his face in the mirror and couldn't look away.

"It's a bitch, isn't it?" Nathan put his elbows on the bar and brought the smell of sun-cooked leather with him. "Seeing what you are and remembering what you were."

"You did time?"

"Vietnam POW. Four years."

Adrian touched the scars on his face and leaned closer. Prison mirrors were made of polished metal and not so great for showing a man his soul. He turned his head one way, then another. The lines were deeper than he'd thought, the eyes wider and darker. "Is it like this for everybody?"

"Thoughtful making? Nah." The bartender shook his head and poured brown liquor into a shot glass. "Most just want to get drunk, get laid, or start a fight. I see most everything." He knocked back the shot, clacked it on the bar as the door grated and light flashed in the mirror. "Don't see much of that, though."

Adrian dragged his gaze from the mirror in time to see daylight spill around a skinny kid. He was thirteen or fourteen, one arm shaking from the weight of the gun in his hand. Nathan slipped a hand under the bar, and the kid said, "Please don't."

Nathan put his hand back on the bar, and everything about him got serious and quiet and still. "I think you're in the wrong place, son."

"Just . . . nobody move."

He was a small boy, maybe five and a half feet tall with fine bones and uncut nails. The eyes were electric blue, the face so familiar that Adrian felt sudden pressure in his chest.

*It couldn't be . . .*

But it was.

It was the mouth and the hair, the narrow wrists and the line of his jaw. "Oh, my God."

"You know this kid?" Nathan asked.

"I think I do."

The boy was attractive, but drawn. His clothes might have fit two years ago but at the moment showed dirty socks and a lot of wrist. His gaze was wide and terrified. The gun looked huge in his hand. "Don't talk about me like I'm not here."

He stepped inside, and the door swung shut behind him. Adrian slipped off the stool and showed both hands. "Jesus, you look just like her."

"I said don't move."

"Just take it easy, Gideon."

"How do you know my name?"

Adrian swallowed hard. He'd not seen the boy since he was an infant, but would know his features anywhere. "You look like your mother. God, even your voice . . ."

"Don't act like you know my mother." The gun trembled.

Adrian spread his fingers. "She was a lovely woman, Gideon. I would never hurt her."

"I said don't talk about her."

"I didn't kill her."

"That's a lie."

The gun shook. The hammer clicked twice.

"I knew your mother, Gideon. I knew her better than you think. She was gentle and kind. She wouldn't want this, not for you."

"How would you know what she'd want?"

"I just do."

"I don't have a choice."

"Of course you have a choice."

"I made a promise. It's what a man would do. Everybody knows that."

"Gideon, please . . ."

The boy's face pinched up, and the gun shook harder as his fingers tightened on the grip. His eyes grew bright, and Adrian, in that instant, didn't know whether to be terrified or sad.

"I'm begging you, Gideon. She wouldn't want this. Not you and me. Not like this."

The gun rose an inch, and Adrian saw it all in the boy's eyes, the hatred and fear and loss. Beyond that, he had time for a single thought, and it was the name of the boy's mother—*Julia*—that slipped, once, through Adrian's mind before thunder spat out from behind the bar and slapped a red hole on the boy's chest. The impact pushed Gideon back a step as his gun hand dropped and blood spread thick as oil through the weave of his shirt.

"Oh." He looked more surprised than hurt, his mouth open as he found Adrian's eyes, and his knees failed.

"Gideon!" Adrian crossed the room in three strides. He kicked the gun away and dropped to his knees beside the boy.

Blood pulsed from the wound. The kid looked blank-eyed and stunned. "It hurts."

"Shhh. Lie still." Adrian stripped off his jacket, balled it against the wound. "Call 911."

"I saved your life, brother."

"Please!"

Nathan lowered a small, silver pistol and picked up the phone. "You remember that when the cops come." He cradled the receiver, and dialed 911. "I shot that boy to save your life."

# 4

Elizabeth's house had always been a sanctuary. Neat and trim, it filled a narrow lot on the historic side of town, a small Victorian under spreading trees that kept the lawn shaded and green. She lived alone, but the place was such a perfect reflection of what she loved about life that she never felt lonesome there. No matter the case or the politics or the collateral damage, stepping through the front door had always allowed her to turn off the job. She could study the oil paintings on the walls, trail her fingers along rowed books or the woodcarvings she'd collected since she was a girl. The house had always been an escape. That was the rule, and it had worked every month of her adult life until now.

Now, the house felt like wood and glass and stone.

Now, it was just a place.

Thoughts like that kept her up most of the night, thoughts of the house and her life, of dead men and the basement. By four o'clock, it was all about Channing, and those feelings spun mostly on the things Elizabeth had done wrong.

*She'd made so many mistakes.*

That was the difficult truth, and it pursued her until finally, at dawn, she slept. Yet, even then she dreamed and twitched and woke with a sound in her throat so animal it frightened her.

*Five days* . . .

She felt her way to the bathroom sink, splashed water on her face.

*Damn.*

When the nightmare let go, she sat at the kitchen table and stared at a manila file that was old and thumbed and dangerous enough to get her fired if it was ever found in her house. She'd spent three hours with it the day before, a dozen more the week before that. She'd had it since Adrian Wall's conviction. Except for newspaper clippings and photographs she'd taken herself, it was an exact copy of the Julia Strange murder file that was stored, now, somewhere in the district attorney's office.

Flipping to a sheaf of photographs, she took out a picture of Adrian. He was in dress blues, younger than she was now. Handsome, she thought, with the kind of clear-eyed determination most cops lose after a few years. The next shot was of Adrian in plainclothes, then another of him on the courthouse steps. She'd taken that one before his trial and liked the way light hung on his face. He looked more the way she felt now, a little worn and a little jaded. But still handsome and straight, she thought, still the cop she'd always admired.

Elizabeth flipped through newspaper coverage and got to the autopsy photos of Julia Strange, a young woman whose murder rocked the county the way few other murders ever had. Young and elegant in life, her beauty was stripped away by bloodlessness, a crushed throat, and the morgue's bright lights. But she'd been lovely once, and strong enough to put up a fight. Signs of it were all over the kitchen: a broken chair and an upended table, a spray of shattered dishes. Elizabeth riffled through photographs of the kitchen, but saw the same things she always saw: cabinets and tile, a playpen in the corner, photographs on the fridge.

There were the usual reports, and she knew them thoroughly. Lab work, fingerprints, DNA. She skimmed the family history: the wife's early days as a model, Gideon's birth, the husband's job. They'd been a perfect family in so many ways: young and attractive, not rich, but doing okay. Interviews with family friends said she was a wonderful mother, that the husband was devoted. Only one witness statement was in the file, and Elizabeth had read that a hundred times as well. An elderly neighbor heard an altercation around three in the afternoon, but she was bedridden, infirm, and not much help beyond establishing a basic timeline.

Elizabeth was a rookie when the murder happened—a uniformed officer four months into the job—but she had discovered Julia's body on the altar of a church seven miles from the edge of town. That it was Elizabeth's childhood church was an uncomfortable but otherwise irrelevant fact. It was a body in a building, a crime scene like any other. Elizabeth couldn't know the effect its discovery would have on her own life. On her parents. Her church. Elizabeth had come that day to see her mother and discovered the body of Julia Strange, instead. She'd been choked to death in the most violent manner, the body undressed, then laid out on the altar and draped to the chin in white linen. No signs of sexual trauma were found, but skin discovered beneath her fingernails contained Adrian Wall's DNA. Further investigation discovered Adrian's prints on one of the shattered glasses in the kitchen and on a beer can found in a roadside ditch near the church. A court-ordered medical exam discovered scratches on the back of his neck. Once the prosecutor established that Adrian knew the victim, it was a hard, fast slide to conviction. He had no alibi and no explanation. Even his own partner testified against him.

Only Elizabeth doubted his guilt, but she was barely twenty-one, and no one took her seriously. She tried to investigate on her own, but was warned off. *You're biased,* she was told. *Confused.* But Elizabeth's faith in Adrian went beyond anything that simple. The second time she tried speaking to the witness, she was suspended. The next time she was threatened with prosecution for obstruction. So, Elizabeth let it go. She sat in the courtroom every day and kept her eyes straight ahead when the verdict came back against him.

No one understood why she cared about Adrian Wall, only that she did. No one got it or possibly could.

Even Adrian didn't know.

She spent another thirty minutes with the file, then heard a knock on her door and made it halfway across the room before realizing she was still in her underwear. "Hang on. I'm coming." Slipping down the narrow hall, she snatched a robe off the back of her closet door and returned to the living room as someone knocked a third time. Putting an eye to the peephole, she saw Beckett's wife on the porch. She was cheery and plump and looking at her face in a small mirror. Elizabeth cracked the door. "Carol, hey. What are you doing here?"

Carol flashed a smile and lifted a small, blue valise. "I come with assistance."

"I'm sorry, what?"

"My husband said you needed help with your hair?" Carol raised her voice as if it were a question.

"My hair?"

Carol pushed in and nudged the door shut with a hip. She examined the house approvingly, then turned her attention to the dark circles under Elizabeth's eyes, the washed-out skin, and cool, quiet frustration. "He wasn't kidding about the hair."

Elizabeth's hand moved unconsciously, three fingers on the jagged bangs. "Listen—"

"You didn't ask me to come, did you?"

"Did he say that I had?"

"Look, I'm sorry. I can tell this is unexpected."

Elizabeth sighed. Carol was a patient soul who'd never had a bad day in her life. "It's okay." Elizabeth smiled and nodded. "I think we both know how your husband is."

"A bit of a control freak, God bless him."

"You should try working with him."

"Right, then." Carol put the case down, her face suddenly businesslike. "So, he didn't ask and didn't tell you I was coming." Hands on her hips, she did a slow look around the living room and kitchen.

"Right, then." The second time was less convincing, but she nodded regardless. "Shower for you. I'll have a coffee while I wait, and then we can fix your hair once you're dressed."

"Look, there's no need—"

"Maybe something conservative."

"I'm sorry?"

"What?"

"You said I should put on something conservative."

"Did I?" Carol looked appalled. "God, no. I'm sorry. I don't know what came over me." She fluttered a hand. "It's the short robe and the long legs. Wait. No. I'm still not saying this right." She took a deep breath and tried again. "You're so pretty you'd look beautiful in anything. We're just a little more modest at our house. Please forgive me. I honestly can't believe I said that. I'm here in your home, unexpected . . ."

Elizabeth held up a hand. "It's okay."

"Are you sure? I would hate for you to think I'm such a prude. It's really none of my business."

"Just give me a few minutes. A shower. Another cup of coffee."

Carol smiled weakly. "If you're positive."

"Five minutes."

In the bathroom, Elizabeth stood in front of the mirror and breathed deeply as her smile drained away. She heard the sound of cabinet doors and dishes clanking, then put both hands on the sink and looked in the mirror. Dyer was right about the weight. She stood five-eight and normally carried enough lean muscle to do the job efficiently and well. Good shoulders. Strong arms. But she looked waifish now, the cheekbones more prominent, the eyes larger and deeper, their irises pale green. Stripping off the robe, she tried to imagine what someone like Carol Beckett saw. The hair was brown and short over a small nose and narrow chin. The skin was pale but clear, the face proportional in all the right ways. Elizabeth knew she was pretty, but a white scar ran across her stomach where a junkie with a knife had cut her from rib to hip bone, and a rough patch discolored her shoulder where she'd gone down on hard concrete. Men seemed to like her, but she didn't kid herself about the deeper truths. She'd broken an arm and four ribs, torn skin going over fences, and been thrown through two different windows. *Thirteen years on the force,* she thought. *And what am I?* It was not a light question. She'd had five serious relationships, and all were dead ends. She was a preacher's daughter and a college dropout, a drinker, a smoker, and a fallen cop. She was under investigation for the deaths of two men and felt no remorse at all. Would she change anything if she could?

*Maybe,* she thought.

*Probably not.*

There were reasons for everything. Why she hated her father. Why she'd become a cop, and why relationships were hard. She could say the same thing about the basement and the shooting and Adrian Wall. Consequence mattered, but so did the reasons.

Sometimes the reasons mattered more.

When she came out of the bathroom, she was clean and damp and dressed as conservatively as she could manage, which meant jeans and boots and a linen shirt. Maybe the jeans rode low on her hips, and maybe the shirt was a bit too tailored for someone like Carol. Elizabeth tried to make light of the whole thing. "Is this better?"

"Much."

Elizabeth saw the Julia Strange murder file on the coffee table and scooped it up. "Don't you have a wedding or something?"

"Oh, you sweet girl. Not for another hour, and this won't take nearly that long."

"Are you sure?"

She said it hopefully, but Carol dragged a chair onto the kitchen floor and patted it with one hand. So, Elizabeth sat and allowed her hair to be cut and sprayed and blown. They spoke of little things, but mostly of Carol's husband. "He loves being your partner." Carol stepped back, made a small movement with a brush. "He says watching you work is a beautiful thing."

"Yeah, well . . ."

"Does he talk about me? When you're in the car, I mean, or on a case. Does he talk about me or the kids?"

"Every day," Elizabeth said. "He plays it like everything else—gruff and close—but there's no mistaking how he feels. Proud of his kids. Loves his wife. The two of you give me hope."

Carol beamed, and a little more energy found its way into her brushstrokes.

"Are you about finished?"

Carol gave Elizabeth a hand mirror. "Take a look."

The hair was brown and bobbed and smooth. It was a little more sprayed than she liked, a little too styled. She handed the mirror back and stood. "Thank you, Carol."

"It's what I do." Carol patted her blue case and was halfway down the stairs when her cell phone rang. "Oh. Would you hold this?" She pushed the case at Elizabeth and pulled a phone from her front pocket. Still on the steps, she said, "Hello." A pause. "Oh, hi, sweetheart . . . What? . . . Yes, I am." She looked at Elizabeth. "Of course. Yes. We're at her house." She pressed the phone against a heavy breast and spoke to Elizabeth. "Charlie. He wants to talk to you."

Carol handed over the phone and Elizabeth looked at the street beyond Carol's broad, powdered face. "What's up, Beckett?"

"Your phone is off the hook."

"I know."

"Your cell phone's off, too."

"There's no one I really care to talk to. What's going on?"

"A kid got shot out by the prison."

"I'm sorry to hear that. Why does it concern me?"

"Because odds are fifty-fifty Adrian Wall's the one who shot him."

Elizabeth felt the world go soft under her feet. She wanted to sit, but Carol was staring at her face.

"There's more to it," Beckett said.

"What?"

"The kid that got shot is Gideon Strange. Look, I'm sorry to be the one—"

"Wait. Stop."

Elizabeth pushed on her eyes until she saw red haze and white sparks. She flashed on every autopsy photo in the Julia Strange murder file, then remembered what Gideon had been like on the day his mother had gone missing. She could see every detail of the boy's living room, the furniture and the paint, the detectives and the crime-scene techs that drifted like smoke from the kitchen. She remembered Adrian Wall—pale as a sheet—and the feel of the boy's hot, squirming body as he'd screamed in her arms and other cops tried to calm his wild-eyed, wailing father.

"Is he alive?"

"Surgery," Beckett said. "I don't know any more than that. I'm sorry."

Elizabeth was dizzy, the sun too bright. "Where was he shot?"

"The high right side of his chest."

"No, Beckett. Where did it happen?"

"Nathan's. The biker bar."

"I'll be there in ten minutes."

"No, you won't come anywhere near this. Dyer was specific. He doesn't want you around Adrian Wall or this case. Obviously, I agree."

"Then why did you call me?"

"Because I know you love the kid. I thought you'd want to go to the hospital, be there for him."

"I can't do anything at the hospital."

"You can't do anything here, either."

"Beckett . . ."

"He's not your son, Liz." She froze, the phone painful against her ear. "You're just the cop who found his mother dead."

That was a hard truth, but who else was closer to the boy? His father? Social services? Elizabeth had been the first on scene when Gideon's mother went missing. It might have ended there, but she'd also found Julia Strange broken on the altar of Elizabeth's father's church, the body so vulnerable in its desecration she'd almost wept. They'd never once met; and yet Elizabeth, even now, felt a kinship between them, a thread that twisted through thirteen years and found its embodiment in the small boy left behind. A man such as Beckett would never understand that. He couldn't.

"Go to the hospital," he said. "I'll meet you there, later."

Beckett hung up, and Elizabeth handed the phone back to Carol, who said a good-bye that barely registered. There was a blur of face, a cough as the car started and made a brushstroke of color in the road. When it was gone, Elizabeth walked to the bathroom, kept her eyes down so as not to see her face, and used the sink to rinse spray from her hair. She was numb, her mind spinning on images of Gideon as a toddler, and then as a boy. She thought she knew everything about him, his wants and needs and secret hurts.

*Why was he at the prison?*

Elizabeth shied from the answer because deep down she knew that, too.

Sitting on the sofa, she opened the murder file and pulled a photograph taken by a crime-scene tech less than an hour after Julia Strange was discovered missing. In the shot, Elizabeth stood in uniform with a red-faced infant in her arms. The Stranges' kitchen was in disarray behind her. Gideon had the fabric on her shirt balled in his tiny fist. As a rookie and the only woman in the house, she'd been given the child to take care of until social services arrived. She didn't know then how she'd react to such need and helplessness. She was a kid herself. She couldn't have.

Elizabeth leaned back, remembering all the days and months she'd spent with the boy in the years that followed his mother's death. She knew his teachers, his father, the friends he kept at school. He called her when he was hungry or scared. At times, he walked to her house, just to do homework or talk or sit on the porch. For him, too, the old house had been a sanctuary.

"Gideon."

A single finger touched his face, and when tears rose in her eyes, she let them run unheeded down her cheeks.

"Why didn't you talk to me?"

But he had tried, she remembered, calling three times in one day, then again, and then not at all. She'd known that Adrian was getting out, and that Gideon knew it, too. She should have anticipated his distress, known he might do something stupid. He was such a feeling, thoughtful boy.

"I should have seen it."

But she'd been at the hospital with Channing, then talking to state police and roaming the halls of her own private hell. She hadn't seen a thing. She'd not even thought of him.

"You poor, sweet boy . . ."

She gave herself that minute to be soft, to feel the guilty fullness of a mother's love when she was not, in fact, a mother; then she put the file away, pushed a pistol into her belt, and drove for the cinder-block bar that sat in the shadow of the prison.

# 5

Elizabeth took Main Street at twice the legal limit. She saw a blur of sidewalks and narrow streets, of wrought-iron fencing and redbrick buildings so weathered they looked like orange clay. She passed the library, the clock tower, the old jail that dated back to 1712 and still had stocks in the courtyard. Six minutes later, she left rubber at the on-ramp for the state highway that turned north past the last remnants of the city, a few outlying buildings rising on her left, then falling away as if sucked into the earth. Beyond that were trees and hills and twisted roads.

*If Gideon died . . .* , she thought.

*If somehow Adrian shot him . . .*

The math was horrible because both of them mattered. The man. The boy.

"No," she told herself. "Just Gideon. Just the boy."

But simple truth was not always so simple. She'd tried for thirteen years to forget what Adrian had once meant to her. They'd never been together, she told herself. There was no *relationship*. And all of that was true.

So, why did she see his face as she drove?

Why wasn't she at the hospital?

The questions came without easy answers, so she focused on the drive as the road dropped into a narrow valley, then crossed the river, the prison like a fist in the distance. Elizabeth kept her eyes on a knot of low buildings that floated in a heat shimmer two miles down the road. Cars were parked in front of the sand-colored buildings. She saw blue lights that spun and flashed, a slash of red where an ambulance lingered. Beckett met the car when she stopped. He was not happy.

"You're supposed to be at the hospital."

"Why? Because you said so?" Elizabeth patted a thick arm, walked past him. "You know better than that." He fell in beside her, the bar thirty yards ahead, cops clustered around the door. Elizabeth glanced at the cop cars. "I don't see Dyer. Is he too scared to show his face?"

"What do you think?"

Elizabeth didn't have to think at all. She'd sat front and center at Adrian's trial and remembered every aspect of Francis Dyer's testimony.

*Yes, my partner knew the victim. Her husband was a confidential informant.*

*Yes, they'd been alone together in the past.*

*Yes, Adrian had once commented on how attractive he found her to be.*

It took the prosecutor ten minutes to establish those simple truths, then he drove the point home in seconds.

*Tell me what Mr. Wall said when making reference to the victim's physical appearance.*

*He thought she was too good for the man she was with.*

*You're referring to Robert Strange, the victim's husband?*

*Yes.*

*Did the defendant make a more specific reference to the victim's appearance?*

*I'm not sure what you mean.*

*Did the defendant, your partner, make a more specific reference to the victim's appearance? Specifically, did he mention whether or not he found her attractive?*

*He said she had the kind of face that could drive a good man to do bad things.*

*I'm sorry, Detective. Could you repeat that, please?*

*He said she had the kind of face that could drive a good man to do bad things. But I don't think—*

*Thank you, Detective. That will be all.*

And it was. The prosecutor used Dyer's testimony to paint a picture of obsession, rejection, and payback. Adrian Wall knew the victim. He knew her house, her habits, her husband's schedule. In his professional duties, he'd grown infatuated with the beautiful wife of a confidential informant. When she refused his advances, he abducted and killed her. His fingerprints were at her house and the murder scene. His skin was under her fingernails. He had scratches on his neck.

*Motive,* the prosecutor said.

*The oldest, saddest kind.*

It could have gone down like that, too. Murder one. Twenty-five to life. The jury debated for three days before handing down the lesser verdict of second-degree murder. Cops weren't supposed to talk to jurors postconviction, but Elizabeth did it anyway. It was a crime of passion, they believed, and done without premeditation. They thought he'd killed her at the house, then taken her to the church as an expression of perverse remorse. Why else the white linen and brushed hair, her place beneath the golden cross? Juror twelve found it strangely sweet, and the verdict came as simply as that. Murder two. Thirteen years, minimum.

"Where is he?"

"Third car." Beckett pointed.

Elizabeth saw hints of a man in the backseat of a police cruiser. She couldn't see much, but the shape seemed right, the tilt of his head. He was watching her; she could tell.

"Don't stop walking."

"I'm not," she said, but that was a lie. Her feet were slowing as she spoke. She tried to pretend it wasn't Adrian in the car, that he hadn't changed her life, that maybe she'd never loved him.

"Come on, Liz." Beckett took her arm and pulled her into motion. "That's Nathan Conroy in the other car." He pointed. "Ex-soldier, ex-biker. This is his place. He says he shot the boy in self-defense, which might be true. When the uniforms got here, they found his gun on the bar, a .32 Walther with one shot fired. The serial numbers were filed, so we're holding him on a gun charge for now. As for his claims of self-defense, there was a Colt Cobra .38 on the floor beside Gideon. It was loaded but unfired. Given what day it is, I'd call it pretty likely the boy came gunning for payback."

"He's only fourteen."

"Fourteen with a dead mother and a fucked-up father."

"Jesus, Charlie . . ."

"Just keeping it real."

"Is the gun registered?"

"Look, you're not even supposed to be here."

"Right, right. Sit at the hospital. Mind my own business. That's not going to work for me."

She neared the bar, her gaze locked on a detective she knew and a bloody spot near the open door. Beckett plucked at her sleeve, but she pulled her arm away and called out to the detective, a soft-voiced, steady woman named CJ Simonds. "Hey, CJ. How're you doing?"

"Hello, Liz. I'm sorry about this. They say you know the boy."

CJ pointed into the gloom, where every cop had stopped to stare. Elizabeth nodded, but kept her lips tight. She stepped inside, going wide to clear the stained floor near the entrance. Out of the heat, she found the bar to be a narrow space that reeked of disinfectant and stale beer. A few uniformed officers tried to look busy, but eyes followed her as she moved around the room, avoiding the blood on the floor, touching a chair, the bar. She was a cop, yes, but the papers had turned against her, which meant half the city wasn't far behind. State cops wanted her for double homicide, and every cop in the room knew it was dangerous for her to be here. She was connected to the kid and to Adrian Wall. She had no badge, no standing; and though no one said a word, a lot of people would burn if the kid died or a news crew rolled up unannounced. Elizabeth tried to ignore the attention, but found the stares so unfair and oppressive she snapped, "What?" No one said anything. No one looked away. "What are you looking at?"

Beckett whispered, "Take it easy, Liz."

But they were the same stares she got from the press and her neighbors and people on the street. Headlines or not, it should be different with cops. They understood the dangers of the job, the feel of dark places; but there was no kinship here.

One patrolman's stare was particularly intent; it moved from her breasts to her face and then back. As if she were not a cop, as if she were nothing.

"Do you have some reason to be in here?" she said. The patrolman looked at Beckett. "Don't look at him, look at me."

The patrolman was eight inches taller, ninety pounds heavier. "I'm just doing my job."

"Well, do it outside." He looked at Beckett again, and Elizabeth said, "He'll tell you it's fine."

"It's okay." Beckett gestured to the open door. "Go on outside. Everyone but CJ."

People filed out. The big patrolman waited until the end and brushed Elizabeth with a shoulder as he passed. The contact was swift, but she felt it all the way down, a large man using his size. She watched him go.

Beckett took her elbow. "No one is judging you, Liz."

"Don't touch me." She was glassy-eyed and slick with sudden sweat. The patrolman had dark hair, shaved at the sides of the neck. His hands were brushed with hair like black wire.

"It's just me," Beckett said.

"I said don't touch me. I don't want anybody touching me."

"Nobody's touching you, Liz."

Outside, the patrolman looked her way, then leaned into his friend and whispered something. His neck was thick, his eyes dark and deep and dismissive.

"Liz."

She stared at his hands, at rough skin and square nails.

Beckett said, "You're bleeding." She ignored him, room fading out. "Liz."

"What?" She flinched.

He pointed. "Your mouth is bleeding."

She touched a finger to the corner of her mouth, and it came back red. When she looked at the patrolman, he seemed worried and confused. She blinked twice and realized how young he was. Maybe twenty.

"I'm sorry," she said. "I thought I saw something."

Beckett started to touch her, but stopped. CJ was looking, too, but Elizabeth was in no mood for troubled eyes or the compassion of others. She glanced a final time at the patrolman, then wiped a bloody finger on her pants. "What does Adrian say?"

"He won't talk to us."

"Maybe he'll talk to me."

"Why would he do that?"

"Of all the cops who knew Adrian Wall, which one never accused him of killing an innocent woman?"

She left the bar at a fast walk. Beckett caught her halfway to the car. "Look, I know you had feelings for this guy . . ."

"I don't have feelings."

"I didn't say you *do*. I said you *did*."

"Okay. Fine." She tried to bluff her way past the slip. "I *didn't* have feelings."

Beckett frowned because he recognized the lie. No matter what Elizabeth said now, her feelings for Adrian had been obvious to anyone who'd cared to look. She'd been young and eager, and Adrian was a rock-star cop, not just smart but telegenic. He caught the big cases, made the big arrests. Because of that, every reporter in town lined up to make him a hero. The rookies loved that about him. A lot of the older cops resented it. With Elizabeth, though, it went deeper, and Beckett had been there to see it.

"Listen." He caught her arm and stopped her. "Let's call it a

friendship, okay? No judgment. No baggage. But, you were closer
to Adrian than you were to most. He meant something to you, and
that's okay. The medals, the pretty face, whatever. But he's been
thirteen years inside the hardest prison in the state. A *cop* on the
inside, you understand? Whether he killed Julia Strange or not—
and to be clear, I'm certain that he did—he's not the man you
remember. Ask any cop that's been around for a few years, and
you'll hear the same thing. It doesn't matter if Adrian was a good
man, once upon a time. Prison breaks a man down and builds him
into something different. Just look at the poor bastard's face."

"His face?"

"My point is that he's a convict, and convicts are users. He'll try
to leverage your relationship, whatever feelings you may still have."

"It's been thirteen years, Charlie. Even then, he was just a friend."

She started to turn, but he stopped her again. She looked at the
hand on her arm, then at his eyes, which appeared dim and sad
under heavy lids. He struggled for the prefect words, and when
he spoke his voice seemed as sad as his eyes.

"Be careful with friendships," he said. "Not all of them are free."

She stared pointedly at his hand and waited for him to release
her arm. "Third car?" she asked.

"Yeah." Beckett nodded and stepped aside. "Third car."


She walked away with an easy stride, and Beckett watcher her go.
The long legs. The eagerness. She carried herself well, but he wasn't
fooled. She'd been deep in the cult of Adrian Wall. Beckett remembered how she'd been at the trial, the way she rode the bench day
after day, straight-backed and pale and utterly convinced of Adrian's
innocence. That set her apart from every other cop on the force.
Dyer. Beckett. Even the other rookies. She was the only one who
believed, and Adrian knew it. He'd look for her in court, first in
the morning, then after lunch and at the end of the day. He'd twist
in his seat, find her eyes; and Beckett—more than once—saw the
bastard smile. Nobody celebrated when the verdict came down,

but it was hard to deny the near-universal sense of grim satisfaction. When Adrian murdered Julia Strange, he put a black eye on every cop that cared about right and wrong. Beyond that, it was a PR nightmare.

*Hero cop murders young mother . . .*

Then there was Gideon Strange, the boy. For whatever reason, Elizabeth bonded to him, too. She'd held him at the funeral as his father wept and was even now involved in the boy's life on a fundamental level. She cared for him, loved him, even. Beckett never understood the reasons, but knowing the depth of her affection, he wondered how she was holding it together.

"Sir." It was CJ Simonds, the interruption hesitant.

"Yes, CJ. What is it?"

She pointed, and Beckett looked past the bar to a dark car on the verge and a group of men beside it. "It's the warden—"

"Yes." Beckett cut her off. "I see that." The warden was in a suit, the guards in uniforms sharp enough to cut paper. Beckett pointed at the cruiser. "Watch Liz. Make sure she's okay."

"Sir?"

"Just . . . watch her."

Beckett crossed the lot, felt heat under his shoes and a fist of emotion in his chest. He'd known the warden for a long time, but the relationship was complicated. He stopped by the car and felt the warden's stare.

"Detective." The warden was sweating in the heat, his smile overly bright.

Beckett ignored the guards and spoke quietly. "What the hell are you doing here?"

The police cruiser was in the shade at the back of the lot. Elizabeth kept her chin down and her eyes sideways as she cleared the hood and circled to the rear door. She saw the top of Adrian's head first; and he was looking down, so deathly still she had the wild thought he was actually dead, that he'd drifted off, alone in the back of the car. Then he showed a scarred face, and eyes that were utterly unchanged. For that second the entire world shrank to a black hole that stripped away all the years of her adulthood. She saw how he'd saved her life and never known it, his gentle manner as he'd stopped on a chill day to ask if she was all right. In that second Elizabeth was seventeen again, alone at the edge of a two-hundred-foot drop, a child looking for the courage to take one more step.

*Are you okay, miss?*

His shoulders were square, the badge on his belt bright gold. She hadn't heard him, hadn't seen him.

*I just . . .* She wore tall shoes that laced above her ankles, a secondhand dress that flapped against her skin. Her gaze settled on the thirty acres of black water that filled the quarry below. *I was just counting.*

It was a stupid thing to say, but he didn't act as if it were. *Counting what?*

*The seconds it would take to fall,* she thought, but said nothing.

*Are you sure you're okay?*

She stared at the badge on his belt and couldn't look away. His fingers, beside it, were still.

*Are your parents here?*

*Down the trail,* she lied.

*What's your name?*

She offered it in a broken voice, and he studied the trailhead at the edge of the woods. It was late and cold and almost dark. The water beneath them looked as hard as metal.

*Parents tend to worry about children up here, especially with dark coming on.*

His gesture took in the mountaintop, the quarry below. She looked at the sucking blackness of all that water, then at the strip of stone at her feet. His face, when she finally looked at it, was beautiful.

*You're sure they're waiting?*

*Yes, sir.*

*Off you go, then.*

He smiled a final time, and she left on legs that were cold and weak and shaking. He didn't follow, but was watching when she glanced back, his eyes lost in the fading light. She waited until trees surrounded her, then ran as she'd never run before. She ran until her body burned and her breath was gone, then she curled up in dry leaves and wondered if God had sent the policeman to pull her back from the thing she'd meant to do. Her father would say yes, that God is in all things; but God could no longer be trusted, not God or her father or boys who said, *Trust me.* That's what she thought as she lay in the leaves, shaking: that the world was bad, but maybe not all of it. That maybe she'd try to live another day. That maybe she could.

Elizabeth didn't believe in God anymore, but looking at Adrian through patrol-car glass, she thought that fate might be real. She'd almost died the day they first met, and here he was again. She wasn't suicidal, but still . . .

"Hello, Adrian."

"Liz."

The door pressed against her hip, but she had no memory of opening it. The world seemed to be his voice, his eyes, the unexpected thumping in her chest. The scars on his face were pale and thin, a half diamond on one cheek and a six-inch line that ran top to bottom beside his left eye. Even with Beckett's warning, the starkness of the scars surprised her, as did the thinness that made the bones of his face sharper than she remembered. He was older and hard, with an animal stillness that disconcerted her. She'd expected something else, furtiveness maybe, or shame.

"May I?"

She gestured at the seat, and he shifted sideways to make room for her to sit. She slipped into the car, felt his warmth in the leather. She studied his face and did not look away when his hand moved to cover the worst of the scars.

"It's only skin," she said.

"On the outside, maybe."

"How about the rest of you?"

"Tell me about Gideon."

It surprised her that he knew Gideon's name. "You recognized him?"

"How many fourteen-year-old boys want me dead?"

"So, he did try to hurt you."

"Just tell me if he's okay."

Elizabeth leaned against the door and didn't speak for long seconds. "Why do you care?"

"How can you ask me that?"

"I can ask you that because he came here to kill you, and because people are not normally so concerned about those intent on doing that kind of harm. I can ask you that because he was fifteen months old the last time you saw him, because he's not your family or your friend. I can ask that because he's an innocent kid who's never hurt a fly in all the days of his life, because he weighs a hundred and fifteen pounds and has a bullet where no bullet should ever be. I can ask you that because I more or less raised him, and because he looks just like the woman you were convicted of killing. So, until I know for sure you're not the one who shot him, we'll do this my way."

Her voice was loud by the time she finished, and both of them were surprised by the outburst of emotion. Elizabeth couldn't hide her feelings when it came to the boy. She was overprotective, and Adrian saw it.

"I just want to know he's okay. That's all. He lost his mother and thinks it's my fault. I just want to know he's alive, that he hasn't lost everything."

It was a good answer, Elizabeth thought. Honest. Fair. "He's in surgery. I don't know more than that." She paused. "Beckett says Conroy is the one who shot him. Is that right?"

"Yes."

"Was it self-defense?"

"The boy came to kill me. Conroy did what he had to do."

"Would Gideon have done it?"

"Pulled the trigger? Yes."

"You sound certain."

"He said it's what a man would do. He seemed convinced."

She studied his fingers, which looked as if they'd been broken and poorly set. "All right. I believe you."

"You'll tell Beckett?"

"Beckett. Dyer. I'll make sure everyone understands."

"Thank you."

"Adrian, listen—"

"Don't."

"What?"

"Look, it's nice to see you. It's been a long time, and you were good to me, once. But don't pretend to be my friend."

They were difficult words, but she understood. How many times had she driven past the prison since his conviction? How many times had she stopped? Gone inside? Not once. Not ever.

"Can I do anything for you? Do you need money? A ride?"

"You can get out of the car." He was looking at Beckett and a group of men standing by a dark sedan on the edge of the road. Suddenly pale and sweating, he looked as if he might be sick.

"Adrian?"

"Just get out of the car. Please."

She thought about arguing, but to what end? "Okay, Adrian." She swung her legs into the heat. "Let me know if you change your mind."

Elizabeth walked away from Adrian and met Beckett halfway across the lot. Behind him, men slipped into the sedan, which turned across traffic and accelerated toward the prison. She recognized a face in the window, a flash of profile, quickly gone. "That was the warden."

"Yes."

"What did he want?"

Beckett watched the car for long seconds, eyes narrowed. "He heard about the shooting and knew it involved one of his prisoners."

"Were you arguing?"

"Yes."

"About what?"

"The fact he has no business on my goddamn crime scene."

"Take it easy, Charlie. I'm just asking."

"Yeah. 'Course. Sorry. Did you get anything from Adrian?"

"He confirms the bartender's story. Gideon came looking for revenge. Conroy shot the boy to save Adrian's life."

"Damn. That's brutal. I'm sorry."

"What are you going to do with him?"

"Adrian? Take a statement. Cut him loose."

"Does Gideon's father know?"

"We haven't found him yet."

"I'll do it."

"He's a deadbeat drunk in a county full of shit-heel bars. Who knows what rock he's crawled under for the day?"

"I can track him down."

"Tell me where you think he might be, and I'll send some uniforms."

Elizabeth shook her head. "We're talking about Gideon. His father should be with him when he wakes."

"His father is an asshole who hasn't done two good things for that boy in his whole life."

"Nevertheless, I'd rather find him myself. It's personal, Charlie. You understand."

"Your interview with the state police is in three hours."

"I said I'd do it."

"Okay. Fine. Sure. Whatever." He was angry, but it seemed everyone was. "Three hours."

"Yep."

"Don't be late."

Late? Maybe. Elizabeth wasn't even sure she'd show up.

Dropping into the car, she thought she was out clean. But Beckett filled the open window before she could put the car in gear. He leaned in, looking swollen in a tight suit. She saw scratches on his wedding ring; smelled shampoo that was probably his wife's. Everything about him was earnest and heavy. The stare. The sound of his voice. "You're in a strange place," he said. "And I get that. Channing and the basement, state cops and Adrian. Hell, the boy's blood's not even dry."

"I know all these things, Charlie."

"I know you do."

"Then what are you trying to say?"

"I'm saying people don't think straight when they get twisted up. That's normal, even for cops. I just don't want you to do anything stupid."

"Like what?"

"Bad men. Dark houses."

He was trying to help, but that was the hard edge of Elizabeth's world: bad men and the things that happen in dark houses.

Putting the prison in her rearview mirror, Elizabeth took her time driving back to the city. She wanted a moment's quiet, but thoughts of Gideon in surgery made that impossible. A .32 was a small bullet, but he was a small boy. Did she blame Nathan Conroy for shooting him? No. Not really. Did she blame Adrian? What about herself?

Elizabeth pictured Gideon's mother, as she'd been—tall and clear-eyed and elegant—then pictured her son in the dark, lying in wait with a loaded weapon in his pocket. Where did he get the revolver, and how did he get to Nathan's? Did he walk? Hitchhike? Was it his father's gun? Jesus, did he really plan to kill a man? The line of thought made her nauseous, but maybe it was a delayed reaction to sight of the boy's blood, or that she'd had three cups of coffee after two days without food, or that she'd barely slept six hours out of the last sixty. Slowing at the river, she pulled onto the verge and called the hospital to check on Gideon's status.

"Are you family?" she was asked.

"Police."

"Hold for surgery."

Elizabeth held, and as she did, she watched the water. She'd grown up near the river and knew its moods: the gentle slide in August, the hard rush that followed winter storms. She'd taken Gideon fishing at times, and it was their place, their thing. But today the river felt different. She didn't see the sycamores or the willows or the ripples in the current. She saw red banks carved away, wounds in the earth.

"You're asking about Gideon Strange?"

Elizabeth played the cop card again and got all the information available. *Still in surgery. Too early for a prognosis.*

"Thank you," she said, then crossed the river without once looking down.

It took twenty minutes to reach the derelict side of things, a seven-mile stretch that began with empty storefronts and ended with shuttered factories and mill houses in their second century. The textile industry had left even before the downturn, same with furniture and the bottling plant and big tobacco. Now, the east side of town was paved with empty factories and broken dreams. As a young cop, Elizabeth had cut her teeth on the east side, but it was worse now. Gangs had moved north from Atlanta, down from DC. Drugs ran up and down the interstate, and bad things multiplied with the trade. Much of the violence happened on the seven-mile stretch, and a lot of poor but decent people were caught in the middle.

That included Gideon.

Turning onto a narrow street, she worked the car between cast-off furniture and old cars until a chalk-yellow house slid past and the hill steepened. Shadows crept out the deeper she went. Cars got rustier; grass disappeared. By the time she bottomed out, the road was in full shade, a ribbon of asphalt running beside a cold stream that broke white over gray stone and bits of shattered concrete. Gideon hadn't always lived in such a desolate place, but when his mother died, Robert Strange started drinking, and the whirl of it took him down. A good job became an occasional job. The drinking got worse. There were drugs. The only mystery was how he managed to keep Gideon in his life at all. But that, in the end, was no mystery. The system was stretched, and Elizabeth loved the boy too much to break the last bit of his heart. Every time she got social services involved, Gideon would beg her to leave him with his father.

*It's my father,* he'd say. *He's all I have left.*

Other than a few months in foster care, he'd gotten his wish. In exchange, Elizabeth stayed involved. She made sure his clothes were clean, that food was on the table. That worked until it didn't. Now, Gideon was fighting for his life, and she had to face the hard question.

*How much of that was her fault?*

Twisting along the valley floor, she found the boy's house on a stony patch beside the creek. It was smaller than most, a faded cube beneath a streaked, metal roof. Piled firewood made the porch sag on one side, and the cinder-block chimney leaned ten degrees out of true; but the stream was what made everything so stark in comparison, all that cold, clean water rushing off to better places.

Stepping from the car, she studied the slash of sky, the stream, the pale, pink house across the street. It was quiet in the shade, and hot. An old car rusted on flat tires. The yard was red dirt.

On the porch, Elizabeth knocked twice, but knew already that no one was home. The house had that empty feel. Inside, she stepped over liquor bottles and engine parts and old mail. She checked the boy's room first. The bed was made, shoes lined against the wall. A single shelf was rowed with books and framed photographs. Elizabeth lifted a picture of Gideon's mother taken on her wedding day. She wore a simple dress and a ring of flowers in her hair. She stood in front of the old church, her new husband young and clean-cut and handsome. The next two pictures were of Elizabeth and Gideon: a picnic in the park, one at the river.

There were no other pictures of his father, and that felt about right. The last was of Gideon and Elizabeth's parents. The boy enjoyed church and sang in the choir. Elizabeth would pick him up on Sundays and take him. She never went in herself—that was an old promise—but her parents loved the boy almost as much as she did. They'd have him for dinner once a month; ask after his grades; watch him in school plays. The reverend was determined to see Gideon through his childhood, and to remind the boy that his father had, once, been a fine man.

Moving through Gideon's room, Elizabeth touched schoolbooks, a turtle shell, a jar of pennies. Nothing had changed, she thought, then she considered the outcome should Gideon die.

*Nothing ever would.*

Closing the boy's bedroom door, she checked the rest of the house, then went looking for his father. Beckett was right about Robert Strange. He drank and was undependable, an otherwise broken man who loved the boy as best he could. He worked part-time for a shade-tree garage far out in the county. The owner was a drunk, which meant Robert could drink, too. He worked off the books, mostly on American cars, mostly for cash. That's where he would be, she thought, at the garage and useless and drunk.

It took eighteen miles of country road to get there, the route twisting past the quarry, the gun range, the ruins of an old theater. She drove past dairy farms and plowed-under fields, turned left, and ran under heavy trees that swayed with the breeze. Two miles into the last stretch of gravel road, she turned onto raw dirt and followed the track to a corrugated shed that sat on a high bank in the last bend of the river. She turned off the engine and stared for long seconds through the glass. Hot cars and stolen tires weren't the only illegal things this far out in the county. There were meth labs and cockfights and trailer-park brothels run by large men with long hair and swastika tattoos. People went missing this far out, and not too many years passed without hunters finding the remains of one poor soul or another. So, Elizabeth took a good, long look around and checked the gun at her back before she stepped from the car.

Even then, she didn't like it. Dogs lolled in the shade. Beyond them, the river hissed along the bank, then flattened and slowed as it spilled across the county line. Elizabeth watched the dogs as she walked. Two of them stayed down, but one found his feet, his head low, a pink tongue hanging out as he panted in the heat. Elizabeth kept one eye on him and one on the shed. Ten feet from the bay door, she smelled grease and gasoline and cigarette smoke.

"Can I help you?"

A man stepped from beneath a truck on a hydraulic lift. He was in his late fifties with close hair and grease-stained shoulders. Six-four, she guessed. Two-thirty. He wiped thick hands on a dirty handkerchief and guarded his expression.

"My name is Elizabeth Black."

"I know who you are, Detective. We do get the papers out here."

Not aggressive, Elizabeth thought. Not helpful, either. "I'd like to speak to Robert Strange."

"Never heard of him."

"He works here four days a week. You pay him cash, off the books. That's his moped under the pecan tree."

She pointed at a yellow moped, and another dog stood up, a whine in its throat as if it sensed tension in the air.

The big man stepped out onto gravel, sunlight hard on his face. "Aren't you suspended?"

Elizabeth counted five men, now, most of them holding back in the dimness of the shed. There'd be warrants out on a few of them: missed court dates, felony charges. "Are you going to make this difficult for me?"

"I'm not sure, yet."

"I just want to talk to him."

"Is it about his boy?"

"You know about that?"

"Glenn's wife works 911 dispatch." He pointed at one of the men. "She told us what happened. The boy comes around sometimes. He's a good kid. We all like him."

Elizabeth studied the shed, the men inside. She thought of Gideon here and could see it. He liked cars and the forest. The river was down the hill. "I want to talk to his father. It's important."

"We don't want any trouble."

"There won't be any."

"Back room, then." He hooked a thumb over his shoulder. "Past the Corvette."

The Corvette sat on a floor jack, front tires off the rims, the bearings pulled. Beyond it was a metal door painted black. Looking at it, Elizabeth felt a tingle in her fingers. The men were still watching her, nobody working. She'd have to the pass through the gauntlet of their bodies, then twist between cars and jacks and lifts. It was dim in the shed. They were staring at her, waiting; and she wondered what was in the back room, if there would be windows or darkness or a mattress-shaped hole in the world.

"Detective?"

Elizabeth started, then pushed into the shed, between the men. To her surprise, they stepped back to make room. Three of them nodded politely and one mumbled the word "Ma'am," before ducking his head as if embarrassed. At the door, she looked back, but no one else had moved, so she touched a handle that clicked as she turned it. The room beyond was just a room, a small, square space with vending machines, a vinyl sofa, and a table with four chairs. Robert Strange sat with both hands on the table, a bottle and a glass between them. The lines in his face seemed deeper than normal. He did not look well.

"Hello, Robert."

"I figured it was you who'd come looking."

"Why?"

"Because it's always you, isn't it?" He lifted the glass and choked on brown liquor. "Is he dead?"

"I talked to the hospital an hour ago. He's in surgery. I'm hopeful."

"Hopeful."

The word leaked out. Elizabeth saw doubt and regret, but darker things, too. She tried to gauge how drunk he was, but he'd always been a quiet, grim drinker. "Do you know why your son was shot?"

"You should leave, Detective."

"He was shot trying to kill Adrian Wall. Are you sober enough to understand that? He was out by the prison. Fourteen years old with a loaded weapon."

"Don't say that bastard's name."

"Where were you when this was happening?" He lifted the glass, but she took it from his hand. "Where did he get the gun?"

"Give me the glass."

"Answer the question."

"Can you, for once, mind your own goddamn business?"

"No."

"He's my son, you understand? Why are you in the middle of that? Why are you *always* in the middle?"

It was an old argument between them. Elizabeth was part of Gideon's life. Robert didn't like it. Looking at him now, Elizabeth studied the bright eyes, the swollen veins. His hands twisted the bottle as if it were her throat. "Did you give Gideon the gun?"

"For God's sake . . ."

"Did you want Adrian dead, too?"

He hung his head and ran fingers through greasy hair. Elizabeth studied the heavy jaw, the veined nose. He was tired and nearly ruined and only thirty-nine. With all the bitterness and regret, it was easy to forget that he was a young man, heartbroken from the death of a beautiful wife. "Did you know what your son was doing?" She asked it more gently. "Did you know he had a gun?"

"I thought . . ."

"You thought what?"

"I was drunk." He pressed fingers against his eyes. "I thought it was a dream."

"What do you mean?"

"Gideon with a gun in his hand." Robert shook his head, dark hair glinting. "It came out of the television. That had to be a dream, right? Guns coming out of TVs. That can't be real."

"Was it your gun, Robert?" His mouth stayed shut, so she pushed harder. "Did you know that Adrian Wall was getting out of prison today?" He looked up, his eyes so suddenly pink and shattered-looking Elizabeth knew the answer. "Jesus, you did."

"It was a dream. Right? How could that be real?"

He buried his face in his hands, and Elizabeth—understanding—straightened.

*Had he really thought it was a dream?*

*Or had some part of him known?*

That was the part of his soul that had him weeping. The part that thought it was real and decided not to call the cops, the part that wanted Adrian Wall dead and was willing to let his son do the dirty work.

"Is my boy alive?" He showed the same pink eyes. "Please say he is."

"Yes," she said. "Twenty minutes ago he was alive." He broke then, sobbing. "I want you to come with me, Robert."

"Why?"

"Because as much as I might hate it right now, Gideon loves you. You should be there when he wakes."

"You'll take me?"

"Yes," she said; and he rose, blinking and afraid, as if condemned to some terrible fate.

# 6

Elizabeth drove Robert Strange to the hospital and got him situated in a waiting room down the hall from the surgical theaters. After a brief talk with one of the nurses, she returned to the place she'd left him. "Gideon's still in surgery. It looks good, though."

"Are you sure?"

"As sure as I can be." Elizabeth pulled twenty dollars from her pocket and dropped it on the table. "That's for food. Not liquor."

The irony was that Elizabeth wanted the drink. She was tired and drained and for the first time in her adult life knew she didn't want to be a cop. But what else was there?

Some other job?

Prison?

That felt real as she drove. State cops. Incarceration. Maybe that's why she took the long drive to the station. Maybe that's why she was thirty minutes late.

"Where the hell have you been?"

Beckett was waiting outside, his tie loose, his face redder than usual. Elizabeth locked the car and considered the second-floor windows as she walked. "What happened with Adrian?"

"He's in the wind." Beckett fell in beside her, deflated by her steady calm.

"Where?"

"Walking down the road, last I saw him. How's Gideon?"

"Still in surgery."

"Did you find his father?"

"He's at the hospital."

"Drunk?"

"Yeah."

They were avoiding the obvious. Beckett came around to it first. "They're waiting for you."

"The same ones?"

"Different."

"Where?"

"Conference room."

"Jesus."

"Yeah, I know."

The conference room was beside the bull pen and glass-walled. That meant the state cops wanted her visible. They wanted every other cop to see. "I guess we do this the hard way."

They took the stairs to the second floor and stepped into the bull pen. People stopped talking and stared. She felt the distrust and condemnation, but tuned it out. The department was taking heat, yes. The newspapers had turned, and a lot of people were angry. Elizabeth understood all that, but not everyone could walk into the dark and make the hard choice.

She knew who she was.

The cops in the conference room, though, were strangers. She saw them through the glass, both of them older and stern. They wore sidearms and state credentials and watched intently as she moved between the desks.

"Captain." She stopped where Dyer waited at the conference room door. "Those are not the same investigators."

"Hamilton and Marsh," Dyer said. "You've heard of them?"

"Should I have?"

"They report directly to the attorney general. Dirty politicians. Crooked cops. They go after the worst of them. It's all they do. Big cases. High profile."

"Should I be flattered?"

"They're a hit squad, Liz, politicized and effective. Don't take them lightly."

"I don't."

"Yet, your lawyer's not here."

"True."

"He says you haven't met him at all, won't return his calls."

"It's fine, Francis."

"Let's reschedule and bring in the lawyer. I'll take the heat."

"I said I'm fine." She laid a palm on his face, then opened the door and went inside. Both state investigators were standing on the other side of a polished table. One's fingertips rested lightly on the wood; the other's arms were crossed.

"Detective Black," the taller one began. "I'm Special Agent Marsh. This is Special Agent Hamilton."

"I don't care about introductions." Elizabeth pulled out a chair and sat down.

"Very well." The one called Marsh sat. The other waited a heart-beat, then sat, too. There was not a kind look between them, not a moment's softness. "You understand you have the right to an attorney?"

"Let's just do this."

"Very well." Marsh pushed a Miranda waiver across the table. Elizabeth signed it without comment, and Marsh pressed it into a folder. He looked at Dyer and gestured at an empty chair. "Captain, would you care to sit?"

"No." Dyer stood in a corner, arms crossed. Beyond the glass, every cop was watching. Beckett looked as if he might vomit.

"All right." Marsh started a tape recorder and gave the date, the time, the names of everyone present. "This interview is in regard to the shooting deaths of Brendan and Titus Monroe, brothers aged thirty-four and thirty-one at the times of their deaths. Detective Black has waived right to counsel. Captain Dyer is present as a witness only and is not participating in the interview. Now, Detective Black . . ." Marsh paused, face neutral. "I'd like to walk you through the events of August fifth."

Elizabeth laced her fingers on the table. "I've given a statement regarding the matter in question. I have no additions or modifications."

"Then, let's consider this discussion one of nuance and color. We simply want to understand what happened a little better. I'm sure you can appreciate that."

"Very well."

"I'd like to hear more about how you came to be in the house where the Monroe brothers died. Channing Shore had been missing for a day and a half. Is that correct?"

"Forty hours."

"I'm sorry?"

"Not a day and a half. Forty hours."

"And police were actively involved in the search?"

"There was speculation she was a runaway, but, yes. We had her description and were involved. Her parents had come to the precinct. They were very concerned."

"They'd posted a reward?"

"And spoken to local television. They were convincing."

"Did you believe her to be a runaway?"

"I believed she'd been abducted."

"Based on what information?" Marsh asked.

"I'd spoken to her parents and been to her house, in her room. I interviewed friends, teachers, coaches. There was no sign of drug or alcohol abuse. Her parents were not perfect, but they weren't abusive, either. There was no boyfriend, nothing unusual on her computer. She was going to go to college. She was a solid kid."

"That was the sole basis of your judgment?"

"She had pink sheets."

"Pink sheets?"

"Pink sheets. Stuffed animals." Elizabeth leaned back in her chair. "The lives of runaways are rarely pink or fluffy."

Hamilton stared at Elizabeth as if she were something dirty. Marsh shifted in his seat. "Channing was eventually discovered in the basement of an abandoned dwelling on Penelope Street."

"Yes."

"How would you describe that neighborhood?"

"Decayed."

"Violent?"

"There have been shootings there, yes."

"Murders?"

"A few."

Marsh leaned forward. "Why did you go into that house alone? Where was your partner?"

"I've explained this."

"Explain it again."

"It was late. We'd been working Channing Shore's disappearance since five in the morning. We were exhausted. Beckett went home for a shower and a few hours' sleep. I went for coffee and a drive. We were going to meet again at five the next morning."

"Go on."

"I received a radio call from dispatch asking me to check out reports of suspicious activity at an abandoned house on Penelope Street. The report indicated activity in the basement, possible screams. I would not normally take a call like that, but it was a busy night. The department was stretched."

"Stretched, how?"

"The battery plant closed that day—three hundred jobs gone in a city that can't afford to lose three. There was rioting. Some burned cars. People were angry. The department's resources were strained."

"Where was Detective Beckett?"

"He's married with kids. He needed the time."

"So, you went alone to a dangerous neighborhood, then into an abandoned house where screams had been reported?"

"That's correct."

"You didn't call for backup?"

"No."

"Is that normal procedure?"

"It was not a normal day."

Marsh drummed his fingers on the table. "Were you drinking?"

"That question is offensive."

Marsh slid a paper across the table. "This is the incident report completed by your commanding officer." He glanced at Dyer. "It says you were disoriented after the shooting. At times, nonresponsive."

Elizabeth flashed back to the moment in question. She was sitting on the curb outside the abandoned house. Channing was in the ambulance, wrapped in a blanket, catatonic. Dyer's hands were on Elizabeth's shoulders. *Talk to me,* he'd said. *Liz.* His eyes faded in and out. *Jesus Christ,* he'd said. *What the hell happened in there?*

"I wasn't drinking. I wasn't drunk."

Marsh leaned back and studied her. "You have a soft spot for young people."

"Is that a question?"

"Especially those who are helpless or abused. It's reflected in your files. People in the department are aware of it. You respond with great passion to young people in distress. You've intervened with authorities, used force on multiple occasions." Marsh leaned forward. "You feel a connection to those who are small and young and unable to care for themselves."

"Isn't that part of the job description?"

"Not if it interferes with the job." Marsh opened another folder and began to spread out photographs of the dead men. They were glossy, full color. Crime-scene photographs. Autopsy photographs. They stretched across the table like a fan of cards: blood and blank eyes and shattered bone. "You went alone into an abandoned house." He touched the photographs as he spoke. "There was no power. Reports of screams. You went alone into the basement." He straightened the edges of the photographs until he had a perfect line. "Did you hear anything?"

Elizabeth swallowed.

"Detective Black? Did you hear anything?"

"Dripping water. Rats in the walls."

"Rats?"

"Yes."

"What else?"

"Channing was crying."

"You saw her?"

Elizabeth blinked, the memory collapsing into something dimmer. "She was in the second room."

"Describe it."

"Concrete. Low ceilings. The mattress was in the corner."

"Was it dark?"

"There was a candle on a crate. It was red."

Elizabeth closed her eyes and saw that, too: melted wax and flickers of light, the hallways and doors and shadowed places. It was as real as in her dreams, but mostly she heard the girl's voice, the broken words and prayer, the way she begged God to help her, please.

"Where were the Monroe brothers at this time?"

"I don't know." Elizabeth cleared her throat. "There were other rooms."

"And the child?" Marsh pushed a photograph forward. It showed the mattress, the wires. Elizabeth blinked again, but the room around her remained blurry. Only the photograph was sharp. The mattress. The memory. "How was Channing?"

"She was as you might imagine."

"Frightened, of course." He placed a single finger on the photo of the mattress. "Wired to a mattress. Exposed. Alone." He removed the photographs, touched two that showed the dead men, their bodies broken and bent and shredded. "These are the ones that interest me the most." He pushed them toward her. "The bullet placement, in particular." He touched one man and then the other. "Both knees shot away." He slid forward a close-up of the shattered knees. "Multiple shots to the groin. Again, both men." Another close-up hissed across the table, this one an autopsy photo, stark and bright. "Did you torture these men, Detective Black?"

"It was dark . . ."

Another photograph slid across the table. "Titus Monroe. Shot in both knees, both elbows."

"Not intentional."

"But painful. Nonfatal."

Elizabeth swallowed, nauseous.

Marsh noticed. "I'd ask you to look at each photograph."

"I've seen these."

"These are not random injuries, Detective."

"I thought they were armed."

"Knees. Groins. Elbows."

"It was dark."

"Eighteen shots."

"The girl was crying."

"Eighteen shots placed to cause maximum pain."

Elizabeth looked away. Marsh leaned back, his eyes blue and cold. "Two men are dead, Detective."

Elizabeth turned her head slowly, her own eyes so flat and emotionless they, themselves, looked dead. "Two animals," she said.

"I beg your pardon."

Her heart beat twice. She spoke with care. "Two *animals* are dead."

"Liz! Jesus!"

Marsh held up a hand as Dyer seemed to lurch forward. "It's okay, Captain. Stand where you are." He turned his attention back to Liz, hands spread on the table. "Did you torture these men, Detective?" He lifted a bloody photograph, placed it gently in front of her. Elizabeth looked away, so he put down two more. They were autopsy photos, close-ups. The wounds were immediate and full color. "Detective Black?"

Elizabeth stood. "We're done here."

"You're not excused."

She pushed back her chair.

"I'm not finished, Detective."

"I am."

She turned on a heel.

Hamilton stood, but Marsh said, "Let her go."

Elizabeth pulled open the door and was outside before Dyer could touch her arm or say a word to stop her. She pushed through the crowd of watching cops, through friends and rivals and faces that seemed strange to her. The room faded to gray as people muttered words she didn't care about or understand. Everything was *the basement.* It was stone and fabric, screams and blood. She heard her name, but it wasn't real. The world was gun smoke and wire and the twine of Channing's fingers . . .

"Liz!"

Slippery skin and pain . . .

"Liz, damn it!"

That was Beckett, still distant. She ignored the brush of his fingers, and only in the fresh air did she realize he'd followed her down the stairwell. There were cars and black pavement, then Beckett's fingers on her wrist.

"I don't want to talk about it."

"Liz, look at me."

But, she couldn't. A car had leaked oil onto the tarmac. Sunlight turned the puddle into melted iron, and that was exactly how she felt: as if all the hardness had been drawn from her bones, as if she, too, were melting away. "Don't call me, Charlie. Okay? Don't call me. Don't follow me."

"Where are you going?"

"I don't know," she said; but that was a lie.

"Maybe you should talk to Wilkins."

"Don't go there, either." Wilkins was the department shrink. Every other day he called. And every other day she declined his services. "I'm fine."

"You keep saying that, but you look like a strong wind will lift you off your feet."

"I'm fine."

"Liz . . ."

"I have to go."

She got in the car and drove to the abandoned house where Channing had been held captive for forty long hours. She wasn't sure why she'd come, but guessed it had to do with photographs and dreams and the way she avoided this bit of town. The structure was a shell under the darkening sky. It sat far back from the road, part of it crushed by a fallen tree, the rest of it obscured behind saplings, milkweed, and high grass. She could smell it through the open window, a whiff of rot and mold and feral cat. The house next door was empty. Three more on the street were dark.

The city was crumbling, she thought.

She was crumbling.

At the porch, she hesitated. Yellow tape fluttered at the door. The windows were boarded up. Elizabeth touched flaking paint and thought of all the things that had died on the other side of the door. *Five days,* she told herself. *I can handle this.* But her hand shook when she reached for the knob.

She stared at it, disbelieving, then snapped her fingers shut. She stood for a long minute, then retreated in disarray for the first time since pinning on a badge. It was just a place, she told herself. Just a house.

*Then why can't I go inside?*

Elizabeth got back in the car and drove, houses flicking past, sun dropping behind the tallest trees. It was only as the road bent in a long, slow curve that she realized she wasn't going home. The houses were wrong, the ridgelines and the views. But, she kept driving. Why? Because she needed something. A touchstone. A reminder of why she'd become a cop in the first place.

When she found Adrian, he was ten miles out of town in a burned-out building that used to be his home. It sat under tall trees at the end of a half-mile drive, a once-fine farmhouse now little more than ash-heap walls and a bone of chimney. She stepped out under a spinning sky, and the wind, on its lips, carried the faintest taste of smoke.

"What are you doing here, Liz?" He stepped from the gloom.

"Hello, Adrian. I'm sorry for just showing up like this."

"It's not really my house, is it?"

"That's not what I meant."

"Then, what?"

"Prison. Thirteen years." She ran out of words because Adrian was the one who'd made her what she was. That made him a god of sorts, and gods terrified her. "I'm sorry I didn't visit."

"You were just a rookie. We barely knew each other."

She nodded because words, again, were inadequate. She'd written him three times in the first year of his incarceration, and each one said the same thing. *I'm sorry. I wish I could have done more.* After that, she'd had nothing else to offer.

"Did you know . . . ?" She turned both palms to finish the sentence. *Did you know your house was burned, your wife gone?*

"I never heard from Catherine." His face was a slash of gray in the gloom. "After the trial I never heard from anyone."

Elizabeth rolled her shoulders against a final rush of guilt. She should have told him years ago that his wife had left, his house had burned. She should have gone to the prison and told him face-to-face. She'd been unable to bear it, though, the thought of him locked up, diminished. "Catherine left three months after your conviction. The house sat empty for a while, then one day it burned. They say it was arson."

He nodded, but she knew it hurt. "Why are you here, Liz?"

"I just wanted to check on you." She left the rest unspoken: that she was looking at murder charges of her own, that she was hoping for insight, and that she might have loved him, once.

"Would you like to come inside?"

She thought he was joking, but he picked his way through scrub and rubble until orange light touched his skin. It was the old living room, she saw. The floor was gone, but fire burned in the fireplace and made sounds as it settled. Adrian added wood, and the light spread. Around her, she saw ash, swept back, and a log dragged in as a seat. Adrian's hands were stained, too; and Gideon's blood still showed black on his shirt. "Home sweet home." He said it flatly, but the hurt was there. His great-great-grandfather had built the house. Adrian grew up in it, then deeded it to his wife to cover his legal bills, if necessary. It had survived the Civil War, his bankruptcy, and his trial. Now, it was this shell, tumbled and damp beneath trees that had seen the sweep of its history.

"I'm sorry about your wife," Elizabeth said. "I wish I could tell you where she was."

"She was pregnant when the trial started." Adrian sat on the log; stared at the fire. "She lost the baby two days before the verdict. Did you know that?" Elizabeth shook her head, but he wasn't watching her. "Did you see anyone out there?"

"Out there?" She indicated the fields, the drive.

"There was a car, before."

He seemed adrift and vague. She squatted beside him. "Why are you here, Adrian?"

Something flickered in his eyes, and it looked dangerous. Anger. Intent. Something sharp and cruel, and then suddenly gone. "Where else would I go?"

He lifted his shoulders, and the vagueness returned. Elizabeth looked deeper, but whatever she'd glimpsed was gone. "A hotel. Some other place."

"There is no other place."

"Adrian, listen—"

"Did you see something out there?"

It was the same question in the same voice; but if he was worried about something in the night the worry didn't show. The fire consumed his attention, even as Elizabeth stood. "Was it horrible?" she asked, and meant prison. He said nothing, but his hands twitched, and scars glinted like ivory in the light. Elizabeth thought of her youth, and of all the times she'd watched him move through the world: the way he stood at his desk and at the range, how he'd worked a witness, a crime scene, the bureaucracy. He'd worn confidence like a smile, and it was strange to see him so still and quiet, his eyes withdrawn beyond the smoke. "Would you like me to stay awhile?"

His eyes drifted shut, and she knew the answer was no. This was a communion, and she, in his mind, was just a kid he'd once known. "It was nice of you to come," he said, but the words were false.

*Go away,* he meant.

*Leave me to suffer in peace.*

# 7

Ramona lost track of time in the blackness of the silo. Her world was damp earth and heat and concrete walls. The door was a metal square that gave a fraction of an inch before the lock outside clanked.

"Somebody . . ."

It was a whisper, her voice already broken.

"Help me."

Something fluttered high in the silo, a bird maybe and trapped, too. Ramona lifted her face, then scratched at the door, her nails torn by rusted screws and cracks in the metal. Another hour passed, or maybe it was a day. She drifted and slept and woke to a spear of yellow light. It flicked the length of her body, and she saw grime on her hands and arms. Hope sparked in her chest, but died when he spoke.

"Time to go, Ramona."

"Water . . ."

"Of course, you can have water."

He pulled her through the door, her feet dragging. It was still night, but barely, the moon a hint of gray as headlights made shadows dance on the silo. She blinked, but his face was a blur.

"Here." He gave her a bottle, and she drank too much, choking. "Let me help." He guided the bottle to her lips, tilted it. She wanted to scream or run, but could barely move. He used a damp towel to wipe black soil from her face and arms. She watched in quiet terror as he lifted the hem of her dress and used the same towel to clean her legs, the touch intimate but chaste. "Better?"

"Why . . ."

"I'm sorry?" He leaned closer, one hand on the soft place behind her knee.

She licked cracked lips. "Why?"

He smoothed hair from her face and stared into her eyes. "Ours is not to wonder why."

"Please . . ."

"It's time to go."

He pulled her up and guided her to the car with torn seats and cigarette burns in the vinyl. The cuffs clinked on her wrists, and he kept a grip on the chain as he belted her inside the car.

"Safe and sound," he said, then walked through bright lights, his shadow rising and falling, then gone. She tugged at the seat belt, but was weak with hunger and heat. He slipped into the car and closed his door.

"I want to go home."

The clock on the dash said 5:47. Beyond the glass, a pale light gathered in the trees.

"The more you cooperate, the easier this will be. Do you understand?"

She nodded, crying. "Where are you taking me?"

He said nothing as he turned on rough dirt and drove out of the woods. At the paved road, he cut the wheel right, color bleeding into the fields as they drove, the sun a dim eye rising.

"Please don't hurt me."

He said nothing, drove faster.

Four minutes later she saw the church.

# 8

Elizabeth dreamed, and the dream was memory. It was night and hot as she moved through the yard of the abandoned house on Penelope Street. A few lights simmered down the road, but they were far and dim. She crossed from the last tree to the side of the house, her feet slipping in wet grass as she pushed through overgrown bushes and pressed her back against ancient clapboards that were cracked and split and wet from the storm. Holding her breath, she listened for noises inside. The caller said he'd heard a scream. What Elizabeth heard was her breath, her heart, and water dripping from choked-out gutters. She pushed along the wall as wet leaves trailed across her face and hands, and streaks of lightning dropped far off in the fading storm. At the first window, she paused. It was below grade, painted black. Two steps past it a sound came and went so fast Elizabeth thought she could be imagining it.

A voice?

A cry?

On the porch, she thought for the last time about calling Beckett or Dyer or someone else. But Beckett was with his family and the city was burning. Besides, if people were inside the house, it would be kids smoking pot or screwing. How many calls like that had she taken in her uniform days? A dozen? A hundred?

She drew her weapon and felt the knob turn. Inside, it was pitch-black, the air heavy with the stink of mold and cat and rotten carpet. She closed the door and turned on her flashlight, sweeping the room.

Rainwater pooled on the floor.

The ceiling was a soggy mess.

She cleared the living room and kitchen, the back rooms and the hall. The stairwell going up was rotted through, so she ignored the second floor and located the stairs to the basement. She kept the flashlight low, her back against the wall. Eight steps down she found a narrow landing, a turn, and then a door that scraped when it opened.

Elizabeth led with the gun. The first room was empty: more water on the floor, mounds of rotted cardboard. She followed a hallway into a square space that felt dead center of the house. Channing was to the right, facedown on a mattress. Beyond her was another hallway, doors to other rooms. A candle burned on a crate.

She should back away; call it in. But Channing was looking at her, eyes desperate and black.

"It's okay."

Elizabeth crossed the room, weapon up as she checked doors, the hallway beyond. The place was a warren of passages, closets, blind corners.

"I'm going to get you out of here."

Elizabeth knelt by the girl. She untwisted the wire where it cut her skin, first one wrist then the other. The girl cried out as circulation returned to her hands.

"Be still." She tugged the gag from Channing's mouth, watched the doors, the corners. "How many? Channing? How many?"

"Two." She sobbed as Elizabeth removed wire from her ankles. "There are two of them."

"Good girl." Elizabeth hauled her to her feet. "Where?" Channing pointed deeper into the maze. "Both of them?"

Channing nodded, but was wrong.

Terribly, awfully wrong.


Elizabeth woke with the girl's name on her lips, and her fingernails dug into the arms of a chair. The same dream came every time she fell asleep. Sometimes, she woke before it got really bad. Sometimes, it went the distance. That's why she drank coffee and paced, why she never slept unless it crept up to drag her down.

"That was fun."

Elizabeth scrubbed both palms across her face. She was soaked in sweat, her heart running fast. Looking around, she saw hospital green and blinking lights. She was in Gideon's room, but didn't remember taking off her shoes or closing her eyes. Had she been drinking? That happened, too, sometimes. Two in the morning, or three. Tired of coffee. Tired of memories.

It was dim in the room, but the clock said 6:12. That meant a few hours sleep, at least. And how many dreams? It felt like three. Three times down the stairs, three times in the dark.

Finding her feet, Elizabeth moved to the bed and stared down at the boy. She'd come in late and found Gideon alone in his room. No sign of his father. No doctors at such a late hour. The night nurse filled her in and said she could stay if she wanted. It broke a few rules, but neither of them wanted Gideon to wake alone. Elizabeth had held his hand for a long time, then sat and watched long hours walk up the face of the clock.

Leaning over the bed, she pulled the sheet to Gideon's chin, flicked the curtain, and looked outside. Dew hung on the grass, and the light was pink. She'd see Channing today, and maybe Adrian. Maybe, the state cops would come for her at last. Or maybe, she'd get in the car and leave. She could take the Mustang top-down and drive west. Two thousand miles, she thought, until the air was dry and the sun rose red over stone and sand and views that went forever.

But Gideon would wake alone.

Channing would be without her.

Elizabeth found a different nurse at the station beyond the door. "You were here yesterday, weren't you?"

"I was."

"What happened to Gideon's father?"

"Security escorted him from the building."

"He was drunk?"

"Drunk. Disruptive. Your father took him home."

"My father?"

"Reverend Black was here most of the day, and half of last night. Never left the boy's side. I'm surprised you missed him."

"I'm glad he could help."

"He's a generous man."

Elizabeth handed the nurse a card. "If Mr. Strange causes problems again, call me. He's too pitiful for regular cops, and more trouble than my father should have to handle." The nurse looked a question, and Elizabeth waved it off. "It's a sad story. And an old one, too."

Elizabeth spent another twenty minutes with Gideon, then drove home as the sun broke above the trees. She showered and dressed, thinking again of the desert. By nine o'clock she was deep into the historic district, twisting down shaded lanes until she reached the street where Channing lived in a centuries-old mansion that towered over gardens and hedgerows and wrought-iron fencing.

The girl's father met Elizabeth at the door. "Detective Black. This is unexpected." He was in his fifties and handsome, a fit man in jeans, a golf shirt, and loafers worn without socks. They'd met more than once, each encounter under difficult circumstances: the police station on the day Channing disappeared, the hospital after Elizabeth brought her out of the basement, the day state police opened an official investigation into the shooting of Brendon and Titus Monroe. A powerful man, he was unused to powerlessness and police and wounded daughters. Elizabeth understood that. It didn't make him any easier to deal with.

"I'd like to speak with Channing."

"I'm sorry, Detective. It's early, still. She's resting."

"She asked me to call."

"Yet, this appears to be a visit."

Elizabeth peered past him. The house was full of dark rugs and heavy furniture. "She very much wanted to see me, Mr. Shore. I think it's important we speak."

"Look, Detective." He stepped outside and closed the door behind him. "Let's forget what's in the news, okay. Let's forget that you're under investigation and that the state police are giving my lawyers hell trying to get to Channing, who for some reason doesn't care to talk to them. Let's put all that aside and cut to the chase. We appreciate what you did for our little girl, but your part in this is over. My daughter is safe at home. We're taking care of her. Her mother and me. Her family. Surely, you understand that."

"Of course. That's beyond question."

"She needs to forget the terrible things that happened. She can't do that with you sitting next to her."

"Forgetting is not the same as coping."

"Listen." For a moment, his face softened. "I've learned enough about you to know that you're a fine person and a good cop. That comes from judges, other police officers, people who know your family. I don't doubt your intentions, but there's nothing good you can do for Channing."

"You're wrong about that."

"I'll tell her you stopped by."

He retreated inside, but Elizabeth caught the door's edge before it could close. "She needs more than strong walls, Mr. Shore. She needs people who understand. You're six feet and change, a wealthy man with the world at his feet. Channing is none of those things. Do you have any idea what she's feeling right now? Do you think you ever could?"

"No one knows Channing better than I."

"That's not the point."

"Do you have children, Detective?" He towered above her, waiting.

"No. I don't have children."

"Let's revisit this conversation when you do."

He pushed the door shut and left Elizabeth on the wrong side of it. His feelings were understandable, but Channing needed a guide through the bitter landscape of *after,* and Elizabeth knew those trails better than most.

Looking up at high windows, she sighed deeply, then threaded between box bushes that rose like walls around her. The path twisted around giant oaks, and when it spit her out on the driveway, she found Channing seated on the hood of her car. Loose jeans and a sweatshirt swallowed the girl's small body. A hood kept her eyes in shadow, but light touched the line of her jaw as she spoke. "I saw you pull up."

"Channing, hi." The girl slid off the car and pushed hands into her pockets. "How'd you get out of the house?"

"The window." She shrugged. "I do it all the time."

"Your parents . . ."

"My parents treat me like a child."

"Sweetheart . . ."

"I'm not a child anymore."

"No," Elizabeth said sadly. "No, you're not."

"They say everything's okay, that I'm safe." Channing clenched her jaw: ninety pounds of china. "I'm not okay."

"You can be."

"Are *you* okay?"

Channing let sunlight find her face, and Elizabeth saw bones that pressed too tightly against the skin, circles beneath the girl's eyes that were as dark as her own. "No, sweetheart. I'm not. I barely sleep, and when I do, I have nightmares. I don't eat or exercise or talk to people unless I need to. I've lost twelve pounds in under a week. It's not fair, what happened in that house. I'm angry. I want to hurt people."

Channing pulled her hands free from her pockets. "My father can barely look at me."

"I doubt that."

"He thinks I should have run faster, fought harder. He says I shouldn't have been outside in the first place."

"What does your mother say?"

"She brings me hot chocolate and cries when she thinks I can't hear."

Elizabeth studied the house, which spoke of denial and quiet perfection. "You want to get out of here?"

"You and me?"

"Yes."

"Where to?"

"Does it matter?"

"I guess not."

Channing got in the car, and Elizabeth drove them out of the historic district, past the mall, the car dealers, and day-care centers. She drove into the country, then to the gravel road that ran deep into the woods before turning up the face of the mountain that rose alone from the hills around the city. Air whistled through the car as they climbed, but neither spoke until they neared the top and the road flattened into a parking lot.

"This is the abandoned quarry." Channing broke the silence, but with little real curiosity.

Elizabeth pointed at a gash in the woods. "Just up that trail. A quarter mile."

"Why are we here?"

Elizabeth killed the engine and set the brake. She needed to do something, and it was going to hurt. "Let's take a walk."

She led Channing into the shade, then up a winding trail that was beaten flat by all the people who'd walked it over the years. It grew steep in places. They passed bits of litter and gray-skinned trees with initials carved into the bark. At the top of the mountain, the trail emptied onto an overlook that offered views of the city on one side and of the quarry on the other. In places, trees grew from shallow soil; in others there was only rock. It was a stark and beautiful place, but the drop into the quarry was two hundred feet straight down.

"Why are we here?"

Elizabeth stepped to the edge and peered down at the vast expanse of cold, black water. "My father's a preacher. You probably didn't know that." Channing shook her head, and Elizabeth's hair lifted in a breeze that rose up sheer walls like an exhalation from the water. "I grew up in the church, in a small house behind it, actually. The parsonage. Do you know that word?"

Channing shook her head again, and Elizabeth understood that, too. Most kids could never understand church as a life, the prayer and dutifulness and submission.

"The church kids would come here on Sundays after church. Sometimes there were a few of us, and sometimes a lot. A couple of parents would drive us up the mountain, then read the paper in the cars while we hiked up here to play. It was good, you know. Picnics and kites, long dresses and lace-up boots. There's a trail that leads to a narrow ledge above the water. You could swim or skim stones. Sometimes we'd have campfires." Elizabeth nodded; saw yellowed memories of a day like this, and of an unsuspecting, narrow-hipped girl. "I was raped under those trees when I was seventeen."

Channing shook her head. "You don't have to do this."

But Elizabeth did. "We were the only two left, this boy and me. It was late. My father was in the car, down the hill. It happened so fast . . ." Elizabeth picked up a rock, tossed it, and watched it fall into the quarry. "He was chasing me. I thought it was a game. It probably started out that way. I'm not really sure. I was laughing for a while, and then suddenly was not." She pointed at the trees. "He caught me by that little pine and shoved needles in my mouth to keep me from screaming. It was fast and awful, and I barely understood what was happening, just the weight of him and the way it hurt. On the walk down, he begged me not to tell. He swore he didn't mean to do it, that we were friends and he was weak and it would never happen again."

"Elizabeth . . ."

"We walked a quarter mile through those woods, then rode home in my father's car, both of us in the backseat." Elizabeth didn't mention the feel of the boy's leg pressed against her own. She didn't describe the heat of it, or how he reached out once and put a single finger on the back of her hand. "I never told my father."

"Why not?"

"I thought it was my fault, somehow." Elizabeth lobbed another rock and watched it drop. "Two months later, I almost killed myself. Right here."

Channing leaned over the drop as if putting herself in the same place. "How close did you come?"

"A single step. A few seconds."

"What stopped you?"

"I found something larger to believe in." She didn't mention Adrian because that was still too personal, still just for her. "Your father can't make it better, Channing. Your mother can't make it better, either. You need to take charge of that yourself. I'd like to help you."

Emotion twisted the girl's face: anger and doubt and disbelief. "Did *you* get better?"

"I still hate the smell of pine."

Channing studied the narrow smile, looking for a lie, the shadow of a lie. Elizabeth thought she would lose her. She didn't.

"What happened to the boy?"

"He sells insurance," Elizabeth said. "He's overweight and married. Every now and then I run into him. Sometimes, I do it on purpose."

"Why would you do that?"

"Because in the end only one thing can make it right."

"What?"

"Choice." Elizabeth cupped the girl's face with a palm. "Your choice."

# 9

Ellen Bondurant married young and well, then at forty-one learned a bitter truth about fading looks and selfish men. At first she was bewildered, then heartbroken and sad. In the end she was numb, so that when her husband presented papers, she signed them. Her attorney said she was being naïve, but that was not the truth, either. The money embarrassed her and always had: the cars and parties and diamonds as large as acorns. All she wanted was the man she thought she'd married.

But he was long gone.

Now, she lived with her dogs in a small house by a creek in the country, and her life had become a simple thing. She trained horses to make money and liked to walk the open spaces when she could: low country by the river if she was feeling contemplative; ridgelines to the old church and back if she wanted views.

Today, she chose the church.

"Come on, boys."

She called the dogs, then set out on foot, the route taking her on a steep angle to a trail that followed a line of hills to the southeast. She felt light as she moved, and younger than her forty-nine years. It was the work, she knew, the early mornings in the saddle, the long hours with longe line and whip. Her skin was leathered and lined, but she was proud of what her hands could do, how they worked unceasingly in snow and rain and heat.

She stopped at the top of the first hill, her house, far below, like a toy dropped behind plastic trees. Ahead of her, the trail curled higher, then leveled for three miles as the ridgeline bent west and the earth fell away on either side. When the church appeared, its stark and stately beauty struck her as it always did: the granite steps, the iron cross, fallen and twisted.

Slipping a bit as the trail dipped into the saddle of the forgotten church, Ellen felt the difference without understanding it. The dogs were agitated, their heads low as they tracked an invisible scent and whined low in their throats. They went halfway around the church, then came back at a run, noses snuffling at the base of the broad steps as they crisscrossed each other's path and fur lifted in strips between their shoulder blades.

She whistled for the dogs, but they ignored her. The largest one, a yellow Lab she called Tom, lunged up the stairs, his nails clicking.

"What is it, boy?"

Grass whispered on her legs, and she noticed tire tracks near the door. People did come here; it happened. But they usually parked on the dirt road or in the gravel lot. These tracks went all the way to the door.

She stopped at the bottom step and, peering up, realized what else was different. The doors were slabs of oak, the handles black iron as thick as her arm. For as long as she could remember, the handles had been chained together, but today the chain was cut, and the right-side door stood ajar.

Suddenly afraid, Ellen looked longingly up the hill. She should leave—she felt it—but Tom stood at the door, a whine in his throat. "It's okay, boy." She caught the dog's collar and stepped through the door. Beyond the threshold, it was dim, the darkness cut by blades of light through boarded windows. The ceiling rose, vaulted and dark, but the altar held her. On either side, boards had been pulled from the windows so that light spilled in and lit it like a jewel. She saw white and red and black; and her first thought was *Snow White*. That was the feeling; a stillness that bordered on reverence, the hair and skin and nails stained red. It took five steps to realize what she was seeing, and when she did, she froze as if her body, entire, had turned to ice. "Sweet Lord." She felt the world freeze, too. "Oh, my dear, sweet, merciful Lord."

Beckett sipped coffee in the back booth of his regular diner. It was a favorite local joint, the booths filled with businessmen, mechanics, and mothers with young children. A plate of bacon and eggs was pushed off to the side, half-eaten. He hadn't slept much and wanted to smoke for the first time in over twenty years. It was Liz's fault. The worry. The stress. She liked to maintain a border between the personal life and the professional. Okay, fine. She wasn't like other partners he'd had, didn't want to talk about the opposite sex or sports or the difference between a good lay and a great one. She kept quiet about her past and her fears, lied about how much she slept and drank, and why she cared enough to be a cop in the first place. But, hey, that was cool. Space mattered—*freaking boundaries*—and that was fine until the lies went from small and harmless to scary, frightful, seriously fuckin' dark.

She was lying.

Channing Shore was lying, too.

To make the problem very real, little birdies were telling him that Hamilton and Marsh had not left town. They'd been to the abandoned house and tried twice to meet with Channing Shore. They'd pulled every complaint ever filed against Liz and were, at that very moment, interviewing Titus Monroe's widow. What they hoped to gain was beyond him, but that they were even having the conversation spoke volumes.

They wanted Liz. That meant they'd get around to him eventually; try to trip him up or turn him. After all, he'd known Liz since she was a rookie. They'd been partners for four years. The problem for them, however, would be simple. Liz was a solid cop. Steady. Smart. Dependable.

*Until the basement . . .*

That thought stuck in his mind as he tried to figure out what Liz was thinking when she'd told the state cops who were out to hang her that the men she'd killed weren't men, after all, but animals. It went beyond dangerous. It was self-destructive, insane; and the absence of an easy explanation troubled him. Liz was a special kind of cop. She wasn't a numbers guy like Dyer or a gung ho head breaker like half the assholes he'd come up with. She wasn't in it for the thrill or the power or because, like him, she was too used up for anything better. He'd seen her soul when she thought no one was looking, and at times it was so beautiful it hurt. It was a ridiculous thought, and he knew it; but if he could ask one question and get an actual answer, it would be why she became a cop at all. She was driven and smart and could have been anything. Yet, she'd thrown the interview, and that made no sense at all.

Then, there was Adrian Wall.

Beckett thought, again, of Liz as a rookie: the way she'd mooned over Adrian, hung on his every word as if he had some special insight every other cop lacked. Her fascination had an unsettling effect, not just because it was so obvious but because half the cops on the force hoped she'd look at them the same way. Adrian's conviction should have ended the doe-eyed infatuation. Failing that, thirteen years of incarceration should have done the job. He was a convict, and broken in a hundred different ways. Yet, Beckett had watched Liz at Nathan's, how she slid into the car with Adrian, the way her breath caught, and how her eyes hung on Adrian's lips when he spoke. She still felt for him, still believed.

That was a problem.

It was all a giant, fucking problem.

Frustrated, Beckett pushed the coffee cup away and signaled for the check. The waitress brought it in a slow, easy step. "Anything else, Detective?"

"Not this morning, Melody."

She put the check facedown as the phone in Beckett's pocket vibrated. He dug it out, squinted at the screen, then answered, "Beckett."

"Hey, it's James Randolph. You got a minute?"

James was another detective. Older than Beckett. Smart. A brawler. "What's up, James?"

"You know an Ellen Bondurant?"

Beckett searched his memory and came up with a woman from six or seven years ago. "I remember her. Divorce case gone bad. Her husband violated a restraining order; smashed up the house, I think. What about her?"

"She's holding on line two."

"That was seven years ago. Can't you handle it?"

"What can I tell you, Beckett? She's upset. She wants you."

"All right, fine." Beckett stretched an arm across the back of the booth. "Patch her through."

"Hang on."

The line crackled with static, then clicked twice. When Ellen Bondurant came on the line, she was calmer than Beckett had expected.

"I'm sorry to bother you, Detective, but I remember how nice you were to me."

"It's okay, Ms. Bondurant. What can I do for you?"

She laughed and sounded forlorn. "All I wanted was to take a walk."

When Beckett hit the drive below the church, he had Detective Randolph back on the phone. "I'm not sure yet." The car stuttered over washboard ruts, the church high above. "Just get everything on standby. Some uniforms, crime scene, the medical examiner. This may be a false alarm, but it doesn't feel like it."

"Is it the same?"

"I don't know, yet."

"Should I tell Dyer?"

Beckett considered the question. Dyer was a good administrator, but not the best cop in the world. He took things personally and tended to delay even if hesitation was dangerous. Then there was the location, the fact Adrian was fresh out of prison, and the chance it could actually be the same. In Beckett's heart he thought Dyer had never fully recovered from his partner's being a killer. Questions had rattled around the department for years.

*How did Dyer miss it?*

*What kind of cop could he possibly be?*

"Listen, James. Francis could get a little twitchy on this one. Let's make sure what we're dealing with first. Just sit tight until I call you back."

"Don't leave me hanging."

Thirteen years had passed since Adrian killed Julia Strange in the same church, but Randolph felt it, too: the dark charge. This could change everything. Lives. The city.

*Liz . . .*

Beckett dropped the phone in a pocket, put both hands on the wheel, and stared through the windshield as the church humped up above him. Even now, the place disturbed him in a deeply fundamental way. The building was old, the grounds overgrown with dog fennel and horseweed and scrub pine. That wasn't the problem so much as the history of the place. It started with Julia Strange. Her murder was bad enough, but even after the church was abandoned, the death lingered like an aftertaste. Vandals broke glass and toppled headstones; they spray-painted the walls and floors with profanity and satanic symbols. For years after that, vagrants moved in and out. They left bottles and condoms and the remains of cooking fires, one of which got out of control enough to burn part of the structure and topple the cross. But, you could see old glories if you looked: the massive stones and the granite steps, even the cross itself, which stood for almost two hundred years before being twisted in the fall. Beckett's religious convictions had not entirely faded, so maybe his discomfort stemmed from guilt for all the wrongs he'd done. Maybe it was the contrast of good and evil, or perhaps from memories of how the church had been, of Sunday mornings and song, his partner's life, before.

Whatever the cause, he was unhappy enough to grind his teeth and clench the wheel. When his car crested the ridge, he saw the Bondurant woman standing in tall grass with two dogs at her side, one of them barking. He hit the brakes and slid to a halt. None of the *wrongness* dissipated.

"They're friendly," she called.

Beckett had yet to meet a Lab that wasn't. He greeted the woman by name, then took in the church and the fields and the distant forest. "You walked up here?"

"My house is that way." She pointed. "Three miles. I walk here a few times a week."

"Did you see anyone?" She shook her head, and he gestured at the church. "Did you touch anything?"

"The door handle on the right side."

"Anything else?"

"The chain was already cut. I stopped long before I got to the . . . uh, uh . . ."

"It's okay." Beckett nodded. "Tell me the last time you were up here."

"A few days. Three, maybe."

"Did you see people, then?"

"Not then, but on occasion. I find trash, sometimes. Beer bottles. Cigarettes. Old campfires. You know how this place can be." Her voice broke at the end.

Beckett reminded himself that civilians didn't see bodies the way cops did. "I'm going to go inside and take a look. You stay here. I'll have more questions."

"It's the same, isn't it?"

He saw fear in her eyes as trees rustled above the church, and one of the dogs pulled against its leash. "Sit tight," he said. "I won't be long."

Beckett left her where she stood and made for the church,

stopping briefly to examine the tire tracks in the grass. Nothing remarkable, he thought. Maybe they could get an imprint. Probably not.

Stepping across the fallen chain, he moved into the dark and heat. Ten feet in it was close to black, so he waited for his eyes to adjust. After a moment, the void gathered itself into a low-ceilinged, dim space with sconces in the walls, a stairwell to the left, and closet doors broken from their hinges. Stepping through the narthex, he fumbled his way to the double doors that led into the nave. Once beyond them, the ceiling soared away, and while it remained dim at his end of the church, light spilled through stained glass at both transepts to illuminate the altar and the woman on it. Colors were in the light—blues and greens and reds—and lines of shadow from iron in the glass. Otherwise, the light speared in like a blade to pin the body where it lay, to put color in the skin and on linen that was white and crisp and ran from feet to chin. Beckett's first impression was of black hair and stillness and red nails, the image so familiar and haunting it transfixed him where he stood.

"Please, don't be the same . . ."

He was talking to himself, but couldn't help it. Light lit her like a jewel in a case, but it was more than that. It was the tilt of her jaw, the apple-skin nails.

"Jesus."

Beckett crossed himself from an almost-forgotten childhood habit, then worked his way past broken floorboards and lumps of rotted carpet. He made his way between tumbled pews, and with each step the illusion of perfection crumbled more. Color fell out of the light. Pale skin dulled to gray, and marks of violence rose as if by magic. Bruising. Ligature marks. Torn fingertips. Beckett took the last, few steps, and, at the altar, looked down. The victim was young, with dark hair and eyes shot through with blood. She was stretched on the altar as Julia Strange had been, her arms crossed on the linen, her neck blackened and crushed. He studied the choke marks, the eyes, the lips that were nearly bitten through.

He lifted the linen to find her nude beneath it, the body pale and unmarked and otherwise perfect. Beckett lowered the sheet and felt a surge of unexpected emotion.

The Bondurant woman was right.

It was the same.

The sun burned through the trees as Elizabeth drove Channing down the mountain. It was quiet in the car until they approached Channing's neighborhood. When the girl spoke, her voice was quiet, yet wound like a coil. "Have you ever gone back to the place it happened?"

"I just took you there. I just showed it to you."

"You took me to the quarry, not to the place it happened. You pointed. You talked about it. We never went near the little pine where the boy knocked you down. I'm asking if you've ever stood on the exact spot."

They stopped in front of Channing's house, and Elizabeth killed the engine. Beyond the hedge, brick and stone rose, inviolate. "I wouldn't choose to do that. Not now. Not ever."

"It's just a place. It doesn't hurt."

Elizabeth turned in her seat, appalled. "Did you go back to the crime scene, Channing? Please tell me you did not go alone into that godforsaken house."

"I lay down on the place it happened."

"What? Why?"

"Should I try to kill myself, instead?"

Channing was angry, now, a wall going up between them. Elizabeth wanted to understand, but struggled. The girl's eyes were bright as dimes. The rest of her seemed to hum. "Are you upset with me for some reason?"

"No. Yes. Maybe."

Elizabeth tried to remember how it felt to be eighteen, to be stripped to the bone and held together with tape. It wasn't difficult. "Why did you go back?"

"The men are dead. The place is all that's left."

"That's not true," Elizabeth said. "You remain, and so do I."

"I don't think I do." Channing opened the door, climbed out. "And I think maybe you don't, either."

"Channing . . ."

"I can't talk about this right now. I'm sorry."

The girl kept her head down as she walked away. Elizabeth watched her move up the drive and fade into the trees. She would make it into the house unnoticed or the parents who didn't know what to do with her would discover her creeping through the window. Neither outcome would help the girl. One of them could make things a whole lot worse. She was still thinking about that when her phone rang. It was Beckett, and he was as twisted up as the girl.

"How fast can you get to your father's church?"

"His church?"

"Not the new one. The old one."

"You're talking about—"

"Yeah, that one. How fast?"

"Why?"

"Just answer the question."

Elizabeth looked at her watch, and her stomach rolled over. "I can be there in fourteen minutes."

"I need you here in ten."

Beckett hung up before she could ask another question.

*Ten minutes.*

He stood by the window in the north transept. Bits of colored glass had been broken out years earlier, but much of it remained. He peered through a hole and watched the world as if he could see the storm coming. Adrian had been out of prison for barely a day. When news of another murder broke, it would go viral. The church. The altar. It was too big, too gothic. The city would call for blood, and everything would come under scrutiny. The sentencing guidelines. The judge and the cops. Maybe even the prison.

*How did the system let another woman die?*

If news of Gideon's shooting broke, too, the storm would spin out of control. Beckett saw how the papers would play it, not just as a story of murder and family and failed revenge, but of systemic incompetence as the first victim's child slips through every crack in the system only to be shot in the shadow of the prison. Someone would figure out that Liz had been at Nathan's, and that would make the cops look even worse. She was the angel of death, the department's largest black eye since Adrian himself. The city was already turning against her. How bad would it get when people learned she'd worked to keep Gideon clear of social services? It was a royal mess, all of it. Dyer would never allow Liz on the scene.

But, Beckett wanted her here. She was his partner and friend, and she still had feelings for Adrian. Beckett needed to fix that.

"Come on, Liz."

He paced to the altar and back.

"Come on, damn it."

Seven minutes later, his phone rang, and James Randolph's number popped on the screen. Beckett didn't answer.

"Come on, come on."

At the ten-minute mark, Randolph called again, then again. When the fourth call made the phone burr in his pocket, Beckett ripped it out and answered.

Randolph was frustrated. "What the hell, Charlie? I've got the ME on hold and eight cops staring at me like I'm crazy."

"I know. I'm sorry." Beckett heard voices in the background, the clatter of gear.

"Are we rolling or not?"

Beckett saw a car on the road. It crested the hill at speed, then slowed. He gave it a five count to make sure, then said, "You can roll, James. Call Dyer, too. He'll be twitchy, like I said. Just tell him it's my call. Tell him it's the same."

"Goddamn."

"One other thing."

"Yeah?"

"Find Adrian Wall."

Beckett then walked outside to meet Liz on the worn, granite steps of her childhood church. Even at a distance, her unhappiness was unmistakable. She was moving slowly, her eyes on the great trees, the fallen steeple. It was going to get ugly, and Beckett hated that.

"I never come here," she said.

"I know. I'm sorry."

They met on the bottom step, and Beckett hated the way doubt colored every glance. The church had been the center of her life for years: the congregation, her parents, and childhood. Though it had never been a rich church, it had been old and influential. Most of that changed after Julia Strange died on the altar. She'd been married in the church; her son was baptized there. Most of the congregation never got past her death or the desecration of their church. The few who persevered insisted on moving to a new location. Elizabeth's father fought the idea, and her mother, in the end, forced the issue: *How can we pray where one of our own died alone and in fear? How can we christen our children? Marry our young people?* Her impassioned pleas swayed even her husband, who broke, it was said, with exceptional grace. What followed was a clapboard structure on a skinny lot in a dangerous part of town. The church continued as best it could, but only a fraction of the congregation made the move. Most drifted off to join First Baptist or United Methodist or some other church. Liz's life changed after that.

Her parents descended into obscurity.

Adrian Wall went to prison.

"We don't have much time," Beckett said.

"Why not?"

"Because Dyer will arrest us both if he finds you here."

He pushed into the interior, and Elizabeth followed him through the darkened narthex and into the light beyond. She moved as if it hurt and kept her eyes down until the balcony passed above her head, and the ceiling rose up. Beckett watched her face as she took in the rafters and the char and the fixtures hung like iron crowns. She turned a bit, but kept her gaze from the altar, let it light first on windows and walls and a thousand shadowed places. He could not imagine her thoughts, and nothing on her face betrayed them. She held stoic and straight, and when she finally faced the altar, it took three seconds for her to acknowledge that she understood what she was seeing.

"Why are you showing me this?"

"You know exactly why."

"Adrian didn't do this."

"Same church. Same altar."

"Just because he's out of prison . . ."

Beckett took her arm and pulled her to the altar she'd known since birth. "Look at her."

"Who is she?"

"It doesn't matter." Beckett said it harsh and hard. "Look at her."

"I have."

"Look deeper."

"There is no deeper. Okay? She's dead. It's the same. Is that what you want to hear?"

Liz was sweating, but it was a thin, cold sweat. Beckett saw enough on her face to understand what she was feeling inside: childhood and betrayal, the hard turns of an ugly disbelief. This was her church. Adrian was her hero.

"Why are you doing this?" she asked.

"Because you're not thinking straight. Because I need you to understand that Adrian Wall is a killer, and that your obsession with him is dangerous."

"There's no obsession."

"Then stay away from him."

"Or what?" There was the spark, the heat. "Why do you hate him so much? He didn't kill Julia Strange. He didn't kill this one, either."

"Jesus, Liz. Listen to yourself." Beckett frowned, frustrated by his inability to do this simple thing. Liz's faith in Adrian Wall had burned a lot of bridges when she was a rookie. Cops distrusted her, thought her flawed and female and irrational. It took years for her colleagues to fully accept her, and longer still for her to walk the station without a chip on her shoulder. Beckett had seen it. He'd lived it. "Try to look at this like a cop. Okay?"

"As opposed to what? An astronaut? A housewife?"

He was making it worse. Same chip on her shoulder. Same bitterness.

"He didn't do it, Charlie."

"Damn it, Liz—"

"I was with him last night."

"What?"

"He wasn't interested in something like this. He wasn't interested in people, at all. He was . . . sad."

"Sad? Do you even hear yourself?"

"You shouldn't have brought me here." She turned and started walking. "It was a mistake," she said, and Beckett knew she was right.

He'd played it ten kinds of wrong.

He'd lost her.

# 10

Elizabeth drove and tried to get her head around what had just happened in the church. Forget the body, the fact of another death. That was too big and too sudden. She'd need time to process what it meant, so she thought about Beckett instead. He wanted to help—she understood that—but she despised the church in a way he could never understand. It was old, that hatred, twined so deeply into Elizabeth's soul that it was hard to stand before the altar of her youth and be objective about anything. She felt small there, and angry and betrayed. That was a tough combination; so, in the quiet of her car, she focused on the one thing that mattered now.

Was she right to believe in Adrian?

They'd never been close in any of the normal ways. He was the man who'd saved her life, a glow in the night of her bitter despair. Because of that, her feelings for him had never been rational. When she thought of him, she saw his face at the quarry, the steadiness and goodwill. Her faith in him only grew when she became a cop. He was bold and smart, cared about victims and their families. Yet, even when she was a cop herself, he'd maintained an aloofness. A smile here. A word there. The gestures were small and in passing, but she could not deny the feelings they'd stirred or the dangerous question such feelings raised.

*Was she obsessed?*

It was a difficult question, but only because she'd never asked it of herself. She was a cop because of Adrian; driven because he, too, had been driven. When his skin turned up under Julia Strange's nails, Elizabeth had been the only one to doubt his guilt. Not his friends or peers or the jury. Even his wife seemed to fade at the end, sitting with her head down, unwilling to meet his eyes or show up for the sentencing. That thought bothered Elizabeth more now than it ever had. Why should she believe in Adrian when his own wife had not? Elizabeth disliked that kind of self-doubt, but her faith in Adrian *had* been blind. She'd been young, desperate to believe; and looking back, that all made sense. But was she blinded, now? Thirteen years had passed, but the murders looked the same. She could blink and lay Gideon's mother on the same altar. What was different from one murder to the next?

She didn't know. That was the problem. They didn't have time of death on the new victim, but based on the body's appearance, she most likely died after Adrian's release from state prison. Elizabeth chewed on that for an hour and disliked the taste of such strong coincidence. She wanted to know if anything tied the new victim to Adrian—witness statements, physical evidence, anything beyond his being a convicted killer fresh off a thirteen-year stretch. Normally she could call a dozen people, but she was suspended, out of the loop; and Francis Dyer would fire her for real if she dug too deeply. She told herself to let it go. Her life was coming apart, and Channing's was, too. Gideon was in the hospital. State cops wanted her for double homicide.

*But, it was Adrian Wall.*

*Her father's church.*

She returned to it without conscious thought, parking on the verge to watch movement high above. The medical examiner was there. So were Beckett, Randolph, and a dozen others—techs and uniforms and somewhere, she thought, Francis Dyer. How could he not be there? Adrian had been his partner. His testimony helped bring him down.

Elizabeth lit a cigarette, then tilted the mirror to study her face. She looked drawn and bloodshot and unsure.

*What if she was wrong about him?*

*What if she'd been been wrong all these years?*

Twisting the mirror away, she smoked half the cigarette and stubbed it out. Something was not right, and it was not the church or the body or anything obvious. Was it the victim? Something about the scene? She watched the church for another five minutes and understood, suddenly, what felt so wrong.

Where was Dyer's car?

He was the captain of detectives; this was a huge case. Dialing Beckett's cell, she waited three rings for him to answer.

"Liz. Hi." His voice fell, and she imagined him stepping away from the body. "I'm so glad you called. About earlier—"

"Where's Francis?"

"What?"

"I don't see Dyer's car. He should be there."

Beckett paused, his breath heavy on the line. "Where are you, Liz? Are you here at the scene? I warned you—"

But Elizabeth wasn't listening. Dyer wasn't at the church. She should have seen it coming. "Son of a bitch."

"Liz, wait—"

But that wasn't going to happen. Turning across the road, Elizabeth put the church in her blind spot and broke every speed limit heading back to town. From a hilltop two miles out, she saw steeples and rooftops and houses that showed white through the trees. Off the hill and in heavy traffic, she went right, then crossed a cobbled street and blew through the other side of town, thinking, *He wouldn't; not yet.* But on the last stretch before Adrian's burned-out farm, she saw flashing lights a mile away. The body was still in the church, and Dyer had already come to arrest his old partner. Resentment. Laziness. Hatred. Whatever the reasons, she saw it like ink on a page. They were going to lock him in a cell and find some reason to keep him there.

"It's not what you think."

Dyer met her when she spilled from the car. He had both hands up, backpedaling as she pushed hard between the cars, the burned-out house ten yards ahead.

"The body's barely cold. You can't possibly have a reason to arrest him."

"Slow down, Liz. I mean it."

She shouldered past uniformed officers, rounded into the same charred room, and saw Adrian, facedown in the soot. Whatever the takedown looked like, it had been violent. His shirt was torn. Smears of blood slicked his hands and face. They'd zipped his ankles and wrists, dropped him in the dirt like an animal.

Three steps in, and Dyer was already pulling her back, his hands like steel on her arm. "I want to talk to him."

"Not a chance."

"Francis—"

"I said that's enough!"

He dragged her outside, cops watching, spots of red in Dyer's cheeks. He pushed her against an oak tree, and she jerked her arm free. "This is bullshit."

"Calm down, Detective." Dyer used the force of his voice, the authority in his eyes. "It's not what you think, and you're not going to talk to him. That means I need you to step away from this arrest." She moved right, and he moved with her. "I mean it, Liz. I'll take you in for obstruction. I swear it."

She pushed forward.

He placed a palm squarely on her chest. The touch was entirely inappropriate, but she saw no discomfort on his face. "I'll cuff you," he said. "Right in front of God and everybody. Do you want that?"

Elizabeth looked at him with new eyes. Such forcefulness was not his normal style. "I'm fine."

"Are you sure?"

She stepped back and lifted her hands. Through the crowd, she saw Adrian in the dirt. His eyes found hers, and she felt a jolt of electricity. "Why is he in full restraints?"

"Because he's a dangerous man."

"Who's under arrest for what?"

"If I tell you, will you behave?"

Resentment gathered in Elizabeth's chest. It was an indulgent word: *behave*. "When have I not?"

"Just stay here. We'll talk when this is over."

"One question."

He turned and held up a single finger.

"What charges?"

Dyer pointed at a red-and-white sign nailed to a blackened timber. In her lifetime, Elizabeth had seen a thousand of them just like it. It was a metal square: two words, simple.

"You're kidding me," she said.

"He doesn't own the property anymore."

Dyer walked back into the house and left Elizabeth on the periphery to watch them haul Adrian to his feet, drag him from the ruins, and stuff him in a car. She watched him go and couldn't hide the emotion she felt. Whatever Adrian was now, he'd been a cop once, and one of the finest, not just capable but decorated, lauded. He'd suffered thirteen years behind bars for a crime she didn't think he committed, and now, here he was, assaulted on ground he used to own.

Cuffed and stuffed.

Arrested for trespass.

Elizabeth left before Dyer could find her for a further discussion. She waited on the road, then followed a line of patrol cars to the station and watched from a distance as Adrian was manhandled from the cruiser and goose-stepped toward the secure entrance. He fought the rough treatment. The treatment got rougher. By the time he disappeared inside, he was fully off the ground: two cops holding his feet, two more at his shoulders as he struggled. Elizabeth sat in silence and stared at the door. She waited for Dyer to make an appearance, but he did not.

*At the church,* she decided. Because that's how it was supposed to work. Investigate first. Then arrest.

She put the car in gear and eased away from the curb, but not before she saw the dark blue sedan parked at the edge of the secure lot. It had blackwall tires and state tags. Hamilton and Marsh, she decided.

Still in town.

Still looking for the rope to hang her.

*There was a knoll that looked down on the church, and a gravel road if you knew how to find it. It bent through the trees and ended in a high glade with uninterrupted views of rolling hills and far mountains. In better times he'd gone there to be alone and think of all the good in the city. Things made sense then, the sky above and everything in its place.*

*But that was a long time ago.*

*He left the car under the canopy and moved through the grass until he could see down onto the fallen steeple and scattered cars. He knew people came to the church—the horsewoman, vagrants—so he knew someone would find the body. But it made him sick to see the police there. After so many years, the church was his special place. No one else could understand the reasons or its purpose, the void in his heart it filled so perfectly.*

*And the girl on the altar?*

*She was his, too, but not as much as the others he'd chosen, not with cops looking at her and touching her and speculating. She should be in the stillness and the dark, and he hated what was happening behind the shards of stained glass: the bright lights and jaded cops, the medical examiner going about his dull, grim business. They would never grasp the reasons she'd died or why he'd chosen her or the incentive to let her be found. She was so much more than they could ever understand, not a woman or a body or a piece of some puzzle.*

*In death, she was a child.*

*At the end, they all were.*

Elizabeth went to the hospital and found that Gideon had been moved out of recovery and into a private room on the same floor. "How is that possible?"

"The cost, you mean?" The nurse was the same from earlier, a pretty redhead with brown eyes and a spray of freckles across her nose. "Your father asked for it as a charitable gesture. It's a slow week. The hospital administrator agreed."

"Why would he do that?"

"Have you ever argued with your father?"

Elizabeth struggled with the unexpected kindness, reminding herself that her father loved Gideon, too. "Is he here now?"

"Your father? He comes and goes."

"How is Gideon?"

"He woke, once, but isn't speaking. Everyone here is pretty much heartbroken for him. He's such a tiny thing, and torn up over his mother. Everyone knows what he was planning to do with that gun, but it doesn't matter. Half the nurses want to take him home."

Elizabeth thanked her and tapped on Gideon's door. There was no answer, so she went in quietly and found him asleep with tubes in his arm and under his nose. A monitor beeped with the rhythm of his heart, and he was so small beneath the sheet, the movement of his chest so barely perceived. In his whole life, the poor boy had never caught a break. Poverty. Borderline neglect. Now he was branded with this other sin. Would he forgive himself? she wondered. And if so, for what? That he'd tried to kill a man or that he'd failed?

Elizabeth stood for a long time, thinking how she might appear from beyond the open door. A stranger could misconstrue her love for the child.

*Why?* one might ask. *He's not even yours.*

There would never be an easy answer, but were Elizabeth forced to offer reasons, they might sound like this: *Because he needs me, because I'm the one who found his mother dead.*

Yet, even that was not the whole truth.

Leaning closer, Elizabeth studied the narrow face and bruised eyes. He appeared eight more than fourteen, closer to dead than to living.

His eyes opened and filled with shadow. "Did I kill him?"

Elizabeth smoothed his hair and smiled. "No, sweetheart. You're not a killer."

She leaned closer, thinking he'd be relieved by the news. Behind the boy's head, though, the monitor started beeping faster.

"Are you sure?"

"He's alive. You did nothing wrong." The monitor spiked. His eyes rolled white. "Gideon? Breathe, honey."

The monitor began to scream. "Nurse!" Elizabeth yelled, but it was unnecessary. The door was already open, one nurse spilling in, a doctor on her heels.

The doctor asked, "What happened?"

"We were just talking . . ."

"What did you say to him?"

"Nothing. I don't know. We just—"

"Get out."

She stepped away from the bed.

"Now!"

The doctor bent over the boy. "Gideon. Look at me. I need you to calm down. Can you breathe? Squeeze my hand. Good boy. Look at my eyes. Watch me. Slow and easy." The doctor breathed in, breathed out. Gideon's fingers were twisted white, his eyes fastened on the doctor's. Already, the monitor was slowing. "Good boy . . ."

"You need to go," the nurse said.

"Can't I just . . . ?"

"You can't help anyone," the nurse said; but Elizabeth knew that was not entirely true.

Maybe she could help Adrian.

It was late afternoon when cops started rolling in from the crime scene at the church. Elizabeth was in the old Mustang when it happened, parked on a side street north of the station. It was hot outside, shadows stretching out from buildings and trees and people walking to their cars. It was a normal day for normal people. Sunset coming. Time for dinner and family, time for rest. For the cops heading to the station, it was still early. Evidence needed to be processed, reports written, plans made. Even with Adrian in custody, Dyer would want uniforms on the street and detectives flogging every thin angle. Whatever his plan, he'd want it rock solid by the earliest news cycle. That meant all hands on deck, and Elizabeth planned to use the chaos to get what she wanted.

She stayed low as the tech van rolled past and turned for secure parking behind the station. Three patrol cars followed, and then Beckett and Dyer and two different attorneys from the DA's office. James Randolph was last: a lump in the window, a glimpse of smooth scalp and unshaven face. That's whom she wanted, a defiant, tough old bastard who thought rules should no more than graze an otherwise honest cop. He'd actually approached her after the basement and suggested she should have ditched the bodies and never said a word about it. She'd thought he was joking at first, but his crooked face seemed serious.

*A lot of woods out there, pretty lady.*

*A lot of deep, quiet, dark-as-hell woods.*

She gave him ten minutes inside the station, then called his cell. "James, hey. It's me." She stared at the window near his desk, thought she saw a shadow move. "Have you had dinner yet?"

"I was about to order takeout."

"Wong's?"

"Am I that predictable?"

"Let me buy it for you."

She heard his chair creak and pictured his feet going up on the desk. "It's been a long day, Liz, and a long night, coming. How about you tell me what you want?"

"You heard about Adrian?"

"'Course."

"I want to talk to him."

Seven seconds ticked past. Cars moved on the street. "Crispy beef," he said. "Don't forget the sticks."

They met twenty minutes later at a below-grade door set flush with the concrete wall.

"Here's how we do this."

He let her into the building. The hall was painted green, the floor was buffed vinyl.

"We go quick and quiet, and you keep your mouth shut. If we pass anyone in the hall, try to look humble, and remember what I said about your mouth. Any talking needs doing, I'm the one that does it."

"I understand."

"I'm doing this because you're a good cop and you're pretty, and because you've never cared that I'm as ugly as an old tire. None of that means I'm willing to lose my job getting you in to see this son of a bitch. Are we clear on that?"

She nodded, mouth tight.

"Good girl," he said, and offered the only smile she was liable to see. "Tight on my six; humble fucking pie."

She did as he asked and wasn't surprised that they made it unseen. They'd come in low and from the side. The action would be at the sergeant's desk near the front of the building and in the detective squad upstairs. The holding area would be a dead zone this late, and they were counting on that. Rounding a final corner, they saw a single guard at a desk near the heavy, steel door. He looked up, and James waved an easy hand. "Matthew Matheny. How's it hanging?"

Matheny crossed his arms, looked at Elizabeth. "What's going on, James?"

"Why don't you catch a smoke?"

"Are you asking or telling?"

"I don't tell you what to do. Come on."

Matheny looked at Elizabeth, his skin washed out in the fluorescent light. Like James, he was in his fifties and bald. Unlike James, he was thin and stooped, a mean-eyed man who, every day, seemed to hate his life a little bit more. "You know who's in there, right? Public enemy number one." Matheny pointed. "She may as well be public enemy number two. That makes this a big goddamn favor."

"The lady just wants a word. That's all."

"Why?"

"What does it matter? It's a word, an exchange of syllables. It's not like we're walking him out of here. Don't be such a girl."

"Why do you always do that? I don't like it, James. I never have."

"Do what? I'm not doing anything."

Matheny stared at Liz, doing the math. "If I say yes, we're even. I don't want to hear about *the day* ever again. It's done. Even if Dyer himself walks in here and finds her. We're even forever."

"Done. Fine."

"I can give you two minutes."

"She wants five."

"I'll give you three." Matheny stood. "He's in the lockdown cell. All the way down on the right."

"Why is he in lockdown?" Elizabeth asked.

"Why?" Matheny dropped keys on the desk. "Because fuck him, that's why."

When he was gone, she raised an eyebrow at James Randolph, who shrugged. "It's a pretty common sentiment around here."

"So, why is he helping us?"

"Matthew shot me on a quail hunt when we were kids. I tend to remind him about it from time to time. It irks him."

"But, a lockdown cell . . ."

"I bought you an extra minute." James unlocked the big door. "Don't make me come in there after you."

Elizabeth stepped into the hall, saw big cages on the right and left, the blank door of the lockdown cell at the far end. She moved deeper, and the hall darkened as old fluorescents flickered and snapped and made her uncomfortable. The place felt too much like prison, and prison, for her, was becoming a little too real. Low ceilings. Sweaty metal. She kept her eyes on the lockdown cell, which butted against the end wall. A grim affair, it had a solid-steel door, and an eight-inch cutout at face height. It was reserved for junkies, biters, the mentally disturbed. The walls and floors were padded with ancient canvas, stained with fecal matter and blood and every other possible fluid. Beyond anger, spite, and small-mindedness, no legitimate reason existed for Adrian's confinement there.

Slipping a bolt, she opened a hinged plate and peered into the cell. For some reason she held her breath, and the silence seemed to radiate outward. No movement in the cell. No sound beyond a whisper.

It was Adrian, in the corner, on the floor. He had bare feet. No shirt. His face was tucked into knees.

"Adrian?"

The cell was dark, dim light fingering its way past Elizabeth's head. She said his name again, and he looked up, blinking. "Who's there?"

"It's Liz."

He pushed himself up. "Who's there with you?"

"It's just me."

"I heard voices."

"No." Liz glanced down the hall. "No one else." He shuffled closer. "Where's your shirt? Your shoes?"

He made a vague gesture. "It's hot in here."

It looked it. Sweat glinted on his skin, beaded under his eyes. Parts of him seemed to be missing. The intellect. Much of his awareness. He tilted his head and sweat rolled on his face.

"Why are you here, Liz?"

"Are you okay, Adrian? Look at me." She gave him time, and he took it. She noticed small twitches in the muscles of his shoulders, the single shudder that led to a cough. "Did something happen after they brought you in? I know it was rough, but were you mistreated? Threatened? You seem . . ." She trailed off because she didn't want to finish the thought, that he seemed *less*.

"Darkness. Walls." He offered a difficult smile. "I don't do well in small spaces."

"Claustrophobia?"

"Something like that."

He tried to smile, but it turned into another round of coughing, another twenty seconds of the shakes. Her eyes moved down his chest, and across his stomach.

"Jesus, Adrian."

He saw her looking at the scars and turned away. His back, though, was as bad as his chest. How many pale, white lines were there? Twenty-five? Forty?

"Adrian . . ."

"It's nothing."

"What did they do to you?"

He picked up the shirt and shrugged it on. "I said it's nothing."

She looked more closely at his face and saw for the first time how bones did not line up as she remembered. Shadows filled the hollow place beside his left eye. The nose was not quite the same. She threw a glance down the hall. She had minutes. No more. "Have they questioned you about the church?"

Adrian put his palms flat against the door and kept his head down. "I thought you were suspended."

"How do you know about that?"

"Francis told me."

"What else did he tell you?"

"To stay away from you. To keep my mouth shut and not drag you into my problems." Adrian looked up, and for an instant the years faded. "For what it's worth, I didn't kill her."

He was talking about the church, the new victim.

"Did you kill Julia Strange?"

It was the first time Elizabeth had ever questioned his innocence, and the moment stretched as muscles tightened in his jaw and old wounds pulled apart. "I did the time, didn't I?"

His gaze, then, was clear and angry. Same Adrian. None of the weakness.

"You should have taken the stand," she said. "You should have answered the question."

"The question."

"Yes."

"Shall I answer it, now?"

The words were flat, but the stare was so intent a throb began at the base of Elizabeth's skull. He knew what she wanted. Of course, he knew. She'd waited every day of his trial for the question to be answered. There would be an explanation, she'd thought. Everything would make sense.

But he never took the stand.

The question was never answered.

"It's what it comes down to, isn't it?" He watched her. "The scratches on my neck. The skin under her nails."

"An innocent man would have explained it."

"Things were complicated, then."

"So, explain it now."

"Will you help me if I do?"

There it was, she thought. The convict Beckett had warned her about. The user. The player.

"Why your skin was under Julia Strange's nails?" He looked away, jawline clenched. "Tell me or I walk."

"Is that a threat?"

"A requirement."

Adrian sighed and shook his head. When he spoke, he knew how it would sound. "I was sleeping with her."

A pause. A slow blink. "You were having an affair with Julia Strange?"

"Catherine and I were in a bad place . . ."

"Catherine was pregnant."

"I didn't know she was pregnant. That came after."

"Jesus . . ."

"I'm not trying to justify it, Liz. I just want you to understand. The marriage wasn't working. I didn't love Catherine, and she didn't much love me, either. The baby was a last, desperate try, I think. I didn't even know she was pregnant until she lost it."

Elizabeth took a step away; came back. The pieces were ugly. She didn't want them to fit. "Why didn't you testify about the affair? The DNA evidence convicted you. If there was an explanation, you should have given it."

"I couldn't do it to Catherine."

"Bullshit."

"Hurt her. Humiliate her." He shook his head again. "Not after what I'd done to her."

"You should have testified."

"It's easy to say that now, but to what purpose? Think about it." He looked every inch a broken man, the face scarred, the eyes a dark stain. "No one knew the truth but Julia, and she was dead. Who would believe me if I claimed adultery as my defense? You've seen the trials same as me, the desperate men willing to lie and squirm and barter their souls for the barest chance of a decent verdict. My testimony would look like a string of self-serving, calculated lies. And what could I possibly get from it? Not sympathy or dignity or reasonable doubt. I'd open myself to cross-examination and look even guiltier by the end of it. No, I stared down that road more than once, thinking about it. I'd humiliate Catherine and get nothing for it. Julia was dead. Bringing up the relationship could only hurt me."

"No one saw you together?"

"Not in that way. No."

"No letters? Voice mails?"

"We were very careful. I couldn't prove the affair if I wanted to."
Elizabeth plucked at the edges. "It's all very convenient."

"There's more," he said. "You won't like it."

"Tell me."

"Someone planted evidence."

"For God's sake, Adrian . . ."

"My prints in her house, the DNA—that all makes sense. I get
it. I was there all the time. We were intimate. But the can at the
church doesn't fit. I was never near the church. I never drank a
beer there."

"And who do you think planted it?"

"Whoever wanted me in prison."

"I'm sorry, Adrian . . ."

"Don't say that."

"Say what? That you sound like every convict I've ever met. 'I
didn't do it. Someone set me up.'"

Elizabeth stepped back, and it was hard to hide the disbelief.
Adrian saw it; hated it. "I can't go back to prison, Liz. You don't
understand what it's like for me, there. You can't. Please. I'm asking
for your help."

She studied the grimy skin and dark eyes, unsure if she would
help. She'd changed her life because of him, yet he was just a man,
and seriously, perhaps fatally, flawed. What did that mean for her?
Her choices?

"I'll think about it," she said and left without another word.


It took two minutes to exit the building. Randolph stayed at her
side, moving her quickly down one hall and then another. At the
same low door on the same side street, he walked her onto the
sidewalk and let the door clank shut behind him. The sky burned
red in the west. A hot wind licked the concrete as Randolph shook
out two cigarettes and offered one to Elizabeth.

"Thanks."

She took it. He lit them both, and they smoked in silence for half a minute.

"So, what is it?" She flicked ash. "The real reason?"

"For what?"

"Helping me."

He shrugged, a misshapen grin on his face. "Maybe I dislike authority."

"I *know* you dislike authority."

"You also know why I helped you. Same reason I'd have helped you bury the Monroe brothers in the darkest woods in the deepest part of the county."

"Because you have daughters."

"Because fuck them for doing what they did to that girl. I'd have shot them, too, and I don't think you should go down for it. You've been a cop for what? Thirteen years? Fifteen? Shit." He sucked hard; blew smoke. "Defense lawyers would have put that girl through hell all over again, and some knee-jerk judge might let them go on a goddamn technicality. We both know it happens." He cracked his neck, unapologetic. "Sometimes justice matters more than the law."

"That's a dangerous way for a cop to look at things."

"System's broken, Liz. You know it same as me."

Elizabeth leaned against the wall and watched the man beside her, how light touched his face, the cigarette, the knotted fingers. "How old are they now? Your daughters?"

"Susan's twenty-three. Charlotte's twenty-seven."

"They're both in town?"

"By the grace of God."

They smoked in silence for a moment, the lean woman, the hump-shouldered man. She thought of justice and the law and the sound his neck made when he cracked it. "Did Adrian have enemies?"

"All cops have enemies."

"I mean inside the system. Other cops? Lawyers? Maybe someone from the DA's office?"

"Back in the day? Maybe. For a while you couldn't turn on the TV without seeing Adrian's face on the screen beside one pretty reporter or another. A lot of cops resented that. You should really ask Dyer."

"About Adrian?"

"Adrian, yeah." James stubbed out the cigarette. "Francis always hated that guy."

When Randolph went back inside, Elizabeth finished her cigarette, thinking. Thirteen years ago, did Adrian have enemies? Who knew? Elizabeth had been so young at the time. After the quarry, she'd managed her final year of high school and two years at the University of North Carolina before dropping out to become a cop. That made her twenty on her first day out of training, twenty and fired up and scared half to death. She wouldn't have known the hatreds or politics; she couldn't have.

But, she was thinking about it, now.

Following the sidewalk to the corner, she skirted a clump of pedestrians, then turned left and stepped into the street. Her car was parked a half block up on the other side. She thought about enemies; thought she was out clean.

That lasted another dozen steps.

Beckett was sitting on the hood of her car.

"What are you doing, Charlie?" She slowed in the street.

His tie hung loosely, shirtsleeves rolled to the elbow. "I could ask you the same thing." He watched her cross the last bit of dark pavement. She gauged his face; it was inscrutable.

"I just stopped by," she said. "You know. Checking on the case."

"Uh-huh."

Elizabeth stopped at the car. "Have you identified the victim?"

"Ramona Morgan. Twenty-seven years old. Local. We think she disappeared yesterday."

"What else?"

"Pretty but shy. No serious boyfriend. A waitress she worked with thinks she might have had plans on Sunday evening. We're trying to pin that down."

"Time of death?"

"After Adrian got out."

He dropped that on her like a rock; watched to see if she could handle it. "I want to talk to the medical examiner."

"That's not going to happen, and you know it."

"Because of Dyer?"

"He wants you isolated from anything to do with Adrian Wall."

"He thinks I'll jeopardize the case?"

"Or yourself. Hamilton and Marsh are still in town."

Elizabeth studied Beckett's face, most of it lost in shadow. Even then, she could see the emotion below the surface. Aversion? Disappointment? She wasn't sure. "Does Dyer hate him?"

He understood the question. She saw it. "I don't think Francis hates anybody."

"What about thirteen years ago? Did he hate anyone then?"

A bitter smile cut Beckett's face. "Did James Randolph tell you that?"

"Maybe."

"Maybe you should consider the source."

"Meaning what?"

"Meaning James Randolph was everything Adrian was not. Plodding. Narrow-minded. He's been divorced three times, for God's sake. If anyone hated Adrian, it was Randolph."

Elizabeth tried to work that piece into the puzzle.

Beckett slid off the car and thumped the fender, changing the subject. "I didn't know you were still driving this rust bucket."

"Sometimes."

"What year is it again?"

She watched his face, trying to catch the angles. Something was happening, and it wasn't about the car. "'Sixty-seven," she said. "I paid for it working summer jobs. It was pretty much the first real thing I ever bought by myself."

"You were eighteen, right?"

"Seventeen."

"That's right. Seventeen. Preacher's daughter." He whistled. "Lightning in a bottle."

"Something like that." She didn't mention the rest: that she'd bought the car two weeks after Adrian Wall stopped her from jumping to her death in the cold, black waters of the quarry; that she would drive it for hours on end; that for more years than she cared to count, it was the only good thing in her life. "What's with all the questions, Charlie?"

"There was this rookie, once." The transition was seamless, as if they'd been speaking of rookies all along. "This would be twenty-five years ago, before your time. He was a nice enough guy, but all elbows and apologies. Follow? Not cop. Not street. Anyway, this poor bastard went through the wrong door on the wrong side of town and ended up with a couple junkies on his chest and the business end of a broken bottle against his neck. They were going to cut his throat, kill him right there."

"Then you came through the door and saved his life. It was your first shoot. I've heard the story."

"Give the lady a gold star. Do you remember the name of the rookie I saved?"

"Yeah. It was Matthew . . ." She looked down. "Shit."

"Finish it."

Elizabeth shook her head.

"Come on, Liz. I gave you the gold star. Matthew what?"

"Matthew Matheny."

"The moral of the story is that a man like Matheny feels more loyalty to the man who saved his life than to the fifty-year-old version of some dumb-ass kid who got peppered in the leg with bird shot. Did you really think I wouldn't find out?"

"Does Dyer know?"

"Hell, no. He'd burn this place to the ground and take you with it. The only thing between here and there is me."

"Then why are you beating me up about this?"

"Because bright and early tomorrow this street will be elbow deep in news crews from as far away as DC and Atlanta. By sunset, it's headline news from coast to coast. We've got dead women draped in linen, a murderer ex-cop, a shot-up kid, and a tumble-down church straight out of some goddamn gothic masterpiece. The visuals alone will take it national. You want to get sucked into that story? Now, when the AG already wants you for double homicide?"

"Who put Adrian in lockdown?"

"What does that have to do with anything?"

"He's claustrophobic. Was it Dyer?"

"Goddamn, Liz. What is it with you and stray dogs?"

"He's not a dog."

"Dog. Convict. Lonely ass kid. You can't save every little thing."

It was an old argument that felt deeper than usual. "What if someone set him up?"

"Is that what this is? Seriously? I told you, Liz. He's a convict. Convicts are players."

"I know. It's just—"

"It's just that he's wounded and alone, right? You don't think he knows that's your weakness?" Beckett looked suddenly resigned, the frustration draining away. "Give me your hand." He took it without waiting, then used his teeth to pull the cap off a pen. "I want you to call this number." He wrote a number on the back of her hand. "I'll call him first. Tell him to expect you."

"Who?"

"The warden. Call him in the morning, first thing."

"Why?"

"Because you're lost in the wasteland, Liz. Because you need a way out, and because you won't believe the things he'll tell you."

# 11

Elizabeth left her partner on the street and drove west until the road crested a high ridge, and the sun flattened like a disk against the earth. Adrian was either lying or not, and Elizabeth could think of only one place to find the answer she needed. So she followed a two-lane out of town and ten minutes later turned onto the long, dark drive of a five-hundred-acre estate that bordered the river where it ran fast and white at the bottom of a tall bluff. Box bushes scraped paint as she pushed into the property. Branches hung low above the drive, and when it dead-ended, she climbed from the car. The house loomed beneath a dimming sky, and she felt the history of it as she stepped onto the porch. George Washington slept here, once. So did Daniel Boone, a half dozen governors. The current resident—though once equally impressive— came to the door in a poplin suit that looked slept in. He was unshaven, his face drawn beneath a cloud of thin, white hair that stirred as the door opened. He'd lost weight since she'd last seen him, seemed shorter, frailer, ancient.

"Elizabeth Black?" He was confused, at first; then smiled. "My God, it's been a thousand years." He squeezed her, took her hand.

"Come have a drink. Have two." The bright eyes twinkled. "Elizabeth Black."

"Crybaby Jones."

"Come in, come in."

He turned into the house, muttering apologies as he cleared newspapers and law books from different pieces of grand, old furniture. Glass clinked as empty bottles and cut-crystal glasses disappeared into the kitchen. Elizabeth wandered the room, her gaze on walking sticks, oil paintings, and dusty guns. When the old man returned, his shirt was buttoned to the collar, his hair perfectly smooth and damp enough to stay put as he moved. "Now, then." He opened a double-door closet that concealed a wet bar and a wall of bottles. "You don't care for bourbon, as I recall."

"Vodka rocks, please."

"Vodka rocks." His hands hovered by a row of bottles. "Belvedere?"

"Perfect."

Elizabeth watched him fix her drink, then mix an old-fashioned for himself. Faircloth Jones was a lawyer, retired. He'd come from nothing, worked weekends and nights to put himself through school, and become—arguably—the finest defense attorney ever seen in the state of North Carolina. In fifty years of practice—decades of cases involving murder, abuse, betrayal—he'd only cried once in court, the day a black-robed judge swore him into the state bar, then frowned disapprovingly and asked the young man why he was so shiny-eyed and trembling. When Faircloth explained that he was *moved by the grandeur of the moment,* the judge asked that he kindly move his wet-behind-the-ears, crybaby self somewhere other than his court.

The nickname stuck.

"I know why you're here." He pushed the drink into her hand, sat in a cracked, leather chair. "Adrian's out."

"Have you seen him?"

"Since retirement and divorce, I rarely leave the house. Sit. Please." He gestured to his right, and Elizabeth sat in a wooden-armed chair whose cushions were covered in faded, wine-colored velvet that had, in places, been worn white. "I've been following your situation with great interest. An unfortunate business: Channing Shore, the Monroe brothers. What's your lawyer's name, again?"

"Jennings."

"Jennings. That's it. A youngish man. Do you like him?"

"I haven't spoken to him."

"Young lady." He lowered the drink onto the arm of his chair. "Water finds a level, as you know, and the state will have its pound of flesh. Call your lawyer. Meet with him tonight if need be."

"It's fine, really."

"I fear I must insist. Even a young lawyer is better than none at all. The papers make your situation quite plain, and I don't pretend to have forgotten the politics of state office. Were I not a million years old, I would have sought you out myself and demanded to represent you."

He was agitated. Elizabeth ignored it. "I'm not here to talk about myself."

"Adrian, then."

"Yes." Elizabeth slipped onto the edge of her chair. It seemed so small, the truth she needed. A single word, a few letters. "Was he sleeping with Julia Strange?"

"Ah."

"He told me as much less than an hour ago. I just want verification."

"You've seen him, then?"

"I have."

"And you asked about the presence of his skin beneath Julia's nails?"

"Yes."

"I'm sorry . . ."

"Don't say no."

"I wish I could help you, but that information is a matter of attorney-client privilege, and you, my dear girl, are still an officer of the law. I can't discuss it."

"Can't or won't?"

"I've dedicated my life to the law. How can I do less when the days that remain are so few?" He drank deeply, visibly upset.

Elizabeth leaned closer, thinking perhaps he might feel the strength of her need. "Listen, Crybaby . . ."

"Call me Faircloth, please." He waved a hand. "The nickname reminds me of better days that hurt all the more for their passing." He settled into the seat as if a hand were pressing down.

Elizabeth clasped her fingers and spoke as if the rest of her words might cause pain, too. "Adrian believes someone planted evidence to implicate him."

"The beer can, yes. We discussed that, often."

"Yet, it was never challenged at trial."

"For that, my dear, Adrian would have needed to take the stand. He was unwilling to do so."

"Can you tell me why?'

"I'm sorry, but I cannot; and for the same reason as before."

"Another woman has been killed, Faircloth, murdered in the same manner and in the same church. Adrian has been arrested. It will be in tomorrow's papers."

"Dear God."

The glass trembled in his hand, and she touched his arm. "I need to know if he's lying to me about the beer can, the presence of his skin beneath Julia's nails."

"Has he been charged?"

"Faircloth—"

*"Has he been charged?"* The old man's voice shook with emotion. His fingers were white on the glass, spots of color in his cheeks.

"Not for the murder. He was picked up on a trespass charge. They'll hold him as long as they can. You know how it works. As for the dead woman, I know only that she was killed *after* Adrian's release from prison. Beyond that, I don't know what evidence they have. I'm frozen out."

"Because of your own troubles?"

"And because Francis Dyer doubts my intentions."

"Francis Dyer. Phhh!" The old man waved an arm, and Elizabeth remembered the way he'd cross-examined Dyer. As hard as Faircloth had tried, he had never been able to discredit Dyer's testimony. He was unshakable on the stand, utterly convinced of Adrian's obsession with Julia Strange.

"They'll hang him for this if they can." Elizabeth leaned closer. "You still care. I can tell. Talk to me, please."

He looked out from under bushy brows, the narrowed eyes very bright. "Will you help him?"

"Trust him or walk away. Those are my choices."

The old man leaned back in the chair and looked small in the rumpled suit. "Did you know that my family and Adrian's have been together on this river for two hundred years or more? No reason you should, of course, but there it is. The Jones family. The Walls. When my father was crippled in the First World War, it was Adrian's great-grandfather who taught me to hunt and fish and work the land. He cared for my parents, and when the Depression came, he made sure we had butter and beef and flour. He died when I was twelve, but I remember the smell of him, like tractor grease and grass and wet canvas. He had strong hands and a lined face and wore a tie when he came for supper on Sundays. I grew up and followed the law and never knew Adrian that well. But I remember the day he was born. A group of us smoked cigars on the porch right there. His father. A few others. It's good land on the river. Good families."

"That's a lovely sentiment, but I need something beyond simple faith. Can you tell me anything more? About Adrian? The case? Anything?"

The last word smelled of desperation, and the old lawyer sighed. "I can tell you that the law is an ocean of darkness and truth, and that lawyers are but vessels on the surface. We may pull one rope or another, but it is the client, in the end, who charts the course."

"Adrian refused your advice."

"I really can't discuss it."

The old man drained his drink, the cherry bloodred in the

bottom of the glass. He declined to meet her eyes, and Elizabeth thought she understood. He knew about the affair. He could have used it to sow doubt in the minds of the jury, but Adrian wouldn't allow it.

"It saddens me, child, to have you here while I have so little of value to say. I hope you can forgive an old man for such a frightful lapse, but I find myself weary."

Elizabeth took his hand, the bones within it light and brittle.

"If you would be kind enough to fix another drink." He retrieved his hand and offered the glass. "My heart aches from thoughts of Adrian, and my legs seem to have lost much of their feeling." Elizabeth fixed the drink and watched him take it. "Did you know that George Washington slept here, once?" He gestured vaguely; seeming tired enough to be transparent. "I often wonder which room."

"I'll leave you alone," Elizabeth said. "Thank you for speaking with me."

She made it to the tall, wide doors before he spoke again. "Do you know how I got my nickname?"

Elizabeth turned her back to the curving staircase and the floor stained black by time. "I've heard the story."

"That flint-eyed judge was right about one thing. Lawyers are not to become emotionally involved. We are to be strong when clients are weak, righteous where they are flawed. It's a simple conceit. Discipline. The law." He looked up from the depths of his chair. "That worked for every client until Adrian."

Elizabeth held her breath.

"We spent seven months prepping his case, sat side by side for long weeks of trial. I'm not saying he was perfect—God knows he was as human as the rest of us—but when he was convicted, it was like something inside me broke, like some vital, lawyerly organ simply stopped working. I kept my face, mind you. I thanked the judge and shook the prosecutor's hand. I waited until the courtroom was clear, then I put my head on the defense table and wept like a child. You asked if there was anything I could tell you, and

I guess that's it. The last trial of Crybaby Jones." He nodded at the liquor in his glass. "A sad old man and tears, like bookends."


When Elizabeth returned to the police station, she marched through the front door without slowing. Adrian was telling the truth—that was the old man's message. Now, she wanted to know what they had on him. Not the trespass. The murder. She wanted answers.

"What are you doing here, Liz?"

She rounded into the bull pen, still moving fast. Beckett worked his large body between the desks, trying to catch her as she narrowed the angle to Dyer's door.

"Liz. Wait."

Her hand found the knob.

"Don't. Liz. Jesus . . ."

But the door was already opening. Inside, Dyer was standing. So were Hamilton and Marsh.

"Detective Black." Hamilton spoke first. "We were just talking about you."

Elizabeth faltered. "Captain?"

"You shouldn't be here, Liz."

Elizabeth looked from Dyer to the state cops. It was hours after dark, too late for the meeting to be random. "This is about me?"

"New evidence," Hamilton said. "We'd like your take on it."

"I won't allow that," Dyer said. "Not without representation."

"We can keep it off the record, if you like."

Dyer shook his head, but Elizabeth raised her hand. "It's okay, Francis. If there's new evidence, I want to hear it."

"Off the record, then. Come in and shut the door. Not you, Beckett."

"Liz?" Beckett showed his palms.

"It's okay. I'm fine."

She tried to tell herself that was true, but Dyer looked ruined. Even Hamilton and Marsh seemed burdened by some unseen weight. Elizabeth worked to hold on to her conviction and purpose. She'd come for Adrian because the old lawyer's certainty was as compelling as any proof she'd ever seen. But the air in the close, crowded office tasted thick and sickly sweet. It was fear, she realized. She was barely three feet into the room, and already afraid. "Am I being charged?"

"Not yet." Hamilton closed the door.

She nodded, but *not yet* meant it was coming, meant it was close. "What evidence?"

"Forensics on the basement." Hamilton's fingers touched a file on the desk. "Is there anything you want to tell us about what happened there?" His voice came from some distant place. "Detective Black?"

Everyone was looking at her, now, Dyer suddenly worried, the state cops so full of inexplicable pity they seemed grotesque.

"We ran DNA," Hamilton said. "On the wire used to bind Channing Shore. The lab identified blood from two different people. One was from the girl, of course, which we expected." He paused. "The second sample came from an unknown person."

"A second person?"

"Yes."

"One of the Monroe brothers," Elizabeth said.

"Both brothers have been ruled out."

"Then the blood came from some other crime. Cross-contamination. Old evidence."

"We don't believe so."

"Then, some other explanation . . ."

"May we see your wrists, Detective Black?" Everyone looked at her sleeves, at the light jacket and buttoned cuffs. Hamilton leaned closer, his expression as soft as his voice. "We're not incapable of sympathy . . ."

Elizabeth kept her hands perfectly still, though her skin seemed to burn. "I don't know what you mean."

"If there's a reason you snapped—"

"I shouldn't be here," she said.

"If there are extenuating circumstances—"

"I shouldn't be here at all."

She hit the door at a fast walk, blood rushing in her ears, the skin still burning. She didn't think about why because she was tired of thinking, same with feeling, remembering, talking. There was a time and a place, and not every goddamn thing mattered. That's what everyone else refused to understand.

The basement was done.

Over.

For an instant, she sensed Beckett behind her, his voice in the stairwell, then on the street. She moved faster, slid into the car, then gunned it, seeing his face as a white blotch, his hands rising and then down. She drove fast and let the car do the talking. Rubber at the corners. Engine on the flats. Her skin still burned, but it was more like shame and rage and self-loathing.

*DNA on the wire.*

Her hand hit the wheel.

She wanted to move and keep moving. Barring that, she wanted to get drunk. She wanted to be alone in the dark, to sit in a chair and feel the weight of a glass in her hand. The memory would still be there, but the colors would dim; the Monroe brothers would fade; the carousel would stop.

Beckett, however, had other ideas. His car hit the driveway twenty seconds behind her own. "What are you doing here, Charlie?"

"I heard what they said." Beckett stopped at the bottom step. "Through the door, I heard it."

"Yeah. So?"

"So, I don't know what to do." He looked as ruined as Dyer as he tried and failed to keep his eyes off the place her hands joined her arms. "Liz, Jesus . . ."

"Whatever they're talking about has nothing to do with me. I'm a cop. I'm fine."

"If something happened—"

"I shot them like I said. I don't regret it. I would do it again. Beyond that, there's no story. Good guys won. The girl's alive."

"And if the girl was talking? If Hamilton and Marsh could get through her father's lawyers?"

"She'd say the same thing."

"Maybe that's the problem. The way things are with you two." He tilted his large head, and shadows moved on the broken landscape of his face. "You make it easy to believe the worst."

"Because we look out for each other?"

"Because when you talk, you use the same words. You should look at your statements. Put them side by side and tell me what you see. Same words. Same phrasing."

"Coincidence."

"Show me your wrists."

"No."

He reached for her arm, and she slapped him so hard the sound itself was like a shot. They froze in the silence that followed. Partners. Friends. Momentary enemies.

"I deserved that," Beckett said.

"You're goddamn straight."

"I'm sorry. It's just—"

"Go away, Charlie."

"No."

"It's late."

She fumbled with keys, and Beckett watched from the fog of his discontent. When the door closed between them, he raised his voice. "You should have called me, Liz! You should have never gone in alone!"

"Go home, Beckett."

"I'm your partner, damn it. We have procedures."

"I said, go home!"

She put her weight on the door, felt the crush of her heart and wood against her skin. Beckett was still outside, standing and watching. By the time he left, she was shaking and didn't know why.

*Because people suspected?*

*Because her skin still burned?*

"Past is past." She closed her eyes and said it again. "Past is past and now is now."

"Is that how you do it?"

The voice came from a dark corner beyond the sofa, and Liz's hand touched checkered wood before she cataloged it. "Damn it, Channing." She took her fingers off the pistol grip, flipped on an overhead light. "What the hell are you doing?"

The girl's feet were pulled up in the well of a deep chair. She wore jeans and chipped polish and canvas sneakers. The same hooded sweatshirt framed her eyes. Bright as they were, the girl still looked haunted, her narrow shoulders rolled inward, a kitchen knife in the knot of a single hand. "I'm sorry." She put the knife on the arm of the chair. "I don't do well with angry men."

Elizabeth locked the door. Crossing the room, she collected the knife and put it on the kitchen table. "How did you get in here?"

"You weren't home." Channing hooked a thumb. "I jimmied the window."

"Since when do you break into people's houses?"

"Never before tonight. You should have set your alarm, by the way."

"Would it have stopped you?"

"I feel safe with you. I'm sorry."

Elizabeth ran water in the sink, splashed some on her face. She didn't know if the girl was sorry or not. In the end, it didn't matter. She was hurting. Like Liz was hurting.

"Do your parents know where you are?"

"No."

"I'm facing indictment, Channing. You're a potential witness against me. It would be . . . unwise."

"Maybe I'll run away."

"No, you won't."

"I could do it, you know." Channing stood and walked along a row of books. "Run away. Check the hell out." The profanity seemed wrong in such a young and flawless mouth, and the girl spoke as if she could see Elizabeth's thoughts. "Tell me you don't think about it. Tell me you weren't *just* thinking about it." Channing flicked fingers toward the door, meaning Beckett and the conversation and the mantra that bordered on prayer. "Leaving this place. Disappearing."

"My problems are not yours, Channing. You're so young. You can do anything, be anyone."

"But, it's not about age anymore, is it?"

"It can be."

"It's too late to go back or stay the same."

"Why?"

"Because I burned it all." A spark flared in Channing's eyes. "The stuffed animals and posters and pink sheets, the photographs and books and notes from little boys. I burned it in the garden, a great, giant fire that almost took everything else with it." She dropped the hood to show cherry-red skin and hair burned away at the tips. "The garden was burning, two of the trees."

"Why would you do that?"

"Why did you get so close to the quarry's edge?"

It was softly said, but broke Elizabeth's heart.

"My father tried to stop me. But I ran when I saw him. I think he hurt himself going over the fence. He was screaming, angry maybe. Whatever the case, I can't go home." The girl's defiance dwindled to desperation. "Tell me I have to leave, and you'll never see me again. I'll burn the world. I swear it."

Elizabeth poured a drink and spoke with her back turned. "Your parents should know you're okay. Text them, at least. Tell them you're safe."

"Does that mean you'll let me stay?"

Elizabeth turned and smiled wryly. "I can't have you burning the world."

"Can I have one of those?" Channing pointed at the drink. "If it's not about the age . . ." Elizabeth poured a single finger in a second glass and handed it over, wordlessly. The girl swallowed it, choking a little. "I saw a bathtub . . ."

She let it hang, and Elizabeth pointed down the hall. "Towels are in the closet."

Elizabeth watched her down the hall, then poured another drink, turned off the lights, and sat in the dark. Twice her cell phone vibrated, and twice she let it go to voice mail. She didn't want to talk to Beckett or Dyer or any of the reporters who found their way to her number.

For another hour, she sat and drank and held herself still. When she finally stood, the bath was empty and the guest-room door was closed. Elizabeth listened, but there was no noise beyond the tick and creak of an old house finding its way deeper into the earth. She checked the locks, anyway. The doors. The windows. Stepping into the bathroom, she locked that door, too, then removed her shirt and examined the cruel, thin cuts on her wrists. They went all the way around and were deeper in some places than in others. Red lines, partly scabbed. Memories. Nightmares.

"Past is past . . ."

She took off the rest of her clothes and filled the tub. She was hiding the truth, yes, but there were reasons. That should make her feel better, but *reason* was just a word.

Like *family* was a word.

Or *faith* or *law* or *justice.*

She slipped into the tub because hot water seemed to help. It warmed her through and made her weightless. Water was good like that, but it was water's nature to rise and fall and rise again; that was its purpose, so that when she closed her eyes, the world fell away, and she felt it again: the basement around her, like fingers on her throat.

*The man was choking her, one arm locked around her neck, his hand tight on her wrist, smashing her gun hand into the wall. Channing was a doll on the floor, screaming as the gun struck concrete three times, four times, then skittered into the dark.*

*Elizabeth felt the gun go, tried to turn.*

*Who was he?*

*Who the fuck . . . ?*

*She could tell he was massive and unwashed, but that was it. He was an arm around her neck, a scrape of whiskers as he squeezed harder and blackness crowded in. She kicked down, looking for the instep, the shin. She flung her head back, but the contact was small and weak.*

*"Shh . . ."*

*Breath found her ear, but she was fading. No blood getting through. Eyes tight.*

*She clawed at his arms, and in the dark there was movement. The second man, broad and hunched. Channing saw him, too, her heels scrabbling in the grime, her back finding the wall.*

*Channing . . .*

*No sound came out. Elizabeth saw her own hand outstretched, the fingers doubling as her vision blurred.*

*Channing . . .*

*The second man snaked big fingers into the girl's hair, dragged her across the floor and into the dimness of another room.*

*Where was the gun?*

*Elizabeth was forced to her knees, saw high-top sneakers and grimy jeans, the place her fingers smeared mold on the floor. His weight settled on her back, pushing her forward, pushing her down. Whiskers ground into her neck, and the same breath licked her ear.*

*"Shhhh . . ."*

*It was longer that time.*

*Then fading.*

*Then blackness.*

In judo, it was called a blood choke or a carotid restraint or a sleeper hold. Cops called it a lateral vascular neck restraint. The name didn't matter. The purpose and function did. Simultaneous compression of the carotid and the jugular could render an adult unconscious in seconds. Do it right, and it didn't take much strength. Do it wrong and it fails or somebody ends up dead. It's not like the movies. You have to know what you're doing to do it right.

Titus Monroe knew what he was doing.

Elizabeth played it over for the millionth time: how it started and ended, the minutes in between. Channing was off the mattress, and they were backing out of the room, the girl's hand hot and wet and twisted into Elizabeth's own. Elizabeth kept her gun trained deeper into the basement. She would shoot if necessary, but the door was empty, the basement quiet behind them. They managed three steps before the girl stumbled and went down, but that was okay. Elizabeth's gun was up, and the last hall was ten feet away. There were some closed doors, some stairs; but they were going to make it.

Elizabeth never heard the door open behind her, never heard him at all; she felt the rush of his arm around her neck, his fingers on her wrist. She felt him and fought and failed, went down into the black, and woke wired to a mattress with her clothes stripped off and her mouth clamped shut. His tongue moved on her ear, her neck; and she fought like an animal would fight, screamed behind his sweaty hand as a red candle burned and his fingers moved across her skin. He was going to rape her, maybe kill her. But even as she fought, she felt as if she were falling, his rough touch fading, the candlelight winking twice, then gone. She heard a voice that was her own, but younger.

*Not again, not again . . .*

The fall could have taken her all the way down, so deep she would not have come back the same or even close. He was going to pound her into the dark and leave her there . . .

Elizabeth settled deeper in the tub, cold and hot and shaking. She'd lost herself when it mattered most. Thirteen years of cop and she'd broken like a plaster mask.

It took Channing to save her.

The girl.

Who was only eighteen.

———

*He was a million pounds of sweat and hair, of muscle and fat and thick, hard fingers.*

*"Fine bitch . . ."*

*His skin slid on hers, but there was little breath in her lungs. She breathed out; he pushed down.*

*"Fine, sweet, hot fucking bitch . . ."*

Elizabeth was all but gone when gunshots blew the dark world into bright, shiny bits. She heard screams and followed them up, eyes blinking as the big man rolled to his feet, shouting something she later understood to be his brother's name.

No answer came beyond the screams, which were agonized and terrible and afraid. They rose from the room next door, ricocheted off concrete walls, and Elizabeth—even now—had no idea how Channing got her hands on the gun. She was simply there, pale in the door, and naked, the gun impossibly large in her tiny hand. Elizabeth saw it slow and clear, but like the dream of a dream; as if it had happened to some person she may have known once upon a distant time.

*The first shot blew his knee to mist. He was still falling when the second knee disappeared, too. He jerked right and left, then dropped where he'd stood, the ruined bones slapping concrete with a heavy, wet sound she would never forget. His screams joined his brother's before turning into a tortured version of barely recognizable words.*

*"Bitch!"*

*He writhed.*

*"Fucking . . . Ahh! Fuck!"*

*Channing shuffled across the floor, a broken mask on her face,*

*too. The eyes looked dark and swollen, the mouth open and sound-*
*less. The gun pulled her arm down, so she staggered once, then*
*stopped above the screaming man.*

*"Channing . . ."*

*The name fell from Elizabeth's mouth, but Channing raised the*
*gun, her face utterly still as the screams ramped louder, and tears*
*tracked through the grime beneath her eyes. She was in shock and*
*filthy, blood running from her wrists to drip off her fingers.*

*"Channing . . ."*

*Elizabeth stopped struggling. The girl stared at the wailing man.*

*"Channing . . ."*

It took forever to use all eighteen bullets: seconds that stretched
to minutes, minutes that felt like hours. In reality, it could have
been no time at all. Elizabeth was not the one to say. She kept
her eyes on Channing when she could; saw the wounded blank-
ness of all who are ruined young. In the end, it was a simple
thing. The gun spoke. Men screamed. When they were dead,
Channing stood for a long time before Elizabeth's words made
any kind of impression.

*The shots will have been heard.*

*Police will come.*

Smoke still hung in the air, and already the world was torn wide
open. Even as sirens rose in the distance, and wire bit more deeply
into her wrists, Elizabeth understood that the police were now on
one side of the rift, while she and Channing stood, forever, on the
other.

That's how fast she made her decision.

How fast her old life ended.

Elizabeth wanted to be done, but images spun out of the dark:
Channing's fingers, shaking red as they stripped off wire, and sirens
drew close. The gathering of clothes and the wiping of the gun,

the story repeated as Elizabeth held the child and forced her to say the words.

Channing was on the mattress.

Elizabeth shot them in the dark.

*"Say it again, Channing."*

*"I was on the mattress. You shot them in the dark."*

At two o'clock, Elizabeth finally climbed into bed. She barely slept, and when she did, she woke soaked in sweat. The third time it happened, she followed an unfamiliar noise and found Channing curled on the bathroom floor. The only light was a flicker from the girl's room, but it was enough to see the bruises and the bite marks, the bandages on her wrists.

"I thought I was going to be sick. I'm sorry if I woke you."

"Here." Elizabeth ran cold water on a washcloth and handed it to Channing. "Let me help you." She helped the girl up. They stood at the counter and in the mirror looked very different, Elizabeth narrow and lithe, the girl shorter, more gently curved. The girl was crying, but seemed unable to move. "Let me." Elizabeth took the washcloth and pressed it against the girl's skin. She wiped away tears and smoothed hair from the pale, cool forehead. "There." She turned Channing to face the mirror. "Better?"

The girl stared at her own face, then at Elizabeth's. "We have the same eyes."

Elizabeth lowered her face until it was even with the girl's, their cheeks almost touching. "So we do."

"It's my fault," Channing said. "What happened in the basement, what happened to you."

"Don't be silly."

"What if it were, though? Would you still be my friend?"

"Of course."

The girl nodded, but seemed unconvinced. "Do you believe in hell?"

"Not for you, I don't." Elizabeth squeezed Channing's shoulders, her voice fierce. "Not for this."

The girl looked down, and the bright eyes closed. "I shot the little one the most because he liked to hurt me the most. That's what the dream was about: his fingers and teeth, that whisper he had, the way he'd hold my eyes open as he hurt me, that deep-down, forever stare."

"He got what he deserved."

"But, I made the choice," Channing said. "The smaller brother was the worst so I shot him the most. Eleven bullets. That was me. My choice. How can you say there's no hell?"

"You can't look at it like that."

"I barely sleep, and it's not for fear of dreams. It's because there's this one second when I wake, this one instant, where I don't remember."

"I know that second."

"But there's another one behind it, isn't there? Another second, and everything comes down so hard it's like being buried alive. I go to bed in fear of that second. I'm eighteen years old, and I've done this thing . . ."

"What thing?" Elizabeth hardened her voice because the girl needed hard. "You saved my life. You saved us both."

"Maybe I should tell somebody."

She meant the police, her parents, a shrink. It didn't matter. "You can't tell anyone, Channing. Not ever."

"I tortured them."

"Don't say that word."

"We could say it was self-defense."

A sliver of hope touched Channing's face, but no juror could understand the truth of what happened. They would have to have been there, to see Channing, naked and filthy in the candlelight, see the blood dripping from her fingers, see her face, shattered, the teeth marks in her skin.

*Eighteen shots . . .*

*Torture . . .*

The trial would force her to live it again, in public and on record. Elizabeth had seen enough rape and murder trials to understand the power of their deconstructive nature. Testimony would last for days or weeks, and the process would eviscerate any innocence the girl had left. She'd be marked for life, possibly convicted.

Elizabeth could hear the prosecutor, now. *Eighteen shots, ladies and gentlemen. Not three or four or six. Eighteen shots, placed to wound and hurt and punish . . .* They'd pursue her for the politics of it, the visuals. "Promise me, Channing. Swear you won't talk about it."

"I don't know who I am."

"Don't say that."

"Can I sleep with you?"

"Anything." Elizabeth hugged her, her emotions undone. "Everything."

She led Channing to the large bed in the corner bedroom on the left side. There was no tough girl left, no anger or pretense or wounded pride. They were survivors—sisters—and as such climbed wordlessly into the same bed.

"Are you crying?" Elizabeth asked.

"Yes."

"Everything will be all right. I promise."

Channing reached out an arm and laid two fingers on Elizabeth's back. "Is that okay?"

"It's fine, sweetheart. Go to sleep."

The touch must have helped because Channing did, her breathing shallow at first, then rhythmic and slow. Elizabeth felt the girl's closeness, the heat of her skin. She felt the stillness of those two fingers, and her own breathing eased. It took a long time, but the room fell away.

Her aching heart slowed.

The carousel stopped.

# 12

Beckett didn't know how to help his partner. Elizabeth was not just wounded but withdrawn, hurting in a way he'd never before seen. Normally, she owned the job. That meant the street, the politics, every impossible decision a cop would ever have to make. She made hard choices and lived with them, unflinching. Even the men she'd dated took a backseat to her unshakable sense of self. If relationships ended, it was because Elizabeth said so. She set the ground rules and the tone, said when it began and when it was over. Some thought she had ice in her veins, but Beckett knew better. Fact was, she felt more than most, but knew how to hide it. It was a survival skill, an asset; but whatever happened in that goddamn basement stripped it right out of her. She was a walking nerve, now—every bit exposed—and Beckett was running out of ideas on how to protect her. Keep her out of prison. Keep her away from Adrian. Those were the obvious things.

*What about the rest of it?*

It was late when he parked outside the house owned by Channing's parents. He wasn't supposed to be here—the lawyers had made that clear—but only two people knew the truth of what happened in the basement, and Liz wasn't talking.

That left the kid.

Problem was, her father was rich and connected and draped in lawyers. Even the state cops couldn't get past the wall. It was one of the biggest questions, really. Why wasn't the girl talking? The lawyers claimed it would be too traumatic, and maybe they were right. Beckett had daughters. He was sympathetic.

*But still . . .*

He peered through the heavily treed yard; saw stone and brick and yellow light. He'd met the father a few times when Channing first disappeared. Not a full-blown asshole, but he liked the word *listen,* as in *You listen to me, Detective.* But that was probably a worried-father thing, and Beckett wasn't about to judge a man for protecting his family. Beckett would do the same thing. His wife. His kids. Make the threat big enough, and he'd tear the city down.

Turning off the car, Beckett walked down the drive and circled to the front porch. A burned smell hung in the air. Music filtered through the glass and stopped when he rang the bell. In the silence, he heard cicadas.

Channing's mother answered the door. "Detective Beckett." She was in an expensive dress, and obviously impaired.

"Mrs. Shore." She was petite and pretty, a slightly weathered version of her daughter. "I'm sorry to bother you this late."

"Is it late?"

"I was hoping to speak with your daughter."

She blinked and swayed. Beckett thought she might fall, but she caught herself with a hand on the wall.

"Who is it, Margaret?" The voice came from stairs in the main hall.

The woman gestured vaguely. "My husband." Channing's father appeared in workout clothes and a full sweat. He wore boxing shoes and wraps on his hands. "He wants to talk to Channing."

The words slurred that time. Mr. Shore touched his wife's shoulder. "Go on upstairs, sweetheart. I'll handle it." Both men watched her unsteady exit. When they were alone, Mr. Shore showed his palms. "We grieve in our own ways, Detective. Come in."

Beckett followed the man through the grand foyer and into a study lined with bookshelves and what Beckett assumed to be expensive art. Mr. Shore went to a sidebar and poured mineral water in a tall glass with ice. "Can I get you something?"

"No, thanks. You box?"

"In my youth. I keep a gym in the basement."

It was hard to not be impressed. Alsace Shore was midfifties, with thick, muscled legs and heavy shoulders. If there was fat on him, Beckett couldn't see it. What he did see were two large adhesive bandages, one protruding from the sleeve of his shirt, the second high on his right leg. Beckett gestured. "Have you been injured?"

"Burned, actually." Shore swirled water in the glass and gestured toward the back of the house. "An accident with the grill. Stupid, really."

Beckett thought that was a lie. The way he said it. The play of his eyes. Looking more closely, he saw singed fingertips and patches on both arms where hair had been cooked away. "You said people grieve in different ways. What, exactly, are you grieving?"

"Do you have children, Detective?"

"Two girls and a boy."

"Girls." Shore leaned against a heavy desk and smiled ruefully. "Girls are a special blessing for a father. The way they look at you, the trust that there's no problem you can't handle, no threat in the world from which you can't protect them. I hope you never see that look of trust disappear from your own daughters' eyes, Detective."

"I won't."

"So certain."

"Yes."

Another difficult smile bent Shore's face. "How old are they now, your daughters?"

"Seven and five."

"Let me tell you how it happens." Shore put down the glass and stood on the broad base of his trunklike legs. "You build your life and your redundancies, and you think you have it covered, that you know best and that you've built the defenses necessary to protect the ones you love. Your wife. Your child. You go to bed believing yourself untouchable, then wake one day to the realization you haven't done enough, that the walls aren't as strong as you think, or that the people you trust aren't trustworthy, after all. Whatever the mistake, you realize it too late to make a difference." Shore nodded as if seeing Channing at those same, young ages—seven and five, and full of faith. "Bringing a daughter home alive is not the same as bringing her home unchanged. Much of the child we knew is gone. That's been difficult for us, and for Channing's mother, in particular. You ask why we grieve. I'd say that's reason enough."

The message seemed heartfelt and sincere, yet Beckett wasn't sure he believed the performance. It felt a little practiced and a little pat. The sternness and disapproval. The jaw tilted just so. What he'd said was true, though. People grieved in different ways. "I'm very sorry for what happened."

Shore dipped his large head. "Perhaps, you could tell me why you're here."

Beckett nodded as if he would do just that. Instead, he walked along a wall of books, then stopped and leaned in. "You shoot?" He pointed at a row of crackled spines. The books were old and well thumbed. *Tactical Marksmanship. Surgical Speed Shooting. USMC Pistol Marksmanship.* There were others, maybe a dozen.

"I also skydive, kitesurf, and race my Porsche. I like adrenaline. You were getting to the point of your visit."

But Beckett didn't like being rushed. It was the cop in him. Situational management, he called it, though Liz claimed it was alpha-male bullshit. *Button pushing,* she'd say. *Pure and simple.* Maybe, there was some of that, too. Beckett tried not to go too deep. The job and his family, old regrets and thoughts of retirement. Usually, that was enough. But he didn't much care for lies or liars. "What it comes down to, Mr. Shore"—Beckett pulled a few of the marksmanship books and started flipping pages—"is that I'd like to speak to Channing."

"She doesn't want to talk about what happened."

"I understand that. But, your daughter's not the only one who came out of that basement changed. Perhaps, others grieve as well. Perhaps, there are larger issues."

"My responsibility is to my daughter."

"Yet, it's not a zero-sum game, is it?" Beckett closed the second book on shooting, riffled through another, then leaned into the shelf where a *Kama Sutra* manual caught his eye.

"Detective Black is your partner?"

"She is."

"Family of a sort." Beckett nodded, and Mr. Shore put down his glass. "Your partner killed the men who took my daughter, and part of me will always love her for that. But even *she* doesn't talk to Channing. Not her. Not the state cops. Not you. Do I make myself clear?"

The stare between them held. Big men. Serious egos.

Beckett blinked first. "The state police will compel her testimony. It's only a mater of time. You know that, right?"

"I know they'll try."

"Do you know what she'll say when the subpoena comes?"

"She's the victim, Detective. She has nothing to hide."

"And yet truth, I've learned, can be a fluid business."

"In this case, you're wrong."

"Am I?"

Beckett opened three of the shooting manuals and left them spread on the desk. The inside jacket of each one showed Channing's signature, beautifully made.

"Those are *my* books."

The father choked as he said it, and Beckett nodded sadly.

That was a lie, too.

Elizabeth woke unable to remember the dream that haunted her; only that it was dark and hot and close. The basement, she guessed.

Or prison.

Or hell.

She shrugged off a weight of blankets and felt cool wood under her feet. At the window, she saw trees like an army in the fog. It was early, barely light. The road ran off into the mist, black and still, then fading, then gone. The stillness reminded her of a morning with Gideon six years ago. He'd called her after midnight. The father was out, the boy alone and sick. *I'm scared*, he'd said, so she'd collected him from the porch of that tumbledown house, brought him home, and put him between clean sheets. He was feverish and shaking, said he'd heard voices in the dark beyond the creek, and that they'd kept him awake and made him afraid. She gave him aspirin and a cool cloth for his forehead. It took hours for him to fall asleep, and as he drifted, his eyes opened a final time. *I wish you were my mother*, he'd said; and the words were light, as if raised from a dream. She'd slept in a chair after that and woke to an empty bed and wet, gray light. The boy was on the porch watching fog roll through the trees and down the long, black road. His eyes were dark when he looked up, his arms wrapped across his narrow chest. He was shivering in the cool air so she sat on the step and pulled him against her side.

*I meant what I said.* His cheek found her shoulder, and she felt the warm spot of his tears. *I never meant nothing so much in all my life.*

He'd cried hard after that, but it was still a favorite memory, and Elizabeth kept it close every day of her life. He never said the words again, but the morning was a special thing between them, and it was hard to look at fog without feeling love of Gideon like a pain in her chest. But this was a different day, so she shook off the emotion and focused on what was coming in the next few hours. Adrian would face court, and that meant media, questions, familiar faces from better times. She wondered if he would seem as torn, and if the cops would have enough to hold him. The trespass charge was weak. Could they charge him with murder? She rolled the footage of his life and knew what she was doing as she did it, that it was easier to worry about Adrian's future than her own. Large as he stood in the halls of memory, his suffering would remain his alone, at least until she faced her own conviction. Yet, that risk was out there, too, and it could happen now: cars in the mist, cops with weapons drawn. What would she say if Hamilton and Marsh suddenly appeared? What would she do?

"You should run."

Elizabeth turned and found Channing awake. "What did you say?"

The girl pushed up in the bed, her eyes catching light from the window, the rest of her dim and shapeless in the gloom. "If we're not going to tell the truth about what I did, then you should leave. Maybe, we should leave together."

"Where would we go?"

"The desert," Channing said. "Some place we could see forever."

Elizabeth sat on the bed. The girl's eyes looked so kaleidoscopic that anything seemed possible. Escape. The desert. Even a future. "Did you know what I was thinking just now?"

"How would I know that?"

Elizabeth waited half a beat, thinking the girl *had* known. "Go back to sleep, Channing."

"Okay."

"We'll talk later."

Elizabeth closed the bedroom door, then took the hottest shower she could stand. Afterward, she tended the wounds on her wrists, then put on jeans and boots and a shirt with tight cuffs. She was in the living room when Beckett showed up at the front door.

"Two things," he said. "First, I was out of line last night. Way out of line. I'm sorry."

"Just like that?"

"What can I say? You're my partner. You matter."

"What's the second thing?"

"Second thing is I still want you to see the warden. He gets in early. He's expecting you."

"Adrian has court."

"First appearances aren't until ten. You have time."

Elizabeth leaned into the door, thinking she was tired and wanted coffee and that it was too early for her to be standing in the door and talking to Charlie Beckett. "Why do you want me to see him? The real reason."

"Same as before. I want you to recognize Adrian Wall for what he is."

"Which is what?"

"Broken and violent and beyond redemption."

Beckett put a big period at the end of the sentence, and Elizabeth thought hard about what he wanted. The prison mattered in the county. It meant jobs, stability. The warden had a lot of power. "He'll show me something I don't already know?"

"He'll show you the truth, and that's all I'm asking. For you to open your eyes and understand."

"Adrian's not a killer."

"Just go. Please."

"Okay, fine. I'll see the warden."

Elizabeth leaned on the door, but Beckett caught it before it closed. "Did you know she's a shooter?"

Elizabeth froze.

"I looked it up last night. Channing is a competitive marksman. Did you know that?" Elizabeth looked away, but Beckett saw the truth. "It's not in your report."

"Because nobody needs to know."

"Doesn't need to know what? That she could strip your Glock in the dark, then put it back together and shoot the dick off a gnat? I dug up her scores. She can outshoot ninety-nine cops out of a hundred."

"So can I."

"She burned down her yard, yesterday. Did you know that, too? The fire marshal says the house could have gone up with it. The neighbor's house, too. People could have died."

"Why do you push, Charlie?"

"Because you're my friend," Beckett said. "Because Hamilton and Marsh are coming for you, and because we need an alternate story."

"There is no alternate."

"There's the girl."

"The girl?" Liz leaned on the door until the center of a single eye was all that showed. "As far as you're concerned, there is no girl."

Beckett disagreed. The bullet placement was *perfect*. Knees. Elbows. Groins. Could the girl have done it? Taken the Monroe brothers out in near dark? Tortured them, first? She was eighteen, weighed all of ninety pounds. Beyond that, he didn't know her at all, so he couldn't say.

But, he did know Liz.

She treated Gideon like a son, the girl like a sister, and Adrian like some kind of fallen saint. She was a sucker for lost causes, and now there were these new questions.

*Could Channing have pulled the trigger?*

*Whose blood was on the wire?*

The questions followed him into the precinct and upstairs. He checked the murder board on Ramona Morgan, but they didn't have much. Burn marks from a stun gun were obvious, but they had no fingerprints, fibers, or DNA. No sexual assault occurred. Death was by strangulation, which apparently happened on or near the altar, and took a long time. There was no sign the body had been moved, but no sign was found of her clothing. Torn fingertips suggested that she'd been held elsewhere and tried hard to escape. Bits of rust had been scraped from beneath her nails and skin. There was no roommate or boyfriend, as far as her coworkers knew. Phone records showed three calls from a burner cell, which was interesting, but at the moment, useless. The medical examiner had promised a full report minus tox screen by the end of the day. In the meantime, the girl's mother was pushing to claim the remains.

"One thing."

The words were quiet, the rest of the thought unspoken.

*I need one thing to tie this to Adrian Wall.*

He needed Adrian to be the killer and felt the need in a way few could understand. But, there was nothing. They'd canvassed neighbors, coworkers, people who liked the same bars as Ramona, the same coffee shops and restaurants and parks. No one could put Adrian and the victim together.

*Could I be wrong?*

The thought was unpleasant. If Adrian didn't kill Ramona Morgan, then maybe he didn't kill Julia Strange, either. That meant his conviction was flawed and that every cop who'd hated him for so long and with such passion was full-on, absolutely wrong.

*No.*

Beckett shook off the doubt.

*That was just not possible.*

Beckett poured coffee and carried it to his desk, his thoughts already spinning away from the murder case and back to Liz and the girl. The distraction was a problem, but Channing mattered to Liz, and Liz mattered to him. So, he started at the beginning. Why was the girl taken? Not why, really. Why her? Why at that time and place? Abduction was rarely as random as most wanted to believe. It happened, yes—a pretty girl in the wrong place at the wrong time—but more often than not, abduction scenarios involved people known to the victim: a workman at the house, a friend of the family's, a neighbor who always seemed so quiet and polite. He pictured Channing, her house, the case. He replayed his conversation with Channing's father.

"Hmm."

Beckett keyed up the sheets on Brendon Monroe and his brother, Titus. They were pretty standard. Weapons charges. Assault. Drugs. Some traffic offenses, two cases of resisting an officer. There were no sex convictions, though Titus had been charged twice with attempted rape. Beckett knew all that, so he keyed on the drug charges. Crack. Heroin. Meth. There was some pharmaceutical stuff, some weed. Beckett didn't see what he wanted, so he rang down to narcotics. "Liam, it's Charlie. Good morning . . . Look, I see your name all over the Monroe jackets . . . What? . . . No, no problem.

Just a question. Was there ever any noise about them selling steroids?"

Liam Howe was a quiet cop. Solid. Dependable. Young. He worked undercover because he looked too fresh-faced to carry a badge. Dealers thought he was a college kid, a rich man's son. "If there was money to be made, they'd sell it; but I don't remember anything about steroids."

"Is there much of that in town these days? Weight lifters? Jocks?"

"I don't think so, but steroids have never been high priority. Why do you ask?"

Beckett pictured Channing's father, sweat-soaked and massive. "Just a thought. Don't worry about it."

"You want me to ask around?"

Beckett's first instinct was to say no, but Channing's father had lied to him twice. "Alsace Shore looks like a juicer. Fifty-five, maybe. Built like a truck. I just wonder if he might have known the Monroe brothers."

"Alsace Shore." The drug cop whistled, low and deep. "I'd use a long stick to poke that bear, especially if you're implying some kind of involvement with the Monroe brothers."

"All I want is information, maybe enough to squeeze him."

"About?"

*His daughter,* Beckett thought.

*The basement.*

"Just ask around, will you?"

"Sure thing."

"And, Liam?"

"Yeah."

"Maybe, keep it quiet."

Liz left Channing a note and the keys to the Mustang.

> *Make yourself at home.*
> *Car's yours if you need it.*

It felt strange sliding into the unmarked cruiser, as if some part of her was no longer a cop. The awkward sensation clung as the sun edged above the trees, and she drove past the old Victorians on her way to the outskirts of town. When she got to the prison, most of it was still shrouded in gloom, only the highest walls dappled pink, the high wires glinting. At the public entrance, a uniformed guard met her at the door. He was early forties, with washed-out eyes and a pale, wide body that had few hard corners. "Ms. Black?"

*Not Detective or Officer.*

*Ms. Black . . .*

"That's me."

"My name is William Preston. The warden asked me to bring you in. Do you have any weapons? Contraband?" Elizabeth's personal weapon was in the car, but a rumpled pack of cigarettes rode in a jacket pocket. She pulled it, showed it to the guard. "That's fine," he said, then walked her to a visitor processing area. "I need you to sign in." She signed, and he slid the paperwork to an officer behind the bulletproof divider. "This way." She went through a magnetometer, and Preston stood close as a two-hundred-pound woman administered a thorough pat down.

"You realize I'm a police officer."

Thick hands went up one leg, then the other.

"Procedure," Preston said. "No exceptions."

Elizabeth endured it: the feel of hands through fabric, the smell of latex and coffee and hair gel. When it was done, she followed Preston up a flight of stairs, then down a hallway to the east corner of the building. He walked with his shoulders down, and the round head tipped forward. His shoes made rubbery noises on the floor. "You can wait here." He indicated a small room with a sofa and chair. Beyond the room was a secretary of some sort, and beyond her a set of double doors.

"Does the warden know I'm here?" Elizabeth asked.

"The warden knows everything that happens in this prison."

The officer left, and Elizabeth sat. The warden didn't keep

her long. "Detective Black." He swept past the secretary, a dark-haired man pushing sixty. Elizabeth's first thought was *Charming.* The second was *Too charming.* He took her hand with both of his, smiled with teeth too white to be anything but bleached. "I'm so sorry to keep you waiting. Detective Beckett has spoken of you for so long and with such passion, I feel as if I've known you a lifetime."

Elizabeth retrieved her hand, wondering at the line between charming and slick. "How do you know Beckett?"

"Corrections and law enforcement are not so dissimilar."

"That's not really an answer."

"Of course, it's not. I apologize." He blinded her again. "Charlie and I met once at a recidivism seminar in Raleigh. We were friends for a time—professional men with similar jobs—then life, as it so often does, took us in different directions, he more deeply into his career and I more deeply into mine. Still, I know a few in law enforcement, your Captain Dyer, for instance."

"You know Francis?"

"Captain Dyer, a few others. A handful of people in your department have maintained an interest in Adrian Wall."

"That doesn't seem entirely appropriate."

"Morbid curiosity, Detective. Hardly a crime."

He gestured to the office beyond the double doors and did not wait for a response. Inside, they sat, he behind the desk, Elizabeth in front of it. The room was institutional, and trying to hide the fact: warm art and soft light, heavy rugs under custom furniture. "So," he said, "Adrian Wall."

"Yes."

"I understand you knew him before."

"Before prison," she said.

"Have you known many on the other side? By that, of course, I mean men who've served lengthy sentences. Not misdemeanor recidivists, but hardened felons. Men like Adrian Wall."

"I'm not sure what Beckett told you—"

"I ask because this is the great difference in our chosen professions. You see the actions that lead men to places like this. The things they do, the people they hurt. We see the change that prison inflicts: hard men made crueler, soft ones unmade entirely. Loved ones rarely get the same person back when the sentence is done."

"Adrian is not a loved one."

"Detective Beckett led me to believe you have certain feelings—"

"Look, this is simple. Charlie asked me to come, so I'm here. I assume there's a purpose."

"Very well." A drawer opened, and a file came out. The warden placed it on the desk; spread his tapered fingers. "Much of this is confidential, which means I will deny ever showing it to you."

"Beckett's seen it?"

"He has."

"And Dyer?"

"Your captain as well."

Elizabeth frowned because it still felt unseemly: the easy smile and the office that tried to be what it was not, the heavy file that should not be so well thumbed. Of course people would have kept track. How could she have presumed otherwise? The deeper question was why she had not done the same.

"Pedophiles and police." The warden opened the file. "Convicts hate both with an equal passion." He handed over a sheaf of photographs. There were thirty maybe; all of them full color. "Take your time."

If Elizabeth thought she was ready, she wasn't.

"The miracle," the warden said, "is that he survived at all."

Taken in the prison hospital, the photographs were a testament to both the fragility and resilience of the human body. Elizabeth saw knife wounds, ripped skin, eyes swollen bloody.

"In the first three years, Mr. Wall endured seven hospitalizations. Four stabbings, some pretty horrific beatings. That one"—the warden waved a finger when she stopped on a photograph—"your Mr. Wall went headfirst down thirty concrete stairs."

The skin was peeled off one side of Adrian's face, his head shaved where staples held his scalp together. Six fingers were clearly broken, as was an arm, a leg. The sight made Elizabeth nauseous.

"When you say he went headfirst down the stairs, you mean he was thrown."

"A witness in prison . . ." The warden turned his palms up. "Few men have the courage to talk."

"Adrian was a cop."

"Yet a prisoner like everyone else, and not immune to the perils of institutional life."

She tossed the photos on the desk, watched them slide, one across the other. "He could have been killed."

"Could have been, but was not. These men, however, were." A stack of files hit the desk. "Three different inmates. Three different incidents. All were suspected in one or more of the attacks on your friend. All died quietly and unseen, killed by a single stab wound, perfectly placed." The warden touched the soft place at the back of his neck.

"How does one die, unseen, in prison?"

"Even in a place like this, there are dark corners."

"Are you suggesting that Adrian killed these men?"

"Each death followed an attack on your friend. Two months later. Four months."

"Hardly proof."

"And yet, it speaks to a certain patience."

Elizabeth studied the warden's face. He had a reputation for being smart and effective. Beyond that, she knew nothing about him. As large as the prison stood in the life of the county, the warden kept to himself. He was rarely seen at restaurants or other gatherings. The prison was his life, and while she respected the professionalism, something about the man made her uncomfortable. The false smile? Something in his eyes? Maybe it was the way he spoke of dark corners.

"Why did Beckett want me to come here? It can't be for this."

"Only in part." The warden used a remote control to turn on a wall-mounted television. The scene that flickered and firmed was of Adrian in a padded cell. He was pacing, muttering. The angle was down, as if the camera was mounted high in the corner. "Suicide watch. One of many."

Elizabeth walked to the set for a better look. Adrian's cheeks were sunken. Stubble covered his chin. He was agitated, one hand flicking out, then the other. It looked as if he was arguing. "Who's he talking to?"

"God." The warden joined her and shrugged. "The devil. Who can say? His condition worsened after the first year in isolation. He was often as you see him here."

"You took him out of the general population?"

"Some months after the final assault." The warden froze the image, looked vaguely apologetic. "It was time. Beyond time, perhaps."

Elizabeth considered Adrian's image on the screen. His face was tilted toward the camera, the eyes wide and fixed, the centers pixelated black. He looked angular, unbalanced. "Why is he out?"

"I beg your pardon."

"He was released on early parole. That could not have happened without your approval. You say he killed three people. If that's true, why did you let him out?"

"There is no proof he was involved."

Elizabeth shook her head. "It's not a matter of proof, though, is it? Parole is about good behavior. A subjective standard."

"Perhaps I am more sympathetic than you imagine."

"Sympathetic?" Elizabeth could hide neither the doubt nor the dislike.

The warden smiled thinly and selected a photograph from the desk. It showed Adrian's face: the ripped skin and staples, the stitches in his lips. "You have your own problems, do you not? Perhaps, that's why Detective Beckett suggested you come, to better understand the proper use of your time." He handed her the photograph, and she studied it, unflinching. "Prison is a horrible place, Detective. You would do well to avoid it."

When Officer Preston took the woman away, the warden moved to the window and waited for her to appear outside. After four minutes she did, stopping once to peer up at his window. She was pretty in the morning light, not that he cared. When she was in her car, he called Beckett. "Your lady friend is a liar." The car pulled away as the warden watched. "I studied her face when she looked at the photographs. She has feelings for Adrian Wall, perhaps very strong ones."

"Did you convince her to stay away?"

"Keeping Adrian Wall alone and isolated is in both our interests."

"I don't know anything about your interests," Beckett said. "You wanted to talk to her. I made that happen."

"And the rest of it?"

"I'll do what I said."

"He really is broken, our Mr. Wall." The warden touched the television, the pixelated eyes. "Either that or he's the hardest man I've ever seen. After thirteen years I'm still unsure."

"What does that even mean?"

"I should explain myself, why? Because we were friends, once? Because I am so generous with my time?"

The warden stopped talking, and Beckett said nothing.

They weren't friends at all.

They weren't even close.


If Elizabeth was looking for further insight into Adrian, she didn't find it in the first moments of court. He entered in full restraints, the nineteenth inmate in a row of twenty. He kept his eyes down, so she saw the top of his head, the line of his nose. Elizabeth watched him shuffle to his place on the long bench and tried to reconcile the man she saw with the video from the warden's office. As disturbing as he'd appeared, he looked ten times better, now— not filled out but heavier, troubled but not insane. She willed him to look her way, and when the brown eyes came up, she felt the same shock of communication. She sensed so many things about him, not just willfulness and fear but a profound aloneness. All that flashed in an instant, then the din of court intervened, and his head dipped again as if weighted by all the stares heaped upon it. Cops. Reporters. Other defendants. They all got it. Everybody knew. Crowded as the room was—and it was packed—nothing brought the thunder like Adrian Wall.

"Holy shit. Look at this place." Beckett slid in beside her, craning his neck at the double row of cameras and reporters. "I can't believe the judge allowed this kind of circus. There's what's-her-face. Channel Three. Shit, she's looking at you."

Elizabeth glanced that way, face expressionless. The reporter was pretty and blond in bright nails and a tight red sweater. She made a call-me gesture and frowned when Elizabeth ignored it.

"Did you see the warden?" Beckett asked.

"You know what? Outside." Elizabeth pushed against his shoulder and followed him off the bench. Eyes tracked them, but she didn't care what Dyer or Randolph or any of the other cops thought. "You know, your buddy the warden is a real asshole."

They rounded into the hall, a sea of people milling around them, parting at the sight of Beckett's badge. Elizabeth crowded him into a corner beside a trash can and a tattooed kid sleeping on a bench.

"He's not exactly my buddy," Beckett said.

"Then, what?"

"He helped me once when I was in a bad place. That's all. I thought he could help you, too."

"Why was he at Nathan's?"

"I don't know. He just showed up."

"What were you arguing about?"

"The fact I didn't want him on my fucking crime scene. What's going on here, Liz? You have no reason to be angry with me."

He was right, and she knew it. Moving to a narrow window, Elizabeth wrapped her arms around her chest. Outside, the day was too perfect for what was coming. "He showed me the tape."

"And the people Adrian killed?"

"The people he *might* have killed."

"You don't think he's capable?"

Elizabeth stared through the glass. Adrian had been gentler

than most, but like all good cops he had steel in his spine and an unflinching will. Could suffering such as his twist those things into something deformed and violent? Of course it could. But, had it? "People are rushing to judgment, Charlie. I feel it."

"That's not true."

"Come on. When was the last time you saw so many cops at first appearance? I counted twenty-three, including the captain. What is it normally? Six or seven? Look at that." She gestured at the crowd gathered at the courtroom door. It was twice as large as one might normally see: spectators and press, the angry, the curious.

"People are scared," Beckett said. "Another woman. The same church."

"This is a witch hunt."

"Liz, wait."

But she didn't. She pushed through the crowd and found another seat in the area reserved for cops. People were still staring, but she didn't care. Could Charlie be right? What was the path when your heart said one thing, and facts hinted at another? Adrian was tried in a courtroom very much like this, convicted by a jury of his peers. But they didn't know everything, did they? There was a reason his DNA was under the dead woman's nails.

*Reasons and secrets, infidelity and death.*

Adrian said no one knew he was sleeping with the victim, but was it really such a blur? What about Gideon's father? If Adrian was sleeping with his wife, Robert Strange may have known. Sex. Betrayal. Wives had been murdered for less. If he framed her lover for the murder, it would be a neat little package: cheating wife dead, boyfriend locked away. But Robert Strange had an alibi. Beckett himself had verified it.

*What about Adrian's wife?*

That was an interesting question. Did Catherine Wall know her husband was cheating? She was pregnant, possibly jealous. She wasn't investigated because no one other than Adrian and his attorney knew about the affair.

What if that was not entirely true?

Against his own attorney's advice, Adrian had refused to take the stand. Had he done so, he could have explained all the things that led to his conviction. He said he kept quiet because he didn't wish to hurt his wife, and because no one would believe him, anyway. What if it was more than that? What if he didn't want to implicate her? Take the stand against her?

*Did Adrian go to prison to protect his wife?*

If Catherine Wall knew of the affair, she had motive to kill Julia Strange. Did she have an alibi? Most likely, no one would ever know. The woman was gone, the case closed. So Elizabeth considered the crime itself. Manual strangulation took some strength. So did lifting bodies, posing them on altars. Could a woman do it?

Maybe.

If she was strong enough. Angry enough.

Maybe she had help.

Elizabeth watched Adrian, but he did not look up again. So, she scrubbed at her face and settled into the drudgery of court as first appearances took over. Prisoners met the judge, had their charges read, waited for lawyers to be appointed. She'd seen it a hundred times on a hundred different days. The first ripple came long before Adrian was even called. It started in front of the bar, and Elizabeth saw it like a breeze over grass. Heads came together; people muttered. She didn't understand until the prosecutor leaned into his assistant and whispered, "What the hell is Crybaby Jones doing here?"

Elizabeth followed the stares and saw Faircloth Jones at a side door beyond the bar. He was frail but elegant, dressed in the same kind of bow tie and seersucker suit he'd worn for most of his fifty years in practice. He stood above a dark-wood cane and held perfectly still until even the judge turned his way. After that, the old lawyer had the stage, crossing the room as if he owned it, nodding at older lawyers, who grinned or nodded back or brooded over old cases and long-wounded pride. The younger lawyers nudged each other and leaned close, each one asking more or less the same question: *Is that really Crybaby Jones?* Elizabeth understood that, too. Faircloth Jones was the finest lawyer to come through the county; yet, he'd not been seen outside his own house in close to ten years. Even the judge accepted the impact of the old lawyer's presence, leaning back in his chair and saying, "Okay. May as well deal with this, now. Mr. Jones." He projected his voice at the row of seated lawyers. "Very nice to see you again."

Faircloth stopped beside the first bench and seemed to bow without doing so. "The pleasure is entirely mine, Your Honor."

"I'd rather not assume, but may I ask . . . ?"

"Adrian Wall, Your Honor. Yes. I'd like to be noted as counsel of record."

The DA rose, large and unhappy. "Your Honor, Attorney Jones hasn't been seen in court for over ten years. I don't even know if his license is current."

"Let's ask him, then. Mr. Jones?"

"My license is quite current, Your Honor."

"There you are, Mr. DA. Quite current." The judge glanced at the rowed prisoners, lifted a finger, and said, "Bailiff."

Two bailiffs culled Adrian from the prisoner's bench. He kept his head up this time and nodded at the old lawyer. Faircloth touched him once on the shoulder, then said, "I'd like to have these cuffs removed, if I may."

The judge motioned again, and the DA could not hide his frustration. "Your Honor!"

The judge held up a hand and leaned forward. "It's my understanding that the defendant is not before this court on a violent offense."

"Second-degree trespass, Your Honor."

"That's it? A misdemeanor?"

"Also, resisting arrest," the DA said.

"Another misdemeanor, Your Honor."

"Yet, there are other circumstances—"

"The only relevant circumstance," Faircloth interrupted the DA, "is that the authorities want my client locked away while they investigate another crime for which they have insufficient evidence to charge. It's no mystery, Your Honor. You know it. The reporters know it." Faircloth gestured at the press bench, which was packed shoulder to shoulder. Some famous faces were there, including some from the big stations in Charlotte, Atlanta, Raleigh. Many had covered the original trial. None of them could take their eyes off the old lawyer, and Faircloth knew it. "While no one would argue with the tragedy of another young woman's early demise, the district attorney is trying to end-run the constitutional restraints of due process. Have things changed so much in my absence, Your Honor? Are we now some kind of banana republic that the state, in all its might and glory, could even contemplate such a thing?"

The judge drummed his fingers and glanced twice at the reporters. He was an ex-prosecutor and generally leaned in that direction. The reporters changed the math, and the old attorney knew it. So did the judge. "Mr. DA?"

"Adrian Wall is a convicted killer, Your Honor. He has no family in the community. He owns no property. Any expectations for an appearance at some later court date would be based on hope alone. The state requests remand."

"For two misdemeanors?" Crybaby half turned to face the reporters. "Your Honor, I implore you."

The judge pursed his lips and frowned at the DA. "Do you intend to file felony charges?"

"Not at this time, Your Honor."

"Mr. Jones?"

"My client was arrested on land that had been in his family since before the Civil War. After thirteen years of incarceration, the impulse to return there is understandable. I'd further argue that any resistance he might have offered at the time of his arrest was in response to police overzealousness. Police reports indicate that twelve officers were involved—and I'd stress that number again—twelve officers on a trespass complaint. I think that speaks clearly to the state's intent. On the other hand, Mr. Wall's family has been in this county since the winter of 1807. He has no plans to leave and is eager to appear before this court so we might offer a vigorous defense to frivolous charges. Given all that, Your Honor, we consider remand an absurd request and ask only that bond be reasonable."

The lawyer finished softly, the room so silent every word carried. Elizabeth could feel tension in the space around her. It went beyond the DA's frustration or Faircloth's dignified air. A woman was dead, and Adrian was the most notorious convicted killer of the past fifty years. Reporters craned where they sat. Even the DA was holding his breath.

"Bond is five hundred dollars."

The gavel came down.

The room erupted.

"Next case."

Outside, Elizabeth found Faircloth Jones on the edge of a crowd. He leaned on his cane as if waiting for her. "It's good to see you, Faircloth." She took his hand, gave it a squeeze. "Unexpected but really, really good."

"Take my arm," he said. "Walk with me."

Elizabeth looped her arm in his and guided him through the crowd. They took the wide, granite stairs, found the sidewalk. A half dozen people spoke a word or touched the lawyer's arm. He smiled at each, dipping his head, murmuring a kind word back. When they were beyond the crowd, Elizabeth pressed his arm against her side. "You made a very nice entrance."

"The law, as you may have surmised, is equal parts theater and reason. The finest scholars might struggle in court, while mediocre thinkers excel. Logic and flair, and leverage where appropriate, such are the makings of a trial attorney. Did you see His Honor's face when I mentioned the reporters? Good Lord. It appeared as if something unpleasant had taken up sudden residence beneath his robe."

He chuckled, and Elizabeth joined him. "It was good of you to

come, Faircloth. I doubt Adrian would have fared as well with a
court-appointed attorney that didn't know or care for him."

Faircloth waved off the compliment. "The smallest thing. One
courtroom appearance among a multitude of thousands."

"You're not fooling me, Mr. Jones." She pressed his arm more
tightly. "I was only one row behind you."

"Ah." He dipped his still-lean jaw. "And you noticed the sweat
stain on my collar. The slight but unfortunate tremor in my hands."

"I saw no such things."

"Indeed?" Humor was in the word, a twinkle so lively she
couldn't help but smile again. "Then, perhaps, my dear, you should
have those lovely eyes checked."

They passed the last edge of the crowd and moved thirty yards
in a slow shuffle, tarmac on the left, sun-cooked grass to the right.
Neither spoke, but he pressed her hand with his arm. When they
reached a bench in a spot of shade, they sat and watched a line of
uniformed officers stand at the balustrade and stare in their direction. They disliked that Adrian was bonding out, that Liz was
sitting with the lawyer who made it happen. "That's a grim spec-
tacle," Faircloth said.

"Not everyone sees Adrian as we do."

"How could they when they barely know the man? Such is the
nature of headlines and innuendo."

"And murder convictions." The old lawyer looked away, but not
before Elizabeth saw the pain she'd caused. "I'm sorry," she said.
"I didn't mean that the way it sounded."

"It's quite all right. It's not as if I've forgotten."

Elizabeth looked back at the officers. They were still watching
her, most likely hating her. "I never visited," she said. "I tried a
few times, but never got past the parking lot. It was hard. I couldn't
do it."

"Because you loved him."

It was not a question. Elizabeth felt her jaw drop, the sudden
flush. "Why would you say that?"

"I may be old, my dear, but I have never been blind. Beautiful young ladies don't sit so devotedly in court without good reason. It was hard to miss the way you looked at him."

"I never . . . I wasn't . . ."

The old lawyer nudged her with a shoulder. "I imply no impropriety. And completely understand why a woman might feel that way. I'm sorry if I made you uncomfortable."

She shrugged once, then shifted on the bench and wrapped her arms around a single knee. "How about you?"

"Visit? No. Never."

"Why not?"

He sighed and stared at the courthouse as another man might stare at an old lover. "I tried at first, but he wouldn't see me. Everyone hurt. There was nothing to say. Maybe he blamed me for the verdict. I never found out. After that first month, it became a matter of simple avoidance. I told myself I'd try again, then a week went by, and then another. I found reasons to avoid that side of town, the prison, even the road that would take me there. I made up lies and stories, told myself he understood, that I was old and done with the law, and that the relationship had been purely professional. Every day I whittled at the truth of my feelings, buried them deep because it hurt like hell, all of it." He shook his head, but kept his eyes on the courthouse. "Adrian was there because of my inadequacy. That's a hard truth for a man like me to accept. So, maybe I drank too much and slept too little. Maybe I turned from my wife and friends and all that ever mattered to me as a man and a lawyer. I lost myself in the guilt because Adrian was, perhaps, the finest man I'd ever represented, and I knew he'd never come out the same. After that, the hatred came like a thief."

"He doesn't hate you, Faircloth."

"I was referring to myself. To the power of self-loathing."

"Do you still feel that way?"

"Now? No."

Elizabeth looked away from the lie. The old man had hurt for a long time. He still did. "How long until he's out?"

"I'll post the bond," Faircloth said. "They'll drag their feet on principle. A few hours, I imagine. He can come home with me, if he likes. I have room and spare clothes and life, still, in these old bones. He can stay as long as he likes." The old man struggled to his feet, and Elizabeth guided him back to the sidewalk. "If you'll help me to my car. It's there." He pointed with the cane, and she saw a black car with a driver by the rear door. They moved down the walk, but Faircloth stopped a few feet from the bumper, one hand white on the cane, the other still on her arm. "He did not seem well, did he?"

"No." Elizabeth frowned. "He did not."

"The perils of confinement, I suppose." The driver opened the door, but the lawyer waved him off, a sudden twinkle in his eye. "Why don't you come by the house tonight? Perhaps between the two of us we can make him feel less forgotten. Shall we say drinks at eight, dinner after?"

She looked away, and he said, "Please, do come. The house is large, and the two of us, alone, insufferably male. It would be so much livelier with your company."

"Then, I'll be there."

"Beautiful. Excellent." He tilted his head skyward and breathed deeply. "You know, I'd almost forgotten how it feels. Fresh air. Open sky. I should appreciate it more, I suppose, today being the first time in eighty-nine years I've risked my own involuntary confinement."

"What do you mean?"

"It's illegal to practice law without a license, my dear." He flashed a wink and an old man's wicked grin. "Mine has been expired for ages."

# 13

He watched the courthouse from a distance and recognized so many faces: the police, the lawyer, even some of the reporters. It was like that when you'd lived in a town as long as he had, when you knew people. He kept his eyes on the woman, though, on the way she moved and kept her eyes down and touched the old man's elbow.

*Elizabeth.*

*Liz.*

So many years, he thought. So many times he'd laid up in the dark knowing it would end with her.

*Did he have the strength to do it?*

He rolled the idea around his mind, taking it apart, putting it back together. Everyone else had been a stranger. He knew the names, yes, where they lived and why he chose them: a multitude of women who, in the end, were as blank to him as water in a ditch.

*Things now were getting complicated.*

*Same town.*

*Familiar faces.*

He settled lower in the seat, watching the line of her jaw, the angle of her shoulders. When she put the lawyer in the limousine, she *looked his way but didn't see him up the street, safe in the car. He watched her walk away and pictured the girl who would be next. The thought made him sick, but it always did.*

*When the nausea passed, he started the car, drove six blocks, and stopped at the curb. Beyond the glass, children ran and played under the gaze of the day-care staff. Most of the women were used up. They slumped on benches and smoked cigarettes under trees. The woman he'd chosen was not like that. She stood beside the slide, smiling as she held a little boy's hand. He was six, maybe, small and happy even though his parents were at work, and none of the other children looked at him twice. He went down the slide, and the woman caught him when he hit the dirt, laughing as she spun him so hard his heels flicked up and showed the bottoms of his shoes.*

*If he had to say why he'd chosen her, he probably couldn't. The look was wrong, except for the eyes, of course, and maybe the line of her jaw. But she lived in the same town as Adrian, and Adrian was part of this.*

*Still . . .*

*He watched for another minute. The way she moved, the eyelashes, black on her skin. She had a good laugh and was pretty and tilted her head a certain way. He wondered if she was smart, too, if she would see through his lies or understand the church as it rose in the distance.*

*In the end, it didn't matter, so he pictured how it would be: the white linen and warm skin, the bow of her neck and the communion as she died. He felt sick again, thinking about it; but already his eyes were brimming.*

*This time, it would work.*

*This time, he would find her.*

*He waited until it was dark, and she was home alone. For an hour, he watched the lights in her house. Then he circled the block and watched for an hour more. There was no movement in the night. No walkers or porch-sitters or idle curious. By nine o'clock he was certain.*

*She was alone in the house.*

*He was alone on the street.*

*Starting the car, its lights off, he pulled forward, then backed into her driveway. The neighboring house was close on that side, but his car settled above an oily spot only ten steps from the porch. There were bushes, trees, pools of blackness.*

*On the porch, he saw her through the glass. On the sofa. Legs curled. He tapped on the glass and watched her eyebrows crease as she came hesitantly to the door. He lifted a hand so she saw it through the pane: a friendly wave from a friendly face. The door opened a few inches.*

*"May I help you?" A trace of doubt flickered, but she would overcome it. She was young and polite and Southern. Girls like her always overcame it.*

*"I'm sorry to bother you. I know it's late, but it's about the day-care center."*

*The door opened another six inches, and he saw that she was barefoot in jeans, and that she'd removed her bra. The T-shirt was worn thin, so he looked away, but not before she frowned and the door's gap narrowed.*

*"The center?"*

*"There's a problem. I know it's sudden. I can drive, if you like."*

*"I'm sorry. Do I know you?"*

*Of course, she didn't. He had nothing to do with the center. "Mrs. McClusky is not answering her phone or her door. I guess she's out." He smiled one of his good smiles. "I just naturally thought of you."*

*"Who are you again?"*

*"A friend of Mrs. McClusky."*

*She looked at her feet—a palm on each thigh—and it seemed as if it might be that easy. "I need shoes."*

*"You don't need shoes."*

*"What?"*

*That was stupid. Stupid! Maybe he was more nervous than he thought, or more frightened of failure. "I'm sorry." He laughed, thought it was good. "I don't know what I'm saying. Of course, you need shoes."*

She looked past his smile and saw the car in the drive. It was dirty and dented and streaked with rust. He used it because he could burn it if he had to or drop it in the river. But it caused these problems.

"We should hurry." He tried again because headlights rose two blocks down the street. Getting the girl in the car was taking too long.

The door closed another inch. "Maybe I should call Mrs. McClusky."

"By all means. Of course. I'm just trying to help."

"What did you say the problem was?"

She turned into the house, going for the phone. The headlights were a block away and would hit the porch in seconds. He couldn't be there when it happened. "I didn't exactly."

She said something about waiting on the porch, but he was already committed. He caught the door, two steps behind her. The phone was across the room, but she didn't go for the phone. She spun and hit the door and drove it into his face. He snatched at her shirt, caught fabric, and felt it tear. But she wasn't running. She lurched sideways, one hand behind the door as she pulled a bat from the crack, then spun and swung it at his head. He threw up an arm, caught the blow on his elbow, and felt a burst of yellow heat. She tried again, but he stepped back, let it pass, then snapped a palm under her chin, clacking her jaw closed and making her eyes roll white.

She swayed, and for a split second he was amazed by the quiet ferocity of her attack. No screaming or crying.

But it was over.

He caught her with one arm and felt the tiny waist, the flutter. Mosquitoes whined as he moved down the stairs to open the hatchback and make space. Back inside, he wiped every surface he'd touched: the edge of the door, the bat. When it was done, he checked the street and carried the girl to the car.

She fit perfectly.

Candy in a box.

# 14

At eight o'clock Elizabeth found Faircloth Jones on the porch of his grand old house. He was alone, with a drink in one hand and a cigar in the other. "Elizabeth, my dear." He rose to press a papery cheek against her own. "If you are looking for our friend, I fear time and circumstance have stolen him away." The porch was dark but for open windows and squares of light. Long-untended box bushes pressed against the rails. Down the bluff, the river moved with the sound of a whispering crowd. "May I offer you something? I know it's not the evening I promised, but I've opened a fine Bordeaux, and there's Belvedere, of course. I also have a lovely Spanish cheese."

"I don't understand. Where has Adrian gone?"

"Home, I fear, and on foot." Faircloth tilted his head down the hill. "It's only a few miles if you know the trails that follow the river. I dare say he knows them well."

Elizabeth sat in a rocking chair, and the old lawyer did the same. "You mentioned circumstance."

"Tight spaces and paranoia, my dear. I brought our friend home as intended, but he was unwilling to remain under my roof or between my walls. Nothing uncivilized, mind you. Lots of thanks and kindness; but, he wasn't going to have it. Apparently, he has every intention of sleeping beneath the stars, and the risk of another trespass charge is no deterrent. Love of place. I believe Adrian suffers unduly."

"He's also claustrophobic."

"Ah, that's very good." The lawyer's eyes narrowed as he smiled. "Not many people ever figured that out."

"I saw him in lockdown." Elizabeth pressed her hands between her knees. "It wasn't pretty."

"He spoke to me of reasons, once, and I had nightmares for a year, after."

"Tell me."

"Adrian had family in some farm town up in Pennsylvania. His mother's parents, I believe. It was a little place, regardless, all cornfields and trucks and dusty brawls. He was six, I think, or seven, wandering about on a neighbor's farm when he went down an abandoned well shaft and wedged tight at sixty feet. They didn't find him until lunch the next day. Even then, it took another thirty hours to get him out alive. There're newspaper accounts out there somewhere if you care to dig them up. Front-page stuff. The pictures alone would break your heart. The most blank-eyed, traumatized look I've ever seen on a child. I don't think he spoke for a month, after."

Elizabeth blinked and saw Adrian as he'd been in the lockdown cell, shirtless in the dark, scarred and sweat-slicked and talking to himself. "Jesus."

"Indeed."

"I think I'll have that drink."

"Belvedere?"

"Please." He shuffled into the house and returned with a glass that clinked as he handed it to her. "You mentioned paranoia."

"Oh, yes." The lawyer reclaimed his chair. "He thought we were followed from the jailhouse. A gray car. Two men. He was very agitated about it. Told me he'd seen the same car on three prior occasions.

I pushed him for motive or cause, and though he refused to discuss it, he did act as if, perhaps, he knew what it was about."

Elizabeth perked up. "Did he elaborate?"

"Not at all."

"Was he believable?"

"His concern was. He was stoic about it, of course, but more than eager to be on his way. He did allow me to find clothes that fit, but I couldn't coax him to linger for love or money. He stripped where we sit; asked me to burn the clothes he'd been wearing, even suggested I consider leaving for my own protection. Wanted me to stay in a hotel for a few days. The very idea."

"Why did he think you unsafe?"

"I know only that my obstinacy upset him. He kept staring off that way." Crybaby pointed left. "And calling me a stubborn fool of a man who was old enough to know who to trust and not. He said I should leave with him. Or, barring that, call the police. At the time, I thought his behavior the height of foolishness."

"At the time?"

The lawyer's eyes glinted in the night. "You came in from town, right? Crossed the river there?" He gestured right, where land fell away. "You crossed the bridge and turned directly into my drive?"

"I did."

"Hmm." He drew on the cigar, thin legs crossed at the knee. "If you look left"—he gestured to a gap in the trees—"you'll see the land rise up to where the road follows the ridge. It's distant, I'll give you; but there's a turnoff there from which you can see the house. Tourists find it from time to time. It makes a nice picture when the leaves peak."

"What, exactly, are we talking about?"

"We're not so much talking as waiting."

"For . . . ?"

"That. Do you hear it?"

She didn't at first, and then she did: a car on the road. The noise grew from a whisper, then the car hit the bridge, and the old lawyer gestured left with his cigar. "Watch the gap." She did what he asked, heard the car, sensed its lights as it climbed through the trees. "Do you see it?"

Lights rounded a bend, rose, and then leveled off. The car was on the ridge, the road shining beneath it. For three seconds, that's all she saw. Then, the car sped past the gap, and Elizabeth saw a second car parked on the verge.

"You saw it?" Crybaby asked.

"I did."

"And the men in it?"

"Maybe. I'm not sure."

"What color was the car?"

"Gray, I believe."

"Thank God." The old lawyer leaned back, finished his drink. "After three cocktails and two hours of staring up that hill, I was beginning to think our troubled friend's paranoia might be contagious."

Elizabeth kept the headlights off until she reached the bottom of the driveway. When the road appeared, she clicked on the lights, and turned left. At the top of the ridge she stepped on the gas and hit the blues when the parked car appeared. It was a Ford sedan and fairly new, judging by the paint. She pulled in behind it and saw the outlines of men in the front, shapes changing as they turned to look back. She kept the lights bright, blues thumping behind the grille as she keyed the license plate on her laptop. What she saw made little sense, but there it was.

The number.

The registration.

Keeping one hand on the grip of her pistol, Elizabeth opened the door and exited, flashlight held high as she kept the weapon low and gave the car's rear bumper a wide berth. Inside the car, both men held still, and she saw them plainly. They wore dark ball caps, the both of them. Elizabeth took in the heavy shoulders and blue jeans and dark shirts. Late thirties, probably. Maybe early forties. The driver kept his hands on the wheel; the passenger's were out of sight. That brought Elizabeth's weapon higher, kept it up as the window slid down. "Is there a problem, Officer?"

She stayed behind his left shoulder, watched the line of his jaw, his fingers on the wheel. "I want to see the passenger's hands. Now." Hands rose from the dark, then settled on the man's lap. Elizabeth checked the backseat, leaned closer. No alcohol smell. Nothing obviously illegal. "Identification."

The driver lifted his shoulders and dipped his head so the cap shielded his eyes against the light. "I don't think so."

The attitude bothered her. Something about his face did, too. It was partially obscured, but an arrogance was there, and an unpleasant softness. "License and registration. Now."

"You're a city officer five miles into the county. You have no jurisdiction here."

"City and county cooperate when called for. I can have a sheriff's deputy here in five minutes."

"I don't think so, seeing as how you're suspended and under investigation. The sheriff won't jump for you, lady. I doubt he'd even take your call."

Elizabeth studied the men more closely. The hair was clipped short, the skin pale. The flashlight washed out their features, but what she saw of the driver seemed familiar: the rounded jaw, and drained-out eyes, the sweat just dry enough to make him look sticky. "Do I know you?"

"Anything's possible."

A smile underlaid the words, the same condescension and easy conceit. Wheels turned in Elizabeth's mind, gears that wanted to mesh. "This vehicle is registered to the prison."

"We'll be leaving, now, Ms. Black."

"Are you following Adrian Wall?"

"You have a nice evening."

"Why are you watching this house?"

He turned the key. The engine caught, and Elizabeth stepped back as gravel sprayed and the car surged onto smooth pavement.

She watched it rise and fall and disappear beyond the next hill. Only then, alone on the road, did the last gear finally click.

*Ms. Black . . .*

She holstered the weapon; checked her math.

Yeah.

She knew the guy.

Adrian did not go to the farm. He followed the river, instead, and listened for a voice on the wind that refused to come. The water spoke. So did the leaves, the branches, the soles of his shoes. Everything that moved gave voice, but none of it offered him what he needed. Only Eli Lawrence knew the guards and the warden and the secret corridors of Adrian's hurt. Eli kept him together in the dark and the cold. He was the steel that held Adrian straight, the steady hands that gathered the threads of his sanity.

"They're following me," Adrian said. "They were at the farm, I think. Now, they're at Crybaby's."

No response came, no voice or touch or flicker of humor. Adrian was alone in the night. He picked his way along the trail, his feet finding the rocks and muddy places, the deadfalls and the moss and the slick, black roots. The bank dipped where a creek trickled in. Adrian held on to a sycamore, the branch of a pine. He splashed through the creek and climbed the bank on the other side.

"What if they're still there? What if they hurt him?"

*They won't bother the lawyer.*

Relief flushed through Adrian like a drug. He knew the voice wasn't real—that it was an echo from prison and the darkness and a thousand horrible nights—but for years it was all he'd had: Eli's voice and his patience, his eyes in the dark like dim, small suns.

"Thank you, Eli. Thank you for coming."

*Don't thank anybody but yourself, son. This little delusion is all yours.*

But Adrian didn't believe that, entirely. "First day in the yard. You remember?" Adrian clambered over a fallen tree, then another.

"They were going to kill me for being a cop. You stood them down. You saved my life."

*More years on the inside than I could easily count. There were still a few who listened to me.*

Adrian smiled at the understatement. There were men alive today who would kill or die for Eli Lawrence. Dangerous men. Forgotten ones. Until the day he died, the old man had been a voice of wisdom in the yard, an arbitrator, a peacemaker. Adrian's life was not the only one he'd saved.

"It's good to hear your voice, Eli. Eight years since I watched you die, and it's still good."

*You're basically just talking to yourself.*

"I know that. You don't think I know that?"

*Now, you're bitching at yourself.*

Adrian stopped where the river widened. People would find it strange, how he talked to a dead man. But the world had grown strange, too, and every sound reminded him of that: the slide of the river, the scrape of pines. He'd known this land as a boy, fished thirty miles in either direction, walked every trail and climbed a hundred trees that hung above the water. How could it be so foreign, now? How could it feel so wrong?

*'Cause you're a goddamn mess.*

"Hush now, old man. Let me think."

Moving down the bank, Adrian slipped his hand into the river. That was real, he told himself, and unchanged. But the sky felt too broad, the trees too tall. Adrian climbed back to the trail and tried to ignore the ugly truth, that only he was different, that the world spun as it always had. He walked and considered that and realized, once, that he'd been standing still long enough for the moon to rise. He held out a hand and watched light spill through his fingers. It was the first moonlight he'd seen in thirteen years, and thoughts of Liz came, unbidden. Not because she was beautiful—though she was—but because the same moon had risen on the night he'd found her at the quarry, and then again on the night she'd made her first arrest. He imagined her in the light. The moon. Her skin.

*Jesus, son. The first pretty woman you see . . .*

Adrian laughed, and it the first honest laugh he could remember. "Thank you, Eli. Thank you for that."

*You're still talking to yourself.*

"I know I am." He started walking. "Most of the time, I know."

The river bent west, and the trail with it. When it twisted again a mile later, Adrian turned away from the low ground and worked his way upslope until he found a dirt road that trended in the right direction. That was good for half a mile. When it, too, turned away from his path, Adrian crossed a band of woods, then a farm with a small, white house, brightly lit. A dog barked twice from the porch, but Adrian knew how to stay quick and quiet, and the night swallowed him before the dog got a good scent. Beyond the farm was a road that took him to an intersection three miles farther. Left would take him into the city. Right would lead to a subdivision on the flats beneath the mountain.

Adrian went right.

Francis Dyer lived right.

When he got to Dyer's house, he checked the name on the mailbox, then rang the doorbell. When no one answered, he peered through the window, saw lights inside and things he remembered: pictures of Dyer as a rookie and the day he made detective, leather furniture and Oriental rugs, rowed guns that looked the same as the last time they'd gone hunting together as partners and friends. That was hard to see because it reminded Adrian of laughter and hot sun, of quiet competition and bourbon drinks and dogs that lay panting and wet when the birds were rowed on the tailgate and the last gun put away in the back of the old truck. It drove home the sad fact that he and Francis had been friends, once; and it reminded him of the trial and disappointment, and of the unpleasant truth that had split them apart.

Everything Francis had said at Adrian's trial was true. Julia had a face that could drive a man to do bad things, and Adrian was, in fact, obsessed. He'd fallen so hard and fast that even now the memory dizzied him. But, it was more than the face. It was visceral, electric, *needful*. They'd both been unhappy, and their first meeting delivered a shock of energy so strong it could have lit the city. Recognition. Desire. The need that even now he felt. They'd fought it, and not just because they were married. Her husband worked for the county and was helping with an embezzlement case that ran into the six figures. Money had been disappearing for years: $5,000 here, $10,000 there. The total was $230,000 at best count. Real money. A serious case.

After a week, it barely mattered.

After a month, he was lost.

Adrian slumped on the porch, feeling her death as if it had happened days ago and not years.

"Ah, Julia . . ."

It had been so long since he'd allowed the luxury of remembrance. It was hard in prison because it made him soft when he could not afford it. Besides, she was dead, and death was forever. So, where did that leave him now? Out of prison and alone, sitting before an empty house and suddenly full to bursting.

Thirteen years!

They filled him up, all those years, all the suffering and pain, the hours to think of things he'd lost and pieces that didn't fit.

"Francis!"

He beat again on the door; knew it was pointless.

*So, wait for him.*

"That's your advice, old man? Wait for him?"

*'Less you plan to beat the door down or converse with an empty house.*

Adrian took a deep breath and forced himself to calm down. He was here for information, an exchange of words. That meant Eli was right. No violence.

"All right, then. We wait."

Adrian found a dark place on the porch and sat with his back against the wall. He watched the empty street and tried to let the anger go. But what else was there?

Answers?

Peace?

*You don't look so good.*

Adrian's lips twisted in the dark. "I don't feel so good, either."

*You can handle this, son. You're bigger than this.*

"I'm an ex-con talking to a dead man. I don't know anything anymore."

*You know my secret.*

"They're watching me."

*Not right now they're not. You can walk this very second. Go anywhere you want. Have anything you want.*

"Maybe I want to kill them."

*We've discussed that.*

"If I don't kill them, they'll find me."

*That's the inmate talking.*

"I don't want to be alone, Eli."

*He's coming.*

"Don't leave me."

*Hush, boy.* The voice flickered, faded. *Motherfucker's right there.*

Adrian opened his eyes as Francis Dyer stepped onto the porch. The suit was dark gray; the shoes glinted. He kept a shooter's stance, weapon level as he checked the corners, the yard.

Adrian showed his hands. "Just take it easy, Francis."

"Who were you talking to?"

"Myself. It happens."

Dyer checked the corners again. His weapon looked like the same revolver he'd always carried. "What are you doing here?"

"I have questions."

"Such as?"

"Where's my wife?"

Tension showed on Dyer's face; turned his fingers white on the gun. "That's why you're here?"

"Part of it."

Adrian started to push himself up, but Dyer didn't like it. "You sit until I say. Hands, again."

Adrian took his hands from the decking and showed his palms.

"This is my house, Adrian. My home. Convicts don't show up at a cop's home. That's how they get shot."

"So do it." Adrian put his hands on the floor; slid his back up the wall until he was standing. It was a small victory. He took it. "Where's my wife?"

"I don't know."

"The farm's burned. Liz says she disappeared."

"I'm surprised she didn't leave sooner."

The revolver didn't budge. Adrian studied the narrowed eyes, the tight lips. Catherine and Francis had been close. Hell, before the murder and the trial, they all had.

"You were her friend."

"I was her husband's partner; that's different."

"You want me to beg, Francis? We were partners for seven years, but fine. You want me to beg. I'm begging. Please tell me what happened to my wife. I won't ask anything of her or ruin her life. I just want to know where she is, that she's well."

Maybe it was the tone of voice, or memories of their partnership. Whatever it was, Dyer holstered the weapon. In the gloom, he was all angles and dark eyes. His voice, when he spoke, was surprisingly soft. "Catherine wouldn't talk to any of us after the trial. Not me or Beckett or anyone else from the department. We tried to keep up with her, but she wouldn't answer the phone or the door. It went that way for three or four months. The last time I went to see her, the place was locked up tight. No car. Mail stacked up on the porch. Two months after that, the house burned. It was too much for her. She left. I think it's that simple."

"But, she still owns the farm."

There was a question there, and Dyer understood. "The county took it two years later. Unpaid taxes."

Adrian leaned against the wall. The land had been in his family since before the Civil War. Losing it to the same people who'd locked him away for thirteen years was an unbearable injustice. "I didn't kill Julia."

"Don't."

"We're just talking."

"Not about her, we're not."

Every angle in Francis Dyer seemed to sharpen. The shoulders. The jaw.

"Tell me about the beer can."

"What?"

Adrian watched him, looking for the lie. "A twelve-ounce Foster's can with my prints on it was found in a ditch thirty yards from the church. It linked me to the murder scene, but here's the thing." Adrian stepped closer. Dyer didn't budge. "I never drank a beer near that church. I never left a can there, I wouldn't. The last time I drank a Foster's was here, in this house, two days before she died."

"You think I planted evidence?"

"Did you?"

"There were other people here that night. Beckett. Randolph. Even Liz was here. I could name fifty people. It was a party. Besides, no one needed to plant evidence to convict you. You handled that part just fine by yourself."

Dyer meant DNA and skin and scratches. That was logical and fine, but the can was first-day evidence. Without Adrian's prints at the scene there'd have been no court order subjecting him to a physical exam, no knowledge of the scratches on his neck, and nothing connecting him to the murder.

"Someone planted that can."

"No one framed you."

"It didn't get there by itself."

"You know what? We're done."

"I didn't kill her, Francis."

"Mention Julia again, and I'll shoot you for real. I mean it."

Adrian didn't blink or back down. He held his ex-partner's gaze and felt all the emotion behind it. "Do you really hate me so much?"

"You know why," Dyer said; and looking in his black and bitter eyes, Adrian did.

Because Francis Dyer had always been jealous.

Because he'd loved Julia, too.

That certainty grew as Adrian walked out of his old partner's neighborhood. The can was peripheral at trial, not a nonevent but almost an afterthought. By then, the prosecutor had scratches on Adrian's neck and skin under Julia's nails; he had prints in the house and Adrian's own partner to testify against him. Those things made a case so strong the beer can at the church was a blip. But, that was the trial, and the early days of the investigation had been very different. Liz had found Julia's body in the old church, and it was like marble on the altar, white and lifeless and clean. Adrian could still feel the rage and sadness that ripped through him when he got the call; he remembered every second—had lived them a million times: the drive to the church and the sight of her there, the love of his life gone lifeless, hardwood under his knees as he'd wept like a child, uncaring.

But, people saw: Francis and other cops. They saw and they wondered. Then a tech pulled Adrian's print, and everything changed. Not just the doubts and dirty looks, but the court-ordered blood sample and the physical exam that found the scratches on his neck. After years behind the badge Adrian was on the outside, a suspect. He lost standing, trust, and, in the end, everything he'd ever loved.

Julia first.

Then life as he'd known it.

That his partner might have been jealous enough to plant evidence didn't occur to Adrian until his first year in solitary. It was so out there and so extreme, a thought born of the smallest memory. Julia lay propped on an elbow, a sheet gathered at her waist. They were in a hotel in Charlotte, tenth floor. Light from the city spilled in, but all else was dark. It was a week before she died, and she was beautiful.

*Are we bad people, Adrian?*

He'd stroked her face. *Maybe.*

*Is it worth it?*

It was an old question between them. He'd kissed her, then, and said, *Yes, it has to be.*

But doubt was in the room, a dark conjuring.

*I think your partner knows.*

*Why?*

*A look,* she said. *A feel.*

*Like what?*

*Like he watches more than he should.*

That was it, a nothing in the night. But nothings grow when the world is eight by six and hours stretch forever. Adrian replayed the memory a hundred times, and then a thousand. Two days later, he added the can to see how the pieces fit. It seemed possible, he'd thought, which was not the same as probable. But the can was not probable, either.

Not with his prints on it.

Not at the church.

Francis had always been insecure, lost at times in Adrian's shadow. That's how it could be with cops. One was first through the door, and one was second. One got the media. One was the hero. But jealousy alone could not explain something as malignant as planted evidence. That required stronger emotions, the minting of a single coin, perhaps, with love bright on one side, and envy black on the other. Spin it fast enough, and what would you see?

A partner grown silent and strange?

A man who watched more than he should?

It still seemed possible, but there was no certainty on the roadside or under the high, dim stars. Nor did conviction present itself between the crumbled walls of his burned-out home. Adrian lit a fire as he'd done before and tried to pace the questions into ordered form. Who killed Julia, and why? Why the church? The linen? The violence that crushed her neck with such utter, irretrievable conviction?

*Could someone else have planted the can?*

In the end, such questions were voices lost in the throng. Adrian was not the same man, and he knew it. His thinking grew muddled, at times. Sometimes, he blanked out. That was a gift from the warden and the guards. Yet, clarity had not deserted him entirely. Open spaces and faces of good intent. These things made sense to him and offered hope of a sort. Liz was his friend—he believed that. So was the lawyer, this land, memories of what it meant to be determined and sure. Had that man gone? Adrian wondered. Had he been carved away in his entirety?

He paced another hour, then found a corner and sat. The night was dark and still, and then gone as if it too was only memory.

He was on a metal bed.

He was screaming.


*"Hold him down. Get the arm!"*

*They got the free arm strapped again, cinched it down as he screamed into the gag, and edged metal flashed red. Adrian tasted blood; knew he was biting his tongue, the inside of his cheeks. The room smelled of bleach and sweat and copper. Blood streaked the warden's face. The ceiling was rusted metal.*

*"Now, I'm going to ask you again." The warden leaned close, his eyes like black glass as metal flashed once more, and a line of fire opened on Adrian's chest. "Are you listening?" Another cut, blood pooling on the table. "Just nod when you're ready to talk. Look at me when I'm speaking. Look at me!"*

*Adrian fought the straps; felt something tear.*

*"It's too much," someone said. "He's bleeding out."*

*"Hand me a needle. Hold his finger." The needle slipped under the nail; Adrian screamed, and his back came off the table. "Give me another." That one went in harder, deeper. "Will you talk to me, now? Look at me. Not at the ceiling. What did Eli tell you?" A hand slapped Adrian's face. "Don't pass out. We'll have to start over. Prisoner Wall? Adrian? Hey. Eli Lawrence. What did he tell you?"*

*Two more blows, Adrian's head rocking. After that, the warden sighed and lowered his voice as if they were friends.*

*"You were close to him, I understand. You feel loyalty for a friend, and I admire that. I really do. But, here's the problem." He smoothed a hand across Adrian's soaking hair, left it on the forehead and leaned even closer. "That old man loved you like a son, and I doubt he would have died with such a secret unshared. Do you see my problem? I need to be sure, and this"—he patted Adrian's forehead; ignored the blood on his own palm—"this is the only way. Will you nod for me now, so I know you understand?"*

*Adrian did.*

*"You don't need to die." The warden removed the gag, and Adrian turned his head to vomit. "This can end. Just give me what I want, and the pain goes away forever."*

*Adrian moved his lips.*

*"What?" The warden leaned closer.*

*Eight inches away.*

*Six.*

*Adrian spit in the warden's face, and after that things got ugly. Deeper cuts. Longer needles. A vision of Eli appeared the moment Adrian thought he would finally break. The old man was a shadow beyond the lights, the only man since childhood that Adrian had ever loved.*

*"Eli."*

*The name was in his head, because all else was screams and blood and the warden's question. Adrian focused on the yellow eyes, the paper skin. The old man nodded as if he understood. "No sin in survival, son."*

*"Eli . . ."*

*"You do what you need to do."*

*"You're dead. I saw you die."*

*"Why don't you give the man what he wants?"*

*"They'll kill me once they know."*

*"Are you sure?"*

*"You know they will."*

*"Then look at my face, boy." The old man blinked and was a ghost beside the bed. "Listen to my voice."*

*"Everything hurts."*

*"See how light it is. See how it floats."*

*"It really hurts . . ."*

*"But that's fading now, son. Falling away."*

*"I've missed you so much."*

*"Steady, now."*

*"Eli . . ."*

*"Just listen to my voice."*

They wanted what Eli had told him, plain and simple. And they ran everything: the phones, the mail, the other guards. That meant they had the power, and they had the time. When a year of knives and needles failed, it got psychological. Darkness. Deprivation. Hunger. Eventually, the inmates themselves were turned against him, one after another until every waking hour became a nightmare. And the rules were simple. *Hurt him. Don't kill him.*

But *hurt* was a big word.

Ambush. Intimidation. Isolation. Friendly faces began to disappear: three men dead in the space of a year, killed by a single stab wound at the base of the skull. Their crimes? Adrian believed. A word in the yard. A place, once, at his table. The true nightmare began in the isolation wing. Once they understood the impact of tight spaces, they got creative; and prison, it turned out, was full of subbasements and old boilers and empty pipes. Adrian shuddered thinking of the pipes, of crevasses so airless and rust-choked that every breath tasted of metal. They liked to shove him in upside down, flood the pipe with water, haul him out. They used rats, at times; and once, they left him in for two days, and it was as if childhood terrors found him in the dark. Adrian went blank for a week after that. Lights turned on and off; food went uneaten. When he came back, it was a slow crawl from an empty place. They gave him a week more, then started the cycle again: in the black and on metal beds, hurt and healed, then in a boiler with rats.

A darker voice came, once. It spoke of endings and peace, told him to give up Eli's secret and let the silence come at last. When that voice failed, they started to think maybe he knew nothing, after all. They left him alone for months: regular isolation, a regular prisoner. At times, Adrian's thoughts were so splintered he wondered if he'd dreamed it all, if the scars came from fights with other inmates, as official records said. There were no more questions. No one looked at him twice.

But then he got out.

Adrian squatted by the fire; he added a few sticks, then moved, slow and silent, into the dark beyond the shell of his house. The fields were tall, so he stuck to the drive, hugged the ditch line, and kept his knees bent. When the road appeared, chalk white under the moon, he slipped into the field and drew close enough to see the car. It was not the same one that had followed him to the lawyer's house. That was gray, and this was black. But, it was real, which meant the memories were real, too.

It wasn't delusion.

He wasn't insane.

At the house, he added a few more twigs to the fire, then stirred the coals until they caught in a sputter of flame.

"Talk to me, Eli." He sat again, ancient trees above and the sky piled up forever. "Tell me what to do."

But Eli was done talking, and that made it a bad night in the ruins. At one point, Adrian levered himself up and crept back to the road. The car was gone, but tracks were there, in the dirt. Even sleepless and pulled apart, Adrian knew what they wanted, and what they would do to get it. That made him not just cautious, but dangerous. The only reason no one had died yet was because he wasn't yet willing, and they remained uncertain.

Did he know Eli's secret or not?

They doubted it because no one should be able to suffer as he had and still keep his mouth shut. Not after so many years. Not after the knives and the rats and seventeen broken bones. What they failed to understand were the reasons. He didn't keep the secret for greed's sake. The reasons were older than that, and simpler.

He did it for love.

And he did it for hate.

Kneeling on the verge, Adrian put his fingers on the tire tracks where they were clearest. He saw cigarette butts, a damp spot in the dirt that smelled of urine. They'd been gone for an hour, maybe more. Had they given up? He doubted it. Laziness, maybe. Maybe they needed cigarettes.

When he returned to the fire, he piled wood until flames leapt higher. Dense clouds had moved in to cover the moon, so even with a fire the darkness pressed in. Adrian watched the flames, but visions still gathered in the dark.

"Fuck those guys, and fuck Dyer, too."

He held on to the anger because it pushed the darkness back. The dirt was real, the burned-out house and the fire. Anger kept all that bright, so he thought of the warden, the guards, how the whole thing could still end bloody. It worked for a while, but he blinked once and the fire burned away as if the eye blink were an hour. He'd drifted as he used to do, blinked and gone away. He tried to shake himself alert, but was heavy; everything was heavy. When he blinked again he saw Liz, distant at first and then close, a face across the smoke, the eyes liquid and troubled and impossibly deep.

"What are you doing here, Liz?"

She moved like a ghost and sat, soundless, on the dirt. The edges of her face were blurry, her hair as weightless and dark as the smoke around her. "Did you know I was going to jump?"

He tried to focus, but couldn't; thought maybe he was dreaming. "You wouldn't have done it."

"So, you knew?"

"Only that you were frightened and young."

She watched him with those impossible eyes. "Was it terrible? What they did to you?"

Adrian said nothing; felt heat in his skin. The eyes weren't right. The way she watched and waited and seemed to float.

"I see the hollow place."

She pointed at his chest and drew the shape of a heart.

"I can't talk about that," he said.

"Maybe, there's some of you left. Maybe, they missed a piece."

"Why are you doing this to me?"

"Doing what? It's your dream."

Her head tilted, a mannequin face on a mannequin body. He stood and looked down.

"You're going to kill them, aren't you?"

"Yes," he said.

"Because of what they did to Eli?"

"Don't ask me to let them live."

"Why would I do that?"

She stood, too, then took his face and kissed him hard.

"Who are you?" he asked.

"What do the papers call me?"

"I don't care if you killed those men."

"Yet you dream of me," she said. "You dream of a killer and hope we are the same."

# 15

He liked morning light because it was so unused. Anything could happen with such soft, pink lips pressed upon the world, and he took a moment—just for himself—before dragging the girl from the silo. She fought harder than most, her skin filthy and her fingers torn bloody at the tips. She kicked and screamed, cuffs clanking on her wrists, both hands locked on a ridge of metal. He pulled until her hips rose off the ground, then sighed deeply and touched a strip of skin with the stun gun. When she went loose, he dropped her legs, then stepped away to blot sweat from his face. Normally, the silo made them easier to work with. Fear. Thirst. This one was a fighter, and he thought that might be a good sign.

When his breathing slowed, he rolled her onto a tarp, then removed her clothes and took his time cleaning her. This was a big part of it, and though she was beautiful in the light, he focused on her face instead of her breasts, on her legs rather than the place they joined. He cleaned dried blood from her fingertips and wiped her face with care. She moved once as the sponge slipped behind her knee, and then again when it touched the plane of her stomach. When her eyes fluttered, he used the stun gun a second time and after that moved more quickly, knowing how the light would harden and age her, how different she would appear if he waited too long. When her skin was scrubbed and dried, he used a silk cord to bind her ankles and wrists, then placed her in the car and drove to the church. Yellow tape sealed the door, but what did seals matter? Or police? Or worry itself?

At the altar, he laid her down and used the same cords to strap her flat, cinching the legs tight, pulling the arms down until the shoulder bones jutted. He moved faster now because she was stirring. He covered her with white linen, folding it just so, making it perfect. By then his vision was blurred, both eyes so full and brimming it was as if no time had passed, and all the years between then and now were glass. Her lips were parted; breath moved. And while some deep part of him recognized the illusion, the weeping part embraced it with profound and terrible joy. He touched her cheek as the eyes fluttered and the pupils dilated. "I see you," he said, then choked her for the first time of what he knew would be many.

It took a long time for her to die. She was crying; he was crying. When it was done, he went under the church, dragging himself to the worn spot beneath the altar, and curling in the earth as he'd so often done. This was his special place, the church beneath the church. Yet, even there he could not hide from the truth.

He'd failed.

Had he chosen poorly? Was he somehow mistaken?

He closed his eyes until the grief passed, then touched one shallow grave after another.

Nine women.

Nine mounds in the earth.

They bent around him in a gentle curve, and it troubled him to take so much comfort from their presence. He'd killed them, yes, but there was such lonesomeness in the world. He touched the earth and thought of the women beneath it. Julia should be here, too, as should

*Ramona Morgan and the girl dead above. It was their place as much as his, their right to lie quiet beneath the church where each heart, in its turn, had slowly and painfully ceased to beat.*

# 16

Beckett got two pieces of bad news in the first ten minutes of the new day. The first was expected. The second was not. "What are you saying, Liam?"

He was in the bull pen. Seven forty-one in the morning. Hamilton and Marsh were behind the glass in Dyer's office. Liam Howe had just walked up from Narcotics. The place was a madhouse. Cops everywhere. Noise. Movement.

"I'm saying it sucks."

Howe dropped into a chair across the desk, but Beckett was barely paying attention. He was watching the state cops, who'd left his desk sixty seconds ago. Now, they were giving Dyer the same earful they'd given him. No sound came through the glass, but Beckett knew enough to catch the big words like *subpoena* and *Channing Shore* and *obstruction*. Playtime was over. They were gunning for Liz and they were gunning hard. Why? Because she wasn't talking to them. Because in spite of their attempts at understanding and moderation, she was still telling them the same thing, which basically amounted to *fuck off*. "You know what?" Beckett swung his feet from under the desk. "Let's walk."

He tossed a final, sour look at the state cops, then guided Howe out of the room and into the back stairwell. Outside, they stood in the secure lot, white sky going blue at the edges, heat stirring in the pavement. "All right, Liam. Tell me again, and give me details."

"So, I did what you asked, right. I pulled some sheets; asked around. There's no indication the Monroe brothers ever sold steroids. Alsace Shore may use them, but if so, he's getting them somewhere else."

Beckett chewed on that for a second, then shrugged it off. "That was a long shot, anyway. What's the twist?"

"The twist is the wife."

Something in the way Howe said it. "She's a user?"

"Oh, yeah. Big-time. Prescription meds, mostly. OxyContin. Vicodin. Anything in the painkiller family. Cocaine on occasion."

"Does she have a sheet?"

The drug cop shook his head. "Everything is scrubbed at the source: connections, favors, whatever. The few times she's been implicated, the charges went away. I only know as much as I do because I took the question to some of the retired guys. Turns out a lot of wealthy housewives walk on the dirty side. The unspoken rule has been to look the other way. Too many frustrations over the years, too many powerful husbands, and too much weight."

Beckett could see it because small towns were like that: connections and secrets, old money and old corruption. What's the harm in a few stoned housewives? Forget the hypocrisy, that drugs were tearing half the city down. "Where did she get the dope?"

Howe shook his head, lit a cigarette. "The story doesn't have a happy ending."

"Tell me."

"We'll call it the story of Billy Bell."


Beckett was at the Shores' house by eight fifteen. Two kinds of bad news. Two different reasons. Alsace Shore knew about the first one. "I've already spoken to the state police, and I'll tell you exactly what I told them. I don't know where Channing is. Even if I did, I wouldn't tell you. Fuck your implications and fuck your subpoena."

The man looked huge in a tailored suit and glossy shoes. In the house beyond him, every light was burning. Beckett saw people in the study to the right: other suits, a woman, small and blond in pink Chanel.

"I'm not here about the subpoena."

"Then why?"

Channing's father leaked aggression like an old tire leaked air, but again, it was hard to blame him. State cops had a subpoena for his daughter and tried to serve it when the sun was still below the trees. It was a cheap trick. Beckett would be angry, too. "She's really not here, is she?"

"Like I told the state cops."

"Do you know where she is?"

"No."

"Do you know, at least, if she's safe?"

"Safe enough." It was grudgingly offered, possibly sincere. "Her mother got a text saying she was okay, but wouldn't be home for a while."

"Is that normal?"

"The text, no. But, she's left home before. Parties in Chapel Hill. Clubs in Charlotte. There've been some boys. Teenage stuff she thinks is dangerous."

Beckett sifted the words, came up satisfied. "May I come inside?"

"Why not? Every other cop in the county has." Shore showed his back, knowing Beckett would follow. In the study, he lifted an arm. "These are my attorneys." Three different men stood. "You remember my wife."

She sat on a sea of dark velvet as if she'd been weighted and sunk there. Pink suit rumpled. Makeup smeared. *Stoned,* Beckett thought. *Numb.* "Mrs. Shore." She did not look up or respond, and from the reactions of everyone else in the room her condition was obviously no surprise. "I'm glad you're here. This concerns you."

That was a bomb in the stillness.

"In what regard?" one of the lawyers asked.

He had white eyebrows and ruddy skin. One of the big firms in Charlotte, Beckett guessed. Five hundred an hour, minimum.

"Let's call it a story for now." Beckett kept his voice level, though he was angry deep down. "A story about dead brothers, bored housewives, and a town full of dirty little secrets."

"I won't allow you to question her."

"I'll do all the talking, and right now we're talking about stories." Beckett pushed past the lawyer, the husband; towered over the wife, instead. "Like all good stories, this one revolves around a central question, in this case the question of how two low-life brothers like Titus and Brendon Monroe ever came into contact with a girl like Channing. Drug dealers. Kidnappers. Rapists. I suspect you know this story." Beckett was unflinching. Mrs. Shore was not. "I'm guessing that it started with drinks over brunch. Five years ago? Maybe ten? Brunch became afternoon wine, then cock-tails at five, more wine with dinner. Four days a week became seven. There would be parties, of course. Weed from a friend, maybe. A doctor's prescription or two. All harmless fun until we get to the stolen pills and the cocaine and the low-life dealers who go with it."

That was his hardest voice, and she looked up, bewildered. "Alsace—"

"You have a gardener," Beckett interrupted her. "William Bell. Goes by the name Billy."

"Billy, yes."

"The last time Titus Monroe was arrested for dealing drugs, he was selling OxyContin to your gardener, Billy Bell. That was nine-teen months ago on a Tuesday. Not only did your husband post Billy's bond, he paid for the lawyer that helped him stay out of jail."

"That's enough, Detective." That was Mr. Shore. Close. Physical.

Beckett ignored him. "Channing wasn't plucked off a street, was she?"

"You said no questions." Shore's voice was loud, but had nothing to do with anger. He was begging, pleading, as his wife sank more deeply into the sofa.

"It's a common enough story." Beckett lowered himself before the broken woman. "Except for the ending." She didn't move, but a tear spilled down a sunken cheek. "Do you know the Monroe brothers, Mrs. Shore? Have they been to this house?"

"Don't answer that."

Beckett tuned out the lawyer. This was about truth, responsibility, the sins of the parent. "Will you look at me?"

Her head moved, but the lawyer pushed between them. "This is a temporary restraining order signed by Judge Ford." The attorney snapped a paper in Beckett's face. "It protects Mrs. Shore from police questioning in this matter until such time as her attending physician is brought before the court and the matter is heard."

"What?"

"My client is under a doctor's care."

Beckett took the paper, scanned it. "Psychiatric care."

"The type of care is irrelevant until a judge rules otherwise. Mrs. Shore is in a fragile state, and under the protection of the court."

"This is dated the twelfth."

"The timing is also irrelevant. You cannot pursue this line of questioning."

"You knew about this days ago." Beckett dropped the paper and squared up on Mr. Shore. "She's your daughter, and you fucking knew."

Outside, the day was too hot and blue for Beckett's mood. The abduction was not random, the bad guys not some passersby who saw Channing on the street.

And the father knew.

*Motherfucker* . . .

"I didn't know until after."

Beckett spun on a heel.

Alsace Shore had followed him out. He looked smaller and shaken, a powerful man begging. "You have to believe me. If I'd known while she was missing, I'd have told you. I'd have done anything."

"You withheld evidence from me, Mr. Shore. It wasn't some *accident* your daughter was taken. What happened to Channing is your wife's fault."

"You don't think I know that? You don't think *she* knows that?" Shore stabbed a finger at the house, and Beckett remembered the man's talk of grief and grieving and things forever changed. "I can't undo what happened to my daughter. But I can try to protect my wife. You have to understand that." Shore's hands rose, clasped. "You're married, right? What would you do to spare your wife?"

Beckett blinked; felt sun like a palm on his cheek.

"Tell me you understand, Detective. Tell me you wouldn't do the same."

Liz was on her second cup of coffee when the banging started. Beckett had left two messages, so she knew it was coming. Another day. Decisions. She opened the door after about the twentieth knock. She was in faded jeans and an old red sweatshirt, her face still pale from sleep, the hair loose and wild on her head. "It's a little early, Charlie. What's the problem? No coffee at the precinct?"

Beckett pushed inside, ignoring the sarcasm entirely. "Coffee sounds good, thanks."

"Okay, then." She closed the door. "Come on in."

Elizabeth poured a cup of coffee and added milk the way he liked it. Beckett sat at the table and watched her. "Hamilton and Marsh got their subpoena. The girl will have to answer their questions about the basement. She'll have to do it under oath."

Liz didn't blink. "Take this." She handed him a cup and saucer and sat across the table.

"They tried to serve it this morning, but Channing was gone. Her parents don't know where she is. She sent a text, though."

"That was considerate of her."

"They say that's not her normal behavior. Sneaking out, yes. Not the texting."

"Hmm." Elizabeth sipped from her own coffee. "How odd."

"Where is she, Liz?"

Elizabeth put the coffee down. "I've told you how I feel about you and this girl."

"She doesn't exist. I remember. Things are bigger, now. You can't protect her. You shouldn't."

"Are you saying it's wrong to try?"

"She's a victim. You're a cop. Cops don't have relationships with victims. It's a rule designed for your own protection."

Elizabeth looked at her fingers on the china cup. They were long and tapered. The fingers of a pianist, her mother once said. If Elizabeth closed her eyes, though, she'd see them bloody and red and shaking. "I'm not sure about rules, anymore." She said it softly and left out the rest. That she wasn't sure about being a cop, either, that maybe—like Crybaby—she'd lost something vital. Why was she doing it if not for the victims? What did it mean if she became one? They were hard questions, but she wasn't upset. The feelings were more of calm and quiet, a strange, still acceptance that Beckett—for all his abilities—didn't seem to notice.

"If I take Channing in, I can keep your name out of it. No obstruction charges. Nice and clean." He reached for her hand, and she watched his fingers on hers. "She can tell the truth, and this can end. The state investigation. The risk of prison. You can have your life back, Liz, but it has to be now. If they find her here . . ." He let that hang between them, but his eyes were deadly serious.

"I can't give you what you want," she said. "I'm sorry."

"And if I force you?"

"I'd say that's a dangerous road to walk."

"I'm sorry, Liz. I have to walk it."

Beckett rose before the last word died. He moved down the short hallway, surprised when she didn't try to stop him. He opened one door and then another, and at the second stared for a long time at tousled hair and pale skin and tangled sheets. When he returned, he sat in the same chair, his features still. "She's asleep in your bed."

"I know."

"Not even the guest room. Your bed. Your room."

Elizabeth sipped coffee, placed the cup on its saucer. "I won't explain because you wouldn't understand."

"You're harboring a material witness and obstructing a state police investigation."

"I don't owe the state cops anything."

"What about the truth?"

"Truth."

She laughed darkly, and Beckett leaned across the table. "What will the girl say if they find her? That she was wired on the mattress when it happened? That you shot them in the dark?"

Elizabeth looked away, but Beckett wasn't fooled.

"It won't work this time, Liz, not with autopsy results, ballistics, spatter analysis. They were shot in different rooms. Most of the bullets went through and through. There are fourteen bullet holes in the floor. You know how that plays."

"I imagine I do."

"Say it, then."

"It plays as if they were on the ground, and no threat at all."

"So, torture and murder."

"Charlie—"

"I can't have you in prison." Beckett struggled, found the right words. "You're too . . . *necessary*."

"Thank you for that." She squeezed his hand and meant it. "I love you for caring."

"Do you?"

He tightened his grip enough to show the strength in his wide palm and in fingers that stopped an inch from her cuff. Their eyes met in a pregnant moment, and her voice caught like a child's. "Don't."

"Do you trust me or not?"

"Don't. Please."

Two words. Very small. He looked at her sleeve, and at the narrow flash of china wrist. Both knew he could lift the sleeve, and that she couldn't stop him. He was too strong; too ready. He could have his answer and, in its wake, find helplessness and truth and the ruins of their friendship. "What is it with you and these kids?" he asked. "Gideon? The girl? Put a hurt child in front of you and you don't think straight. You never have."

His grip was iron, his hand squeezed so tight she had little feeling left in her fingers. "That's not your business, Charlie."

"It wasn't before. Now it is."

"Let me go."

"Answer the question."

"Very well." She found his eyes and held them, unflinching. "I can't have children of my own."

"Liz, Jesus . . ."

"Not now, not ever. Shall I tell you how I was raped as a child? Or should we discuss all that came after, the complications and the lies and the reasons my father, even now, won't look at me the same? Is that your business, Charlie? Is the skin on my wrists your business, too?"

"Liz . . ."

"Is it or isn't it?"

"No," he said. "I guess it's not."

"Then let go of my hand."

It was a bad moment that caught like a breath. But he saw her clearly, now. The children she loved. The string of broken relationships and the withdrawn, cool way she often held herself. He squeezed her hand—once and gently—then did as she asked.

"I'll try to keep them away." He stood and seemed every inch the clumsy giant. "I'll do what I can to conceal the fact she's here." Elizabeth nodded as if nothing were wrong; but Beckett knew her every look. "Channing's scores are public record," he said. "You can't hide that she's a shooter. Sooner or later someone will figure it out. Sooner or later they'll find her."

"All I need is for it to be later."

"Why, for God's sake? I hear what you're saying, okay? The kids and all. I get it. I see what it means to you. But this is your life." He spread the same thick fingers, struggling. "Why risk it?"

"Because for Channing it's not too late."

"And for you it is?"

"The girl matters more."

Elizabeth lifted her chin, and Beckett understood, then, the depth of her commitment. It wasn't a game or delay for its own sake. She would take the heat for Channing. The murders. The torture. She would go down for the girl.

"Jesus, Liz . . ."

"It's okay, Charlie. Really."

He turned away for an instant, and when he turned back he was harder. "I want a better reason."

"For what?"

"Look, I've made mistakes in my life, some really big ones. I don't care to make another one now, so if there's a reason you're doing this—something beyond childhood wounds and raw emotion—"

"What if there is?"

"Then I'll do everything I can to help you."

Elizabeth measured his sincerity, then pulled up both sleeves and lifted her arms so he could take it all in: the fierce eyes and conviction, the raw, pink wounds and all they implied. "I would have died without the girl," she said. "I would have been raped, and I would have been killed. Is that reason enough?" she asked; and Beckett nodded because it was, and because, looking at her face, he knew for a fact that he'd never seen anything so fragile, so determined, or so goddamn, terrible beautiful.


When he was gone, Elizabeth pushed the door shut and watched him all the way to his car. His stride was slow and steady, and he drove away without looking back once.

When she turned, Channing was in the hall. A blanket wrapped her like a package. Her skin was creased from sleep. "I'm ruining your life."

Elizabeth put her back to the door and crossed her arms beneath her breasts. "You don't have that power, sweetheart."

"I heard what you said to him."

"You don't need to worry about that."

"And if you go to prison because of me?"

"It won't come to that."

"How can you know?"

"I just do." Elizabeth put an arm around the girl's shoulder. Channing wanted a better answer. Elizabeth didn't have one. "Did you sleep okay?"

"I was sick again. I didn't want to wake you."

Elizabeth felt a stab of guilt. She slept so well with the girl warm beside her. "You should eat something."

"I can't."

The girl looked as fragile as glass, the veins powder blue in her arms. She looked how Elizabeth felt. Even the skin beneath her eyes was smudged.

"Get dressed. We're leaving."

"Where?"

"You need to see something," Elizabeth said. "And then you're going to eat."

They took the Mustang, top down. Heat was already spiking in the day, but dense trees shaded the streets, and the lawns in Elizabeth's neighborhood were thick and green. It made for a pleasant drive out, and Elizabeth watched the girl when she could. "Why the desert?"

"Hmmm?"

"You said once that we should go to the desert. I found it odd," Elizabeth said, "because I'd had the same thought just before that, and I'm not sure why. I've never considered the desert, never thought

I'd want to live there or even visit. My life is here. It's all I've ever known, but I lie awake at night and imagine wind like it came from an oven. I see red stone and sand and long views of brown mountains." She watched the girl. "Why do you suppose that is?"

"It's simple, isn't it?"

"Not to me."

"No mold, no mildew." Channing closed her eyes and turned her face to the sun. "Nothing in the desert smells like a basement."

They were silent after that. Traffic thickened. Channing kept her eyes closed. When they reached the commercial district, Elizabeth edged onto a ramp that spit them out six blocks from the square. They passed office buildings and cars and homeless people with loaded carts. When the square appeared, they circled the courthouse and turned onto Main Street, which was dotted with a few shoppers and people in suits. They passed a coffee shop, a bakery, a lawyer's office. Channing eased the sweatshirt hood over her head and sank into the seat as if people frightened her.

"You'll be fine," Elizabeth said.

"Where are we going?"

"Here."

"What's here?"

"You'll see."

Elizabeth parked at the curb, then opened the door and met Channing on the sidewalk. Together, they passed a hardware store and a pawnshop. The door after that was glass with wood trim painted dark green. Letters on the glass said SPIVEY INSURANCE, HARRISON SPIVEY, BROKER AND AGENT. A bell tinkled as they pushed into a small room that smelled of coffee and hair spray and wood polish.

"Is he in?" Elizabeth asked.

No preamble. No hesitation. The receptionist stood, the gap of a sweater gathered in one hand, her soft face turning bright red. "Why do you come here?"

Elizabeth said to Channing, "She always asks me that."

"You're not a client, and I don't think for a second that you're a prospective one, either. Is it a police matter?"

"That's between Mr. Spivey and me. Is he in or not?"

"Mr. Spivey comes in late on Fridays."

"What time?"

"I expect him any moment."

"We'll wait."

"Not here, you won't."

"We'll wait outside."

Elizabeth turned and left, Channing at her heels as the bell tinkled again, and the receptionist locked the door behind them. On the sidewalk, Elizabeth stepped into a shaded alcove. "I feel bad about that. She's a nice enough woman, but if her boss won't tell her why I come, then I won't either."

"If you say so." The girl was still small, still sunken in the sweatshirt.

"Do you understand whose office that was?"

"You don't need to do this."

"You need to see how things can change. It matters. It's important."

The girl hugged herself, still doubtful. "How long do we wait?"

"Not long. That's him."

Elizabeth dipped her head as a car rumbled past. In it, a man tapped his hands on the wheel, mouth moving as if singing. Two hundred feet farther, he pulled into an empty spot and climbed out, a thirtysomething man, thick in the middle, thin on top. Otherwise, he was strikingly handsome.

"You don't have to say a word." Elizabeth started walking. "Just stay beside me. Watch his face."

They moved up the sidewalk, and in spite of what she'd said to the girl, Elizabeth felt the narrow finger of her own shame. She was a cop and a grown woman, yet even at a distance suffered the memory of his weight and the taste of pine, the heat of his finger on the back of her hand. She'd had nightmares for years, come close to killing herself from shame and self-loathing. But none of that mattered, anymore. This was about life after, about strength and will and lack of compromise. It was about Channing.

"Hello, Harrison."

He was walking head down and twitched as if her voice carried a live current. "Elizabeth. God." His hand covered his heart as his feet dragged to a stop. He licked his lips and looked nervously at his office door. "What are you doing here?"

"Nothing, really. It's just that it's been a while. This is my friend. Tell her good morning."

He stared at Channing and flushed bright, hot red.

"Can you say hello?" Elizabeth asked.

He mumbled something, and sweat beaded on his face. His eyes flicked from Channing to Elizabeth, then back. "I really need to . . . uh . . . to . . . you know . . ." He pointed at his office.

"Of course. Business first." Elizabeth stepped aside and gave enough room for him to edge past. "Have a nice day, Harrison. Always great to see you."

They watched him shuffle to his office, open the door with his key, and disappear as if sucked inside.

When he was gone, Channing said, "I can't believe you just did that."

"Was it cruel?"

"Maybe."

"Should I be the only one to remember what he did?"

"No. Never."

"What did you see when you looked at his face?"

"Shame. Regret."

"Anything else?"

"I saw fear," Channing said. "I saw a great, giant world of fear."

That was the point, and it sank into the girl as Elizabeth drove them to an old diner on a stretch of empty road on the far side of the county. Blacktop ran off, unbroken, the sky domed above them.

The girl ate in neat bites, smiled twice at the waitress, but in the car, later, looked drawn. "If you tell me everything will be okay, I'll believe you."

"Everything will be okay."

"Do you promise?"

Elizabeth took a left and stopped at a light. "You're just wounded," she said. "Wounds heal."

"Always?"

"If you're strong." The light turned green. "And if you're in the right."

They rode in silence after that, and the day seemed brighter. Channing found a song on the radio; let an open hand drag in the rush of air. This would be a fine day, Elizabeth decided, and for a while it was. They returned to Elizabeth's house, and the minutes folded around them. The porch was shaded, the silence between them easy. When they did speak, it was of small things: a young man on the street, a hummingbird on the feeder. But when Channing closed her eyes, Elizabeth recognized the tightness in her lids, the way her arms banded white across her ribs. Elizabeth remembered the feeling from childhood, and it was one more thing between them, this sudden fear of flying apart. "Are you okay?"

"Yes and no." The girl's eyes opened, and the chair stopped rocking. "Do you mind if I take a soak?"

"Take your time, sweetheart. I'm not going anywhere."

"Promise?"

"Open the window if you like. Call me if you need anything."

Channing nodded, and Elizabeth watched her enter the house. It took a minute, but the window scraped open, and she heard water run in the old porcelain tub. For long minutes she tried to find her own peace, but that, too, was impossible.

Her father made certain.

She watched his car ease down the shaded lane and tried to stifle the deep unease its presence created. He avoided parts of her life. The police station. This street. When they did meet, it was in her mother's presence or on some neutral ground. The policy suited them both. Less resentment and raw nerve. Less chance of an argument. Because of that she met him now as far from the house as she could, and he seemed to want it the same way, stopping twenty feet from the porch and shading his eyes as he climbed from the car.

"What are you doing here?" Her words grated harshly, but they often did.

"Can't a man visit his daughter?"

"You never have."

Tapered hands went into the pockets of black pants. He sighed and shook his head, but Elizabeth wasn't fooled. Her father did nothing without purpose and wouldn't be at her home without some powerful reason.

"Why are you here, Dad? Why now?"

"Harrison called me."

"Of course," she said. "And he told you of my visit."

Her father sighed again and fastened his dark eyes on hers. "Is compassion still beyond you?"

"For Harrison Spivey?"

"For a man who has known nothing but regret for sixteen years, for a decent man struggling to rectify the sins of his past."

"Is that why you're here? Because I've seen no struggle."

"Yet, he raises his children and is charitable and seeks only your forgiveness."

"I won't be lectured about Harrison Spivey."

"Will you talk about this?"

He pulled photos from the front seat and dropped them on the hood of his car. Elizabeth picked them up and felt a twist of sudden nausea. "Where did you get these?"

"They were given to your mother," he replied. "Who is now heartbroken beyond any power to console."

Elizabeth flipped through the stack, but knew what images were there. They came from the autopsy and the basement, full color and graphic. "State police?" She saw the answer on her father's face. "What did they want?"

"They were inquiring about odd behavior, confession, expressions of regret."

"And you let them show these to Mom?"

"Don't be angry at me, Elizabeth, when your choices alone brought us to this place."

"Is she okay?"

"Your vanity and need to rebel—"

"Dad, please."

"Your obsession with violence and justice and Adrian Wall."

The words were loud enough to carry, and Elizabeth glanced at the house, knowing Channing must have heard. "Please lower your voice."

"Did you kill these men?"

She held the stare and felt the weight of his condemnation. It was like this between them and always would be. The old and the young. The laws of God and those of men.

"Did you torture and kill them as the state police claim?"

He was tall and straight and so ready to believe the worst. Elizabeth wanted to share the truth if only to prove him wrong, but she thought of the girl in the house behind her and remembered how it was to be helpless in the dark, to be a child again and nearly broken. Channing saved her from that fate, from monsters that go bump in the night and the emotion that wept like blood from every part of her. That mattered more than her father, her pride, or anything else, so Elizabeth kept her back straight. "I killed them, yes." She handed the photos to her father. "I would do it again."

He sighed deeply, frustrated and disappointed and sad. "Do you know nothing of regret?"

"I think I know more than most."

"Yet, what you sound is prideful."

"I am only what God and my father have made me."

They were bitter words, and he looked away from them. His daughter was a killer, and unrepentant. That was the truth he accepted. "What shall I tell your mother?"

"Tell her that I love her."

"And the rest of it?" He meant the photographs and Liz and her confession.

"You once told Captain Dyer that the cracks in me are so deep God's own light can't find the bottom. Do you really believe that?"

"I believe you are but a short fall from hell itself."

"Then we have nothing to discuss. Do we?"

"Elizabeth, please—"

"Good-bye, Dad."

She opened his car door, and the moment ended badly between them. He glanced a final time at her face, then nodded wearily and slipped into the car. Elizabeth watched him back onto the empty street and drive away. When he was gone, she looked at the bathroom window, then crossed the yard and sat again on the porch. When Channing came out, she was in the same clothes, but her hair was wet and her face flushed with heat. She kept her eyes on the dusty floor, and that's when Elizabeth knew for sure. "You heard all that?"

"Bits and pieces. I didn't mean to eavesdrop."

"It's okay if you did."

"I'm a guest in your house. I wouldn't do that." The girl sniffed and showed the big eyes. "It was your father?"

"Yes."

"You lied to me," Channing said.

"I know I did. I'm sorry."

"You said you never told him what that boy did to you."

"You're upset."

"I thought we were friends, that you understood."

"We are. I do."

"Then why?"

"Why the lie?" Channing nodded, and Elizabeth took a moment because some doors were hard to open, and others impossible to close. When she spoke, it was done softly and with care. "I came up in my father's church," she said. "Raised on prayer and abstinence and piety. It was a spare childhood, but one I believed in, God's love and the wisdom of my father. I didn't realize I was so

sheltered, that I was naïve in a way kids today could never understand. We didn't have television or the Internet or video games. I
didn't go to movies or read fiction or think about boys the way
another seventeen-year-old girl might. The church was my family,
and it was very close. You understand? Protected. Insular."
Channing nodded, and Elizabeth turned her chair to face the girl
straight on. "After Harrison attacked me, I didn't tell my father for
five weeks, and only then because I had no choice. When I did it,
though, I felt dirty and small. I wanted him to make it right, to
tell me I would be okay and had done nothing wrong. Mostly, I
wanted Harrison to pay for what he did."

"Did he?"

"Pay? No. My father called him to the church and made us pray
together, the two of us side by side. I wanted justice, and my father
wanted some kind of grand redemption. So we spent five hours
on our knees asking God to forgive the unforgivable, to fix a thing
that could never be fixed. Two days later I tried to kill myself at
the quarry. My father never did call the police."

"That's why you don't get along?"

"Yes."

"It seems like more. So many years. That kind of poison."

Elizabeth stared at the girl, marveling at her perspicacity. "There
is more. Why we don't speak. Why I went to the quarry." Elizabeth
stood because, after so many years, this was the meat of it, the
thumping, blood-filled core. "I was pregnant," she confessed. "He
wanted me to keep it."

# 17

Gideon woke in a hospital bed, the room dim and cool around him. For an instant he was lost, then remembered everything with perfect clarity: the morning light and Adrian's face, the pain of being shot, and the feel of an unmoving trigger. He closed his eyes against the disappointment and listened to the voice that rose from the corner of the room. It was his father, who was quiet at times, but not always. Gideon heard the mumbling and the disjointed words and wondered why he felt such sudden pity. Other than the pain from being shot and the bed in which he lay, nothing had changed since the night he'd set out to kill Adrian Wall. His father was still useless and drunk, and talking to his dead wife.

*Julia,* he heard.

*Julia, please . . .*

The rest of it was all mumbles and mutterings. Long minutes of it, then an hour. And all the while Gideon lay perfectly still, feeling the same strange and poignant pity. Why was it like that? The curtains were pulled so it was dark in the room, his father more a shape than a man. Long arms around his knees. Shaggy hair and jutting elbows. Gideon had seen the same shape on a thousand nights, but this was different somehow. The old man seemed desperate and harder and sharp. Was it the mumbled words? The way he said her name? The old man was . . . what?

"Dad?"

Gideon's throat was dry. The bullet wound ached.

"Dad?"

The shape in the corner went quiet, and Gideon saw eyes roll his way and glint like pinpricks. The odd moment felt more so for the length of it. Two seconds. Five. Then his father unfolded in the gloom and turned on a lamp.

"I'm here."

His appearance shocked the boy. He was not just disheveled but gray, the skin hanging on his face as if he'd lost twenty pounds in a few days. Gideon stared at the deep lines on his father's cheeks, the crueler ones at the corners of his eyes.

He was angry.

That was the difference.

His father was hard and bitter and angry.

"What are you doing?" Gideon asked.

"Watching you and feeling ashamed."

"You don't look ashamed."

His father stood and brought a stale smell with him. He hadn't bathed. His hair was greasy. "I knew what you were going to do." He put a hand on the bedrail. "When I saw the gun in your hand, I knew."

Gideon blinked, remembering his father's face, and the crown of flowers in his hands. "You *wanted* me to kill him?"

"I wanted him to die. I thought for a minute it wouldn't matter how that happened, whether you killed him or I did. When I saw you with the gun, I thought, well, maybe this is right. It was a flash of a thought. Like that." He snapped his fingers. "But then you ran and were gone so damn fast."

"So you do hate him?"

"Of course I do, him and your mother."

There was the anger, and it wasn't just at Adrian. Gideon ran the last hour in his head: the way his father had said her name over and over, the thrust of it like a blade. "You hate her?"

"*Hate* is not the right word—I loved her too much for that. That doesn't mean I could forgive or forget."

"I don't understand."

"You shouldn't. No boy should."

"How could you hate her? She was your wife."

"On paper, maybe."

"Stop talking in riddles, okay!" Gideon rose up in the bed, pain spreading under the bandages. It was the first time he'd ever raised his voice to his father or expressed his own frustration. But so much of it was inside him, the filthy house and poor food and distant father. Mostly, though, it was the silence and dishonesty, the way his father drank himself stupid, yet had the stomach to curse and groan if Liz came by to help with homework or make sure milk was in the fridge. Now, he was talking about *on paper* as if he were not some kind of paper man, himself. "I'm fourteen years old, but you still ignore me when it comes to her."

"I don't."

"You do. You turn away if I ask about what happened or how she died or why you look at me sometimes like you hate me, too . . . Are you angry that I didn't kill him?"

"No." His father sat, and none of the tension left him. "I'm angry because Adrian Wall is alive and free, and your mother's still dead. I'm upset that you're shot and in this place, and that, when it came down to it, you were the only one of us with the courage to look her killer in the face and do what needed doing."

"But, I didn't do anything."

"That's not the point, son. The point is you had the gun, and I'm just the chickenshit who let you take it. Adrian Wall stole everything from me that ever mattered. Now, look at you, all shot through and small, and somehow bigger than I ever was. And why is that? Because I saw you with that gun and went weak inside for all of ten seconds. Ten goddamn seconds! How could I not be bound up and turned around and choking on the kind of anger that comes from that?"

Gideon heard the words, but thought they were bullshit. His father had half the night to stop him. He could have gone to the prison, gone to Nathan's. "And my mother?" he asked. "What did she ever do to make you mad?"

"Your mother." Gideon's father turned his face away, then pulled a bottle from his pocket and drained a third of it. "When things got hard between us, we'd go to the church and pray. No reason you'd know that, but we did. If we argued about money or you or . . . other things. We'd kneel and hold hands and ask God to give us strength or commitment or whatever the hell we thought we needed. We were married in that church, and you were baptized there. I always figured if one place could fix us, then that'd be it. Your mother disagreed, but she would go to humor me. Goddamn." He shook his head and stared at the bottle. "She'd kneel at that altar and say the words just to humor me."

"I still don't understand."

"Then, I'll say one last thing and leave it at that. As much as I loved your mother and as pretty as she was . . ." He shook his head and drained the bottle dry. "The woman was no kind of fucking saint."

After the run-in with her father, Elizabeth left Channing at the house and pointed the old car at skinny roads that ran wild into the country. It'd been like that since she was a kid: confrontation, then speed, sometimes for hours, and more than once for days. The next state. The next county. It didn't matter. The wind felt good. The engine's scream. But no matter how fast or how far she drove, there was nowhere to go and no white tape marking the end. It was the same empty escape—the same race—and when it was done, Elizabeth's world was no more than her father claimed, just violence and the job and her fascination with Adrian Wall. Maybe he was right about that life. He'd called it pointless once, an embarrassment of lightless rooms. She was thinking of that now, of decisions and the past, and of the only child she would ever conceive.

*It was nine at night when she told her parents the first real lie: "I'm tired," she said. "I'm going to bed."*

*Her father looked up from the kitchen table, and the notes he'd made for Sunday's sermon. "Good night, Elizabeth."*

*"Good night, Father."*

*Such words had been said all the nights of her life. Dinner and homework, his lips dry on her cheek. A week had passed since she'd told the truth of what had happened at the quarry, and supposedly there was peace between them. She didn't see it, though. She saw his hand on the boy's shoulder, the way he'd told his own lies, saying, "Prayer and contrition, young man. These are stones in the path to God's right hand."*

*Elizabeth watched her father return to his notes. First gray was in his beard, hair thinning on the crown of his head.*

*"Come here, baby girl."*

*Elizabeth went to her mother, who was warm and smiling and smelled of bread. The hug she offered was soft and long, so complete Elizabeth wanted to fall into it and never leave. "I don't want this baby."*

*"Hush, child."*

*"I want the police."*

*Her mother squeezed harder and spoke in the same guarded whisper. "I'll talk to him."*

*"He won't change his mind."*

*"I'll try. I promise. Just be patient."*

*"I can't."*

*"You must."*

*Elizabeth pushed away because her own decision was so suddenly hard inside her she feared her mother might feel it.*

*"Elizabeth, wait . . ."*

*But, she didn't. She pounded the stairs, went to her room, and squeezed her legs together until lights were off in the house. When the time came, she went through the window and onto the roof, then down the great oak that had shaded her room since before she could speak.*

*A friend with a car waited at the end of the drive. Her name was Carrie, and she knew the place. "Are you sure about this?"*

*"Just drive."*

*The doctor was slick skinned and Lithuanian and unlicensed. He lived in a trailer at the bad end of a bad trailer park and wore his hair long and parted in the middle. His front tooth was gold, the rest of them as shiny and brown as old honey. "You are the preacher's daughter, yes?"*

*His eyes moved up and down, gold tooth flashing as he pushed a damp cigarette into the center of a narrow smile.*

*"It's okay," Carrie said. "He's legit."*

*"Yes, yes. I helped your sister. Pretty girl."*

*Elizabeth felt a cold ache between her legs. She looked at Carrie, but the doctor had his fingers on her arm. "Come." He moved her toward the back of the trailer. "I have clean sheets, washed hands . . ."*

*When it was done and she was in the car, Elizabeth was shaking so hard her teeth chattered. She hunched above the place she hurt. The road was black, and white lines flicked past, one after another and endless. She settled into the hurt, and into the hum of tires. "Should there be this much blood?"*

*Carrie looked sideways, and her face turned as white as the lines on the road. "I don't know, Liz. Jesus."*

*"But, your sister—"*

*"I wasn't with my sister! Jenny Loflin took her. Shit, Liz! Shit! What did the doctor say?"*

*But Elizabeth couldn't think of the doctor, not of his dead eyes or filthy room or the way he touched her. "Just get me home."*

*Carrie drove fast to make it happen. She got Elizabeth to the house and onto the porch before something else broke inside and stained the porch like a flood.*

*"Jesus. Liz."*

*But Elizabeth couldn't speak, watching instead from the bottom of a lake. The water was clear and warm, but getting dark at the edges. She saw fear on her friend's face, and black waters pushing in.*

*"What do I do, Liz? What?"*

*Elizabeth was on her back, everything warm around her. She tried to raise her hand, but couldn't move at all. She watched her friend pound on the door, then turn and run and spray gravel with the car. The next thing she saw was her father's face, then lights and movement, then nothing at all.*

Elizabeth eased up on the gas, watching mile markers slide past as she played it out again: long days in the hospital, the silent months that followed. She blamed herself when the nights got long. For not wanting the baby, for the dead place inside her. How old would the child be had she kept it?

*Sixteen,* Elizabeth thought.

*Two years older than Gideon. Two years younger than Channing.*

She wondered if that meant something, if God indeed paid attention, and her father had been right all along. It was doubtful, but why else did she find these children? Why were the connections so immediate and unshakable?

"A psychologist would have a goddamn field day."

The thought amused her because psychologists ranked about the same as preachers, which meant pretty low. What if she was wrong about that? If she'd gone for therapy as her mother wanted, then maybe she'd have finished college and married. Maybe she'd have a career in real estate or graphic design, live in New York or Paris, and have some fabulous life.

Forget it, she thought. She'd done good work as a cop. She'd made a difference and saved some lives. So what if the future was shapeless? There were other things and other places. She didn't have to be a cop.

"Yeah, right."

Those were her thoughts as she approached a creek with two boys fishing from the bridge. Her foot came off the pedal, and she moved past, parking beyond the bridge to watch. The smaller boy went into his cast, and for a moment everything hung in perfect balance: the rod all the way back, small arms flexed. He was nine, she guessed, his friend pointing at a deep-looking pool beside a willow tree and a slab of gray stone. The baited hook flicked out, landed perfectly. They nodded at each other, and she marveled that life could be so simple, even for a child. It gave her a moment's peace, then the phone rang, and she answered.

It was Channing.

She was screaming.


Channing had stood on the porch and shaded her eyes as Elizabeth backed from the drive and accelerated down the street. The poor woman had been apologetic and calm, but Channing understood the sudden need to move and do and think wild thoughts. She felt the same thing when her mind went to the basement, like she could scream or rock in the dark or punch the walls until her fingers bled. Anything was better than stillness, and acting normal was the one impossible thing. Conversation. Eye contact. Anything could open the door.

She watched the street for another minute, then went inside and wandered the house, liking everything about it: the colors and the furniture, the comfortable clutter. A bookshelf covered an entire wall of the living room, and she walked its length, opening one book and then another, picking up photographs of Elizabeth and some small boy. In most of the pictures he was young—maybe two or three. In others he was older, shy looking and thin, and close at her side. He had troubled eyes and a pretty smile. She wondered who he was.

Turning from the photographs, Channing locked the door, poured a glass of vodka from a bottle in the freezer, and made her way to the bathroom at the end of the hall. She locked that door, too, and wondered if she'd ever relax behind a door that wasn't bolted. Even here and safe, she felt as if her clothes were too thin and certain muscles had forgotten how to unclench. The vodka helped, so she took a sip, started the bath, and then lifted the glass again. She made the water very hot and waited for steam to rise before undressing in a careful, controlled manner. It wasn't that she hurt—the stitches, the bite marks—but that she feared her eyes might betray her, that they'd find the mirror by mistake and linger on the bruises and dark thread and the tight, pink crescents his teeth had left. She wasn't ready for that.

Sinking into the bath, though, she thought of what Elizabeth stood for, of her patience and strength and will. Maybe it was the vodka, or something more. Whatever the case, Channing climbed from the tub before the water cooled. She kept her eyes up this time and confronted the mirror with a steadiness she thought she'd lost. She started with wet hair and the water on her skin, then looked at the bruises and marks and the ribs that showed too plainly. But it wasn't enough to simply look. She needed to see, and that's what she tried to do, to see not just the person she'd been or was, but the woman she wished to be.

That woman looked a lot like Liz.

It was a good thought that didn't last. Someone was banging on the door.

"Jesus—"

Channing jumped so hard and fast she slammed her hand against the sink. It wasn't a knock at the door, but a hard, brutal pounding.

"Shit, shit—"

She shoved a leg into her jeans, fabric sticking on wet skin, the other leg going in just as hard. The pounding got louder and more intense. Front door, she thought, over and over, and hard enough to shake the house. Channing pulled on the sweatshirt, thinking telephone, Liz, run. It was panic, pure instinct. She could barely breathe, and it took all her strength to open the bathroom door.

The hall was dim, no movement. The pounding got even louder.

Creeping into the living room, she risked a glance through the window. Cops were in the yard—blue lights and guns and hard-faced men wearing Windbreakers that said SBI.

"This is the state police!" A loud voice at the door. "We have an arrest warrant for Elizabeth Black! Open up!"

Channing twitched away from the window, but not before someone saw her.

"Movement! Left side!"

Guns came up, squared on the widow.

"State police! Final warning!"

Channing ducked sideways, saw men on the porch. They wore helmets and body armor and black gloves. One of them had a sledgehammer.

"Break it."

An older man pointed at the lock, and Channing screamed when the hammer hit. The sound was like a bomb, but the door held.

"Again!"

This time the frame buckled, and she saw bright metal. Six men stood behind the hammer, soldiers in a row with fingers tight above the triggers. The old man nodded, and the hammer struck a third time, the door breaking from its frame.

"Move! Move! Move!"

Channing felt the rush, but was already moving. She snatched up the phone and sprinted left.

"Movement! Back hall!"

Someone else yelled "Freeze!" but she didn't. She hit the bathroom in a skid; slammed the door and locked it. They'd clear the house before they broke the door, but it was a small house, and she was already dialing.

One ring.

Two.

She sensed men, tight-packed in the narrow hall. It was the stillness, the silence.

*Please, please . . .*

The phone rang a third time, and Channing heard the click. She opened her mouth, but the door exploded, and the world was guns and men and screaming.

As hard as Elizabeth drove the car before, she pushed it to breaking now, turning off the crumbled road and onto a state highway, cars slashing past as the needle touched 105. The wind made so much noise she could barely think. But what could she think about anyway?

The girl wasn't answering.

Screams. A dead phone. But, she'd heard other things, too. Hard voices and shouting and breaking wood.

Elizabeth dialed the house, but the line was off the hook. She tried the girl's phone again, but that failed, too.

"Damn it!"

Three tries. Three fails.

Desperate, she called Beckett. "Charlie!"

"Liz, where the hell are you? What's that noise?"

She could barely hear above the wind. "Charlie, what's happening?"

"Thank God. Listen. Don't go to your house!" He was yelling to be heard. "Don't go home!"

"What? Why?"

"Hamilton and Marsh . . ." She lost a sentence or two, then he was back. "Word just hit the street. They have an indictment, Liz. Double homicide. We just found out."

"What about Channing?"

"Liz . . ." Static. "Don't . . ."

"What?"

"State police locked us out—"

"Charlie! Wait!"

"Don't go to your fucking house!"

Elizabeth hung up in numb disbelief. It wasn't the warrant or that she'd be arrested. State cops were at her house, and so was the girl who'd saved her life, Channing, who was eighteen and hollowed out and liable to confess anything. Already, five minutes had passed.

"Too much time."

She pushed the old car until the needle touched 110, then 115. She watched for slow movers and cops; squeezed the wheel hard and said her first real prayer in a dozen years.

*Please, God . . .*

But, it was over by the time she got there. She saw it from a block out: no lights at the house, no cars or cops or movement. She came hard anyway, locking up the brakes and rocking into the drive.

"Channing!"

She took the yard at a run, saw tire tracks in the grass, and the door broken in its frame. On the porch she hit the door with a shoulder, felt it rock on a single hinge. Inside, she found out-of-place furniture, dirty footprints, and the bathroom door, blasted off the hinges, too.

She was too late.

That was real.

She checked the house, anyway. Bedrooms. Closets. She wanted to find the girl, hidden maybe, or tucked away. But she was kidding herself, and she knew it. The warrant wasn't for Channing, but they had a subpoena, and Hamilton and Marsh would use it, were probably talking to her now.

*What happened in the basement?*

*Who pulled the trigger?*

In a fog, Elizabeth stepped outside and wedged the door shut behind her. They had the girl, and the girl would talk. Whether from guilt or naïveté or the desire to help Elizabeth, Channing would eventually break.

Elizabeth couldn't let that happen.

The shooting was too political, too racial. They'd burn her down to make an example.

"I saw it happen."

The voice came from beyond the hedge, and Elizabeth recognized the neighbor who lived to the right, an elderly man with a '72 Pontiac station wagon he polished on weekends as if it were made of something more precious than steel and paint. "Mr. Goldman?"

"Must have been twenty cops. Assault rifles and body armor. Goddamn Nazis." He pointed and ducked his head. "Sorry about your door."

"There was a girl . . ."

"A small one, yes. Two tough old bastards hauled her out."

"You saw her?"

"Hard to miss, really, hanging between them like she was, all bright-eyed and flushed and kicking like a mule."

For a hard flat second Elizabeth didn't know what to do. She couldn't go to the station with a murder warrant on her head. It was beyond even Dyer to help her, now. Hamilton and Marsh had their indictment. That meant they'd pick her up and drop her in a hole. Even if she won at trial—which was doubtful—she'd be vilified by the national press, picked apart, and stripped to her bones. It was an angry nation and she was another white cop on the wrong side of a shooting. It couldn't play otherwise, not with fourteen bullet holes in the floor.

And that was best-case scenario.

Worst case, Channing would talk. That meant time mattered, and not the kind that would be counted in days.

Hours, she thought. Minutes.

*Would the girl even fight?*

Elizabeth's paralysis snapped like a glass rod. She started the car and had Channing's father on the line before she reached the first turn. He would move heaven and earth, but his lawyers were in Charlotte. That would take time. So, she went the only place that made sense: around the city, across the river. Box bushes took paint off the car, but she found the old lawyer sitting in the same chair on the same porch. He offered pleasantries, but she shut him down before he could rise from the chair. "No time, Faircloth. Just listen, please."

She started too fast, too shaky.

"Slow down, Elizabeth. Catch your breath. Whatever it is, we'll handle it. Sit down. Tell me from the beginning."

"It needs to be privileged."

"Very well. Consider me your attorney."

"You're not licensed."

"Then consider me a friend." She hesitated, so he spoke carefully to make his point. "Anything you tell me I will take to my grave unless you instruct otherwise. You cannot shock me or dissuade me or make me anything less than your ally."

"I'm not the only one at risk."

"Five decades before the bar, my dear, and you would not believe the secrets I have kept. Whatever the problem, you have come to the right place."

"Very well." She took a deep breath and focused on his hands, on the class ring and creases and parchment skin. He leaned into her words, and she told him everything, her eyes never leaving the crooked fingers, her words rising from some dim, far place. She started with the subpoena for Channing and her own indictment, then moved to the horrible truth of what really happened in the basement on Penelope Street. It hurt like being naked in the cold, but there was no time left for shame or self-pity. She told him everything and let her wrists show to make it real. He interrupted only once, when he whispered, "You poor dear girl."

Even then she couldn't look him in the face. It was the shame of it, as if she weren't just naked but nailed to a board. "I don't know what she'll say, Faircloth, only what will happen if she tells the truth."

"And you wish to put her interests above your own."

"Yes."

"You're certain of that? If she tortured those men—"

"That's on me. My decision."

"May I ask why?"

"Does it matter?"

"Not if you understand the consequences of what you're asking me to do. The indictment has your name on it, not hers. You're risking prison—"

"I'll never go to prison. I'll run first."

"As your friend and lawyer, I feel compelled to advise you that such plans rarely work out."

"Just keep her from talking, Faircloth. I'll live with what comes after."

"Very well. One thing at a time." He patted her hand. "You were right to come to me, Elizabeth. Thank you for that, for that trust."

"What can we do for Channing?"

"For starters, don't panic. Even if she confesses everything, we can argue the shooting is justified. She's a child, and traumatized. Prosecution is not a foregone conclusion. Conviction is not even worth discussing."

"Eighteen rounds. You've seen the papers. You understand the context."

He nodded because he did. Things were different since Baltimore and Ferguson. Everything was racial; everything was watched. That made the deaths of Brendon and Titus Monroe not just public but political, especially with allegations of torture and retribution. If the attorney general had to shift targets, he certainly could. The cop, the rich girl; at this point it didn't matter. Win or lose, the machine needed a body.

"Even if she's acquitted," Elizabeth said, "you know what a trial would do to a girl so young. She won't recover."

"Give me a dollar." The old lawyer held out a hand.

"What?"

"Make it two."

"I have a twenty."

"That's fine." He took the bill. "A ten-dollar retainer for you, and another for the girl. In case anyone asks. Do you have a cell phone?"

"Of course . . ."

"Give it to me." Elizabeth handed it over. He removed the battery and the SIM card, then handed everything back and smiled to take away the sting. "Cops make bad fugitives. It's the mind-set."

"Jesus."

She stared at the phone. Crybaby was already moving.

"Get a burner phone when you can. Call me with the number." He shrugged on a wrinkled coat. The rest of him was in faded jeans and boat shoes without socks. "I'll deal with the girl first, then we can talk about this indictment. Her father is Alsace Shore?"

"You know him?"

"I know his lawyers. They may complicate matters, which doesn't matter so long as they keep her from talking. We'll see when I get there. Will your friends on the force help the state police find you?"

"Beckett's on my side. Dyer, too, I hope. Everyone else is a wild card."

"Then, you should leave, immediately. Do you have a safe place to go? A friend in another town? Family?"

The question almost ruined her. How could she admit the truth? That most of her friends were cops and would arrest her on sight, that even family was a shelter built on sand. "Right now, you and Channing are all I have."

The old man took her hand, and she felt kindness in the heat of his fingers. "Allow me to make a suggestion. I have a fishing cabin on the lake. It's on Goodman Road, not far at all. I haven't been there in forever, but a handyman keeps it open for me. You should go there. Just for now," he assured her. "Just so I can find you."

"Shouldn't I be doing something?"

"Let me find out what's happening. Then we can make a plan."

"All right. Come on. I'll drive you."

"No. Stay out of the city. Stay away from people. I'll call the car service." He guided her off the porch, and she stopped on the second step. "Be quick, Elizabeth. They may have tracked your phone, already."

He was eager, but she needed this single moment, just to be sure. "Why are you doing this?"

"Because you have pretty eyes and a lovely smile."

"Don't joke, Faircloth."

"Very well. I'm helping you because Adrian spoke of you often, and because I've followed your career since his trial, because you are thoughtful and kind and unlike other detectives, because I find you to be a most admirable woman." A twinkle glinted in the old man's eyes. "Have I not told you that?"

"And if you're charged for practicing without a license?"

"Until you showed up the other day, I'd not been out of my house for over a decade. Now, I've been to court, breathed fresh air, and helped a friend that needed help. I'm eighty-nine years old, with a heart so weak I'm unlikely to live another three. So, look at me." He lifted his arms so she could take in the old jeans and flyaway hair, the coat he could have used for a pillow. "Now, ask again if I give a good goddamn about being charged with anything."

# 18

Beckett watched the circus unfold. Alsace Shore. The lawyers. They were in the lobby beyond the glass, arguing, posturing. The Charlotte attorneys made the most noise, but that made perfect sense: $1,500 an hour between the three of them, the client right there and just as red-faced. Only Crybaby Jones seemed at ease. He stood a few feet to the side, both hands on his cane, his head tilted attentively as detectives tried to explain that none of them, in fact, represented Channing Shore.

"She doesn't want a lawyer. She's waived the right—"

"She's too young for that. I'm her father. *These* are her lawyers. Right here! Right now! I demand to see her!"

"Sir, I need you to calm down, and I'll explain again. Your daughter's eighteen. She doesn't want a lawyer."

But Alsace Shore was not the calming kind. He had his own suspicions, Beckett thought. And, why not? He knew what Channing could do with a gun. That meant he knew the danger she was in now, that one wrong word could change her life forever. Beckett felt sick from the thought, but mostly that was about Liz. He'd made a promise and wasn't sure he could keep it.

"How long has this been going on?" Beckett leaned into the sergeant, who shrugged.

"An hour."

"Has Dyer been out?"

"Shit rolls downhill. You know that."

"Call me if it gets worse."

Beckett left the front desk and worked his way toward the interview rooms. Hamilton and Marsh had the girl in isolation with the local cops frozen out. Uniformed troopers barred the door. Even Dyer was banned, and that made the tension unmistakable, as if the AG thought the locals were covering for one of their own and only the state cops knew right from wrong, as if God himself wanted Liz to fry.

It tied Beckett into knots.

Liz was clean.

How could they not see that?

But they didn't. Occam's razor. The obvious explanation. Whatever. The truth was a coal he wanted to puke from his chest.

*The kid is the goddamn shooter!*

Twenty feet from the troopers, Beckett stopped and checked his watch. They'd had the girl inside for ninety-three minutes. The all-points on Liz was two hours' old, and every detail was on the wire. Name. Description. Vehicles. Elizabeth was officially wanted for double homicide. Every cop in the state was looking for her, and that was not the worst part.

*Suspect considered armed and dangerous.*

*Approach with caution.*

"Where's Dyer?" Beckett caught a uniformed officer by the sleeve as she passed. She pointed, and Beckett bulled through the hall, people scrambling to get out of his way. He found Dyer near the conference room. "Where've you been?"

"Making phone calls."

"Have you seen this?" Beckett pushed a copy of the all-points at Dyer.

"It's why I'm making calls."

"Those state cops are going to get her killed."

"What do you want me to do, Charlie? They have an indictment for double murder. She's on the run and armed, and the state cops know it."

"She didn't kill anyone."

Dyer's eyebrow went up. "Are you sure?"

"Just find her."

"I have people on the street."

"Send more. We need to be the ones to find her. Us. Her people."

"She could be out of the county by now, out of the state."

"Not Liz." Beckett was certain. "Not with Channing Shore in custody."

Dyer crossed his arms. "Is there something I should know?"

Beckett looked away and choked on the same hot coal. "All I can say is, she's got a crazy-strong connection to this kid."

"Like the Gideon thing?"

"Stronger, maybe."

"That's not possible."

A day ago Beckett would have said the same thing. Now he wasn't so sure. "There's a connection there, Francis. It's deep and instinctual. Primal, even. She won't leave the girl."

"Whatever the case. Best thing we can do is to bring her in and straighten this out through channels. Counseling. Lawyers. Everybody runs dark at times, and anybody can snap. All we can do now is work the fallout."

"You really think she killed those men?"

"*Animals,* Charlie. That's what she said."

"Francis—"

"Let's just get her home and safe. Deal?"

"Sure. Yeah. Deal."

Beckett watched Dyer all the way to his office, then talked to the first trooper he could find. "I want to talk to Hamilton." The state cop was six-three and solid, unflinching in the brimmed hat and dove-gray uniform. "Don't give me that dead-eye, state-cop fucking stare. Go find him."

It took a few minutes. When Hamilton came out, Beckett didn't waste time. "Is she talking?"

"That's why you brought me out here?"

"Has she given you anything? Yes or no?"

Hamilton studied Beckett's face, thinking about what he saw on it. Determination maybe. Maybe desperation. "She's staring at the table. Hasn't said a single word."

"You've had her for two hours."

"She's a tough little nut."

"Walk with me." Beckett moved for the back stairs.

Hamilton trailed along. "There's nothing I can do for your partner. You know that."

Beckett led him into the break room downstairs. "You want a Coke?"

"Indictment, man. Come on. My hands are tied."

"It's all right. Have a Coke."

Beckett fed a bill into the machine, pushed a button, and waited for the bottle to drop. When it did, he opened it and took a sip. "What does your boss want?"

"Your partner tortured and executed two men. What do you think he wants?"

"Reelection."

"Funny."

"Will he take the case capital?"

"Death penalty. Life in prison. Do you really think it matters?"

"Yeah." Beckett bought another Coke. "Damn straight." Beckett handed over the bottle, then bent for his change to buy time. When he straightened, the decision was made. "I can make her talk."

"Channing? I seriously doubt it."

"Do you want to know what happened in the basement or not?"

"Of course, I want to know."

"Give me five minutes alone with her." Beckett sipped from the bottle, and his eyes were flat. "The kid will fucking talk."

When Beckett walked into the interview room, the girl sat alone at a metal table. He sat across from her, empty-handed. Channing kept her head down, but Beckett saw a pearl of blood at the quick of her nail, the places she'd chewed her bottom lip raw. "I'm Detective Beckett. I'm Elizabeth's partner." She stirred at the name, but kept her eyes down. "I know you're Liz's friend. I know you care. I'm her friend, too." Beckett put his elbows on the table. "Do you believe me?"

"I believe you're her friend."

"That's good. Thank you for that. Do you understand that there's an arrest warrant with her name on it?"

"Yes."

"That she's charged with double homicide for what happened in the basement?"

The girl nodded.

"That means she could go to prison for life and might be executed. Do you understand that, too?"

"Yes."

"Do you think that's fair?"

Nothing.

Stillness.

"What if she gets hurt when they arrest her? There're a dozen state patrolmen in the county looking just for her. Every cop in the state has her picture. What if she gets shot or wrecks a car or hurts somebody trying to elude arrest? What happens to her, then? Life on the run? Life with nothing? You understand that North Carolina is a death-penalty state?"

"She told me not to say anything."

"I know she did. And I know why, too." The girl looked up at that. "It's okay. I know what happened."

"She told you?"

"I'm a cop. I figured it out. Others will, too." The girl looked away, and Beckett waited for her to look back. "Does the name Billy Bell mean anything to you?" It did. He saw it in the twitch of her hands, and in the sudden flush he knew was shame. "He works as a gardener for your parents. I spoke to him this morning."

"So?"

She was on the edge, and Beckett made his voice hard because *on the edge* meant nothing. He needed her broken.

"Billy bought drugs for your mother. Mostly, he bought them from Brandon and Titus Monroe. Pills. Cocaine. That went on for years. That's fact. But you knew that, didn't you? That your mother's a user. That your gardener had a connection. You wanted to meet that connection. You and your friends. You wanted to be bad. You wanted the thrill." Channing tensed, a moment of terror in her eyes. That's when Beckett knew he was right. "Do you know what an affidavit is?"

"Maybe."

"It's a sworn statement, admissible in court. Billy Bell signed one this morning. Would you like to read it?"

"No."

Beckett withdrew a folded paper from his pocket and placed it on the table. "You would have never been in that basement if you and your friends hadn't wanted to walk on the wild side. But that's what happened, isn't it? You bought drugs from the Monroe brothers, and they came back and they took you. It wasn't random. They didn't find you on the street."

"It was just the once. Please. We just wanted to try it."

"Drugs?"

"Marijuana. Just the once."

"And they came back for you."

She nodded, small.

"What happened in that basement was your fault." Beckett leaned forward and challenged her with every ounce of cop he had. "What happened to Liz was your fault, too. I've seen her wrists. I see how she's falling apart."

A sound escaped the girl's throat.

"It's time to tell the truth, Channing. To take responsibility for what happened in that basement."

"What happens to Elizabeth if I do?"

He leaned back in the chair. "Liz walks free. Her life goes on."

The girl turned her head, but Beckett wasn't finished. "Looking away is the easy part," he said. "It always has been. The only real question is if you'll let Liz die with a needle in her arm because you and your friends decided to get high. You okay with that? Look at me. This is your chance to do what's right. Right here. Right now."

The girl took her time. He let her have it.

"Does Liz know you're doing this?"

"I told her I wouldn't."

"Then why are you here?"

"Because I look out for people I love, no matter the cost."

"You love her?" Channing asked.

"Other than my wife she's the best friend I've ever had."

Channing considered his words for another long minute, and Beckett saw the instant she broke. "I'll do it on one condition."

"What?"

Channing told him what she wanted.

Beckett looked at the two-way glass, then shrugged and pushed a notepad across the table. "All right."

The girl smoothed cuffed hands across the page.

Beckett held the pen where she could see it. "But, I want all of it."

"Everything."

"On camera and uncensored."

"For her," Channing said; and Beckett nodded.

"For Liz." He gave her the pen. "Because she would do the same for you."


Beckett watched the girl write, then took the page and folded it into a pocket. Two minutes later he was on the other side of the glass, and Marsh was setting up a video camera to take the girl's statement. She looked small but determined.

Hamilton saw the emotion on Beckett's face. "What did she give you?"

"A note," Beckett said.

"May I see it?"

"It's for Liz. It's personal."

"I don't care."

"You want the note, you fucking shoot me." Beckett's face said he was deadly serious.

Hamilton could push it, but why bother? He had the girl, and she was going to talk. "How did you know?"

"About Billy Bell?" Beckett shrugged. "I talked to the gardener this morning. I thought the mother was the only one buying drugs. Turned out it went deeper."

"That's not what I meant. How did you know Channing would talk?"

"Maybe I didn't."

"I saw your face at the drink machine. You said you could break her in five, yet you did it in two. You were certain."

"Liz loves the kid." Beckett studied the girl through the glass, the delicate features and swollen eyes. "I figured maybe the kid loved her back."

Hamilton didn't buy it. He leaned against the glass and watched Beckett's face. "I've seen husbands kill their wives; mothers turn on sons. Channing and Detective Black barely know each other. It has to be more than that."

"Maybe."

"You have a theory?"

"Maybe she *needed* to confess."

"Why?"

"They say familiarity breeds contempt." Beckett put his hands on the glass, thinking of his wife and the warden and his own bitter mistakes. "Who do we know better than ourselves?"

When the tape was running, it began. Questions came, and the girl spoke haltingly. How she met the Monroe brothers. Where she was when they took her. The state cops walked her through it, and as surprised as they were by the story she told, no one doubted the truth of what she said. The details were too strong, the emotions too real. She spoke of the candle, the mattress, the things they did to her. In places she broke, and in places she froze. The tale of abuse was so hard to hear it shook everyone listening. Forty hours, the child was gone. Forty hours at the hands of monsters. Eventually, she got to the part that tore out the final piece of Beckett's heart.

Even Hamilton was pale by then, sitting rigidly when he asked the question. "How did you get your hands on the gun?"

"I wouldn't do what he wanted me to do. The smaller one. Brandon Monroe. I wouldn't do it, so he hit me again, bit me again." She stopped; collected herself. "The next time he did that, I bit him back, right here." She touched the soft spot above her hip bone. "He got angry and threw me against a wall. When he came for me, I tried to crawl away, but he dragged me by the foot. I was scraping at the floor, trying to hold on to something. The gun was just there in the dark."

"Where was Detective Black at this time?"

"In the other room."

"Could you see her?"

"Yes. Sometimes."

"Can you be more specific?" She shook her head; kept shaking it. A full minute passed. "This is what you're here for," Hamilton said. "This is what we need."

A tear slipped down her cheek, and she scrubbed it away. "Elizabeth was on the mattress."

"Was she awake?"

"Yes."

"Was she wired?"

The girl said nothing. Another tear fell.

"We need to understand the level of her incapacity, Channing. If she was able to act? Why she didn't? You tell us she's not the shooter . . ."

The girl looked at the two-way glass, and Beckett, on the other side, felt the stare all the way down in his soul.

He'd made this happen.

He'd done it.

"She was wired to the mattress," Channing said. "Facedown . . ."

Twenty minutes later Beckett hit the door, and Francis Dyer followed him out into the hall. People stopped and stared. They knew what was happening. Not specifics, but they knew. "What the hell have I done?" Beckett pushed into an empty office. Dyer followed. "Jesus Christ, Francis. Liz will never forgive me."

"You saved her life. No charges. No prison. You did what cops are supposed to do. You got to the bottom of things."

"I made her a victim."

"Titus Monroe did that."

"You think she'll be a cop again? You think she'll just get over it? People will see that testimony. Every cop in here will know what happened, that I broke the most important part of her."

"You didn't—"

"That's bullshit, Francis. We all have our armor; we all need it." Beckett dragged his hands through his hair. "She'll never forgive me. Not for this. Not after I promised."

"Why don't you get out of here? Take the day. Take a drive."

"Yeah. Sure. A drive."

"I'll need the affidavit, though."

"What?"

"Billy Bell's affidavit. The one you showed the girl."

"Jesus, man. There is no affidavit." Beckett laughed a ragged laugh and withdrew the same piece of folded paper from his pocket. "This is a blank page. I just pulled it off the printer."

# 19

Crybaby called it a cabin, but that was not accurate. The driveway cut through private forest for over a mile, ending on a bluff above a mirrored lake that blurred into the feet of distant mountains. The cabin, made of stone and wood, was massive and so permanent looking it could have been carved from the earth itself.

Elizabeth climbed from the car and took it all in: the hundred-year oaks, the plunging views. "'The cabin's yours,' he says. 'Have a drink, relax.'"

That wasn't going to happen.

She followed a walkway to the back of the house. Bushes were overgrown, but the grass had been cut often enough to hold the forest back. She found the key where he'd said it would be, beneath a flat rock on the other side of the empty pool. Unlocking the main door, Elizabeth disengaged the alarm and entered the house, passing through a vaulted foyer and into the main room, where a wall of glass framed views of the lake and mountains. The fireplace was large enough to sit in. She saw sheeted furniture, books, a table long enough to feed thirty people. Dust covered everything, with tracks where the caretaker had been through on previous occasions. She followed them into the kitchen, then upstairs, and outside onto an upper balcony that felt like the roof of the world.

"Damn, Crybaby."

She'd forgotten the magnitude of his success, the raw power he used to wield both in and out of court. Back inside, she studied photographs that stretched back six decades or more: Crybaby with past presidents, celebrities, the woman who'd been his wife. The distraction bought five minutes peace, then she moved onto the porch that faced the drive. It was fifteen feet deep and forty long. A dozen rocking chairs were turned upside down to protect them from the wind. Righting one, she dragged it to the low, stone wall that fronted the drive. The old lawyer would follow the drive, so that was the place to wait.

But, waiting was hard.

She sat. She paced.

The soft, warm day ate her alive.

The first sign of his arrival came midafternoon: a sudden stillness in the forest, then the hum of tires. By the time the limousine appeared in the clearing, Elizabeth was off the porch and in the drive. Her hand was on his door before the vehicle came to a complete stop.

"What?" She read his features the instant she saw them. "What went wrong?"

The old man extended a hand. "Help me, if you would." She helped him from the car. He looked tired in the wrinkled jacket and put more weight on the cane than usual. "Are you hungry? We stopped for a few things . . ."

"I'm not hungry. Where's Channing?"

"Take my arm."

"Faircloth, please."

"Take it. Walk with me." He firmed as he moved, guiding her to the shade of the porch. "Would you?" He gestured at a second chair, and she turned it over for him. Dropping into the chair, he told her, "Sit, sit." She ignored the chair beside him, choosing instead to settle on the stone wall so their knees nearly touched. "We used to have such parties here. People would come from all over, you know. Europe and Washington and Hollywood."

"Faircloth . . ."

"We thought it the ultimate expression of a life well lived. Powerful friends. A job that mattered. Look at it now, emptiness and dust, all those exciting people dead or close to it." He craned his neck to look at the stacked-stone pillars, the massive beams. "I offered the place to my wife when she left. She refused to take it, though, knowing how much I loved it. She said it was a manly space and needed a man inside it. That was good of her, don't you think? That kindhearted lie."

"You're stalling, Crybaby."

"Perhaps."

"It's bad, then?"

"Your partner convinced her to do the noble thing."

"Beckett? What?"

"He felt he had no choice, not with the indictment. He asked me to tell you as much in the hope you might find a way to forgive him."

"Forgive him?" Elizabeth stood. The betrayal was too much. "He did exactly what I asked him not to do."

"That may be so, but when I describe the young lady's actions, I don't use the word *noble* lightly. Channing confessed to make sure you were safe and well. No threats were made against her, no leverage or offers of leniency. She offered the truth for a splendid reason, and that is rarely a simple thing."

"Is she in state custody or local?"

"Local for now. Charging decisions remain unmade."

Elizabeth stared into the forest. Charging decision or not, she saw how it had to be. The girl would be in processing, now. Stripped of her clothes. Examined. Violated all over again.

"She wanted you to have this." A piece of paper appeared in the old lawyer's hand.

Elizabeth took the folded page. "Do you mind?"

"Of course not. By all means."

Elizabeth walked to the far end of the porch. The note was in a beautiful hand, and brief.

> *Dear Elizabeth,*
>
> *You told me wounds heal, but only if we're strong and if we're right. I try to be strong, and think maybe I can be, but nothing I do will ever make things right. You were in that basement because of me, and not in the way you think. Your partner can explain. He figured it out, and I know you would too, in time. The thought of that is more than I could bear, worse even than the memories of what we suffered together. Please, don't hate me for telling the truth about what happened. I love what you tried to do, but I pulled the trigger and nobody else. It's my fault, all of it. Please, don't be angry. Please don't hate me.*

Elizabeth read the note a second time, then let her gaze fall to the lake. How could she hate her? They were sisters. They were the same.

"Are you quite all right, my dear?"

"I don't think I am."

Crybaby appeared beside her. "The indictment against you has been rescinded, and the state police have no further interest in you. I can take you home if you like. Your car will be fine until tomorrow."

"May I stay for a while?"

"As long as you wish. I made no joke about provisions. There's food, liquor. Enough for a week, if you like." She nodded, and he pressed closer. "Was there comfort?" he asked. "In the young lady's note?"

"No. Not really."

"Then let me tell you a thing I've learned in my eighty-nine years. This house, the friends and memories—I'd trade it all for a chance to do what that young woman just did: a noble act, freely undertaken. How many of us have such a chance? And how many the courage to take it?"

"You're the kindest man I've ever known. I'm sure you've had many chances."

"To put one's freedom above my own? To risk my life for another I barely know?" He shook his head, serious. "What I see here is the rarest of things, and the loveliest: her sacrifice and yours, what you've tried to do for each other. One in a million would do the same. One in a hundred million."

Elizabeth studied the keen eyes and white brows, the lines that furrowed his face as if to show every hard decision he'd ever made. "Do you really believe that?"

"With every ounce of my soul."

She looked away and swallowed in a dry throat. "You're a good man, Faircloth Jones."

"I'm an old fart, actually."

Elizabeth folded the note and took his arm. "You said something about liquor."

"I did."

"Is it too early for a drink?"

"Not at all, my dear." Crybaby leaned on the arm and steered for the door. "I have found, in fact, that on days such as this the whiskey lamp is most always lit."

# 20

Beckett didn't go for a drive. He went to the gym in the basement of the precinct. It wasn't much of a facility, but his wife had been after him about his weight, and the next hour came down to two possibilities: sling some steel or seriously hurt somebody.

Minutes. Seconds.

He was that close to losing his shit.

Opening the locker, Beckett stripped off his suit and put on gray sweats and old sneakers. He loaded steel plates on the long bar and didn't worry about the noise as he grunted through more reps than he'd pulled in a long time. Curls, bench, squats. After that, he hit the machines. Triceps, lat pulls, leg extensions.

There was no peace, though.

Too many things moving.

A cold shower broke the sweat, but his mind was still hot as he took the stairs up and rounded into booking.

"Detective Beckett?" a voice called out, and Beckett saw the new girl brought in to work the phones. Laura? Lauren? She pushed past two bloodied men cuffed to a bench and met Beckett halfway across the room. "I tried your cell. I'm sorry."

"It's okay. I was working out."

"Two messages in the past hour. This is from the warden." She handed him a pink slip with a number on it. "He wants you to call his cell. He said it's his fifth message and that he expects to hear from you this time."

Beckett crumpled the paper; tossed it into a can. "What else?"

"A call came into the tip line twenty minutes ago. No name. He asked for you specifically."

Beckett processed that. The only active tip line he knew about had been set up for the Ramona Morgan case. The number was in the papers, on local TV. "What'd he say?"

She made air quotes as she spoke. "'Tell Detective Beckett there was movement at the church.'"

"That's it? Movement?"

"It was strange."

"Any ID on the phone?"

"Disposable cell. The voice was muffled, definitely male. He said one other thing, but it was even stranger."

Beckett looked the question.

She flinched a little. "Sorry. The connection broke so I missed part of it, but I think he said, 'Not even the house of God requires five walls.'"


*Five walls.* Beckett didn't like the sound of that. Four walls to hold up the roof. What was the fifth?

*Adrian Wall?*

Beckett decided to take a drive, after all. He rolled down the windows to wash out the heat, then worked his way through downtown and past the sprawl. Tip lines had been known to cause more trouble than they were worth, especially in high-profile, violent cases. Nut jobs came out of the woodwork when the press got hot. False reports. Copycats. General hysteria. He'd been around long enough to see it all, but something about the tone of this one bothered him.

*Not even the house of God requires five walls.*

Beckett drove until he saw the church on a distant hill. When he crested the ridge, he circled the east side and parked where he'd parked before. Light slanted through the trees. A hot wind blew.

"Shit."

The tape was down. The door stood open.

He got out of the car, and his hand settled on the butt of his weapon as he studied blank windows and blind corners, the dark trunks of massive trees. There *had been* movement at the church. No kind of doubt. He took the stairs, the sun hot on his shoulders. He met the same dark inside, the same smell. He pushed through the narthex, into the nave; and for an instant it was as if no time had passed, either.

"Jesus Christ."

Beckett crossed himself from old habit and pushed deeper into the nave, thinking, *Wrong, wrong, this is so fucking wrong.*

The woman was dead on the altar and hadn't been that way for long. No flies or discoloration; the hair still shone. Even then, he caught the first hint of a sour smell. It was oily and familiar, a death smell; but that's not what made Beckett's stomach turn. He tried to lift one of the victim's arms; found her in full rigor with no sign of dissipation. Three hours at least. No more than fifteen. He lifted the linen to confirm she was nude beneath, took a final look at her face, then pushed outside to find fresh air. The stairs were worn smooth, yet he almost fell going down. From the bottom, it was a twenty-yard stumble, the Johnson grass and dog fennel as high as his waist, the day already different from what it had been. Beckett drew in a breath that burned, then bent as if he might vomit. He closed his eyes, but the world kept spinning. It wasn't the church that made him sick. It wasn't the red eyes or crushed neck, or even its being the third woman dead on the same damn altar.

Beckett knew the girl.

He knew her really well.

———

Forty minutes later, he had the same team back at the church: techs, medical examiner, even Dyer.

"What do we think about this?" Dyer had already asked the same question a dozen times. "Why the church? Why this church?"

Beckett had been there a dozen times, too, as if repeating the same thing over and over might offer some magical revelation. He shrugged. "It was Adrian's church."

"It was mine, too. Same with five hundred other people. Hell, I saw you here once or twice."

"I don't have snakes in my head. I'm thinking Adrian does."

Dyer didn't respond. He circled the body as if unsure what to do. Even now, he had the team on hold outside. He wanted Beckett, alone in the church. The two of them. The body.

"This could start a panic," Dyer said. "You realize that."

"Maybe."

"There's no maybe. The town is already on edge. Any chance we can keep this quiet?"

Beckett thought of all the people outside. Fifteen? Maybe more? "I don't see how."

"So we make no mistakes. We go by the book."

"'Course."

"You say you knew her?"

"Lauren Lester. She worked day care at St. John's, lived on a side street in Milton Heights. She used to watch my kids. My youngest still talks about her."

"Are you too close to this, Charlie?"

"I'll be fine."

"Tell me again about the caller. 'Five walls'? He had to mean Adrian."

Beckett shrugged. "Or wants us to think he did."

"It's the closest thing we have to an ID."

"'Five walls. House of God.' It's not an ID, Francis. It's crazy talk."

"Whoever called knew there was a body."

"Or put it there."

"I want Adrian in for questioning."

"Amen to that."

"Tell me what you need."

"Everything, Francis." Beckett dropped a hand on Dyer's shoulder and squeezed. "I want everything."


Beckett got the cadaver dog an hour before sunset. It came in the back of a marked cruiser, a black Lab named Solo on loan from the SBI office in Charlotte. "Hey, Charlie. Sorry about the holdup." The handler was a young woman named Ginny. Early thirties. Athletic. She opened the back door and let the dog out. "You know that helicopter crash up in Avery County?"

"The tourist thing?"

"We're still pulling bits and pieces off the mountainside."

"Jeez . . ."

"Yeah, I know. Quite the production you have here."

Beckett examined the scene with fresh eyes. Nineteen cars. Two dozen people. The body was gone, but crime-scene techs were scouring the church even as uniformed officers combed the grounds.

"Where's Captain Dyer?"

"I don't know," Beckett said. "Some kind of PR push, probably. You understand what's happening here?"

"Just that you found another body."

"I want to make sure it's the only one. Dog's not too tired, is he? The crash and all?"

"You kidding? Look at him."

Beckett did. The animal was bright-eyed and eager.

Ginny seemed eager, too. "Just tell me when."

Beckett studied the sky, the line of dark trees. The sun would be down soon. The dog whined. "Do it," he said.

Ginny slipped the leash.

———

*He watched it happen from the same knoll across the valley. The dog. The way it moved.*

*Please, God . . .*

*He pushed the binoculars against his eyes. This part was not supposed to happen. The body on the altar, yes. But not his special place.*

*Not the others.*

*The dog moved up one side of the church, and back down the other. It stopped, backtracked, continued. The handler tracked it, light and quick herself. The dog's agitation was unmistakable.*

*The church.*

*It was all the animal cared about. Back and forth, head down.*

*No, no, no . . .*

*He broke cover; couldn't help it. Beckett was involved, now. He was unmistakable. The size. The shaggy head. His arm went up, and uniformed officers jogged for the church. Where was the dog?*

*No!*

*The dog plunged into a clump of bushes. Beckett was there. The handler.*

*No! No!*

*The dog was in the bushes.*

*Scrabbling.*

*Digging.*

"All right. Back him off, back him away." Beckett was in the bushes, the dog scratching at a small door in the foundation of the church. Two feet by two. Peeled paint. Wooden. "You have him?"

Ginny clipped the leash on the collar. "We're good."

When the dog was clear, Beckett examined the door. It was warped, and swollen. He dragged it open and peered into the dark space beyond. "Crawl space. Looks big." He stood; found Ginny. The dog, beside her, was seated but intent on the door. Another whine sounded deep in its throat. "Your dog's impatient."

"That's not a big enough word." She ruffled the dog's coat. "He wants under that church in the worst possible way."

# 21

Faircloth Jones could not remember the last time he'd felt so fine. It was the purpose, he decided, the warm-in-his-bones belief that people needed him.

An old client.

A pretty woman.

He watched her across the rim of his glass. She was worn out. "Can I get you anything else? Another drink? Are you hungry, yet?"

They were in big chairs flanking the cold fireplace. Elizabeth had her shoes off, her feet drawn up beneath her. She smiled, and the old man felt another flutter.

"I think I'll sleep," she said. "Just for a bit. Will you stay?"

"Do you know what should happen?" He leaned forward, put his glass on the hearth. "A gathering."

"There are just the two of us."

"Exactly."

He stood, grinning.

"Are you going?"

"Adrian should be here." Faircloth removed a quilt from the

cabinet and clutched it to his narrow chest. "It's five o'clock now. You sleep for a few hours. Take a shower if you like. I'll rescue Adrian from the tragic ruins in which I am certain he sits and collect takeout on the way back. We can have the dinner we should have had before. A celebration of life."

"I'm not really in the mood to celebrate."

"Yet even the most put-upon must eat." He spread the quilt on her lap and lowered himself beside her. "You're safe here. There's nothing you need to do. No one is looking for you."

"What about Channing?"

"Your young friend is beyond our reach for now; but tomorrow is another day, and her father's lawyers are very skilled. I'll approach them in the morning and suggest a council of war. There is a path, my dear. I assure you of that, and of every possible effort."

"Thank you, Faircloth." Her eyes drifted shut. "Thank you so very much."


The old lawyer crossed the drive, his cane snapping out as the limousine driver climbed from the car. "A short drive," Faircloth said. "A few more hours, then I'll have you home to your family."

"No family." The driver opened the rear door. "No rush at all."

"Very well." Faircloth settled into the soft leather. "Highway 150, then north."

The driver worked the back roads to Highway 150, then circled the city and followed directions to the blacktop that ran to Adrian's farm. Faircloth watched the sun flash red in the gaps between the hills, the shadow and light like days flicking past. "Just over the next hill. A long drive on the right."

The limousine crested the hill, slid down the back side until the road leveled. "Sir?" Faircloth leaned forward as the driver pointed through the glass. "Is that what you mean?"

Faircloth saw the drive, a half mile of crushed gravel that ran through the fields and under trees. Hints of the ruined house were just visible. The car, however, was crystal clear, a gray sedan that blocked most of the drive. Faircloth was pretty sure he'd seen it before.

The driver's foot came off the gas. "What do you want me to do?"

"Pull up behind it. Right on the bumper." The driver did as he was told. They could see men in the sedan, the driver watching in the rearview mirror. "Let's sit tight for a minute. I want to see what they do."

The moment stretched. No one moved.

"Sir?"

"All right." Faircloth pushed his door open. "Let's see what this is all about." He got a single foot on the ground before the sedan's engine caught.

"Careful," the driver said, but his voice was nearly lost as an engine revved and the sedan surged onto the blacktop.

Faircloth choked on dust as it sped away, the metal of it glinting beneath a falling sun. "That was interesting." The lawyer settled back into the car.

"I got the plate number if you want it."

"Good man. Hold on to it for now."

"Down the drive?"

"Indeed."

The limousine moved slowly over cattle guards and washed-out gravel. It crossed a creek and passed beneath an oak tree larger than any other Faircloth had ever seen. The ruined house was desolate in the gloom. Faircloth saw a hint of fire, and then Adrian, very still in the place a wall had once stood. There was no welcome in his face.

"I'll tell you what." Faircloth handed the driver $50. "Go get yourself some dinner. I'll call when I'm ready to leave."

"Thank you, sir." The man accepted the money. "You have my card?"

The old lawyer patted his coat pocket. "I'll call you."

"Sir?"

Faircloth hesitated, one hand on the door.

"Are you sure about this?" The driver meant the gloom and the ruins, the car they'd chased away, and Adrian's murky form. "It'll be full dark soon, and he doesn't seem the most trustworthy sort. No offense if I'm wrong, but this doesn't feel like the right place for a man like you."

Faircloth looked at Adrian, scarred and thin in ill-fitting clothes. "It's the perfect place. You go have a nice dinner."

"Yes, sir." The driver nodded with great hesitation. "If you say so."

"Go ahead, now. I'll be fine."

Faircloth climbed from the vehicle and watched it leave. When the dust settled, he hunched above the cane and watched Adrian approach. "Hello, my boy. I thought I'd find you here."

"Where else would I go?"

"It's a large world, is it not?" Adrian moved out from beneath the trees, and Faircloth met him on the edge of the drive. "I should think you, of all people, might dislike how history lingers in places such as this."

"Maybe I have unfinished business."

"Do you?" Faircloth lifted an eyebrow in what he knew from long years at trial to be his most penetrating gaze. "Perhaps we should speak of that, as I just saw the same, gray car stationed at the end of your drive."

"I'm sure you did."

"Do you know who it is?"

"You honestly think I should tell you?"

"You're upset." The old lawyer was genuinely surprised. Adrian carried tension in his shoulders and in the line of his jaw. The normally warm eyes were anything but. "We're friends, are we not?"

Adrian's head turned, and Faircloth watched him stare across the choked-out fields. The hardness was all in him, as if he'd somehow frozen solid. But, there was sadness, too, the bitter reflections of a deeply wounded soul. "You never visited."

"I tried . . ."

"Not the first month, Crybaby. Those were dark days, my choice. I mean the thirteen years, after. You were my lawyer, my friend."

No forgiveness was in his voice. What he said was fact, indisputable.

"I was too old for that level of appellate work. We discussed as much."

"Were you too old to be my friend?"

"Listen, Adrian." The old man sighed and faced him straight on. "Life changed for a lot of us when you went away. Liz threw herself into life and the living of it. For me, it was the opposite. I didn't care to see colleagues or be with friends. I didn't care to *care*. Maybe, it was depression. I don't know. I felt as if the sun had cooled or the blood in my veins had somehow thickened. I've become adept at analogies and could offer a hundred. Yet, it was my wife, I think, who said it best. She stuck it out for two years, then told me that, even at seventy-two, she was too young to live with a dead man. After she moved out, I barely left the grounds. I had my food delivered, laundry taken out. I drank, slept. Until this week, I'd barely left the house in ten years."

"Why?"

"Why, indeed?" A ghost of smile touched Faircloth's lips. "I think maybe I was heartbroken."

"Not over me."

"Over the law, perhaps, or the irretrievable failings of a system I could not improve. Maybe I lost faith. Maybe I just got old."

"I sent letters asking for help. Heartbroken or not, how could you ignore me?"

"I didn't."

"You did."

"You misunderstand, dear boy. I never got any letters."

Adrian thought about that; nodded once. "The letters were intercepted." He nodded again. "Of course, they were intercepted. They would have had to do that. Stupid. Stupid."

He was talking to himself at the end. Faircloth keyed on something else.

"Who do you mean when you say *they*?"

"Don't look at me like that."

Adrian flashed the dark eyes, and Faircloth thought he understood. He knew prison; had other clients take the long walk. There was always a certain amount of disassociation and paranoia.

"I didn't imagine it," Adrian said.

"Then, let's talk about it. The letters. This mysterious car."

Adrian stepped more deeply into the gloom. Faircloth saw his back, the tilt of his head.

"Adrian?" The old man shifted above his cane. "My friend?"

Adrian ignored the question and looked out at the gathering dark. Without living it, no one could grasp the full truth of what had happened inside. Even Adrian lost track of what was fact and fiction. Was the sky really so dark? Was the old lawyer even there? He thought the answer was yes to both, but he'd been wrong before. How many times had he felt green grass and a warm wind only to open his eyes and find the blackness inside a boiler? The cold and close of a half-frozen pipe? Even friendship itself smelled of false promise. His wife had left him. His colleagues. His friends. What reason did he have to trust the old lawyer's intent?

Only the guards were real.

Only the warden.

Adrian thought again he should kill them. How could he live if they lived, too? How could he ever heal?

"Where are you going?"

Adrian stopped walking; unaware he'd even started. "I'm not the best company right now, Faircloth. Give me a few minutes, okay?"

"Of course. Whatever you want."

Adrian didn't look back. He walked into the field because the sky was largest there, the night's first stars the brightest. He thought the openness would help, but it made him feel small and voiceless, a forgotten man in a world of billions. Even that was okay for a moment. He understood voicelessness and knew more than most about being alone. Survival boiled down to resolution and will; and when such things failed, it hinged on stillness and Eli's words, on the simple act of *going away.* But Adrian didn't want to do that anymore. He wanted his life back, and to confront the ones who'd carved it down to such a thin, poor thing.

What would that look like?

*A conversation?*

He doubted it; and doubt was the reason he spent his hours in the shell of what had once been a proper life. The rage was so great it was a living thing, a creature in the cage of his chest. He wanted to hurt and kill, and then bury it all.

But, there was this thing.

This memory of what he'd been.

Adrian pushed into the field and felt grass on his skin. He'd been a decent man, once. Not perfect. Far from it. But, he'd done the job as best he could; he'd been a friend, a partner, a mentor; he'd loved one woman and failed another. It was a complicated life that seemed more so now, when all he wanted to do was kill five men and plant them so deep in the ground only the earth would remember.

What would Crybaby say about that?

Or Eli?

That was the other thought that kept him from violence. Eli Lawrence wanted Adrian to walk away and build a life. Such was the purpose of every lesson he'd ever taught—to make it through the day, the yard, the rest of his sentence.

*No sin in survival.*

Adrian woke each day with those words on his mind; fell asleep with them on his lips.

*No sin.*

But walking away felt wrong. The warden had been at Central Prison for nineteen years. How many inmates had died in that time? How many had gone insane or disappeared without a trace? Adrian couldn't be the only one, but he didn't kid himself about the risks, either. The warden. The four guards. Adrian knew their names and where to find them; yet they showed no fear at all. They'd appeared at court, and after the boy was shot; they'd followed him to the lawyer's house, and then to his own farm. Did they really think him so weak and broken?

Of course they did.

They were the ones who broke him.

"That's not me, anymore."

But it was.

Memories. Nightmares.

"Stop it."

It could have been a scream, but wasn't. Awake or asleep, it could happen anytime. Memories marched in from the dark: the table and the rats, Eli's death and the questions that came over and again. It was part of being broken, how the horrors rose like water.

"That's not my life."

But it felt like it.

When the final wave receded, Adrian was still on his feet, alone in a field he'd known as a boy. There were no walls or ceilings or cold metal. It should have been over, then; that was the pattern.

But then he saw the car.

It rolled past the field and flashed red where the road met the drive. He heard the engine, the tires. Then it went dark.

"Motherfuckers."

He cut through the field without thinking, and when he reached the road, he stopped. They wore plainclothes, but he knew them. Stanford Olivet and William Preston. Adrian recognized the haircuts, the movements, their faces when a cigarette lighter sparked. They brought it all back, and for an instant, the memories almost rode him down: their smiles like a flicker, their thick hands on his wrists and ankles, holding him as the straps cinched tight, then reaching for the blades, the needles, the sack of rats that moved as if it had a life of its own.

Adrian wanted to pull them from the car, to pound their faces and break his hands doing it if that's what it took. He told himself to move, to do it now; but another image rose. He saw the same men and the same faces, but there when he'd spilled like a dead man from the boiler in subbasement two. Something like pity had been

on their faces, a whispered *Jesus Christ* as they'd shaken rats from
his skin and carried him to a place with light and air and water.

*Poor bastard,* they'd said.

*Poor sorry, stubborn son of a bitch.*

Suddenly, it was too much, the rage and fear, the weight of
submission.

*Do what you're told.*

*Eyes down.*

And that was just regular fear, regular prisoners. Adrian's
damage ran deeper, and only now did he grasp its magnitude. He
was a free man, yet nothing that mattered had changed. He saw
their faces turn his way, their eyes as they recognized him. Olivet
said something, and Preston smiled again, a thick man with pale
lips and small, round eyes. The smile was knowing, and why not?
He knew every inch of Adrian's body, the smell of his blood and
the sound of his screams, the places cut and uncut. Adrian felt a
rush of blood, then a click as some part of him shut down.
Heaviness. Numbness. He saw the car doors open, but from a
distance. The world went nearly black, and when light returned,
Officer Preston had a retractable steel baton in his hand. "What
are you doing, prisoner Wall?"

*Prisoner . . .*

"You think you can just walk up on us like that? You think
you're entitled to that choice?"

Adrian's lips moved, but no sound escaped.

Preston tapped Adrian's chest with the baton. "I want to know
what he told you." He raised his voice the littlest bit. "Eli Lawrence.
You know what I want."

"We're just supposed to watch him," Olivet said. "Just in case."

"Quit whining."

"This is not the place, man. Come on. Cars could come by.
Witnesses."

Preston flicked his wrist so the baton snapped out. He swung
it in a blur; struck Adrian in the neck, then hit so hard on his
kneecap that everything went away but the pain. Adrian ended

up on the ground with gravel in the back of his head. He wanted to move but couldn't, tried to breathe but his lungs were frozen solid.

"Damn it, Preston," Olivet's voice came down. "We're supposed to watch him."

"Just hang on." Joints popped. Adrian saw Preston's face, and a thick hand that came in to slap his cheek. "Are you in there? Hello. You in there, you stupid bastard?"

"Come on, man. This is just pitiful."

"Hey!" Two more slaps. "Where is it? Huh? What did Eli Lawrence tell you?"

Adrian rolled on his side. Preston put a foot on Adrian's throat. "Inside or out, it doesn't matter. You talk to me when I say."

Adrian felt the pressure, but it all seemed distant. The stars. The pain. The man was right. Inside. Outside. There was no winning.

"He's dying, man."

"No, he's not."

"I think you crushed his throat. Look at him."

The foot backed off, and air leaked in. Adrian was spread in the dirt and unmoving, his vision down to a spot of color.

"I'm tired of this Mickey Mouse crap."

Pressure returned, and as Adrian's heels scraped in the dirt, a part of him dug for the fighter he'd once been. He used to fight. On the block, in the yard, the first time they strapped him down or shoved him in the pipes. He believed in the fight, but this time he was dying; he felt it.

But the world, it seemed, was not entirely done with him. Crybaby Jones hobbled from the dark like the ghost of brave old men everywhere.

"You leave that man alone!"

His cane swung up and down, hit Preston on the nose and burst it like a plum. He swung again, and Olivet danced back. Crybaby tried once more but there was no third chance against men like these. The old lawyer was almost ninety and dropped like a dead man from a single blow.

"Jesus!" Preston cupped his gushing nose. "Where did he come from?"

"That's the lawyer."

"I know it's the lawyer, you stupid shit! He didn't get out here on his own." Preston pulled a gun from his belt and pushed it at Olivet. "Check the house. Make sure there's no one else. Take the car. Hurry."

Preston pressed a handkerchief against his nose, then dragged the lawyer from the drive so the car could speed past. Adrian felt the dust, the gravel. He tried to crawl to Faircloth's side, but he was choking.

"Stay put." Preston put the boot on Adrian's throat.

The car was back in seconds. "No one there." Olivet slammed the door. "It's all burned out and empty."

"Give me the gun. Take him." The boot came off, and Adrian watched helplessly as Preston took Faircloth by the ankle and dragged him down the drive. The old man was conscious, but barely. One hand came up as he disappeared into the gloom, and Preston's voice rose. "You're the one worried about cars, Olivet, so let's go."

"Go, where?" Olivet asked.

"Just bring him."

Olivet dragged Adrian to his feet. The night stopped spinning. "Don't make me use this." Olivet flashed another baton. "You know how he is when he gets like this."

"Crybaby . . ."

"Don't talk. Just move."

A hand settled on Adrian's back and shoved hard enough to make him stumble. He kept his feet the first time. The second push took him down; after that, Olivet dragged him, too.

It wasn't far.

Preston had the old man on his back, twenty yards down the drive. "See. No cars. No worries."

"What are you doing, Preston?" Olivet dropped Adrian on the drive. "This is not what the warden wants."

"Ask me if I care."

"He won't talk. You know that. We've been down this road before."

"We didn't have the lawyer before."

"Come on, man." Olivet stepped forward, but Preston was already on his knees with a thick arm around the old man's neck. "We're just supposed to watch. Just in case."

"Look at him, though." He meant Adrian. "Look at him and tell me I'm wrong. He'll break for the lawyer."

"I'll kill you." Adrian found his knees. "Crybaby . . ."

"Hold him," Preston said. "Make him watch."

Olivet brought the baton across Adrian's throat and held him up. Five feet away, Preston did the same thing to the old man. Crybaby struggled, but it was feeble: thin legs dragging in the dirt, spotted hands on Preston's arm. Adrian tried to say his name, but Olivet had all his weight on the baton.

"We'll start slow."

Preston took the old man's pinkie in his fist, and Adrian watched Faircloth's face as the finger broke. He knew how much it hurt, but the old man didn't scream.

Adrian drew in a blade of air, managed, "Stop it. Don't."

Preston took another finger.

"I'll tell you."

"I know you will."

The second finger broke, and when Crybaby screamed, Adrian did, too. He kicked and struggled as Olivet threw his full weight on the baton, and the night went red, then black, as Adrian choked and clawed and went down in the dark.

When he came to, he was alone where he'd fallen. No baton on his throat. Breath scraping in. He had no idea how long he'd been unconscious, but it felt like a long time. Ten minutes? Longer? His throat was dry; blood sticky on his lips. He rolled to his knees, heard voices, and looked up. Olivet and Preston stood above the old lawyer, who was twitching in the dirt, both eyes rolled white as his heels drummed and spit gathered at the corners of his mouth.

"I don't know, man! I don't know!" Olivet looked scared. "A heart attack? A fucking seizure?"

"How much longer will he do that?"

"I don't know."

"He's freaking me out. Make him stop."

"You're kidding me, right?"

"I can't watch it anymore." Preston pulled a gun and pointed it. "I'll kill him right here. I swear to God I will. I'll shoot him in the head. I'll fucking kill him."

He cocked the hammer, and it was as if the lawyer heard. The legs stilled. The hands stopped twitching. The old man gasped three times, and a final shudder rolled the length of his spine. Adrian saw it happen, and the silence behind that final breath slammed the door on thirteen years of fear and submission. His legs were still numb, but he didn't give a shit. Life. Death. All that mattered was Preston's face and the weight of his own gathered fists. The guards turned when he stood, and for a moment showed an utter lack of fear. They thought him the broken man, and why not? After years in the pipes and on the metal bed, it's all they'd ever known of him, the screams and withdrawals, the dark holes of the prison and the faint scratchings of a forgotten man. He was the inmate who maybe knew a secret, and that's how they saw him still—a final mistake—for there was no prisoner left in Adrian's soul and nothing where he stood but the fighter.

"Preston?" Olivet understood first, looking once at Adrian, then stepping back. "Preston?"

But Preston was slow to understand and slow with the gun. He didn't see the rage or hate, so Adrian opened his throat and let it out. He howled as he charged, and though Preston managed two shots, they both flew wide. Then Adrian was on him, driving hard enough to lift him from his feet and move him through six feet of empty air. The gun spun away when he hit dirt, then there was only the fight and the fighter, the spray of blood and teeth as Adrian gave and gave, then went after Olivet and gave some more.

# 22

Beckett slid through the small door, and it felt wrong somehow, the underside of a church. He felt the weight of it above him. A hundred and seventy years. That's how long the building had stood.

"Okay." He reached back. "Give me the light."

Someone handed in the big flashlight, and he shone it around. The pillars were fieldstone, the timbers as thick as his waist. He saw spiders and termite mounds and bits of old debris. The space was immense and low and dark as pitch.

"Someone's been here."

The drag marks were obvious, as if a man had pulled himself through the dust, not once but many times. The track bent past the first stone pillar, then angled for the front of the nave. Beckett shifted his bulk in the tight space.

James Randolph was hunched in the open square, the sky beyond him dark purple. "You sure about this?"

"Why? You want to do it?"

"No, thanks. After fifty-four years I'm close enough to damnation as it is. Looking for bodies under a church might just push me over the edge."

Beckett shone the light on the tracks. "Drag marks point that way."

"The altar's that way."

"The thought occurred to me." Beckett shone the light around some more. Clearance between the dirt and timbers was two feet or less. "I'm a little big for this. If I get stuck or call you, you come running."

"Not a chance in hell."

Beckett didn't know if Randolph was serious or not. He twisted around again, got on his belly. "Just find Dyer," he said. "Get him outhere."

After that, it was just Beckett and the dark space under the church. He stayed clear of the drag marks and after the first pillar, angled to the right, earth and stone gouging his elbows, ruining his shoes. None of that registered because fifty feet in he was feeling the same kind of religious dread as Randolph. How many people had been married or christened or mourned in the church above his head? Thousands over the years, and all the while this raw, rough place was beneath them, this musty, crude, dirt-strewn slit of an oven.

Beckett squeezed beneath another beam.

How far was he, now? Seventy feet? Eighty?

He stopped where a pillar had collapsed and the floor joist sagged. The clearance was barely a foot, so he worked his way around. Even then, wood scraped his shoulders, the top of his head. He choked on sifting dust, and when he cleared the other side, he saw the graves.

"Holy . . . God."

He crossed himself again and felt the kind of chill that only comes once or twice in a lifetime. The graves were little more than mounded earth, but bones protruded from five of them. Finger bones, he thought. A dome of skull. The graves made a narrow arc around a depression large enough to hold a grown man curled on his side.

Yet, it wasn't the bones alone that bothered him

Beckett closed his eyes and took a deep breath, trying to fight the sense of earth pressing up and church bearing down.

"Breathe, Charlie."

Claustrophobia had never been a problem, but he was under the altar—directly beneath it. So were the graves.

Nine of them.

"Come on, come on."

He rolled on his side and imagined all the people who'd moved through the church in the last 170 years. He felt them like ghosts above his head, the infants and the prayerful, the newlyweds and the newly dead. Lives had turned on the altar above him, and bodies here, in this place . . .

It was a desecration.

Beckett closed his eyes, then looked up at the massive joists. They were black with age, thick as a man's waist.

He almost missed the bit of color.

It was small and faded, no larger than a quarter. He shone the light on it, thought it was the corner of a photograph wedged above the joist. He saw a bit of green, and what might have been stone. Pulling on latex gloves, he reached up and eased the photograph from the crack. It was old, washed out in the flashlight's glare. It looked like a woman beside the church. He tilted it; saw how wrong he was.

Not a woman.

Not quite.

Twenty minutes later it was full dark outside, the air alive with mosquitoes. Floodlights stood around the crawl-space door, and moths the size of Beckett's thumb flicked into and out of the light. Beckett and Randolph stood in the fluorescent hum. They were waiting for Dyer.

"They're getting anxious," Randolph said. He meant the medical examiner, CSU, the other cops.

Beckett didn't care. "Nobody goes in until Dyer sees it."

"You don't look so good."

"I'm fine." But he wasn't. The discovery changed things, maybe everything.

"You say there're nine?"

"Yes."

"I'd like to see them."

"Just mind your own business."

"This *is* my business."

"It's like I told you." Beckett pinched a mosquito from his neck; rolled blood between a thumb and finger. "We wait for Francis."


When Dyer showed up, he looked haggard, his shadow climbing the wall as he entered the ring of lights. He didn't say anything at first, choosing instead to study the boarded windows, the small, square hole behind the ratty bush. "I told you *by the book*."

"I know."

"That means no cadaver dog without clearance from me."

"I know that, too."

"So what?" Dyer's hands found his hips. "We didn't have enough bodies for you? Not enough pressure?"

"What I've found . . ." Beckett shook his head. "I'm not sure Adrian's our killer."

"You button that right now." Dyer studied all the faces watching, then led Beckett to a quieter place at the far edge of the lights. "What do you mean you're not sure?"

"We don't know how long these remains have been under the ground. What if they're only five years old or ten? Adrian's been locked up longer than that."

"If he murdered one, he could murder another nine or another fifty. Maybe Julia Strange wasn't the first."

"Or maybe we have another killer on our hands."

"They could just as easily be old," Dyer said. "Maybe those bodies have been there for a hundred years or two hundred. Maybe the church was built above them for some reason we don't understand."

"The graves aren't that old."

"How can you know that?"

Beckett snapped his fingers and waited for a tech to bring a set of disposable coveralls. "Put these on," he said. "I'll show you."

Under the church, Beckett pointed. "Stay clear of the drag marks."

"There're two sets."

"One of them is mine."

"The other looks fresh."

"It was here before me."

"Don't tell me that."

"That's only part of it. This way."

Beckett went in front. He looked back twice, but Dyer was sliding easily beneath the joists. When they reached the graves, Beckett stopped and let Dyer move up beside him. Shadows danced, and bones flashed gray. Dyer froze when he saw the graves.

"We're directly beneath the altar. Here." Beckett handed Dyer a pair of latex gloves and put on a pair himself. "I count nine graves, laid out in a two-hundred-degree arc." Beckett pointed his flashlight at the bones, the bit of skull. "You see the hollow place in the center?"

"It looks fresh, too."

"Recently disturbed." Beckett shifted so he could see Dyer's face. "Someone comes here."

Dyer frowned. He slid a few more inches in the dry, red earth and put his light on each grave in turn. "They could still be old."

"Look at this." Beckett shone his light on the photograph wedged above the joist. "I found it twenty minutes ago."

"What do you mean you found it? Like that?"

"I wanted you to see it the way it was, so I put it back." Beckett snapped open an evidence bag and reached for the photo, gentling it out and sealing it in the bag. "Do you know who that is?"

Dyer took the photograph and studied it for long seconds, tilting it, smoothing a thumb across the slick plastic. He looked once more at the hollow place, the gray bones, and the mounded earth. "Liz can't know about this," he said. "Not yet."

# 23

Elizabeth couldn't sleep. She came close more than once, but every time she drifted, she jerked awake thinking she'd heard Channing's voice, or Gideon's. Once that happened, her imagination kicked in, and she saw them as they probably were: Channing in general population, Gideon in a narrow bed. They were still her responsibility, so it seemed wrong to be tucked under a soft blanket with long views of purple water. So instead of sleeping, Elizabeth prowled the house. She walked long halls beneath carved beams. She fixed another drink, then stepped onto the deck and thought of other times and other waters.

The car, when it came, was like a voice in the woods.

Elizabeth walked back through the house and onto the rear porch in time to see the limousine roll to a stop.

"Where's Mr. Jones?" She met the driver, a big man with large features, beside the car. Seen up close, she thought he seemed afraid. How long since they'd left? Twenty minutes? Less?

"You're the cop, right? The one that's in the papers?"

"Elizabeth Black, yes. Where's Faircloth?"

"He told me to have some dinner."

"Yet, you're here."

"Truth be told, ma'am, I'm worried. I've been driving Mr. Jones these past days. He's a nice man, and gentle. Always the kind word, the bit of advice. He's an easy man to care for, and—well—that's the problem."

"Where is he?"

"See, he wanted me to leave him there."

"At the old farm?"

"I didn't want to do it. I told him the man there was not his sort, not with the scars and hard looks and darkness coming down."

"He's at the farm, now?"

"Yes, ma'am."

"And you came to me, why?"

"Because after twenty years driving all kinds of people into all kinds of situations, I've learned to trust my feelings, and those feelings tell me that was a bad place, ma'am, a dangerous, bad place and not right at all for a gentleman like Mr. Jones."

"It's good of you to worry. I mean that. But, Adrian Wall's no danger."

"The old man thought that, too, so I figured it might be the case." The big head tilted, the thick hands twisted white. "But, then there was the car."

*The car.*

Elizabeth turned out of the drive.

*Gray,* he'd said. *Two men.*

That was bad enough: a gray car with two men, parked at the end of Adrian's drive. It had to be the same, first at Crybaby's house, now at Adrian's. But that wasn't the worst of it.

*They left before I dropped the old man, but I think I passed them later.*

*Later?*

*Like they were going back.*

*How far?*

*Three miles, maybe. Edge of town, and driving fast. That's why I asked if you were police. 'Cause it wasn't right, is all. The car. The way they looked at us. 'Cause they were fast moving at the old man, and 'cause something about 'em just scared me.*

They worried Elizabeth, too. William Preston had a dark streak. She'd sensed it at the prison, and on the road above Crybaby's estate. He had the wrong kind of interest in Adrian Wall. Prison guard. Ex-prisoner. It wasn't right. There was an arrogance there, not just complacency but the unmistakable sense of easy violence. That's what thirteen years of cop told her, that someone like Preston had no business anywhere near a man as fragile as Faircloth Jones.

Not after dark.

Not on an ex-con's burned-out farm.

Elizabeth's lights split the gloom as she drove. Tarmac. Yellow paint. In the darkness beyond, houses ghosted past, flickers of gravel and light, cars in silent drives. She was alone on the road, just her and the wind and the last line of bruised sky as full night descended. She crossed a wide creek, then crested a final hill before the road flattened and the farm road snaked in from the right. She made the turn—tires drifting—and saw the fight from a distance, not sure exactly what it was: a car in the drive, figures moving in the slash of her lights. Two men were on the ground, Adrian fighting with a third. Fifty feet closer, she saw that *fighting* was the wrong word. Adrian swung again, and the man went down with Adrian on top, his fists rising and falling and slinging red. The ferocity of it was so extreme that even parked and close Elizabeth sat frozen. Adrian had no expression, the face beneath his fists so pulped and bloody, it barely looked human. She saw Crybaby, motionless, another man down and crawling. For a second more she sat transfixed, then spilled from the car, knowing only that someone would die if she didn't do something.

"Adrian!" she yelled, but he didn't react. "You're killing him." She caught an arm, but he ripped it free. "Adrian, stop!"

He didn't, so she drew her weapon and struck his head hard enough to drop him in the dirt. "Stay down," she said, then ran to Faircloth Jones and gently rolled him. "Oh, God." He was unconscious and so white he looked bloodless. She found a pulse, but it was irregular and thin.

"What happened to him?"

Adrian dragged himself to his knees, head low as he stared at his hands, at the split knuckles and bits of teeth wedged under the skin.

"Adrian! What the hell happened?"

His gaze slid to the second guard, Olivet. He was on his belly, still crawling. Four feet away, Preston's gun glinted in the dust. Adrian staggered to his feet and stepped on Olivet's hand as it reached for the gun.

"*He* happened." Adrian picked up the gun and pointed it at Preston. "William Preston."

"That's Preston? Jesus, Adrian. Why?"

"He was torturing Crybaby."

"Torture? How? Wait. Never mind. No time for that. We need a hospital, and we need it now." Elizabeth cradled the old man's head. "It's bad." She leaned into his breath; could barely feel it on her cheek. "We need to go now."

"Take him."

Elizabeth looked at Preston. The face was broken a dozen different ways. Blood bubbled at his lips. He was unrecognizable. "What about him?"

"Call an ambulance. Let him die. I don't care. He's not riding with Crybaby."

"Help me, then." They got the old man in the backseat of Elizabeth's car. His head lolled. He weighed less than a child. "Come with me."

Olivet moved again, so Adrian put a foot on his neck. "I'm not finished here."

"Adrian, please."

"Go."

"I don't know what's going on, but Faircloth needs a hospital, and he needs it now."

"Go on, then."

"We need to talk."

"Fine. You know the old Texaco east of town? The one on Brambleberry Road?"

"Yes."

"Meet me there."

Elizabeth took a final look at the scene, at beams of yellow light and the two guards, down and broken. "Are they going to die?"

"I haven't decided yet."

Elizabeth struggled with the answer. Adrian seemed cold and untouchable and every bit a killer. He pointed the gun at Preston, and she hesitated: lawyer in the back, half-dead prison guard bubbling in the dust. Would Adrian do it? Pull the trigger? She honestly didn't know.

"Time's wasting, Liz."

*Shit.*

He was right. Only the lawyer mattered. "Brambleberry Road," she said. "Thirty minutes."

Elizabeth reversed down the drive and sensed Adrian's stillness as he watched her go. She braked at the tarmac and in a swirl of dust saw him dragging Olivet by the collar, over the gravel and into the gloom, heading for the same gray car.

She waited for a shot that didn't come.

Behind her, the lawyer was dying.

Adrian propped Olivet against the front tire, just behind the burning lights. He was hurt, but nothing like Preston. That meant a broken orbital and bloody nose. Maybe a cracked rib, based on the way air whistled past his teeth. Adrian had seen worse, experienced worse. He put the muzzle against the guard's heart and used just enough pressure to keep him upright. The man was crying.

"Please, don't kill me."

The words put an unfeeling twist on Adrian's face. How many times had he begged, only to be cut again, beaten again? He thumbed the hammer and thought about blowing Olivet's heart through an exit wound the size of a grapefruit.

"I have a daughter."

"What?"

"A daughter. She's only twelve."

"That's supposed to save you?"

"I'm all she has."

"You should have thought about that before."

"I'm sorry—"

"Don't."

"You don't know the warden. You don't understand."

"You don't think I know the warden?" The night darkened as Adrian loomed above the guard. "His face. The sound of his voice."

"Please don't do this."

"Were other prisoners killed? Others besides Eli Lawrence?"

"I'm sorry about the old man. He wasn't supposed to die. None of it was supposed to be like this."

"Yet, it is. You tortured Eli. You tortured me."

"I did it for my daughter. We needed money. Child care. Medical stuff. I was going to do it just the once, one time, and that was it. But they wouldn't let me go. The warden. Preston. You don't think I have nightmares? That I hate my life? Please. She's everything. She'll be all alone."

A girl. Twelve years old. Did that make a difference? After all he'd suffered, Adrian had two of the five men responsible and could cut the number to three. Preston dead. Olivet, too. That would leave the warden and Jacks and Woods. If he moved fast enough, he could kill them, too. Tonight. Tomorrow. Temptation was a burn, and though Eli chose this time to be silent, Adrian knew what Eli would say if he decided to speak.

*Let the hate go, boy.*

*Freedom. Fresh air.*

*That's enough.*

*It's everything.*

Here was the brutal irony. Adrian had never killed anyone. Not as a cop, not in the yard or on the cellblock. He'd pulled thirteen hard years and had more reason than most to kill a whole host of men. But, he felt the old man out there, the yellowed eyes and patience, the simple kindness that had kept him alive when any other man would have lain down and quit.

*Don't do it, son.*

But, the gun didn't move. It pressed so hard against Olivet's chest Adrian felt the man's heart beat against the metal.

"Please . . ."

The trigger tightened under Adrian's finger. It was too much, too many years. It had to happen, so the trigger had to move. Olivet must have seen the decision in Adrian's eyes, for his mouth opened, and in the stillness of that final moment, of the long, hard second that would be his last, a noise rose in the darkness beyond the field.

"Sirens," Olivet said. "Police."

Adrian turned his head and saw lights far away. They were blue and thumping and moving fast; but he had time if he wanted it. A minute. Ninety seconds. He could pull the trigger; take the car.

Olivet knew it, same as him. "Her name is Sarah," he said. "She's only twelve."


Elizabeth passed the cops two miles over the bridge, but didn't slow. They blew past her in the other direction: two patrol cars and an unmarked unit she swore was Beckett's. They were moving fast—maybe eighty on the narrow road—and she knew they were going for Adrian. At speed like that there had to be a reason, but stopping or turning was not an option. Nothing mattered but the lawyer.

Reaching back, she found his hand. "Hang on, Faircloth."

But no answer came.

She flew through town and hit the hospital parking lot at speed, the slick tires squealing as she bumped over the curb and rocked to a stop at the emergency-room door. Suddenly, she was inside and yelling for help. A doctor materialized.

"Outside. I think he's dying."

The doctor called for a stretcher, and at the car they lifted him. "Tell me what happened."

"Trauma of some kind. I'm not sure."

"Name and age."

"Faircloth Jones. Eighty-nine, I think." Doors slid open. The gurney clattered as they rolled him inside. "I don't know his next of kin or emergency contact."

"Any allergies? Medications?"

"I don't know. I don't know."

"I need to know more about what happened."

The doctor was confident and sure, Elizabeth the opposite. "I think he was tortured."

"Tortured? How?"

"I don't know. I'm sorry."

The physician scribbled a note as the stretcher rolled. "And, you are?"

"Nobody." She stopped at a second set of sliding doors. "I'm nobody."

He didn't argue. There was too much to do, too many ways a man that age could die. "Room four!" he yelled.

Elizabeth watched them go.

When she returned to her car, she slipped behind the wheel and felt how the nurses stared after her. The doctor may not have recognized her, but others did. Would this make the papers, too? Angel of death. Tortured lawyer. For an instant she cared, but only for that instant. She got out of the car and walked back inside, approaching the first nurse at the first counter. "I need a phone."

The nurse pointed, terrified.

Elizabeth crossed the gleaming floor and lifted the courtesy phone from its cradle. Her first instinct was to call Beckett, but he was at Adrian's farm—she knew it. Instead, she called James Randolph.

"James, it's Liz." She eyed the nurse, the security guard, who looked just as nervous. "Tell me what's happening. Tell me everything."

James Randolph had never been shy or slow. The phone call took less than a minute, so that when Elizabeth left for Brambleberry Road, she knew everything Randolph did about the grim, dark underbelly of her father's church. It turned the world upside down.

*New victims linked in death.*

*More bodies in the place she'd learned to pray.*

She saw it as if she were there, but Randolph's final words haunted her more deeply.

*The whole world's looking for him, Liz.*

*Every fuckin' body.*

He was talking about Adrian, and why not? Fresh bodies on the altar. Nine more under the church. Elizabeth had to ask herself again how much she trusted him. She said it was an easy question— that he was still the same man and that nothing *real* had changed. But she saw Preston's face when she closed her eyes and wondered if, even once, he'd begged for mercy.

*Every fuckin' body.*

Elizabeth turned onto Brambleberry Road and checked the pistol on the seat beside her. It was not the Glock she preferred, but when she pulled behind the old gas station and got out of the car, the gun went with her. She told herself it was smart, and only reasonable; yet the safety moved under her thumb. It was the silence and the darkness, the still trees and the scrub and the gray car bleeding into night as it sat under a tree at the back of the lot. The place had been old when she was a kid and was ancient now, a dirty cube on an empty road, a scratch mark that stank of chemicals and rust and rotting wood. Elizabeth understood why Adrian chose it, but thought if it came to dying, the old gas station was as good as any place she'd ever seen. Maybe it would open in the morning, and maybe not. Maybe a body could lie beside it forever, seasons rolling one across the other until the old bones and concrete looked like a single patch of broken pavement. That's exactly how the place felt. As if bad things could happen here. As if they probably would.

"Adrian?"

She stepped over shattered glass and cinder block to where a sliver of light spilled through a crack at one of the rusted doors. Up close, she saw a pry bar and twisted metal. The lock was broken.

"Hello?"

No one answered, but she heard water running beyond the door. Opening it, she saw a single bulb above a grimy sink and a metal mirror. Adrian stood over the smudged porcelain, washing his hands in water that ran red. His knuckles were swollen and split, and Elizabeth felt her stomach turn as he pulled a bit of tooth from beneath the skin and dropped it in the sink.

"It's just what prison does. It's not who I am."

She watched him work more soap into the cuts and tried to put herself in his shoes. How would she fight if every fight were to the death? "Crybaby didn't deserve what happened to him," she said.

"I know."

"Could you have stopped it?"

"You don't think I tried?" He was looking at her in the mirror, his face blurred in the filthy metal. "Is he alive?"

"He was alive when I left him." Adrian looked away, and she thought she saw something soft. A blink, maybe. A flicker. "What did they want with you? Those guards?"

"Nothing you need to worry about."

"That's not good enough."

"It's personal."

"And if Crybaby dies? Is that personal, too?"

He straightened and turned, and Elizabeth felt the first real fear. The eyes were so brown they were black, so deep they could be empty. "Are you going to shoot me?"

Elizabeth looked at the gun, forgotten in her hand. It was pointed at his chest, her finger not on the trigger, but close. She tucked it away. "No, I'm not going to shoot you."

"May I be alone, then?"

Elizabeth thought about it, then gave him what he wanted. She would help him or not—she didn't really know. But this was not the time to worry or plan. Crybaby was dying or dead, and as much as she wanted to know Adrian's heart, what she really wanted was to breathe and be alone and grieve for the places of childhood. "I'll be outside if you need me."

"Thank you."

She eased the door closed but stopped at the end, watching through the crack as Adrian stared long in the mirror, then soaped his hands again, the water running red and pink and then clear. When it was done, he spread fingers on the sink and lowered his head until it was perfectly still. Bent as he was, he looked different yet the same, violent and held together and still somehow lovely. It was a foolish word—*lovely*—but that, too, came from childhood so she gave it a moment. He was lovely and undone, every tortured inch a mystery. Like the church, she thought, or Crybaby's heart or the souls of wounded children. But childhood was not all good, nor were its lessons. Good came with the bad, as dark did with light and weakness with strength. Nothing was simple or pure; everyone had secrets.

What were Adrian's secrets?

How bad were they?

She watched a moment more, but there was no insight in the filthy room with the metal mirror and the dim, greenish light. Maybe he'd killed two men in the drive of his old farm, just shot them dead and left them there. Maybe he was a good man, and maybe not.

Elizabeth lingered, hoping for some kind of sign.

She left when he started crying.


When the door opened again, Elizabeth was beside the shuttered pumps in front of the old station, watching taillights fade a mile down the road. "Are you okay?"

Another car appeared in the distance, and Adrian shrugged.

She watched the lights swell and spill across his face. "You need to leave," she said. "Leave town. Leave the county."

"Because of what just happened?"

"That's part of it. There's more."

"What do you mean?"

She told him about the discovery of another body on the altar, and of the graves beneath the church. It took some time. He struggled with it. So did she.

"They're looking for you," she said. "That's why they went to the farm, to arrest you if they could."

He used a thumb to massage one knuckle, then another, did the same with the other hand. "How old are the graves?"

"Nobody knows yet, but it's the big question."

"And the one on the altar?"

"Lauren Lester. I met her once. She was nice."

"The name means nothing to me." Adrian scrubbed both palms across his face. He felt numb and cold and disconnected. Two women murdered since his release. Nine more bodies found beneath the church. "This can't be happening."

"It is."

"But why? Why now?"

Elizabeth waited for him to speak of conspiracy and the beer can, and how maybe this was part of some elaborate setup. To her relief, he said nothing. This was too big for that. There were too many bodies. "What about the guards?"

"Do you think I killed them?"

"I think you're troubled."

Adrian smiled because *troubled* seemed such a small word. "I didn't kill them."

"Should I take your word?"

She was small on the roadside, unflinching in the way any good cop should be. Adrian walked to the car and opened the trunk. Olivet was inside.

"Why did you bring him here?"

He dragged the guard out; dropped him on the tarmac. Elizabeth was alarmed, but Adrian was unswayed. He pulled the weapon from his waistband, sank into a crouch, and watched Olivet stare at the revolver as if to read the future. Adrian understood that, too, that fascination.

"I wanted to kill him," Adrian said.

"But you didn't."

He saw her pistol from the corner of his eye and smiled because she'd come so far from the frightened girl she'd once been. The gun was unholstered, but low and steady. She was steady.

"Answer a question," he said.

"If you give me the gun."

"The men who died in the basement. Did they not deserve to die?"

"They did."

"Do you feel regret?"

"No."

"And if I told you this was no different?" He put the gun against Olivet's chest and saw Elizabeth's rise beside him.

"I can't let you kill him."

"Would you shoot me to save this man?"

"Let's not find out."

Adrian studied Olivet's face, the fear and bruising and the sunken eyes. It wasn't the daughter that saved him at the farm. It wasn't blue lights or sirens. Adrian could have killed him and gotten away. Even now his finger felt the curve of the trigger. There was a reason though, and it still mattered.

"If I wanted him dead, he'd be dead already."

Adrian lowered the hammer and placed the revolver on the ground. Elizabeth stooped to retrieve it, but he kept his attention on Olivet, leaning close until their faces were inches apart. "I want you to give the warden a message."

"Yes." Olivet tried to swallow, but choked. "Anything."

"You tell the warden you're alive because of Eli Lawrence, and that it won't be like this the next time. Tell him if I see him, I'll make it personal. I'll make it like it was for me." The guard nodded, but Adrian wasn't finished. "Daughter or not, the same thing goes for you. Do you understand?"

"Yes. God, yes."

Adrian stood and studied Liz's posture, her face. Her fingers were still white on the pistol grip, but he could live with that. What mattered was that she was there at all, that she'd come back when she didn't have to, and that she'd exercised restraint where no other cop would have. It was a small thing in a large world, but in the dim light before the old station Adrian felt less alone than he had in a long time, not at peace but not destroyed, either. He wanted Liz to understand that, to know she meant something to him and that it wasn't something small. "You have questions," he said. "I'm not sure I can tell you everything, but I'll try."

"That would be nice."

"Will you come with me?"

"What?"

"You said it yourself. I have to leave this place."

"Where would we go?"

"It's a secret," he told her, and Liz looked down the darkened road. Secrets were dangerous; both of them understood that. But he could tell that she was hurting, and that her life, too, was at a crossroads. "Please," he said; and she looked at him with those clear and telling eyes. "I'm tired of being alone."

They took Elizabeth's car because cops had found Preston, and the gray car would by now be flagged. Adrian directed her to a road that went east, and they rolled through the night in silence, small towns sliding past, the emptiness between them black and flat and whiskered with pine. "Tell me I'm not crazy," Elizabeth said, once.

"Maybe the good kind," he said, and that seemed to fit. She was alone with the man who'd saved her life. He was wanted for murder, and wind was in her hair and nothing else mattered. That was crazy, but she thought it needed to be. Everything else she loved

was beyond her help. Channing and Gideon and Crybaby. They'd
face prison or heal or die, and Elizabeth could affect none of it.
Circumstance had stripped that power from her and left her here
with this man, in this place of darkness and speed and screaming
wind. She could touch the moment and the man beside her, and
that was it. Her own wants were strange to her. Was she a cop or
a fugitive, a victim or some peculiar, new thing?

What about the feelings in her chest?

She risked a glance, but Adrian's eyes were closed, his face tilted
up so wind lifted his hair and streamed it backward. She felt a
moment's connection; and that was the thing, she decided, the one
thing she knew for sure. Adrian had a story, and she was going to
hear it, to know what and why and if anything remained of what
she'd once thought to love.

"Tell me the story."

"When we're not moving," he said. "Once we're still."

"Okay." She frowned and felt the road through the wheel, the
hum of rubber, and the movement of old springs. "Then tell me
one true thing."

"Just the one?" Humor rose in his eyes, a flash quickly gone.

"It'll do for now."

"Fair enough," he said. "I'm happy that you came."

"That's it?"

"It's the truth."

She let him have the moment and the silence that followed. It
was his game, and she'd agreed to play. Tomorrow, after all, was
time enough for reason. Not to say they didn't play things smart.
They stayed off the main roads and watched for cops, passing like
ghosts through one small town and then another. After a final,
long stretch of empty road, he said, "This'll do."

He meant a low-rent motel, lit up in the night ahead. Elizabeth
slowed the car, then turned into the lot and drove past a dozen
old cars brushed with road dust and red neon. The motel was low
and long, with an empty, concrete pool and lime stains seeping
from the mortar. "What town is this?"

"Does it matter?"

They were on the edge of something small, but there were a hundred towns like that in the coastal plains, some of them wealthy, most of them poor. This felt like the latter. "Get us two rooms." Elizabeth parked in front of the office, dug some bills from her purse, and handed them over. "Try for something in the back, preferably at the far end. I'll be back in a few minutes."

Adrian took the money but didn't move. Pale blue doors stretched off to the left. Ten feet away, an ice machine rumbled and clanked. "Where are you going?"

"Do you trust me?"

He looked at the motel, frowned.

"Twenty minutes," she said, and waited until he got out of the car. When he was gone, she drove into town and found what she expected to find: silent streets and shuttered buildings, small men passing bottles in brown paper bags. There were no restaurants, so she bought beer and food at a convenience store that smelled of fried chicken and sweet tobacco. When she took change from the woman behind the counter, Elizabeth asked, "What town is this?" The woman named the town, and Elizabeth visualized a map in her head. Halfway to the coast. A lot of empty space and skinny roads. The name sounded right. "What's here?"

"How do you mean?"

"I don't know. A college? Industry? When people think of this place what comes to mind?"

"Hell if I know." The woman used her teeth to draw a cigarillo from the box. "Not much around here but poor people and swamp."


When Elizabeth returned to the motel, she entered the lobby and inquired about room numbers from the old man working the desk.

"You mean the scarred fella?"

"Yes."

He looked her up and down, then shrugged as if he'd seen it all. "Nineteen and twenty. Left side around the back."

"May I use your phone?"

"I got phones in the rooms."

"I'd rather call from here."

"Long distance?"

"Maybe."

A mean glint rose in his eyes, so she put $10 on the counter and watched the bills disappear.

"Ten dollars buys five minutes." He pushed a rotary phone across the counter and shuffled into a back room.

Elizabeth dialed a number from memory and got the hospital switchboard. "I'd like to inquire about a patient."

"Are you family?"

Elizabeth played the police card, offering her name and badge number, and telling the woman what she wanted. "Mr. Jones is in ICU. Just a moment."

The phone clicked, and an ICU nurse answered Elizabeth's questions. Faircloth was alive, but critical. "A stroke," she said. "A bad one."

"Jesus. Faircloth." Elizabeth pinched her eyes. "When will you know if he's okay?"

"I'm sorry. Who are you again?"

"A friend. A good one."

"Well, we won't know anything until tomorrow, at least. Even then, it's more likely to be bad news than good. Is there anything else I can tell you?"

Elizabeth hesitated because she was hurting for Faircloth, and because the next part was slippery.

"Ma'am?"

"Yes, I'm sorry. Do you know anything about a man found beaten on the roadside north of town? Early forties. Thickset. Uniformed officers would have called it in or transported him directly."

"Oh, yeah. Everyone's talking about that."

"What are they saying?"

The nurse told her, and Elizabeth may or may not have said

good-bye. She hung up the phone, walked into the night, and sat for long minutes in the car. Crybaby was still alive—the best possible news—but William Preston was not. He spent an hour in surgery, then died on the table, beaten to death, the nurse said, by an as-yet-unidentified person.

*But, that was coming.*

Elizabeth turned the key and felt a hot wind on her neck.

*When Olivet told his story that was definitely coming.*


Adrian sat on the edge of the bed with his back straight. He was worried, but not about normal things. He was going to lose her, Elizabeth, who, other than Crybaby Jones, was the only person alive who'd kept faith in him during the trial. He'd find her face first thing in the morning, front row as they led him in, shackled. He'd look for her, too, at day's end. A final glimpse before they took him away. A nod that said, *Yes, I believe you did not kill her.*

But, that was a long time ago, and there were other issues, now. Olivet. Preston. He'd seen the way she looked at him, his bloody hands. She wanted him to be the same. He wasn't.

"What do I do?"

He was talking to himself, the room, the ghost of Eli Lawrence. Nobody answered, so he waited for the sound of her car beyond the glass, and only as it came did Eli finally speak.

*Stand tall, boy.*

Adrian closed his eyes, but felt the room around him. "She saw what I did."

*So?*

"You saw how she looked at me."

*You're only what prison made you. You already told her that.*

"And if she doesn't believe?"

*Convince her.*

"How?"

Eli didn't answer, but Adrian knew what he would say.

*Tell her the truth, son.*

*If she's all you have left, then tell her everything.*

Adrian thought that made sense but had no idea how to do it. She'd think him delusional or untruthful or both. It was all so jumbled and fragmented: the things that were real, the things imagined. How could she possibly believe that, for years, his waking hours had been worse than the worst nightmare? She couldn't. She wouldn't.

A minute later, she knocked on the door.

"You came back." He smiled, trying for a joke as he stepped aside to let her in.

She put a bag on the dresser, and bottles clanked. Something was different. She was stiff, unyielding.

"What?"

"Officer Preston is dead."

"Are you certain?"

"He died in surgery."

Adrian tried to get his head around that. The beating had been about Crybaby and past hurts and blind rage. He'd not meant to kill the man, but he wasn't sad about it, either. "Is this where you arrest me?"

"If that was the case, I wouldn't be here alone."

"Then, what?"

"Give me your hands."

She stepped closer and took his hands. The skin was split, but the bleeding had stopped. She held the crooked fingers, looked at the swollen knuckles, the stippled nails.

"About Preston—"

Elizabeth shook her head, stopping him. "Take off your shirt."

He looked down, ashamed.

"It's okay. Go ahead." She released his hands, and his fingers were clumsy on the buttons. Elizabeth kept her eyes on his face, and when the shirt came off, she guided him to the lamp. "It's okay," she said again; but he flinched when she touched the first scar, tracing its length, and then touching a second. "So many."

"Yes."

He knew what she'd find if she took the time to count: twenty-seven on his chest and stomach, and untold more on his back and legs. When she put her hands on his hips, he said, "Please, don't." But, she gentled him like a child, then turned his back to the light and traced a scar that ran from left shoulder blade to right hip. "Elizabeth—"

"Be still."

She didn't rush. Her fingers followed one scar, then another, a journey that twisted across his back and left him naked in his soul. How long since he'd been touched without pain in its wake? How long since the simplest kindness?

"All right, Adrian." She touched him a final time, both palms cool and flat on his skin. "You can put it back on."

He slipped into the shirt, small tremors still moving in the muscles of his back.

"You want to tell me about it?" She meant the scars, so he turned away, not just because she'd doubt the story, but because that's what prison had taught him. Don't rat. Don't trust. Keep your shit together. Elizabeth seemed to understand, sitting on a narrow chair and leaning forward, her eyes intent, but still soft. "Your scars didn't come from fights in the yard."

She didn't make it a question.

He sat on the bed, so close their knees almost touched.

"Shanks are stabbing weapons. Most of those scars come from long cuts with a thin blade. Did Officer Preston do it?"

"Some of it."

"And the warden."

Again, it wasn't a question; and he shied from the directness of her stare. He didn't talk about the warden. That was primal. Even the guards spoke his name in a whisper.

"The warden tortured you."

"How do you know that?"

"His initials are carved into your back in three different places." She watched his face. He kept his eyes down, but felt the sudden flush. "You didn't know that, did you?" Adrian's head moved, and

Elizabeth leaned so close he felt her breath. "What did they want from you, Adrian?"

"They?"

"The warden. The doctor. The two guards I know about. They tortured you. What did they want?"

Adrian's head was spinning. She was so close. The smell of her hair and skin. She was the only person since Eli to ever care, and Eli had been dead for eight years. It was making him dizzy. The truth. A woman. "How do you know these things?"

"You have ligature marks on both wrists. They're faint, but clear enough to someone who knows what they look like. Most of the wounds were stitched, which means the doctor was in on it. Otherwise, you'd have gotten word out through the infirmary. A phone call. A message. Whatever they wanted, they didn't want you talking to anybody else." Elizabeth took his right hand in both of hers. "How many times were your fingers broken?"

"I can't talk about this."

"That's scar tissue under your nails, those white lines." She touched a nail, and her hands were gentle. "I won't take you back," she said. "If you tell me your secrets, I'll keep them."

"Why?"

"Because I'm your friend. And, because there are larger things happening here. The warden. The guards. Whatever else is going on in that godforsaken prison. That doesn't mean others aren't looking for you—state police, FBI even. Killing a prison guard is like killing a cop. It'll be worse even than before. You can't go back. Not ever. You know that, right?"

"Yes."

"Do you want to tell me what they did?"

"Don't the scars tell you enough?"

"Can you tell me what they want?"

"No." He shook his head and met her gaze at last. "I need to show you."

# 24

Beckett went home at five in the morning. His wife was asleep, so he crept in quietly and undressed by the shower, nudging aside the ruined shoes, leaving his clothes in a heap. Stepping in, he let hot water sluice off the dirt and smell and traces of William Preston's blood. Beckett had seen a lot of carnage in his day, a lot of beatings.

But this . . .

The man's face was just gone. The mouth. The nose. When Beckett closed his eyes, he saw it again, the drag marks and the stumps of teeth, the spilled blood clotted with dust. Preston had been dead now for hours; and the death had catalyzed what was shaping up to be the largest manhunt Beckett had ever seen. SBI. Highway Patrol. Every sheriff's office in the state. Dyer was talking to the feds, and literally screaming every time some bureaucrat dared a no. That was the dangerous heart of it. People were worked up, angry, eager.

And Liz was in the middle of it. The manhunt. The frenzy. She mattered in so many ways, and the world, it seemed, wanted her life ripped to shreds. The Monroe brothers. Now this.

"Jesus . . ."

Beckett scrubbed his hands across his face, but barely recognized himself. He felt sick in his heart, and not from the shattered face or the gray bones or the slick, vinyl bags birthed from beneath the church.

It wasn't even about Liz.

He braced his hands on the shower wall, water beating down, but none of it hot enough or hard enough. He thought of Adrian's trial and of all the women dead in that goddamn church.

*It had to be Adrian.*

But what if it wasn't? What if the bodies in the crawl space were only five years old? Or ten? If Adrian wasn't the killer, did that mean his conviction paved the way for someone else to hunt and kill for thirteen more years?

Nine women under the church.

Lauren Lester.

Ramona Morgan.

Beckett felt them like a weight, as if their souls were stone and steel and stacked eleven deep on the crown of his head.

"Sweetheart . . ."

That was his wife's voice. Distant.

"Charlie?"

It was louder that time, cutting through the steam as the bathroom door swung open.

"Hang on, honey." Beckett dashed water from his eyes and peered past the curtain. Carol was in the robe she always wore, her hair tousled from sleep. "Hey, baby."

"Why are you in the guest bath?"

"I didn't want to wake you."

"Are you all right? You look a little green."

"It's just the heat, the shower."

"You seem upset."

"I said it's the shower!" She shrank away from his voice, and he apologized immediately. "It's been a long night. I'm sorry. I didn't mean to be so abrupt."

"It's okay. I can tell you've had a long night. Do you want some breakfast?"

"Ten minutes?"

"I'll be in the kitchen."

Beckett finished the shower, then shaved and put on fresh clothes. He studied his face until it was steady, then went to the kitchen to find his wife. She looked beautiful as he walked in, a little heavier than the month before, a little more lined and tired. But he didn't care about that. "How's the love of my life?"

She turned from the stove, and her smile faded when she saw that he was fully dressed. "You're going back to work?"

"I have to, baby. No choice."

"Is it that awful man?"

For an instant Beckett feared she saw his thoughts too clearly, that she somehow *knew.* But it was the television, he realized, Adrian's face on the silent screen, his photo inset beneath a long shot of the abandoned church.

"He's part of it."

"I can't believe he's been in our house, eaten at our table."

"That was a long time ago, baby."

She picked up the remote and switched off the set. Lines deepened at the corners of her mouth. "Were you with Liz all night?"

"Not this time."

He slipped an arm around her shoulders, squeezing. She'd always been jealous of the time he spent with his pretty partner. He'd tried for years to make Carol understand that Liz was a friend, and nothing more. But Carol could not accept how much their marriage meant to him, or the lengths he would go to protect it. That was the thing about guilt. Everyone had some tucked away, the only question being how much and how much damage had it done.

He kissed the top of her head; poured a cup of coffee.

"So, where were you last night?"

"The church. Adrian's place. The hospital."

"Is that because of the poor guard who was beaten to death?"

Beckett hesitated. "You know about that?"

"Yes."

"We kept his death out of the news. We were very specific. Doctors. Nurses. We shut that all down. How do you know about it?"

"Oh. The warden stopped by last night."

"What?" Beckett stood so fast his chair scraped across the floor and toppled. "He was here?"

"Jesus, Charlie. You spilled your coffee."

"That doesn't matter. What did he want?"

"He was very upset." Carol dropped paper towels on the spilled coffee, then righted the chair. "He said the dead guard's name was Preston, and that he had a wife and a son, and that they were friends. The warden feels responsible. I assume he wanted to talk to you about it. It's all so horrible."

"When was here?"

"What?"

"Goddamn it, Carol. When? What time?"

"You're scaring me, Charlie."

Beckett released his fists; knew his face was red and swollen. "I'm sorry, Carol. Just tell me when."

"I don't know. Midnight, maybe. I remember he was apologetic about the time. He said he'd been trying to reach you all day, and that you weren't returning his calls. He said he'd come by again this morning."

"Son of a bitch."

Beckett crossed the room, flicking the curtain to peer outside. It was still dark, but the car was already at the curb. "Wait here."

Carol said something, but Beckett was in the hall, then out the door. He kept his stride steady; it wasn't easy. "What the hell are you doing here?"

The car door was barely open when he said it. The warden didn't seem to mind the aggression. "Get in, Charlie." He wore a dark suit. Beckett didn't move. "Your wife looks concerned. Wave to her."

The warden leaned forward and smiled as he waved a hand at the window. It took Beckett a few long seconds, but he did the same.

"Now, get inside."

Beckett slid onto the leather seat. The door closed and the world got real quiet. "Don't ever come to my house," Beckett said. "Don't you ever come to my house when I'm not there. Midnight? What the hell were you thinking?"

"You weren't returning my calls."

"My wife doesn't need to be involved in this."

"Really, Charlie? I think we both know better than that."

"That was thirteen years ago."

"What's the statute of limitations on embezzlement? What about evidence tampering? Or perjury?" The warden wasn't exactly smiling, but it was close.

"Are you watching my house?"

"Not me, no. I just arrived." The warden lit a cigarette and gestured at a second car down the block. "But, I do like to check on things I own."

"You don't own me."

"Don't I?"

Beckett swallowed his anger, thinking how even the smallest pebble could start an avalanche. "We were friends, goddamn it."

"No. *William Preston* was my friend. We were friends for twenty-one years, and now he's dead, his face so badly beaten his own wife won't recognize the corpse."

"What do you want?"

"A prisoner killed one of my guards, one of my closest friends. That doesn't happen in my world. Understand? It breaks the natural order of things. What do you think I want?"

"I don't know where Adrian is."

"But you'll find him."

"Let's get a few things straight." Beckett turned in his seat, large enough to fill the space, and frustrated enough to be dangerous. "You don't own me, and threats are only good to a point. You asked me to keep Liz away from Adrian. Fine. I helped you with that because she's not thinking straight and shouldn't be near him anyway. You want inside track on where Adrian goes and what he does.

That's fine, too. He's a killer, so fuck him. But you stay away from my wife. You stay away from my wife and my house. That's the deal."

"That *was* the deal. It's different, now."

"Why?"

"Because prisoners don't kill guards. Not in my world. Not ever."

It was said so flatly and coldly that Beckett felt an actual chill. "Jesus, you're going to kill him."

"I let you have Olivet so you could issue a warrant, a BOLO, an APB. Whatever you needed. Whatever it took. But this is how it plays between the two of us. You find Adrian for me, and your secret stays safe. Otherwise, I'll rip it all down. Your world. Your wife's world."

"She doesn't need to know about any of this. I'll handle Adrian."

"Handle? No." The warden laughed, and it was bitter. "What do you know about handling a man like Adrian Wall? Nothing. You can't. So, here's what's going to happen. You find out where he is and you call me. You call me first, and no one needs to know about your wife's sins or the things you've done to protect her. She won't like prison, and you won't either. I can promise you that."

Beckett sat silent for a long moment. It was coming apart; he could feel it. "You were supposed to be my friend."

"I was never your friend," the warden said. "Now, get the fuck out of my car."

Beckett did as he was told. He stood in the road, hands clenched as the SUV rolled away, and the second one followed. Most times he could pretend his life was his own, that he'd never spilled his guts to a devil dressed as a friend. But he had. He'd been distraught and trusting and overwhelmed with guilt. Now, he was this half man, this slave. He reminded himself there were reasons, then thought of his wife, who was forty-three and gentle and lovely to her bones.

She was in the kitchen when he found her, a ring of blue flame on the stove. "Are you okay?"

"Yeah, sure baby. I'm fine."

"What did he want?"

"Nothing you need to worry about."

"You sure?"

"All is well. I promise."

She bought the smile and the lie, standing on her tiptoes to kiss his cheek. "Grab the bacon for me?"

"Sure."

Beckett opened the fridge and saw the beer can on the top shelf. "What is this?"

His wife looked up from the stove. "Oh, that. The warden brought it for you last night. I told him you don't drink beer, but he said you'd like that one. Isn't it Australian?"

"Foster's. Yes." Beckett put the beer on the counter. It was cold. He was cold.

"It's a shame, really."

"What's that?"

She cracked an egg in the pan, and the edges cooked solid. "You two were so close, once."

# 25

He woke early because he could feel it out there. Endings. Exposure. Police were pulling bodies from beneath the church, and they'd find something eventually. A fingerprint. DNA.

The photograph . . .

Lying in the dark of his bed, he worried most about the people close to him. Would they understand?

Maybe, he thought.

Maybe that was the last piece.

Feeling his way through the house, he went to the bathroom, flicked a switch, and blinked in the sudden light. Whose face was this staring back, whose doubt-filled, aging features? He frowned because life had not always been this way. There'd been youth and promise and purpose.

That was before the break.

The betrayal.

He'd learned since then to hide the emotions that drove him. Smile if expected. Say the right things. But inside him was this raging desolation, and it was not enough to simply live with it. He had to *wear so many masks. They slipped on and off with such ease that he forgot at times who he really was.*

*A good man.*

*A bad one.*

*Spreading his hands on the sink, he stared at the mirror until he found the right face staring back. If an ending was near, he intended to confront it without distraction or regret. It was a new day. He would not fear.*

*In the shower, he scrubbed himself not once, but twice. Afterward, he put on lotion and combed his hair. He shaved with great care and found the appearance appropriate. If the day was to be an ending, so be it.*

*Smooth and slick he'd come into the world.*

*Smooth and slick he'd leave it.*

# 26

Channing was alone in the corner of a crowded cell when the guards came for her. They called her name from beyond the bars, and a dozen inmates looked at her when she stood. Some were apathetic, and others angry that she was leaving and they weren't. No one moved or made it easy for her. One of them touched her hair as a bolt scraped in the lock, and a guard said, "Court."

They put the chains on her then: ankles and waist, her wrists shackled in front. She tried to walk and almost fell. The chains were loud as she learned the shuffle that kept her on her feet and between the guards. She kept her eyes down and listened to the rattle as dim walls slid past and hard fingers dug into the bones of both arms. The guards spoke again and pointed, but she was adrift in a sea of faces. They put her on a bench, and she saw her father and lawyers and a judge. Voices rose and fell, and she heard them all, but from the depths of a haze. The talk was of money and terms and court dates to come. She missed most of it, but one thing stuck.

*Manslaughter.*

*Not murder.*

It was her age, they said. The circumstances. She saw pity in the judge's eyes, and in the bailiffs who treated her as if she were four years old and made of glass. When the shackles came off, they took her through the back to avoid the media camped like an army out front. She rode in a long car and nodded when the lawyers spoke and then looked at her expectantly. "I understand," she said, but did not. Court dates and criminal intent and plea bargains. Who cared? She wanted to see Liz and take a shower. Jail smell was all over her, the reek of it. She tried to be tough, but didn't believe it. The guards called her *prisoner Shore*. The worst inmates liked to touch her skin and call her *China*.

"China . . ."

"Did you say something, sweetheart?"

She ignored the question and a block from the house met her father's eyes by accident. He turned away when it happened, but not before she saw the revulsion. She was not his little girl anymore, but she kept her head up. "I killed them like I said."

"Don't talk like that."

She couldn't grasp that either, the denial and disbelief. He'd seen the autopsy photos. She'd confessed not once, but multiple times. The lawyers were making some kind of argument, she knew. Insanity maybe. But, if the judge asked, she'd say it again.

*I killed them like I said.*

There was comfort in that, but not the kind any man in a suit could understand. She hung on to all the things that made her different from them and kept her gaze level as they drove through the second army of reporters camped at her driveway. The car pulled around back, and even when her father opened the door and helped her out, he kept his gaze averted.

"Your mother will be happy to see you."

She followed him inside and watched the lawyers peel off at the study. "Has she seen the photographs, too?"

"Of course not, no." He looked at her then because it was the first thing she'd said that, in his world, felt normal. "She has a surprise for you. Why don't you go on up?"

He stayed below as the staircase drew her from one floor to the next. Her mother was in a chair by the bedroom door. "Hello, sweetheart."

"Hi, Mom."

A hug died stillborn and awkward. One smelled of white wine and lotion, the other of jail.

"I did something for you. It wasn't easy, but I think you'll like it. Would you like to see?"

"Okay."

Her mother turned the knob and pulled Channing into the bedroom. "Don't you just love it? Please tell me you do." Channing turned a circle where she stood. Everything was as it had been before she'd burned it. Posters. Pink bedding. "I knew you'd want things to be just the way they were."

"I can't believe you did this."

"Do you like it?"

"Like it?" Channing was speechless and close to hysterical laughter. "How could I not?"

"That's exactly what I told your father. 'She's still our little girl. How could she not?'"

Channing looked from one wall to the next. She wanted to scream and run. The pillow beneath her fingers was slick and smooth and pink as a baby's skin.

"Now," her mother said, "how about some hot chocolate?"


Channing's mother floated down the stairs and into the kitchen, where she turned knobs and opened cabinets. Gas stove on, cocoa and organic milk, the frosted cookies her daughter had always liked. It was her fault: Titus Monroe, the drugs, the hollow place in her daughter's eyes. She'd brought those horrible men into their lives. But, she could make it right. Channing would forgive her.

Finishing in the kitchen, she balanced the tray and knocked once on her daughter's door. "Sweetheart?" The door opened to her touch, but the room was empty. "Channing?" She put the tray on the bed and checked the bathroom.

Nothing.

No one.

"Baby girl?"

She listened carefully, but there was no sound in the house, and but a single thing that moved. So, she sat on her daughter's bed and she watched it: the curtain by an open window, and the world like a painting beyond.

Channing knew every backyard and side yard in her block, so getting past the reporters was easy. Escaping the rest was a little harder.

*Hot chocolate?*

*Pink sheets?*

She darted through a formal garden, then slipped out a driveway and onto the sidewalk. With a last look up the road, she turned her back to the reporters and kept walking. She couldn't go back because if she did, she'd be forced to play the game. People would shy from her eyes or pretend nothing bad had happened. There'd be luncheons and teas and stolen liquor. But, her father would never take her to the range again. He'd never share a joke or treat her like an adult. The fog would spread as court dates came and went and lawyers told her not to worry. She'd nod and be polite, and then one day split wide open. Only Liz could relate, but when Channing tried her cell, it went straight to voice mail. She tried again, then hung up and walked faster. Liz lived on the other side of town. By the time she got there, it was still early. Ten o'clock, she thought, or a bit later.

No one was home.

Beyond the glass, the house was dark, the broken door wedged in its frame. For a moment Channing felt dread like a flashback, the memory of shattered doors and rifles and screaming cops. The house felt unsafe, but she had nowhere else to go. Family. Friends. They could never understand what the Monroe brothers had made of her. Was she really this cold-blooded thing?

She looked at her hands, and they were steady.

What did that mean?

Rocking the door from its frame, she checked again for Liz, then lifted a glass from the cabinet and the same bottle of vodka from the freezer. Cops wouldn't come this time—that part was done—but what about the rest of it? She was eighteen years old and looking at real time. Maybe the lawyers could save her and maybe not. Worst case, they said, was five years or seven. But she didn't want to be somebody's china doll, not even for a day.

Taking the bottle onto the porch, she choked down a fast glass, then sat and slowly drank another. She told herself Liz would come, that it was only a matter of time and that she would know what to do. But that didn't happen. Cars passed. The sun walked up the sky. The truth was hard, but in an hour seemed softer. In another, she was pleasantly drunk. That's why she was slow to stand when a beat-up car turned into the drive, and a man climbed out. That's why she was unafraid, and that's why she got caught.

*He knew about Channing Shore. She'd been in the papers and on TV, so everyone did. More important, she mattered to Elizabeth, Liz, Detective Black. The names tripped through his mind as if a single word, and images followed: Liz when she was younger, then as she was today. Channing had a lot of Liz in her face. There was a connection, and he believed in connections. Mostly, though, it was the eyes, and the eyes were the windows to the soul. That wasn't speculation or poetic fancy. He knew how to do it, to break a person down and hold them so long the eyes became windows, in fact. That was the moment that mattered. Breath fails; the heart slows. What rises then is the innocence, the soul.*

*He thought about that as he stared at the girl, alone on the porch. The first time he'd passed by, her eyes were downcast, so he'd driven past a second time and then a third. Eventually, he'd parked two houses away, where he could watch and wait and think about it.*

*He'd allowed the cops to find the last two bodies, and that was part of the plan—because Adrian, too, should suffer. But, they'd found the bodies under the church. That was his fault because he'd not thought things all the way through. He'd been overconfident, and now the church was lost.*

"*I can still make this work.*"

*But it was simpler before: rise from bed, smile, say normal things. When the time came, he'd go to other towns, find other women. That kept things clean.*

*But this . . .*

*It was the media and the attention, all the cops and cop theories, and how big it all was. They were using words like* serial killer *and* psychopath *and* insane. *No one could understand the truth of it—that it wasn't about hate, that he didn't have to do it.*

*So, why was he looking at the girl and thinking of white linen?*

*Because God was like that sometimes.*

*Complicated.*


Channing knew more than most rich girls did about junk cars, and the reasons for that were simple. She liked working-class boys. At school, the clubs. Even when she snuck out to college parties, she tried to find the part-timers and the scholarship kids. She didn't like the buff-nailed, pale-skinned players who were like every boy she'd known growing up rich. She preferred the tattooed and rough-handed ones, those too raw and ready to care if her family had money or not. All those boys wanted were the good times, the escape; and she was the same way. That was before the basement, but she still knew the cars: the slick rubber and throaty engines, the rust buckets and the beaters.

"Do I know you?" He was backlit by the sun, a grown man in cap and dark glasses. Something about him was familiar, but she was deep in the vodka, and the world was a comfortable blur.

"I don't know." He stopped five feet away, the car behind him still running. "Do you?"

A bell was ringing in the back of her mind. He was confident. She didn't like confident.

"Are you alone here?"

She looked at his car, a thirty-year-old Dodge spitting blue smoke. Nothing was right. She felt it, now. The burble under the hood. The man who looked familiar but not really. "This is a cop's house."

"I know who lives here. I don't believe she's home."

He wore work boots and a flannel shirt. The bell was ringing louder. Ninety-five degrees and a flannel shirt. "I can call her."

"Go ahead."

Channing dug the cell phone from her back pocket and managed six digits before the stun gun appeared in his hand.

"What's that?"

"This?" He tilted it. "This is nothing."

She saw dull teeth when his lips twitched, then a hint of profile as he checked the street on either side. Channing pushed another button. "It's ringing."

He took the bottom step.

She stood. "Don't come any closer."

"I'm afraid I must."

She turned for the door, caught her foot on the last step, and went down hard. She touched her head and the fingers came back bloody.

"You have beautiful eyes."

He took the final step and leaned above her.

"Very expressive."

Channing woke in a car that smelled of gasoline and pee and dried-out rubber. It was the same car, the Dodge. She was beneath a tarp in the back, but recognized it from other cars she'd known, the way it ran rough and tilted on the curves, brakes grinding like metal on metal. Her head was jammed against gasoline cans, a greasy floor jack, and what felt like a cardboard box full of rocks.

She tried to move, but plastic ties cut her wrists and ankles. That terror was sharp and real because she understood what that kind of helplessness meant.

Not the theory of it.

The reality.

It wasn't supposed to happen again. She'd promised herself a million times. *Never again. I'll die first.* But truth was different. It was hard plastic and gasoline, her blood in the carpet of a filthy car.

Then there was the crazy.

*No church, no church . . .*

He said it over and over, loud and soft and loud again. Springs crunched as he rocked on the seat, and she pictured hands pulling on the wheel, his back striking split vinyl hard enough to make the car rock. He was familiar, somehow. Had she seen him somewhere? The television? The newspaper?

She didn't know; couldn't think.

She twisted her wrists, and the plastic cut. She worked harder and felt pain sharp enough to slice her open. It felt exactly the same.

*The wires . . .*

*The plastic . . .*

Before she knew it, she was thrashing against the cardboard, the sides of the car. She felt as if she were screaming, but was not. In her mouth, she tasted blood.

"Please, don't do that." The craziness fell out of his voice. The words were soft.

She stopped. "What do you want? Why are you doing this?"

"Ours is not to wonder why."

"Please . . ."

"Hush, now."

"Let me go."

"I don't want to hurt you, but I will."

She believed him. It was the voice, the sudden, crazy calm. She held still as the car turned right, rose up, and thumped over railroad tracks. Metal rattled behind her, as the car angled back down.

The tarp shifted, and through a crack she saw tree limbs and phone poles and arcs of black cable.

*West,* she thought. *They were moving west.*

But what did that matter? They were moving faster, now. No sounds of other cars, no billboards or signs. When the car slowed, it made another turn, then jolted over broken ground for what felt like miles. They were off the road, deep in the green. More metal clanked, and her head felt too small for the truth spinning inside it, that God had made this special hell for her, to be taken not once, but again. It couldn't be coincidence, not twice. So swaying in the back of the car, lying horrified in the stink of it, Channing made herself a promise that, live or die, scared or not, it wasn't going to be like the last time. She would kill first, or she would die. She swore it twice, and then a dozen times.

Two minutes later, a silo blotted out the sun.

# 27

Elizabeth drove through the morning fog and felt as stretched and thin as a character in an old movie. Everything was black and gray, the trees ghostly in the mist, and only the road gritty enough to be real. Everything else seemed impossible: the man beside her and the way she felt, the cool, damp air, and hints of swamp beyond the road. Maybe it was the silence or the invisible dawn, the sleeplessness and uncertainty, or the delusory nature of what she was doing.

"This is very hard for me."

Elizabeth glanced right and knew Adrian was speaking of trust. They'd slept in separate rooms and woken to awkwardness and unexpected silence. He was embarrassed by what she'd learned, and she was undone by the memory of his skin. It wasn't the tactile nature of it that haunted her dreams, not the ridged scars or the hard planes or even the resilience of it. She'd dreamed of minute tremors, and of the will it took to force that kind of stillness. She'd seen so many victims over the years, people ready to break or run or simply fold. But he'd stood perfectly still, only his eyes moving as she'd asked him to trust and then touched the most damaged parts of him. Those were the dreams that held her down, long visions of nakedness and heat and reluctant faith.

A fever dream, she thought. That's what Adrian had always been.

Only, now he was not. He watched the water beside them, the glimpses that were black and slick beyond the trees.

Elizabeth asked, "Can you tell me why we're here?"

He didn't say anything at first. Tires hummed, and sudden ripples stirred the water. She thought it was a snake, the way it moved, or the spined back of some enormous fish.

"This is an old swamp," he said. "Half a million acres of cypress and black water, of alligators and pine and plants you won't find anywhere else in the world. There're small islands if you know how to find them, and families that go back three hundred years, hard people descended from escaped convicts and runaway slaves. Eli Lawrence was one of them. This was his home."

"Eli Lawrence is someone you knew in prison?"

"Knew? Yes. But it was more than that."

"What do you mean?"

Adrian watched the forest for a long minute. "Have you ever been in prison?"

"You know I haven't."

"Then, imagine you're a soldier behind enemy lines. You're alone and cut off, but you can see others out there in the mist and the dark, all the people that want to hurt or kill you. You're so cold and scared you can't sleep or eat—you can barely breathe. But maybe you hurt a few of them first, and maybe you get lucky enough to survive the first day, the first night. But everything piles up, the sleeplessness and the cold and the goddamn, awful fear. Because nothing you've ever known could prepare you for being so utterly alone. It drains you from the inside out, renders you down to something you don't even recognize. But, you manage a few days, maybe even a week. There's blood on your hands by then, and you've done things, maybe terrible things. But you cling to hope because you know there's a line out there somewhere, and that everything you've ever loved is on the other side of it. All you have to do is get there, and then it's over. You're home and you're alive, and you think that before long it'll be as if the horror was a dream, and not your life."

"I can see that."

"Being a cop on the inside is the same thing, but there's no line anywhere, and it's not days but years."

"And Eli Lawrence helped you?"

"Helped me. Saved me. Even after they killed him."

Adrian's voice broke, but Elizabeth thought she saw parts of it. "When you say *they* killed him?"

"Preston and the warden, Olivet and two others named Jacks and Woods."

"Guards?"

"Yes."

The road curved left. Elizabeth downshifted, then accelerated through the back of it.

"Eli was my friend. And they killed him for what he knew, not for being a thief or a killer, but for this thing that he alone could tell them. They came on a Sunday and took him. I didn't see him for nine days after that, and when he did come back, it was only to die." Adrian kept his eyes on the swamp, on stalking birds and black lilies. "They broke half the bones in his body, then brought him back thinking he'd tell me the secret he'd refused to tell them. I watched him drown in his own blood and held him as it happened. After that, I was next."

"I'm so sorry," she said; but he didn't care for her pity.

"I wanted them to pay for what they did. I've had dreams of killing them."

"But, you let Olivet live."

"That was Eli, too. That mercy."

"What about William Preston?"

Adrian looked at his swollen hands and nodded once. "I'm fine with that, too."

He said nothing else for twenty minutes. He pointed left or right, and she made the turns as the road dwindled to broken pavement, then gravel and soft, black earth. Elizabeth wanted to know more, but was patient. Besides, broken as it was, the road into the swamp was his confessional, not hers.

"Do you know where we are?"

"Yes."

She considered the unbroken forest. "There're no signs or markers."

"It took seven hours for Eli's lungs to fill with the blood that drowned him. Every word was an agony for him. I couldn't forget them if I tried. He wanted me to find this place."

"Because . . . ?"

"Slow down," he said. "This is it."

Elizabeth stopped in the center of the old road. They were thirty miles from the nearest town, deep in the woods that bled into the swamp. The place he meant was a gash in the trees beside a mound of tumbled stone and a fallen sign that was no more than a square of rusted iron. "Are you sure this is it?"

"It fits what he told me."

Elizabeth didn't like it. The track was overgrown, but not completely. At some point people used it. "What's down there?"

"The reason for everything."

Elizabeth didn't like the answer, either. She looked up and down the empty road, then into the gloom beneath the trees, seeing shadows and vines and broadleaf plants the size of a child. The whole place felt bottomless and forgotten.

"You're sure about this?" Adrian nodded so Elizabeth eased onto the track, scraping through the deepest ruts before the ground smoothed enough to go faster than a walk. "How far?"

"There's an old mill and deep water. A mile or so, he told me. The road should end there."

Elizabeth pushed in; trees closed above them. "This is where he lived?"

"Born here; lived here. His mother died in childbirth, and it was just him and his father. No electricity or plumbing. They didn't even own a car."

It took a long time to cover the mile. When the track broke from the trees, it bent to an abandoned mill that stood beside the rowed teeth of a rotted dock, and water that stretched off in the mist. The mill was ancient. The roof was gone, but bits of paddle wheel remained where a creek pooled behind an impoundment, then broke white over bits of stone. Elizabeth stopped next to the building; saw moss on the wall, and moisture dripping. Adrian got out of the car, and something splashed far out in the mist.

"He used to talk about his childhood here, about family and disappointment, the hard life of a shoeless boy."

Elizabeth peered into the mill. The floors were rotted out, the walls bare stone. "How long ago are we talking about?"

"Eli was born in the shadow of the First World War, but never knew the actual date. The mill was closed when they lived here and had been since the 1800s. They were basically squatters: Eli's father, his grandfather before that. They fished the swamp and hunted, poached cypress for the sawmills, grew some crops. There were other families around, but mostly on the low, small islands far out in the swamp."

"What are we doing here, Adrian?"

But he would not be rushed. He touched the wall of the mill, took a dozen steps toward the rotted dock, and spoke with his hands pushed deep in his pockets. "You have to understand this was an old man talking, ninety or better and looking back on a hard life without phones or power or radio. He'd been decades in prison by the time we met, but could talk about this place like he'd seen it yesterday. He hated it here, you see: the heat and mosquitoes, the lonesomeness and mud and life on the water. He'd be the first to tell you he was young and arrogant and wanted better things. When he spoke of it, though, he was like a poet, the words rough and ready but just . . . perfect. He talked of black mud, and I could smell it. I knew what rattlesnake tasted like, having never tasted it. Same with the suckers and the gars, the catfish and the bullhead."

Adrian paused, and she thought he might be smiling.

"There was a blues club twenty miles down the river, just an open-air shed, really. He'd have to hitch to get there, but there were women at the club, women and liquor and reasons to fight. Every time he'd scrounge a few dollars he'd disappear for days, then come back hungover and bruised and smelling of strange women. His father wasn't like that. He was a hard man, practical and unforgiving. They argued about Eli's choices, and it got violent at the end. When Eli left for the last time, he was twenty years old, broken and bloody and stripped down to nothing. You'd have to know him like I did to understand how strange that image seems. He had this stillness about him, this quiet."

"Why are you telling me this?"

"Because Eli came back one more time. It was sixteen years later. His father was dead or gone—he never knew for sure—but he came back that last time. Right here," Adrian said. "Shot twice and half dead, but here for a reason."

"What reason?"

"That's the question, isn't it?" He looked at the mill, then up the length of the creek that fed it. "Let's take a walk."

"Are you joking?"

"It's not far."

He set off along the creek, and Elizabeth fell in behind him. They clambered around the impoundment and circled the pool, pushing into the forest as the mist thinned and the swamp fell away. They followed the creek for half a mile, then came to a fork where two smaller streams joined at a rocky outcrop. The waterfall was not big—maybe four feet tall. That's when Adrian told her the rest. "In 1946 Eli Lawrence was a young man living on the coast. He was a hustler, a two-bit crook, and like everyone else in that world he dreamed of the big score—him and his friends—of the one job that would put them on easy street for life. In September of that year, Eli thought he'd found it."

They were following the right-hand stream, the bank falling until mud sucked at their shoes. "They had inside information on an armored car running from a bank at the docks in downtown

Wilmington. They knew the routes, the times. Nothing they'd ever done, though, prepared them for that kind of job. Both of Eli's friends died in the shoot-out. One of the guards was killed. The other took three bullets, but lived. Two different bystanders were shot. It was a bloody mess."

"What happened to Eli?"

"He escaped with a hundred and seventy thousand dollars, and two thirty-eight-caliber slugs in his back. He made it here without seeing a doctor. How he managed, I don't know. The wounds were infected by then, the bullets working around where they shouldn't. When he finally went for help, the doctor patched him up and turned him in. Eli got life without parole."

Elizabeth stepped across a gulley. Adrian stopped and pointed. "Does that look like an island to you?" He waded in without waiting for an answer. The water rose to his waist, and then he was out on the other side. "Are you coming?"

Elizabeth stepped in and felt water in her boots, then higher. She pulled herself up the opposite bank, and they picked their way through brambles and scrub until they reached the center of the island and the tree that dominated it. The tree was massive. Its gnarled limbs spread out, some dipping low enough to touch the ground. Age blackened the trunk, yet it rose tall and gnarled, a giant above roots so thick they buckled the earth. "What is this place?"

"All I know is that Eli played here as a boy." Adrian touched the trunk and circled to the other side. "And that after sixty years in prison, it was the only place in the world he ever truly missed. Just this island. Just the tree."

"I've never seen a tree like this."

"He said that from the top he could see the ocean."

"That's eighty miles."

"He wasn't much for exaggeration. If he said he could see it, he probably could."

Elizabeth craned her neck but couldn't see the tree's crown. It rose, enormous and ancient. She tried to imagine a boy climbing it, then perching high enough to see a gleam of ocean eighty miles away.

"What are you doing?" Elizabeth circled the tree and found Adrian on his knees, digging in a hollow spot where rot had long ago invaded the trunk. She watched him scrape in the loose soil, and it felt wrong: the place, the reason. "Please tell me this is not about stolen money."

"Yes and no."

"What does that mean?" He said nothing. "Can you just stop for a minute?"

Adrian rocked back on his heels. Soil stained his hands and left a smear on his face when he wiped sweat from his eyes. "It's not about money or greed, but about the warden and the guards and a man I loved more than life itself."

"I'm listening."

"The warden came to the prison nineteen years ago. By that time, anyone who knew about Eli or the armored car was dead or forgotten. Eli was just an old man destined to die inside. He was a statistic, a number. Just like anyone else. Eight years ago that somehow changed."

"How?"

"Newspaper clippings. Eli's file. I don't know. But, the warden figured out about the shooting and the car, and the fact no one ever found the money." Adrian spread his hands above the hole he'd dug. "This is what Eli died for. This is why they tortured me."

"For money?"

"I said it's not about that. It's about Eli's life and his choices, about courage and will and a final act of defiance."

"Call it what you will, Adrian, your friend died for money."

"Because he refused to be broken."

"For a hundred and seventy thousand dollars."

"Well, that part's not exactly true."

"I'm tired of riddles, Adrian."

"Then give me a minute." He kept digging. When finally he stopped, he leaned in shoulders deep and heaved out a jar, dropping it with a thump. The top was rusted away, the glass smeared with dirt.

Elizabeth pointed. "Is that . . . ?"

"The first of thirty."

She reached for the jar, but stopped short.

"Go ahead."

She plucked out a single coin, smearing dirt with a thumb until it glinted yellow. "How many?"

"Coins? Five thousand."

"You said he stole a hundred and seventy thousand dollars."

"Gold was thirty-five dollars an ounce in 1946."

"How much is it, now?"

"Twelve hundred dollars, maybe."

"So this is . . ."

"Six million," Adrian said. "Give or take."

# 28

Stanford Olivet let his daughter sleep in and started pancakes when he heard the shower run upstairs. It was just the two of them, and today he wanted to hold her close, spend a little time. The kitchen around him was neat and clean, a smell in the air of batter and coffee and gun oil. The .45 was beside the stove. Before that it was beside his shower, and before that, the bed. Olivet was terrified, and not of Adrian Wall.

"Good morning, sweetheart."

"Pancakes. Yes." His daughter moved down the stairs. She was twelve, a tomboy who loved archery and animals and sports cars. She kept her hair short, avoided makeup. Already, she could drive better than most adults. "Are you going to the range?"

She meant the gun. The .45 wasn't his duty weapon, but a military-grade pistol he'd bought secondhand at a surplus store. "I thought I might."

"How's your face?"

She rounded the kitchen island and kissed him gently on the cheek. He had stitches, bandages. Four teeth were loose. "It's okay."

"I hate that your job is so dangerous."

He let the lie stand: that two prisoners jumped him at bed check. Not that Adrian Wall had almost killed him, then inexplicably chosen to let him live. "What do you want to do this morning?"

"I don't know. What do *you* want to do?"

He slid pancakes onto a plate, and she forked a bite.

"Car in the driveway." She pointed with the fork.

He saw it, too. "Shit."

"Daddy!"

"You stay here." He went to the door and took the gun with him.

The warden was already out of the car. Jacks and Woods stayed by its side. "You're supposed to be at work."

"I thought—"

"I know what you thought." The warden pushed into the house. "You thought a few bruises bought you a day off. This is not that day."

Olivet closed the door and trailed the warden into the kitchen. His daughter stopped eating when the warden pointed. "Isn't she supposed to be in school?"

Olivet placed the gun on the counter, but kept it close. "It's okay, honey. Why don't you take breakfast upstairs and watch TV."

The girl disappeared upstairs, and the warden watched her go. "The limp is barely noticeable. How many surgeries was it? Four?"

"Seven."

"Still in remission?"

"I don't like it when you come here."

"I'm offended."

"I don't like you bringing them here, either."

"See, this has always been the problem with you, Stanford. You think you're above this somehow, that your money and conscience are somehow clean. What's your share, now? A half million dollars? Six hundred thousand?"

"My daughter—"

"Don't use her as an excuse. How much did that boat in your driveway cost, or the watch on your wrist? No. You're no kind of hero." The warden dipped a finger in the syrup and licked it. "We've been doing this for a lot of years, you and I. The money and drugs, the dirty prisoners and their dirty little crumbs."

"Don't talk about that here. Jesus. My daughter is right upstairs."

"I don't give a shit about your daughter." The voice was like ice. "You let Adrian Wall kill my best friend."

"I didn't *let* him do anything."

"You didn't *stop* him, either. How should I feel about that? Preston's dead and you're not. Are you a coward, Stanford? Did you beg and crawl as William Preston stood firm and died for the trouble?"

"It wasn't like that."

"Then tell me how it was."

The moment spooled out, and there was hatred there, years of it. Olivet broke first. "Adrian doesn't know anything," he said. "If he did, he'd have told us years ago. That makes following him not just needless, but stupid. He's broken and unpredictable, and we're the ones who broke him. You can't control a situation like that, which means we should have never been on that roadside in the first place. If anything got Preston killed, it was you, your inflexibility and ego and greed."

"Say that again."

"You shouldn't be in my house."

"Here's what's going to happen." The warden smiled a cold, bright smile and stepped close. "We're going to find Adrian Wall, just the four of us. We're going to hunt him down, and we're going to kill him. Then I'll decide if I need to kill you, too."

Olivet glanced at the gun, but the warden was fast and sure, and the gleam in his eyes was like a dare.

*Think of the girl.*

*Of living through the next two minutes.*

"How do we find him?" Olivet cleared his throat and stepped away from the gun. "He could be in Mexico by now. Anywhere."

"He was with the woman last night?"

"Yes."

"He's not in Mexico."

The warden spoke with familiar arrogance. Olivet looked up the stairs and thought he saw a shadow on the wall—his daughter, listening. "Listen," he whispered. "I'm sorry about what I said."

"Of course you are. I understand." The warden picked up the .45, dropped the magazine, and ejected the shell. "We all make mistakes, say things we don't mean." He pushed the .45 flat against Olivet's chest, kept pushing until Olivet stepped backward and struck the sink. "But my friend is dead, and you're not. That means no one walks away from this. You understand? Not you, not me, and sure as hell not Adrian Wall."


Liz followed Adrian back to the mill, each with a jar of coins tucked in the crook of an arm. She slogged through the creek and did the math. Five thousand coins in thirty jars. One hundred and sixty-five to the jar. Maybe one seventy. What was that?

*Two hundred thousand dollars per jar?*

Liz couldn't get her head around that. After thirteen years as a cop, she had $4,300 in the bank and $15,000 in a brokerage account. She didn't care about money—that had never been her thing—but the thought of $6 million buried in a swamp made her head spin. People had died for it, and people had killed. That made it blood money. Did the stain adhere to Adrian?

She watched him move through the green: the muddy pants and narrow waist, the sure, steady movements.

"You okay back there?"

"Yes," she said, and decided that she was. Eli Lawrence was dead, his crime paid for. William Preston deserved what he got, and who was she to judge, anyway? She'd lied about a double murder and harbored not one fugitive but two. "What do you plan to do, now?"

Adrian pushed beyond the last trees and waded through the stream that fed the mill. When he spoke, it was at the car. "Go away, I guess." He took the jar from her hands and put it on the ground beside the other. "Find a place, some other life. It's what Eli always wanted."

Elizabeth let her gaze move across the swamp. Mist was burning off; light fingered through. "What about the warden?"

"I don't need it anymore." He smiled, and she knew he meant revenge.

"And the gold?"

"This'll get me started." He dipped his head at the two jars. "The rest will be there when I come back for it."

Elizabeth looked away from the trust implicit in that statement.

"Come with me," he said.

"You're joking."

"I'm not."

"My life is here."

"Is it really?"

That was a tough question because he knew the answer almost as well as she. The town had turned against her; the job was pretty much over. "It's been a long time, Adrian, since we knew each other."

"I'm not asking you to marry me."

She smiled at the joke, but felt the undercurrent, too. Things between them had shifted, and she thought it had to do with what they'd endured the night before. Maybe it was a tenderness born of touch, or the simple warmth of mutual understanding. Maybe they were both quietly alone, and eager to be something else. Whatever the case, his eyes were less guarded, the smiles a bit quicker. She felt a quickening, too, but feared it was the childhood crush, the fever dream. He was grinning and wounded and hand-some in the yellow light. And were it truly that simple, she might have been tempted.

*Find a place, some other life . . .*

"I don't want to be alone," he said; and it moved her to hear him speak that difficult truth. But others mattered, too. Gideon. Channing. Faircloth.

"I'm sorry," she said.

But at the motel he said, "Reconsider." The smile was back, but the recklessness and easy grace were gone. He seemed needful and nervous, and that was the bitter side of loneliness.

"I'm happy for you, Adrian. That you're letting go."

"But you won't come with me?"

"I can't. I'm sorry."

"Is it because you saw me beat those men?"

"No."

He looked away, stiff-featured. "Do you think I'm a coward? For leaving?"

"I think you're allowed to move on."

"Olivet said there were other prisoners with other secrets. What if that's true? What if there are others suffering as I did?"

"You can't go back," Elizabeth said. "And it's not just the murder warrant. No one will take your word over the warden's. With the guards in his pocket, he's unassailable. It's the genius of what he's doing."

"Because prisoners lie and prisoners die."

"Exactly."

Adrian flushed, the dark eyes troubled as he watched cars blow past on the dusty road. "Maybe I *should* kill him."

"Find a place," she said. "Make that life."

His chin dipped, but not in agreement. "No one outside the prison understands how dangerous the warden is. They don't know what he does or the pleasure he takes in doing it. I'm not sure how I'll feel about that a month from now, or a year. What if Eli was wrong?"

"Even if he was, it hardly matters. Every cop in the state is looking for you, and you need to think that through. If you get picked up for Preston's murder, you'll end up in the same prison under the same warden." He shook his head, but she persisted. "Look at me. Adrian, let me see what I can do. If he's made mistakes, we might get lucky. Some other prisoner. A guard willing to talk. Be patient. As it happens, I've recently met some people in the state police."

He lifted an eyebrow, and his mouth tilted. "Is that a joke?"

"Maybe."

There it was again: the smile, the unexpected flutter. "Okay," he said. "I'll go."

"Good."

"But I'll wait a day in case you change your mind."

"I won't."

"Here. This motel."

"Adrian—"

"It's a lot of money, Liz. You can have half of it. No commitments. No strings."

She held the gaze for a lingering moment, then rose to her toes and kissed his cheek.

"That feels like good-bye," he said.

"That was for luck." She took his face and kissed him long on the lips. "That's the good-bye."


The drive out was hard. She told herself he'd be fine, that he'd manage. But, that was only half the problem. She tasted the kiss, the way he'd kissed her back.

"You barely know him, Liz."

She said it twice, but if knowing was in a kiss, then she knew him pretty well—the shape of his mouth, the softness and small pressures. He was just a man, she told herself, a loose end from the distant past. But her feelings for him had never been that simple. They showed up in dreams, lingered like the taste of his kiss. Even now they worked to confuse her, and that was the thing about childhood emotions: love or hate, anger or desire—they never stayed in the box.


It took time to leave the low country and cross the sand hills, heading west. By the time she reached the center of the state, she'd channeled the confusion into a narrow space behind the walls of her chest. It was an old space, and her feelings for Adrian filled it from long practice. Life now was about the children and Crybaby and what remained of her career. So she took a deep breath and sought the calm center that made her such a good cop. Steadiness. Logic. That was the center.

Problem was, she couldn't find it.

Everything was the kiss and wind and thoughts of her hands on his skin. Adrian didn't want to stay locked away. She didn't want him locked away, either.

"Pull yourself together."

But she couldn't.

The carousel was turning: Adrian and the kids, Crybaby and the basement. Whom was she kidding when she said life could go back to what it had been?

Herself?

Anyone at all?

When she crossed the city line, she stopped at a strip mall to replace her cell phone. The clerk recognized her face from the papers, but didn't say anything about it. His finger rose once. His mouth opened and closed.

"I don't need a smartphone. Cheapest thing you have as long as it calls and texts."

He set her up with a flip phone made of gray plastic.

"Everything's the same? Passwords? Voice mail?"

"Yes, ma'am. You're good to go."

She signed the receipt, returned to the car, and sat beneath blue sky and a pillar of heat. Punching keys, she called voice mail. Seven were from reporters. Two were from Beckett and six more from Dyer.

The last was from Channing.

Elizabeth played it twice. She heard scraping sounds and breathing, then three words, far and faint but clear.

*Wait. Please. Don't.*

It was Channing's voice. No doubt. Faint as it was, the girl sounded terrified. Elizabeth played it again.

*Wait.*

*Please . . .*

She didn't hear the third word that time, disconnecting the phone instead and gunning out of the lot. Channing would have bonded out by now—as wealthy as her father was, there could be little question of that—but where would she go?

Elizabeth called Channing's cell phone and, when she got no answer, steered for the rich side of town. Her father's house had tall walls, privacy. He'd want to keep her there and buttoned down. Maintain control. Avoid the media.

The last part was a joke. Elizabeth saw the news trucks from two blocks out. It wasn't the A-list talent—they'd be at the church or the station—but it was a lot of energy, even for a double killing. It was the optics of race and politics, of torture and execution and Daddy's little girl. No one recognized Elizabeth until she turned for the drive, then the shouting started.

"Detective Black! Detective!"

But, she was through the line before anyone got organized. Fifty feet up the drive she hit private security. Two men. Ex-cops. She recognized them both. Jenkins? Jennings? "I need to see Mr. Shore."

One of the men approached the car. He was in his sixties; wore a decent suit. A four-inch Smith rode his belt. "Hey, Liz. Jenkins. Remember?"

"Yeah. 'Course."

He leaned into the window, checked the seats, the floorboards. "I'm glad you're here. Mr. Shore's pretty upset."

"About what?"

"Your timing."

"That makes no sense."

"What can I say?" Jenkins keyed the radio, told the house she was coming. "Everything's a bitch when your kid goes missing."

"What?"

He stepped back rather than answer the question.

*Missing kid?*

That couldn't be good.

"Straight up to the house. Mr. Shore's waiting for you."

Elizabeth took her foot off the brake, the drive twisting past statuary and formal gardens. The short distance felt longer. By the time Elizabeth parked, Alsace Shore was on the bottom step. He wore jeans and another expensive golf shirt. Twenty feet out, she could see the flush in his neck. "How dare you wait so long?" He stormed across the cobbled drive. "I called the department three hours ago!"

Elizabeth climbed from the car. "Where's Channing?"

"You're supposed to tell *me* that." He was coming undone. No question. Behind him, his wife huddled in the open door.

"How about we start at the beginning?"

"I've explained this twice, already."

"Do it again." His mouth snapped shut because she was cold and hard, and people rarely used that tone with him. Elizabeth didn't care. "Tell me everything."

It was difficult for him to do, but he swallowed his pride and told her about the drive from court and the awkwardness between them, about the pink room, the hot chocolate, and the open window. "She's not thinking right. It's like she's a totally different person."

"I think she is."

"Don't be flip."

"She's snuck out before," Elizabeth said.

"Yes, but not like this."

"Explain."

He struggled, and other emotions broke through. "She was in a dark place, Detective. Resigned. Untouchable. It was as if she'd given up on everything she'd ever been."

"She's in shock. Are you surprised?"

"Jail, I suppose. The threat of prison."

"It's not just jail, Mr. Shore. I warned you about this before. She was abused until she broke, then killed two men in defense of her own life. Did you think to tell her you understood? That maybe you'd have done the same thing?"

He frowned, and she knew he had not. "You've seen the photographs?"

"I don't need to see them, Mr. Shore. I was there. I lived it."

"Of, course. I'm sorry. This day . . ."

"Did she take anything with her?"

"No. I don't think so."

"Leave a message of any kind?"

"Just the open window."

Elizabeth studied the girl's window, remembering her own childhood room and the one time she'd gone down the tree beside it. "She's not a minor, Mr. Shore. The police won't consider her missing until she's been gone for at least twenty-four hours. If anything, they're worried she's jumping bail, which means any looking they do is the kind you probably don't want."

"I don't care. I just want her found."

Elizabeth held his eyes and saw that he was begging. "Do you have any idea where she might have gone? Friends? Places? Something she kept secret or didn't want you to know about?"

"Honestly, Detective, the only person or thing she seems to care about is you."

Elizabeth saw it then, so clearly.

"I love her, Detective. I may not show it, not with the houses, the career, the issues with my wife. I may not show it, but my daughter is my life." He put a palm across his heart, the red now in his eyes. "Channing is my life."

Elizabeth had seen it a thousand times before: people taking others for granted until the others were gone. He was close to tears when she left, a large man, breaking.

She felt the smallest sympathy.

Back at the street, reporters collected at the end of the drive, cameras up and the questions louder. Three of the boldest blocked the exit, and Elizabeth accelerated so there would be no confusion about her intent.

There wasn't.

When she was through she moved faster, skirting the center of town this time, then turning down a narrow one-way street lined with white picket and wisteria. That was the back way into her neighborhood, and it shaved a few minutes off her time, the old car complaining at the first ninety-degree turn. The next street was hers—a shaded lane—and she raced its length without apology or regret. Everything felt wrong, not just Channing's message but Elizabeth's choices, too. She should have kept the girl closer, never left town. Explanations rose in her mind, the possibility of lost phones or resentments or miscommunications. But, nothing was that clean.

*Wait.*

*Please.*

*Don't.*

Elizabeth made the driveway and left the car running. She found a broken bottle on the porch, and a glass turned on its side.

"Channing?"

The door grated on its broken hinge, and she moved through the empty house, calling the girl. She checked the backyard, then searched the house again. No note. No sign. Back outside, she took her time on the porch, finding a flowerpot out of place and a dark smear she knew was blood. She touched the stain, then tried Channing's cell again and found it ringing in a bush beside the porch. She stared at it, disbelieving, then broke the connection.

The girl was gone.

# 29

By the time Elizabeth reached the station a lump of dread had settled in her stomach. Something was wrong, and it was something bad. The message and the blood, the broken bottle and the lost phone. Channing went to Elizabeth's house, but would have stayed there. She had no doubt. The girl was in trouble. But nothing meaningful could be done without access to police resources, and that could be a problem.

The place was crawling with FBI and state police and enough media to make the collection at Channing's house seem small by comparison. She parked across the street, a hundred feet down. The feds were unmistakable with their black cars and stenciled Windbreakers. The SBI investigators were only a shade less obvious. Taking out the new phone, she called James Randolph, who answered on the first ring. "Jesus, Liz. Where are you?"

"I'm parked out front. What's happening?"

"You haven't heard?"

"No. Nothing."

"Christ. Listen." He paused a beat. "Can you meet me in back?"

"Yes."

"Two minutes."

He hung up, and Elizabeth took a right turn to avoid the camera crews and reporters. She worked a wide route, traveling extra blocks to approach the rear of the station from the other side. At secure parking, she keyed the pad and waited as the gate rolled open on heavy-gauge wheels. She saw Randolph on the steps, a cigarette pinched between thin lips. He dipped his head left, and she turned for that corner of the lot, meeting him in a shady place beneath a locust tree that rose from an empty lot on the other side of the fence. "Goddamn, Liz. Where have you been?"

"Good to see you, too." She exited the car. He was worked up, and that was rare for him. James had been around long enough to see most everything. "Can I have one of those?"

"What? Yeah. Sure."

He shook out a cigarette, and she watched his face as he lit a match. She wanted him settled. "Thanks." She leaned into the match. "You okay?"

"Yeah, sorry. Things have been crazy."

"Because of Adrian?"

"Yes and no."

"The dead guard?"

"What? Oh. Him." Randolph raised his shoulders. "Yeah, I guess that's part of it, him being murdered and all."

"What's happening here, James?" He held the gaze; drew hard on the cigarette. "James?"

He flicked the butt; looked miserable. "Ah, shit."


They went through the secure door, and Randolph talked as they followed the long hall and took the stairs up. He told her about the investigation at the church. "Nine more bodies."

"What?"

"Yeah, that's the final count. We dug 'em up, hauled 'em out. They're with the medical examiner, now. Listen, I know this is hard for you, more victims in such a special place."

She stopped him with a raised hand. Everyone considered it her father's church, her childhood home. It hadn't been like that for a long time, but this was too big.

*Nine more bodies?*

*Nine?*

"Are you okay?"

"I will be. Tell me what else."

He led her to a corner near the evidence room. For the moment, it was quiet. Just the two of them, his voice. "Look, this thing's huge, right? SBI is in from Raleigh, feds down from Washington. It's alphabet city with a million eyes looking for the smallest mistake. They're saying it could be the biggest serial killer in the history of the state, and that puts pressure on everybody. Right or wrong, your name's wrapped up in that, now, and I don't mean a little bit. I mean *deep*, Liz, like seriously *deep*."

"Because of the church?"

"Because everyone thinks you left here with Adrian Wall. Because they don't understand the motive or relationship, and because cops get nervous when they can't trust other cops."

"When I left with Adrian, he was charged with misdemeanor trespass that everyone knows is bullshit."

"Yeah well, since then he beat Officer Preston to death."

"People know me here, James. They trust me."

Randolph looked away and actually blushed.

Elizabeth didn't understand at first, but then she did. It was the basement. She'd forgotten that everyone knew the story, now; knew she'd lost control and lied about it, that she'd been subdued and stripped naked and bound like an animal in the dark.

"They think you're damaged goods. I'm sorry."

Elizabeth stared at the floor and felt her own sudden flush. Three doors down, the room was full of FBI and state police and pretty much every cop she'd ever known. "Do you believe that?"

"No." He didn't hesitate. "I don't."

"Then, why the face?"

"Because there's more."

"More of what?"

"The bad stuff," he said. "The really bad."

He wanted her to see the murder board, but it was in the conference room, and that was at the end of the bull pen. "I'm sorry," he said, because going to the conference room meant a long walk through a crowded room, a minute at least with every cop there watching.

"I came here to see Dyer."

"You need to see this first." He led her the rest of the way down the hall. Outside the bull pen door, Randolph kept his eyes on her face and away from her wrists. "It's just a thing," he said."

But it wasn't. He opened the door, and the stares hit as silence spread out like a cone. She worked between the desks, and through the silent men. Eyes followed. The whispers began. Halfway through the room, Randolph took her elbow, but she shrugged it off. Let them stare. Let them judge.

When they made it to the conference room, Randolph closed the door and lifted an eyebrow. "Okay?"

"Yes."

He led her to the far wall, where a half dozen whiteboards were lined end to end. She saw dates and notes and photographs, so much information it was a blur. "Don't look at the board, yet. Look at me." Randolph stood between her and the board. "Thank you. Now listen. Dyer might show up any minute. He'll be angry, so expect it. You're not supposed to be here, and I'm sure as hell not supposed to be showing you this. You need to see it, though, because it will matter to you."

"Okay."

"Forget the bodies *in* the church. This is about the bodies *under* it. Nine of them. All female, all exhumed and with the medical examiner, but we've identified two so far. The first is Allison Wilson—"

"Wait a minute. I know Allison. I grew up with her."

"I know you did."

"She's one of the nine?"

"She is, but that's not the bad news."

Elizabeth held up a hand because she was struggling with the information. She remembered Allison, a pretty girl a year ahead of her in school. She'd made decent grades, smoked cigarettes, and played bass in a grunge band. She'd disappeared a few years after Elizabeth became a cop, but no one made anything of it. The home life was bad; there were rumors of a boyfriend out of state. People assumed she'd run off with him. Now, here she was, dead under the church. By itself, it was a lot to handle; but there was something else, some other problem . . .

"Liz?"

Elizabeth closed her eyes, seeing the girl as she remembered her: strawberry hair, pretty eyes . . .

"Liz." Randolph snapped his fingers. "Are you with me?"

Elizabeth blinked. "Yes. Allison Wilson. Do you know when she died?"

"Not yet."

"Adrian didn't kill her."

"I completely agree."

Elizabeth grew still because his certainty didn't fit. Cops doubted Adrian to the point of hatred. Since Julia Strange, that's what they did. She narrowed her eyes, looking for the trick. "What's changed?"

"The second body."

"What about it?"

Randolph waited a beat, then stepped left to reveal a photograph on the board. "I'm sorry about this. I'd tell Adrian the same thing if I could."

"Oh, my God." Elizabeth stepped closer to the photograph, knowing the smile, the eyes, all of it. "How could this be?"

"We don't know yet."

She touched the photo, remembering the woman as she'd been: beautiful and quiet and somewhat sad.

Catherine Wall.

Adrian's wife.

Elizabeth didn't wait for Francis Dyer to come looking. She found him in his office, on the phone. Beckett was there, too. "Is there something you want to tell me?"

Dyer met her eyes, still on the phone. "No, she's here now. I'll handle it. Thanks for the heads-up." He settled the phone on its receiver. "Apparently, you made quite an entrance." He gestured at Beckett, who closed the door. "That was the FBI agent in command. He wants to know what a suspended detective is doing poking around in what is now the heart of a multijurisdictional operation."

"When were you going to tell me?"

"I'm asking the questions," Dyer said.

"When?"

"Liz, listen—"

She swung to Beckett, hands fisted on her hips. "Don't tell me about task force protocol, Charlie. I know the protocols. I don't care about that." She turned back to Dyer, her voice tight. "When did you plan to tell me that Adrian Wall is in the clear?"

"He's not."

"His wife is a victim. She died *after* his incarceration."

"Adrian beat a prison guard to death with his bare hands." Dyer leaned back and touched his fingertips together. "He may as well have killed a cop."

Elizabeth turned away, reeling from the injustice of it all. Adrian went to prison for something he didn't do. Now, he was wanted for killing a guard he should never have known. "He's lost thirteen years, and now his wife."

"I can't change the fact he killed William Preston. Officer Olivet has given a sworn statement. We'll have DNA soon." Dyer opened a drawer and removed her service weapon and shield, placing them on the desk. "Take them."

"What?"

"Take them back, and tell me where to find Adrian Wall."

Elizabeth considered the badge and understood the offer. She could be a cop again, and word would descend from on high: Liz is in the fold; Liz is one of us. But, readmission came with a price, and the price was Adrian Wall. "What if I told you Channing Shore was missing?"

"I'd tell you she's a grown woman, free on bond. She can go anywhere she wants. Take the badge."

"What if I told you she was in trouble?"

"Do you have some proof of this? Something concrete?" Elizabeth opened her mouth, but knew it was pointless. A smear of blood. A lost phone. "Take the shield. Tell me where to find Adrian Wall."

His palm was on the badge and the gun, his fingers spread. He didn't care about Channing. He wanted Adrian. That's all he wanted.

She pointed at Beckett. "What about you?"

"I think she's an unhappy young woman, and she'll turn up when she's ready. This is more important."

"So it's all about Adrian?"

"Officer Preston had a wife and kids. I have a wife and kids."

Elizabeth stared from one man to the other. There was no give or doubt. "If I give him to you, I want help with Channing."

"What kind of help?" Dyer asked.

"Resources. Manpower. I want her name on the wires. I want her found, and I want it a priority. Local, state, and federal."

"Do you know where to find Adrian?"

"I do."

"And you'll tell me where he is?"

"If you help me find Channing."

Dyer slid the badge across the desk. "Take it."

"I want to hear you say it."

"I'll help you find her."

"All right." Elizabeth picked up the badge; clipped it on her belt. She lifted the weapon, checked the loads.

"That's the easy part." Dyer pushed pen and paper across the desk.

Elizabeth looked once at Beckett, then wrote down an address and room number.

"Don't hurt him," she said.

Then slid the paper back across the desk.

# 30

Channing felt as if she were dying, and that was all about the heat. It filled the silo, pressed her into the dirt. After so many hours, she didn't have any tears left, or sweat. She had the dark and the heat and a single question.

*When was he coming back?*

That was the only thing that mattered. Not why it would happen or where she was, but when?

When would he come?

She rolled onto her knees, her face flat against the hot soil. She could taste it on her lips and in her mouth; feel it in her nostrils.

"One more time."

She straightened, and the plastic ties cut her again. Same pain. Same slickness. The earth tilted in the blackness, but she got to her feet, hands still behind her back, ankles still lashed together.

"I can do this."

She'd already fallen fifty times, or a hundred. It was pitch-black. She was bleeding.

"Okay."

She shuffled an inch, didn't fall.

"Okay, okay."

She tried a hop and kept her balance. She did it two more times, and that was the most she'd managed without going down. That was the pattern. Stand. Fall. Spit out the dirt.

There had to be an exit.

Something sharp.

She tried again and fell as an ankle twisted, and her body whiplashed. She couldn't catch herself, and her face hit hard enough to drive dirt into her throat. She rolled, choking.

"Elizabeth . . ."

The name was like a prayer. Elizabeth would know what to do. Elizabeth would want her strong. But, Channing felt terror like a palm on her back.

*The basement.*

*Now this.*

The palm pressed hard enough to drive everything good right out of her. She'd killed two men, so maybe this was just, to be alone in this place.

Sliding through the dirt, she covered an inch at a time, first on her side, then on her stomach. She was sobbing quietly as she did it, but, at the far wall, pulled herself up and felt her way along it, finding vertical beams every ten feet, each of them as rusted as everything else. It took an hour, or maybe two; but the fourth beam had a narrow edge where metal had rusted away enough to make it sharp.

*So sharp . . .*

Channing backed against it, working her wrists, the zip ties. Skin went with the plastic, but she didn't care.

Now!

It had to be now!

The plastic parted with a snap, and her arms swung like deadwood as she sobbed again and waited for them to burn. When she could move them, she lay on the ground and used the same sharp metal to strip the ties from her ankles. After that, she followed the curve of the wall until she found the door. Made of solid steel, it opened half an inch before the chain outside snapped tight. She stared out with a single eye, saw dirt and grass and trees. Afternoon, she thought, yellow light. She called for help, but knew he'd chosen the silo for a reason. That meant no one was coming. No one was there.

Channing pushed fingers through the crack a final time, then dragged herself up to explore the silo again. The structure was ancient and rusted and crumbling. She went around the perimeter from the door all the way back, tripping twice, then circling again. She found the ladder on the second trip. The lowest rung was high above her head, so she almost missed it, her fingers grazing it once, then coming back. When she pulled it made a clanking sound, and bolts scraped in the concrete. She dragged herself onto it, finding enough strength to reach the third rung, and pull her knees onto the first. When she stood, everything swayed. The ladder was skinny, barely a foot wide. Moving carefully, she climbed another rung, then a dozen more. Twice, the ladder groaned, and each time she froze, thinking it would pull from the wall or drop away beneath her. She managed another twenty rungs before she froze from all the blackness that tried to drag her down. Only the weight on her hands and feet told her which way was up and which was down. Channing closed her eyes and counted to ten.

*The ladder was solid; the ladder was real.*

Ten feet later, the first rung came off in her hand.

It broke quickly, and she spun into the dark, screaming as something in her shoulder stretched and tore. It took a mad scramble to get her feet back on the ladder, another rung in her hands.

But, the damage was done.

She felt all the space below and pushed a cheek so hard into the ladder it ached.

"Please."

It was a useless plea, no more substantial than the air beneath her feet. Channing was alone and going to die. She'd fall or he'd kill her.

That simple.

That sure.

But did it have to be? Would it be like that for Liz?

Taking a breath, she forced herself past the empty space where the broken rung had been. It wasn't easy. The metal was rusted thin, and her mind painted every rung the same.

It would break.

She would fall.

Already, she was fifty feet up, maybe sixty. How tall was the silo? Eighty feet? A hundred? She counted rungs, but lost track when the ladder shifted in the concrete. She held her breath for a hundred count, then started again, thinking, *Please, please, please . . .*

She was still thinking that when she reached up, and her hand struck the dome of the roof. It was inches from her face, and she couldn't see it.

So black.

So still.

But the ladder was there for a reason; there had to be a hatch.

She pushed against the roof and found the hatch easily because it wasn't latched or locked. A line of yellow appeared, fresh air spilling in as she pushed harder and the crack widened. Channing drove the hatch until it fell backward and struck the roof with a clang. Light burned her eyes. Fresh air was a gift. She clung until she could see, then clambered onto the roof, finding handholds and a place for her feet. A breeze blew, and the forest walked away beneath her. Miles of it. Many miles. She leaned out, thinking there should be another ladder going down; but it had broken off years ago. She saw bolts snapped clean, and a tangle of ladder twisting away from the silo halfway down. Everything else was sloping roof and sheer sides. She climbed to the top of the dome to be sure; but there was never any real doubt.

Inside or out, she was just as trapped.

Elizabeth made sure Channing's name and photograph went out to every officer in the county. The FBI stepped up, and so did the state police. That was politics, Francis Dyer holding up his end of the bargain. When it was done, she returned to the conference room. The stares still lingered, but not all of them were distrustful. Maybe, it was the badge. Maybe, the novelty was wearing thin. Whatever the case, she put her back to the glass wall and focused on what she had. There was the message, the blood on the stoop, the broken glass, and the abandoned phone.

Could Channing's disappearance have something to do with the church?

Elizabeth came back to that repeatedly. Too much coincidence, she thought. Too many moving parts. Other women had disappeared; others were dying.

Was there a connection?

Elizabeth combed through the files, the evidence. She worked it all, then ran it again going all the way back to Adrian's conviction, looking first at Julia Strange, Ramona Morgan, and Lauren Lester. They were found in the church, on the altar. What did they have in common? Why were they chosen? They were different ages and backgrounds, different heights and weights and builds. What about the ones found beneath the church? What about Allison Wilson and Catherine Wall?

Photographs of all five women hung from the murder board, and Elizabeth walked the line, studying their faces. Adrian was convicted of killing Julia Strange. Did the others die because the wrong man went to prison?

She walked the line again. Some of the victims were buried, and others posed as if meant to be found. Was that about Adrian?

The questions piled up, yet Elizabeth found herself staring most often at the photograph of Allison Wilson. Something bothered her, and it wasn't a small thing.

"They look like you."

Elizabeth turned to see James Randolph. "What did you say?"

"I said they look like you." He crossed the room and stood beside her at the whiteboard. "Julia Strange. All of them." He touched one photo, then another. "Something about the eyes."

Sixty miles away, armed men gathered in an empty lot two miles from a decrepit motel that rented rooms by the hour. Stanford Olivet was among them, though he did not wish to be.

"The room is in the back. You know the target." That was Jacks. He checked the loads in a Sig Sauer .45, then holstered it. "He's fast and strong, and liable to freak when he sees us. That means we get him down fast and we get him in the van."

"I don't like this," Olivet said.

"When do you ever?"

Olivet looked from Jacks to Woods. They didn't care for him. They never had. "The cops have the same address. You know that, right? They could be here any second."

"Fuck the cops."

"You're joking."

"Just get in the van."

Jacks shoved Olivet through the rear door and rolled it shut. When everyone was in the van, it lurched from the lot and rolled fast until the motel appeared around a bend in the scrub. The building was old, the earth around it sandy and baked. For an instant, Olivet peered into the haze behind them. The warden was out there somewhere. Ten miles away, or twenty. Somewhere safe, Olivet thought. He wouldn't take a chance like this, not with cops coming, too.

"Here we go." Woods twisted in the seat. "Slick and fast and get the hell out."

The van rocked into the parking lot and turned for the back. Olivet rolled a ski mask over his face, said, "Come on guys, masks."

But Jacks wouldn't have it. "Uh-uh. You saw what he did to Preston. I want that son of a bitch to see our faces when we come through the door. I want him afraid and aware. I want to see it register."

Olivet wanted to argue, but they were already past the office and nearing the side of the motel. The parking lot was empty, the pool full of green slime. They rounded into the rear lot, backed up to the door, and spilled from the van, Woods with a sledge,

Jacks with the .45 out of the holster and low against his leg. Nobody said a word. They squared up on the door and, when the lock burst, took the room in a silent rush.

It was empty, the bed rumpled.

"Shower."

Jacks pointed, and they fanned out around the bathroom door, everybody's gun up now, Jacks counting down to three as water stopped running and he eased the door open. Steam rolled out. They saw gray tile, a shower curtain, and clothing on the floor. For that instant, the tableau held, then plastic rings scraped, and the curtain slid back. Behind it was a man in his thirties, and a girl ten years younger. She screamed when she saw them. The man screamed, too. He was skinny, with eyes too large for his face. The girl covered herself with the shower curtain.

Woods said, "Ah, hell."

"You." Jacks centered the .45 on the man's face. "How long have you been here?"

"Please, don't hurt us. There's money—"

"How long have you been in this room?"

"Two days. Jesus, don't shoot me. We've been here since the day before yesterday. Two days. Two days."

"You're certain?"

"Of course, yes. God. Please—"

Olivet saw it coming a second before it actually did. He opened his mouth, but there was no stopping it. The .45 spoke twice: sprays of blood on tile, bits of brain and bone.

"Damn it, Jacks! Why'd you do that?"

"They saw our faces."

"Whose fault is that?"

Jacks ignored Olivet. He collected the casings, then closed the bathroom door and pulled Olivet from the smoke-filled silence. "Get in." He pushed Olivet at the sliding door. "Just get in and shut the hell up."

In the van and accelerating, Olivet skinned off the mask and watched the motel fade into the same, dull haze. He heard sirens rise and watched state police cars blow past in the other direction. There were four of them moving fast; and that's how close it was, he thought.

Seconds.

By the time he turned around, Jacks had a cell phone to his ear. "It's me, yeah. He wasn't there . . . No, I'm sure. Wrong motel, wrong room." The needle crossed fifty-five, then sixty. "Tell your cop buddy the woman lied."

Some people were blessed with the ability to forget bad things. Elizabeth lacked that particular skill, so if she chose to face the ugliness straight on, she could close her eyes and see the past with perfect clarity: the sounds, the slant of light, the way he moved. The memory was about *after*.

It was about Harrison Spivey and her father.

It was about the church.

*Sunlight struck the cross, but it was rosy through the glass and made her think of blood: the blood in her skin, the memory of it between her legs. That color on the cross was wrong, but there it was, salvation and sin and the face of the boy who'd raped her. His reflection twisted in the metal, but it was real, like he was real, a hot-skinned, grass-smelling boy who used to play games and wink in church and be her friend. He knelt beside her as she listened to his lies and pretensions of remorse. He said the words because her father told him to; and like the follower she'd always been, Elizabeth said them, too.*

*"Our father . . ."*

*Damn you for letting this happen to me.*

*She kept the last part to herself because that's what her life had become, a veil of normalcy stretched across a well of hurt. She ate and went to school and allowed her father to pray by her bed, to kneel in the dark and ask God to forgive her.*

*Not just the boy.*

*Her.*

*She lacked trust, he said. Trust in God's purpose, and in her father's wisdom. "The child you carry is a gift."*

*But, it was no gift, and the boy kneeling in her father's church was no giver. She could see him from the corner of her eye, the beads of sweat on his neck, the fingers squeezed white as he repeated the words of prayer and pressed his forehead so hard against the altar she thought it, too, might bleed.*

*They spent five hours on their knees, but there was no forgiveness in her.*

*"I want the police."*

*She said it many times, a whisper; but her father believed in redemption above all things, so urged her to stillness and heart and greater prayer.*

*"There is a path," he said.*

*But there was no such thing for Elizabeth. She had no God to trust, and no father, either.*

*"Take his hand," her father said; and Elizabeth did. "Now, look in his eyes and tell him you find it in your heart to forgive."*

*"I'm so sorry, Liz." The boy was crying.*

*"Tell him," her father said. "Show him your eyes and tell him."*

*But she could not do it, not now and not ever, not if heat was salvation itself and she was offered all the fires of hell.*

The painful memory filled Elizabeth with equally painful questions. She couldn't see the whole picture, but possibilities were lining up: the church, the altar, the women who looked like her.

Could a teenage rapist grow into something worse?

Maybe.

But, had he?

After that day at the church, Harrison Spivey spent three summers working for her father. Mowing grass. Painting. Digging graves with the ancient backhoe. To him it was penance, and to her one more reason to leave. Yet he'd spent hours kneeling at that altar, knew every inch of the grounds and building. She needed to confirm something else, too—something to do with Allison Wilson. Elizabeth picked up her keys, surprised when she turned and bumped into James Randolph. She'd forgotten he was there.

It was the memory.

The burn.

"I can't let you go just yet." His hand settled on her arm. She looked at it. "Please, you need to see this one last thing." Her eyes rose to his face. He looked old, but alert and scrubbed and sincere. "Here," he said. "Sit."

He took the other chair and looked out at the cops in the bull pen. He sat close enough for her to smell the aftershave, the mint on his breath. Were people watching? That was his concern. "There's orders," he said. "And then there's orders." His hand went into a jacket pocket. "You're not supposed to see this. Dyer thinks you'll freak or something, so he sent the word down. Me, I think you need to know. Safety and shit. Common sense."

Elizabeth waited. The hand stayed in the pocket.

He flicked another glance through the glass, and when the hand came out, it held an evidence bag. Elizabeth couldn't tell what was in it, but it was flat and small and looked as if it could be a photograph. "Beckett found this under the church. It was wedged behind a floor joist above the bodies. Only a few people know about it." Randolph pressed slick plastic against her leg, said, "Keep it low."

He moved his hand, and Elizabeth trapped the plastic with three fingers. She saw the back of the photograph. The paper was yellowed, the edges tattered. "Under the church?"

"Right above the bodies."

She turned it over; stared for long seconds. Randolph watched her face. She couldn't move or speak.

He gave her a moment, then tilted his head so he could look at it straight on. "I didn't think it was you, but Dyer says it is. He says he knew you from church and childhood, that even that young and long-haired he knew it was you the second he saw it. I'm guessing you're what? Fifteen?"

"Seventeen."

The word was an exhalation of loss. The photograph was faded and cracked and water-stained. In it, she wore a plain dress with her hair drawn back and tied with a black ribbon. She was walking near the church. Wasn't smiling. Wasn't sad. She wasn't there at all. Not really.

"Do you remember this photograph?"

She shook her head, and it was not a total lie. She'd never seen the photograph, but she knew the dress, the day. "Did you find fingerprints?"

"No. We're thinking gloves. Are you okay?" She said she was, but tears were on her face. "Jesus, Liz. Breathe."

She tried, but it was hard. She remembered the walk by the church.

Five weeks after she was raped.

The day before she killed her baby.


Elizabeth was still glassy-eyed when she stepped into the bull pen. In seconds, everyone was looking at her, but she barely noticed. She was thinking of a black ribbon in hair that hung halfway to her waist. As a girl, her ribbons had always been blue or red or yellow—the only real colors she was allowed. But she'd twined a black one in her hair that single day, and her thoughts were trapped there on that ribbon, as if she could touch it or take it back.

"Liz!"

She heard her name from across the room, and even that seemed faint.

"Hey!"

It was Beckett, working his big body through the room. She blinked, surprised by the urgency of his movements. He was bulling the crowd, and the crowd was angry. A buzz was in the air, and it wasn't like before. The whispers were back, the distrustful looks.

*Shit . . .* She knew what that meant, too.

"Liz, wait—"

But she didn't wait. She couldn't. The hallway door was twenty feet away, and she was moving—fifteen feet, then five, Beckett still coming. Her hand was on the knob when he caught up and took her arm. She tried to pull it away, but he didn't let go. "Walk with me." He pushed her into the hall and then into an empty stairwell. The door clanked shut, and it was just the two of them, Beckett squeezing hard, the look on his face desperate enough to keep her quiet. He was frightened, and it wasn't a normal kind of fear. "Just keep walking. Don't talk to anybody. I mean it."

He led her down a flight, then into another hallway and to a side exit. He hit a metal door with his shoulder. It crashed against the wall, and they were outside. "Where are you parked?"

She pointed, and he dragged her in that direction. "Dyer knows?"

"That you lied about the motel, yeah."

"I guess word spreads fast."

"You think?"

She looked up and saw faces in the windows, watching. A few men were on cell phones. One was snapping his fingers and pointing. "How bad is it?"

"Dyer's about to sign a warrant for your arrest. Obstruction. Accessory. You made him look like a fool."

Elizabeth saw it, of course. She'd lied about Adrian, and the lie had caught her out.

"Tell me where he is."

"I don't know," Elizabeth said.

"You're lying."

"What if I am?"

"Tell me where Adrian is, and maybe I can make this go away. Talk to the state cops. Convince Dyer to rescind the warrant. You have to give me something, though. A real address. A phone number."

"Francis will settle down."

"He won't."

"So I made him look foolish." They reached the car. Elizabeth pulled her arm free. "I gave him a bullshit address. So what?"

"People died."

"What?"

"State police went to the motel you gave us. They found two people shot dead in the shower. The room still smelled of gun smoke. That's how close it was."

"I don't understand."

Beckett took her keys, opened the car, and got her inside. "Tell me where to find him."

"I can't."

"Can't or won't?"

Elizabeth kept her eyes straight ahead; felt the intensity of his stare.

"I need him, Liz. You can't understand how badly. But please. I need you to trust me."

Beckett was hurting. Was it jealousy? Anger?

"Trust? What trust?" She started the car and let him twist. "You should have told me about the photograph."

"James Randolph." Beckett's jaw clenched. "He showed you?"

"Yeah, he did. It should have been you."

"Liz—"

"Partners, Charlie. Friends. You don't think I had the right to know?"

"Francis didn't want you to know about the photograph. Okay? He said you were vulnerable and weak and that nothing good could come of it. He made a good argument, and I agreed with every bit of it. You're not thinking straight. You're a danger to yourself and everyone around you."

"You still should have told me."

"I couldn't."

"Yeah, well"—she put the car in gear—"I guess that's where we're different."

# 31

Elizabeth went to her parents' house and found them pulling weeds from an overgrown flowerbed by the parsonage.

"Sweetheart." Her mother saw her first and stood. "This is an unexpected surprise."

"Mom." Her father stood stiffly. "Dad."

He pulled off work gloves and beat dirt against his pants leg. "I'll leave you two to talk."

"Actually, this concerns you, too. It's about Harrison Spivey."

The preacher's eyebrows came together, but more worry was in his face than anger. Talk of Harrison rarely happened. They looked away instead. They judged and nursed wounds and pretended.

"I won't talk about a parishioner behind his back unless it's to his benefit. You know that."

How many times had Elizabeth heard as much: togetherness and trust, a raft of days in the palm of God's hand?

"What's this about, sweetheart?" Her mother's worry was impossible to miss.

But Elizabeth had little time for explanation. "Childhood. I remember something about Harrison Spivey and Allison Wilson."

"Allison Wilson? What in the world . . . ?"

"They dated?" Elizabeth said. "There was a fight?"

"They never dated, dear. And it was hardly a fight. He asked her to homecoming, as I recall—"

"And she laughed at him," Elizabeth remembered. "She said he was churchbound and uptight and hopeless. Kids at school made fun of him."

"He was quite obsessed with her, the poor boy."

"What about me?"

"I'm sorry?"

"*Obsession* is a specific and powerful word." Elizabeth pictured the photo found under the church, the tattered image of her as a seventeen-year-old girl, pale-skinned and aching and thin as a waif. "After it was all said and done—after Dad found me on the porch, after the hospital and prayers and recrimination— would you use that same word to describe his feelings for me? He raped me, after all. Held me down. Stuffed pine needles in my mouth—"

"Elizabeth. Sweetheart—"

"Don't touch me." Elizabeth stepped away, and her mother's hand drew back. "Just answer the question."

"You're shaking."

But Elizabeth would not be swayed. Dark wheels were turning; she felt them. "He worked at the church. On the grounds. In the buildings. You opened your home to him. You pray with him. You know him. Did he talk about me then? Does he talk about me now?"

"Tell me what this is about."

"I can't."

"Then I'm not sure we can help you. We've worked so hard, you understand? To forgive the sins of youth, to build on the future. Harrison is not the boy you remember. He's done such good things—"

"I don't want to hear that!" Elizabeth couldn't help the outburst. Even now, her feelings for her parents were complicated: pain and love, anger and regret. How could such things live side by side for so long?

Her father spoke as if he understood. "It wasn't the choice you think, Elizabeth. I didn't choose Harrison over you, but love over hate, hope above despair—the lessons I've taught you since birth: to embrace the difficult path, to accept hard choices and hard love, to be penitent and live in the hope of redemption. I wanted that for you and for him. Can't you understand that? Can't you see?"

"Of course I can, but it wasn't your choice to make! To forgive or not was up to me! Your job was something different, and you didn't do it. You didn't protect me. You didn't listen."

"Nor did I walk away from my family, the church."

"Actually, you did. You did walk away."

"And this is God's punishment," he said. "To see my only daughter grown bitter and hateful and hard."

"I'm not having this conversation."

"You never do. You can barely look at me."

"Mom? May I speak to you in private?"

"Sweetheart—"

"Over here. Away from him."

Elizabeth walked away from her father, found a place in the shade where she could turn her back and not face a burning sun.

Her mother touched her shoulder. "Don't think this is easy for him, Elizabeth. He's a complicated man, and he grieves. We both do, but it's a hard world full of hard choices. He's not wrong about that."

"Don't make excuses for him." Elizabeth stopped her mother with a raised hand. "Just tell me if Harrison Spivey owns a farm or commercial property. A hunting cabin, maybe. Anything not easily found."

"Just the house on Cambridge, and it's nothing grand."

Elizabeth looked at the steeple, at the white paint and the gold cross that looked as cheap as foil. "Was he obsessed with me?"

"He prays for you, here and at home. He prays with your father."

Elizabeth felt cold fingers in the shade. "Is there anything else you can tell me?"

"Only that he was wrong, sweetheart, and that he has sought forgiveness with all his heart. That's what makes you right in your way, and your father right in his. It's what makes this all so awful."

After that, Elizabeth was alone. She had a theory, and it was tied so deeply to her own past that she had trouble looking at it straight on. Harrison Spivey had an intimate connection to the church, to her, and to her family. He could be violent, obsessed.

*The victims looked like her.*

Was Randolph right about that? She didn't know. Maybe some of them. All she knew for sure was that Channing was gone, and the clock was ticking. Arrest. Death. They were out there, spinning. And if a voice spoke of caution, it did so from the deepest corner of her mind. Too many years led to this, too many sleepless nights and buried hurts. The word *Providence* rose, yet even that felt dangerous. This was not about her, she told herself, but about finding the girl.

Then why did that voice, too, sound so distant? It whispered in the drive and drowned in the rush of her blood. She was on the porch of Spivey's house, but it could have been the quarry or the church or the back of her father's car as the boy laid a finger on her skin as if daring her to look up or say a word about the thing he'd done. Elizabeth felt all of that, bottled it, and directed it. No one had to get hurt, and no one had to die.

But, goddamn, she felt it.

The feeling took her through the door without knocking; through the kitchen and into the living room, gun holstered, but warm under her palm. She saw the wife and children in the back-yard, which was good, because she had no plan beyond making the man talk. She flicked a glance left; saw a dining-room table, framed photographs, golf clubs in the corner. The normalcy of it stoked the resentment. Could a killer kill and then play golf?

She felt the answer in her skin; heard an echo of the voice and tuned it out. Noise came from the back hall so she turned in that direction, her footsteps soundless on deep carpet. She found him behind a desk littered with papers, a broad, soft man with a pencil in one hand and fingers on an old-fashioned calculator that rattled and clicked. The sight was so pedestrian it pulled her from the moment long enough to see the danger of what she was doing. The obsession was hers, but when he looked up, he had the same eyes and lips, the same hands that had been so quick with pine needles and buttons and torn fabric. "Hello, Harrison."

He took in the gun, and his first glance, after, was through the window and at his children. "Elizabeth. What are you doing?"

She stepped into the room; watched his face and his eyes, his hands on the desk. Behind him, two dozen photographs hung on the wall: Harrison at different groundbreaking ceremonies, a golden shovel in his hand; Harrison with a group of women, and others with suited men. Everyone was at ease and happy and smiling.

"Where is she?"

"Who?"

"Don't fuck with me, Harrison."

"I don't know what's going on, Liz." He spread his hands. "I don't know why you're here with a gun, and I don't know what you're talking about. Please, don't hurt my children."

She stepped closer, emotion like a wind as she remembered sneaking from the house so she could spread her legs in a trailer park abortion mill and let the pervert who called himself a doctor push cold steel past her cervix. That's what Harrison Spivey did for her. That's what she knew of children. "Where is she?"

"You keep saying *she*. I don't know who you're talking about."

"I introduced you to her on the sidewalk. Channing Shore. I introduced you and now she's gone."

"What? Who?"

"They found Allison Wilson, too. Under the church. Murdered."

"What in God's name does that have to do with me?" He looked genuinely appalled, but psychopaths could do that. Dissimulate. Misdirect. Entire lives could be made of lies, with only the dark center holding.

Elizabeth wanted to see his center. "Here's what we're going to do. We're going to leave quietly. Your family is outside; they won't even see us. We're going to find someplace private, you and I, and we're going to have a discussion. What that discussion feels like is up to you."

"I'm not going to do that."

"Get up."

"Maybe, this is how it had to happen." He leaned back in his chair, and the strength surprised her. He seemed suddenly resolved, with none of the fear she saw on those rare occasions she went to his office or tracked him on the streets. "You really don't know me at all, do you, Liz? What I've done with my life. How I've tried to atone." He gestured at the wall behind him. "Do you even see what's right in front of you?"

Elizabeth let her gaze run across the photographs, seeing how they were the same, but different, picking up detail she'd missed.

"Six clinics. In six different cities. A decade of work. Fifty cents of every dollar I've ever made, and this is just the beginning."

Elizabeth looked at the construction sites and finished buildings, at Harrison with his golden shovel and smiling women. Her certainty wavered. "Those are . . ."

"Clinics for battered women." He finished the thought when she trailed off. "Abused wives. Prostitutes. Rape victims. I don't know why you think I took this girl, but I promise you I did not. I have a wife and daughters. They're my life, Liz. I'd make yours different if I could. I'd take it all back." Elizabeth's confidence broke; none of this was expected. "Speaking of which . . ."

"Hi, Daddy." A little girl stepped in from the hall. She was three or four, with a pretty voice and no fear at all of strangers with guns.

"Come here, sweetie." The girl hopped on her father's lap as a wave of dizziness threatened to sweep Elizabeth away. Harrison wrapped his arms around the child, clasped his hands, and pointed with fingers pressed together. "Guess who this is." The girl pulled her legs onto her father's lap. "This is the woman we pray for every Sunday. The one whose forgiveness we ask God to grant."

"You told your children?"

"Only that Daddy did a bad thing, once, and was sorry." He squeezed the girl harder. "Tell Detective Black your name."

"Elizabeth."

"We named her for you."

"But you run from me when I see you on the streets. You barely speak."

"Because you frighten me," he said. "And because I am ashamed."

Elizabeth stared at the little girl. The room was still spinning. "Why would you give that beautiful child my name?"

"Because some things should never be forgotten." He smoothed the girl's unruly hair. "Not if we hope to live better lives."

*He stayed off the streets as much as he could. Even then he worried someone might recognize the car, his face in the car. He'd never seen cops like this. They were everywhere. Local cruisers. Sheriff's deputies. State police. They were on the streets and overpasses. There'd been talk of roadblocks, and that made him nervous. If they searched the car, they'd find tape and a stun gun and zip ties.*

*He couldn't explain that.*

*How could he?*

*Pulling into a gas station, he threw away the tape and plastic ties. The stun gun he kept because some things needed keeping. The linen and silk ropes were someplace safe. Nevertheless, he sat low in the car as a line of state cruisers flashed by. Things were building, and he could feel them out there, the same endings and inevitabilities. There was a chance he'd walk away and continue, but he was tired of killing and carrying secrets. It had been with him for so long. The weight built, a woman died, and for months after he was depressed.*

*He wasn't supposed to be a killer.*

*Watching the state police fade, he sat straighter as a young father came out of the convenience store and lingered by his car. He had a child in his arms, a boy maybe six months old. He watched the father kiss the child and thought that's how life was meant to be. But nothing was that pure anymore, so he drove for the road and looked once in the mirror as the kiss broke and both seemed to smile.*

*The father.*

*The son.*

*He turned into traffic, not eager yet, but accepting.*

*The silo was seven miles away.*

Elizabeth saw the same cops and felt some of the same fear. Her thoughts, though, were very different.

*Could it be an act?*

She ran the question for the tenth time and came back with the same answer.

*She didn't think so.*

*He had daughters, a wife.*

"My God."

Her hands were still shaking. She'd been planning to steal the man from his children, take him to the woods, and break him. It wasn't academic or some dark fantasy. She'd been minutes away from doing it. Cuffs. Car. Some wooded place.

She caught a glimpse of her eyes in the mirror; found them haunted and bruised. She felt out of control, dangerous. But Channing was still out there, and that, too, was real. What choice did she have but to walk the road?

She stopped at a traffic light, watched cops at a checkpoint.

*What if the road disappeared?*

*What if she was already lost?*

Gideon was shot, and Channing gone. Crybaby was alive or dead—she didn't know.

And, there was Adrian.

Elizabeth turned away from the checkpoint, working the back

roads toward her house. She needed to know if cops were there, or if Channing—by some miracle—had returned. She was two minutes out when the phone vibrated in her pocket. "Hello."

"Is it true?"

"Adrian? Where are you?"

"Is it true they found my wife under the church?"

Elizabeth saw another marked car. They were everywhere. "Don't come here."

"Somebody killed her."

"I know. I'm sorry."

"She didn't deserve that, Liz. We may not have worked at the end, but she was a gentle soul, and alone because of me. I can't just sit here."

"The police are looking for you."

"You, too," he said. "Your face is all over the news. They're linking you to the dead guard. They say you're an accessory to murder."

Elizabeth went silent. She didn't think it would really happen. Not Dyer. Not this fast. "Stay away from me," she said. "Stay away from this place."

She disconnected before he could argue, then made the last turn before her neighborhood. Parking a block away from her house, she worked through a line of trees, approached from the rear, and slipped inside. She knew at once the house was empty, but checked it anyway. Every room. Every door. A dozen messages clogged her machine, but none were from Channing.

*What to do?*

The cops could be a mile away, engines wide open. If they found her, she'd face jail and trial and prison. That meant she had to move, and do it now. So, she collected cash and clothing and spare weapons. She stuffed it all into a bag, working faster because speed kept her safe from the truth: that she had nowhere to go, and no way to find the only thing that really mattered.

*Channing . . .*

That was the arrow that brought her down, and she felt it as if it were real, a sudden pain that made her sit on a kitchen chair, hands open and upturned, eyes wide but not really seeing. Channing was gone, and Elizabeth had no way to find her.

Two minutes later a car rolled into the drive.

It wasn't Channing.

Beckett's illusions fell apart when the warrant hit the wires. Until then he'd believed the world might still correct. They'd catch the killer, and Liz would come home. The warden would somehow disappear. Never mind the dead couple in the motel, or that he'd gotten them killed. That was too big, and he had nowhere to put the guilt.

*How could he know Liz would lie?*

He couldn't.

But, the couple was still dead. That was still on him.

"Where's Dyer?" He grabbed the first cop he saw, a uniformed officer plying the crowded halls same as him. State cops. SBI. It was as if someone had kicked apart a nest of ants. Everyone was angry and full of grim intent. Serial killer. Guard killer. People felt it same as Beckett, long falls and acceleration.

"Dyer's gone," the uniform said. "Thirty minutes, maybe."

"Where?"

"No idea."

Beckett let him go and checked Dyer's office for the third time. He wanted the warrant quashed before Liz got hurt. But the office was empty. No answer on the cell. He tried Liz, but she wasn't answering, either. She was angry; didn't trust him.

Shit, he couldn't blame her.

"I'm on my cell." He flung the words at one of the switchboard operators. "Tell Dyer to call me if he shows up."

Beckett pulled the coat off his chair and shrugged it on as he stepped outside, taking in the news crews and cops and all the bright, moving colors. Forces were gathering against him. Old pressures. Old sins. He needed something, and it had nothing to do with the job.

Taking the steps down, he ate up the sidewalk in long strides, took the car across town, and stepped out at the hair salon two blocks from the mall. Inside, it smelled of chemicals and lotions and blown hair. Beckett nodded at the receptionist, then walked past mirrored stations and long looks and found his wife wrist deep in hair the size of a basketball. "Can I talk to you?"

"Hey, baby. Everything okay?"

"I just need a moment."

She patted the woman in the chair. "Give me a sec, sugar." Beckett led his wife to a quiet space beside the rear wall. "What's up?"

"I was thinking of you and the girls, that's all. I wanted to hear your voice."

She studied his eyes, sensing something. "Are you okay?"

"Things are coming together. The case. Some other things. I wasn't sure when we'd talk."

"You could have called, silly man."

"Maybe. But I couldn't do this over the phone."

He kissed her, and she leaned back, embarrassed but not unhappy. "Goodness." She looked at the crowded room and smoothed herself. "You should come here more often."

He ran a hand across her cheek and left his deepest thought unshared, that the kiss was in case he never returned at all. He gave a smile that said he'd loved her as long as he'd known her, that he accepted her and all her faults, and that he, too, was imperfect. He said all those things with a single smile, then tilted her back and kissed her again. Was it a forever good-bye? He didn't know, but wanted her to feel it just in case. So he kissed her as he hadn't done in a dozen years. He made sure the touch lingered, and by the time he left her breathless and flushed, half the ladies in the place were whistling.

The vehicle was a black Expedition with state plates. For a second it sat, silent; then doors opened and four men stepped out.

Elizabeth knew two of them, so checked the weapon at her back before stepping onto the porch. "That's close enough."

The warden stopped fifteen feet from the bottom step. The man to his right had a battered face, and a limp. Stanford Olivet. She recognized him. The other men were in plainclothes, but probably guards. Jacks and Woods, she guessed, both of them armed.

"Detective Black." The warden spread his hands. "I'm sorry to be here under such trying circumstances."

"What circumstances would those be?"

"I know you're friends with the lawyer, and with Adrian Wall." He turned his lips down and shrugged. "I know there is a warrant for your arrest, and one, of course, for Adrian."

Elizabeth felt the rail against her hips and kept a hand near the concealed weapon. She knew the warden now, what he was.

"I don't know where Adrian is."

"Is that right?"

"I assume that's why you're here."

The warden stepped closer, looking up through dark lashes. "Did you know that William Preston stood up at my wedding eighteen years ago? No, of course not. How could you? Nor could you know that I am the godfather to his children. They're twins, by the way, and fatherless, of course. I love them like my own, but it's not the same, is it?"

Elizabeth said nothing.

"So, tell me, Detective." He took another step. "Was my dear friend alive when you left him beaten and bloody on the roadside?"

"I think you should leave."

"The coroner says he aspirated four teeth, and half a pint of his own blood. I try to imagine how that would feel, to drown on blood and road grit and teeth. The doctors say he might have lived had he made it to the hospital at the same time as the lawyer. It troubles me that he died for want of a few minutes, so let me make my question very plain. Was it your decision to abandon him to such a horrible death?" He was seven feet from the porch, then five. "Or did that choice belong to Adrian Wall?"

The gun appeared in Elizabeth's hand.

"Four on one, Detective."

His voice was soft, but Elizabeth saw Jacks and Woods move closer, too. They wanted Adrian and intended to get him. Whether they sought revenge for Preston's death or a chance to finish what they'd started in prison, she didn't know or care. A wild disregard had taken root inside her. It was the arrogance and corruption, the readiness of his smile. "Adrian told me what you did to him."

"Prisoner Wall is delusional. We've established this."

"What about Faircloth Jones? Eighty-nine years old and harmless. Was *he* delusional?"

"The lawyer is irrelevant."

"What?"

"Immaterial," the warden said. "Of no real meaning or worth."

Elizabeth's hand tightened on the pistol, all confusion gone. Nothing burned inside but sudden anger, and that was all right. He'd said *four on one* but was unarmed, himself, and Olivet looked broken. That made Jacks and Woods the immediate threats, and she'd play those odds all day long. The gun was in her hand; clear lines of fire. The warden was still smiling because he thought she was a cop and would behave as one. But, that's not what she was. She was Adrian's friend and Faircloth's, an exhausted woman on the narrow edge of something bloody.

"I want the man who killed my friend."

He made it a threat, but Elizabeth ignored it. She'd take the one on the right first because he looked eager, and she tracked better right to left. She'd drop the second before his gun cleared the holster, then take Olivet and the warden. All she needed was a reason.

"Last time, Detective. Where is Adrian Wall?"

"You tortured him."

"I deny that."

"You carved your initials into his back."

"That sounds difficult to prove."

He was baiting her, smiling. She kept her eyes on Jacks and Woods. She wanted a twitch.

*Please, God . . .*

*Give me a reason . . .*

"Is everything all right over there?"

That was the neighbor, Mr. Goldman. He stood by the hedge, nervous and worried. Behind him was the same '72 Pontiac station wagon, and beyond that, his wife. She stood on the porch with a telephone in her hand and a look on her face that said she was a heartbeat away from calling 911. Elizabeth kept her eyes on the guns because things could go downhill fast, and if the slide started, it would start there.

"Last chance, Detective."

"I don't think so."

The warden looked at the neighbor, the wife with the phone. "You can't hide behind an old man forever." He showed flat eyes and the same white teeth. "Not in a town like this."

# 32

He valued the silo because, like him, it had been made for a particular purpose. It did the job day after day, year after year. Nobody thanked it or even noticed. Now, it was broken down and forgotten, the fields around it grown over with trees, the farmhouse little more than a dark spot in the soil. How many years since someone had cared about it?

Seventy?

A hundred?

He'd discovered it as a boy and in all the years since had never seen another soul come near it. Rumor was some paper company in Maine owned the full ten thousand acres that surrounded it. He could find out for sure if he wanted—a deed of some kind would be buried in a courthouse drawer. But, why bother? The woods were deep and still, the clearing as quiet and lonesome as any place he'd ever known. Concrete was crumbling. Steel was rusted through.

But the structure still stood.

He still stood.

Not all the women made it to the silo, but most did: the fighters and strong-willed, those that needed time to soften. A few had been *ready to die from almost the moment he took them, as if they'd wished him into existence, or as if some vital part of them shut down at the mere thought of an ending. They were inevitably a disappointment. But weren't they all?*

*Yes, in fundamental ways.*

*Then, why bother?*

*Slowing where a red oak hung an arm across the road, he turned onto the narrow track at the property's edge and nudged deeper into the trees, stopping when he got to the gate he'd installed years ago. Out of the car, he opened the big lock and dragged the gate open. The road behind him was empty, but he moved quickly, pushing the car deeper into the trees, then sliding the gate closed. Once inside, he considered the question again. Why bother at all?*

*Because failures built one upon the other.*

*Because all roads led to Elizabeth.*

*"It is in suffering that we are withdrawn from the sway of time and mere things, and find ourselves in the presence of profounder truth."*

*It was one of his favorite quotes.*

*"Profounder truth . . ."*

*"The sway of time and mere things . . ."*

*The car bounced through the scrub, and he felt hope's fitful rise. He loved Elizabeth, and Elizabeth loved the girl. He thought this one would work and in the shadow of the silo felt more convinced than ever.*

*"The sway of time and mere things . . ."*

*Out of the car, he studied the tree line and the clearing. Nothing moved; no one was there. Opening the car, he removed the tarp, the bucket, and ten gallons of water. He'd prefer to give this one another day in the silo, but things were moving fast and would end with Elizabeth.*

*That would happen soon.*

*He felt it.*

*He dreaded it.*

*Fishing out the stun gun, he closed the door and threw another*

*glance around the clearing. It was small in the trees, a slash of grass
and weed and old machines rusted solid.*

*He looked at the silo, the lock on the chain.*

*The key made a lump in his pocket.*


Channing thought he would never come. After hours on the ladder,
her muscles were burning, her tongue, dry and swollen. She hadn't
counted on the heat, the constant strain. She was eight feet up,
but thought she'd be invisible when the small door opened.

Bright light outside.

Constricted pupils.

Most people would be blind when they stepped into the dark,
and she was counting on that, praying quietly as engine noises
rose beyond the wall. She told herself this was not the basement.
She wasn't tied up and wasn't the same person. But, it was a hard
line to hold.

He was here.

He'd come.

She heard a chassis bottom out, the grind of an engine, and
how it ticked in the stillness, after. He would expect to find her
tied and helpless, worn down by heat and fear. But, that's not how
it was going to happen. The broken rung was rusted, yes, but still
steel, still solid in places. He'd come in headfirst, blinking.

She held her breath as the chain clattered through the handles,
and her legs started shaking. She couldn't help it.

*Oh, God, oh, God . . .*

Who was she kidding? He would drag her off the ladder as if
she were nothing. He would drag her down and rape her and kill
her. She saw it as if it had already happened, because in so many
horrible, unforgettable ways it already had.

"Elizabeth . . ."

The chain made a final scrape.

He was coming.

When the door opened, she saw his shadow, sensed his movement. He stooped beyond the door, but nothing happened for twenty seconds, a minute. Then a flashlight clicked on and shot a spear of light into the silo. It brushed the far wall, then touched bits of plastic and settled there. After a few seconds, the light disappeared. "Are you on the ladder, child?"

*No . . .*

"I had a young lady fall off the ladder, once. Don't know how high she was when it happened. High enough to break her neck, at any rate. Did you make it all the way to the roof? It's a pretty view from up there."

Channing started crying for real.

"In the wintertime, you can see the old church across the valley, like a smudge on the hillside." He turned on the flashlight, swept the interior a second time. "Do you like a church? I like a church."

The light clicked off.

"Why don't you come on down?"

His clothing rustled.

"I can lock the door and let you cook, if you like. It wouldn't be pleasant, I promise. You still with me up there?"

Channing scrubbed the tears away.

Gripped the rung tighter.

*He wasn't bothered in the slightest. Some got out of their restraints, and some didn't. Those that did usually found the ladder; and that was part of it, too: the will to overcome darkness and fear, then the realization that the roof, too, was a trap. It was a difficult combination for most: the ladder in blackness, then fresh air and sunshine, a world of hope, and then the loss of it. Some got clever, and that was fine, too.*

*It wasn't just the heat that broke them.*

Channing forced herself to stop crying. She couldn't go up the ladder and couldn't stay where she was.

That left *down*.

"If you make me lock this door again, I might have to let you cook in there for a good long time." Channing didn't move. "Three days. Four days. I'm not sure when I can make it back, and I'd rather you not die pointless and overhot."

"Okay, okay." Her voice shook and cracked. "Don't lock the door. I'm coming down." She moved one foot, then another; made it to the bottom rung. That left six feet to the ground. She sensed him in the door. "I don't think I can do it."

"I'm sure you'll manage."

She'd have one chance. She needed him close. "I hurt my ankle."

"'Profounder truth,'" he said, and she had no idea what he meant. He stayed where he was, hunched in the door and watching. If she lowered herself gently, he'd see the rung in her hand, so Channing stepped out and dropped. She kept the bar close and folded at the waist to hide it, steel ripping skin from her stomach as she landed. She cried out, but that was okay.

*She needed him close.*

"Oh, God . . ." She curled in the dirt, praying he'd think it was her ankle, that he wouldn't see the blood. She felt it though, hot on her stomach, and soaking the shirt. She rocked onto her hands and knees. He was through the door.

Coming.

"It's my ankle . . ."

His shadow moved closer. Hair swung across her face, and when he touched her, she swung the rod with everything she had. It struck something hard. A shoulder. An arm. She didn't know, didn't care. She felt the shock and saw a slash of red in the gloom. She hit him again, stumbling once and falling toward the door. His hand caught her ankle, and she fell facedown, the door just there, light burning her eyes as she pulled herself through, kicking back twice, hitting some part of him as she fell out into the grass, smelling it, feeling it tear beneath her fingers. She dragged herself faster, finding her feet and falling again as the car rose in front of her and seemed to spin. She was dizzy, her legs not right as she lurched at the car thinking, *Keys, road, escape*. Halfway there, she risked a look back.

He was coming fast.

She wasn't going to make it, falling against the car as she left a smear of blood and ran for the door on the other side. She heard a thump and saw him on the hood, sheet metal buckling as he leapt and caught her and tried to drag her down. She shrugged out of the shirt, felt the bloodstain slide across her face, and ran for the trees. It was what she had, shadows and hope and desperation.

He had the speed.

He caught her three steps into the woods, cupped the back of her head, and slammed her face into the trunk of a tree. Something burst; she tasted blood. He did it again, flung her down; and though his face was swollen and stained with blood of his own, it was the eyes that sucked all the heat from the day.

They were that dark and empty.

That terribly unforgiving.

# 33

Adrian sat in a broken-down room staring at a small fortune in gold. Half a million in the room. Another five and change still in the dirt. He thought of Elizabeth's last words. *Stay away from me. Stay away from this place.*

Could he really do that?

The only feelings he'd known were fear and lonesomeness and rage. The love was for a dead man, and that had been a shadow for so long he didn't know what to do with the feelings he had now.

Liz was real.

She mattered.

Flicking the curtain, he peered out at a fifteen-year-old Subaru he'd rolled off a dirt lot in exchange for a handful of coins. He'd been ready to leave before news of his wife broke. He was going to go west—Colorado or Mexico—but things were different now. His wife was dead, and there was this thing in Liz's voice, a quiet desperation not every man would recognize.

"What do I do, Eli?"

He touched his lips where Liz had kissed him.

Eli didn't answer.

———

*The girl passed out as he carried her to a shady place beside the car. The tremble stopped, and she went limp on his shoulder, a tiny thing he could lift with a single arm. But she was a fighter, and there was clarity in the fighters.*

*They were more like Liz.*

*The eyes went deeper.*

*He put the girl in the grass and checked himself in the mirror. His neck was cut low, near the collarbone. He touched a bloody lump on his scalp, then pulled an old towel from the car and pressed it against his neck. The cut hurt, but he accepted the pain because he'd hurt the girl, too. It was the shock of pain and wounded pride. They drove him to needless harm, yet that was the cycle. Sin feeds sin. The spiral draws deeper and down. He studied the girl's face, swollen and bloody, and it wasn't the first time he'd hardened himself. Julia Strange was not an easy kill, either. He'd found her in the church, alone and on her knees. No one was supposed to be there, and even now he wondered what his life would be had he left a step sooner. But she'd heard him and turned. And when she'd looked at him with those bottomless eyes, the sight of her anguish jolted him. She'd been beaten and humbled, but the hurt ran more deeply than the swollen jaw or bloody lip. It plumbed the depths of her eyes and rendered her into something . . . more. The glimpse lasted but a moment, but he saw the hurt, and beneath the hurt, the innocence. She was a child again, and lost. He wanted to take away the pain; that's how it started. But he didn't know what he'd find in her eyes, or what the finding would do to him. Even now it was a blur: the whirl of emotion, the feel of her skin beneath his fingers. That's where it started; she was the first. Thirteen years later, it would end with Elizabeth. It had to, so he hardened himself.*

*But for now there was the girl.*

*He was gentle as he stripped and cleaned her. He kept his thoughts chaste, as always, but wanted to be done because already it felt wrong. The altar he'd made was in the trees and was only of plywood* and sawhorses. He tried to keep the frustration in check, but she didn't look right when he roped her down and spread the linen. Too much yellow was in the light, and not enough church. He wanted the pinks and reds, the vaulted hush. He dragged a hand through his hair, trying to convince himself.

He could make it happen.

It could work.

But the girl was a mess, her face battered from the tree, a red stain where her stomach wound leaked through the linen. He was bothered because the purity mattered, as did the light, the location. Would it work like this? He pushed the question down. He was here. So was she. So he leaned close, hoping to find what he needed at the bottom of her eyes. It never happened fast. It took trial and error, his hands on the neck not once or twice, but many times.

He waited for her to wake, then choked her once so she would know it was real. "We'll start slowly," he said; then choked her like that so she would have no doubt. He took her to the edge of blackness and held her there. Small movements of his hands, whispers of air. "Show me the girl. Show me the child." He let her breathe once, then rose to his toes and leaned into it as she fought and choked. "Shhh. We all suffer. We all feel pain." He put more weight on his hands. "I want to see the real you."

He choked her long and deep, then hard and fast. He used every trick he'd ever learned, tried a dozen times more, but knew it wouldn't work.

The eyes were swollen shut.

He couldn't see her.


Channing didn't know why she was still alive. She knew pain and darkness, thought she was in the silo, then realized there was movement, too. She was back in the car. Same smell. Same tarp. She touched her face with bound hands and realized most of the darkness came from swollen eyes. She could barely see, but knew she was dressed and breathing and alive . . .

A strangled sound escaped her throat.

*How long?*

She relived his hands and the blackness, the yellow trees and his hungry face.

*How long had he tried to kill her?*

She swallowed, and it was like glass ripping her throat. She touched her neck and curled more tightly in the dim, blue space.

Where was he taking her?

Why was she still alive?

Those worries ate at her until a more disturbing one twisted through the tangle of her thoughts: his face beneath the trees. No hat. No glasses. He'd looked different in a way she couldn't process; but sober now, and desperately alive, she remembered where she'd seen him.

*Oh, God . . .*

She knew exactly who he was.

The revelation terrified her because the truth of it was so perverse. How could it possibly be him?

But it was, and it wasn't just the face. She knew the voice, too. He was making calls as the car worked from one street to the next, making calls and muttering angrily between them. He was looking for Liz and getting frustrated that he couldn't find her. No one knew where she was; she wasn't answering her phone. He called the police station, her mother; and once—through a crack in the tarp—Channing saw the blur of Elizabeth's house. She recognized the shape, the trees.

The Mustang was gone.

Channing sobbed after that and couldn't help it. She wanted to be in the car with Elizabeth, or in her house or in the dark of her bed. She wanted to be safe and unafraid, and only Liz could make that happen. So she said the name in her mind—Elizabeth—and it must have leaked through into the real world, because suddenly the car slowed to a hard, rocking stop. Channing froze, and for a long moment nothing happened. His voice, when it came, was quiet. "You love her, don't you?" Channing squeezed into a ball.

"It makes me wonder if she loves you, too. Do you think she does? I think she probably must." He went quiet, fingers drumming on the wheel. "Do you have a phone? I've been trying to reach her, but she won't pick up. I think she might answer if she saw your number."

Channing held her breath.

"A phone."

"No. No phone."

"Of course not. No. I'd have seen it."

A long silence followed, heat under the tarp. When he started driving again, Channing watched a stretch of buildings and trees, then a span of chain-link stained with rust. The car started down, and she felt the sun disappear, caught glimpses of yellow houses and pink ones, the long slide into some dim hollow. When the car stopped again, he turned off the engine and silence filled everything for another terrible minute.

"Do you believe in second chances?" he asked.

Channing smelled her own sweat, the fog of her breath.

"Second chances. Yes or no?"

"Yes."

"Will you be useful to me if I ask?"

Channing bit her lip and tried not to sob.

"Useful, damn it! Yes or no?"

"Yes. God. Please."

"I'm going to take you out of the car and carry you inside. There's no one around, but if you make a sound, I'll hurt you. Do you understand?"

"Yes."

She felt the car rock and heard the hatch open. He lifted her, still in the tarp. They crossed bare dirt, went up stairs and through a door. Channing saw little until the tarp came off; then it was his face and the four walls of a dingy bath. He put her in the tub and cuffed an ankle to the radiator beside it.

"Why are you doing this?"

"You wouldn't understand."

He stripped silver tape off a roll.

She watched it, terrified. "Please, I want to! I want to understand!"

He studied her, but she saw the doubt. It was in there with the crazy and the sadness and the grim determination. "Be still."

But she could not. She fought as he slapped tape across her mouth and wrapped it twice around her head.

When it was done, he stood above her, looking down. She was small in the tub, and horrified, a tiny thing the color of chalk. She said she wanted to understand, and maybe she did. But no one looking in could appreciate the beauty of what he was trying to do. She'd use the same words as the cops. *Serial killer. Dangerous. Deranged.* Only Liz—at the end—would understand the truth that drove him, that he did these things for the noblest reason of all, the love of a precious girl.

Gideon liked the hospital because everything was clean and people were nice. The nurses smiled; the doctor called him "Sport." He didn't understand a lot of what was said and done, but followed parts of it. The bullet had made a small, clean hole and hit no organs or major nerves. It nicked an important artery, though, and people liked to tell him how lucky he was, that he'd made the hospital just in time and that the surgeon had stitched him just right. They liked to make him feel good, but sometimes, if he turned his head fast enough, he'd catch the whispers and strange, sideways looks. He thought that was about what he'd tried to do, because Adrian Wall was all over the television and he was the boy who'd tried to kill him. Maybe it was about his dead mother and the bodies under the church. Or maybe it was about his father.

The old man had been fine for the first day. He'd been calm and quiet, and even respectful. At some point, though, that changed. He got moody and sullen and short with the nurses.

His eyes were red all the time, and Gideon woke more than once to find him staring out from under the bill of an old cap, lips moving as he stared at his son and whispered words Gideon couldn't hear. Once, when a nurse suggested his father go home and get some sleep, he came to his feet so fast the chair scraped. There'd been a look in his eyes, too, something that scared even Gideon.

After that, none of the nurses lingered when the old man was in the room. They didn't smile and tease out stories. But it worked out in a way. Gideon's father stayed away most of the time. When he chose to appear, he curled on the chair or slept. At times he stayed under a hospital blanket, and only Gideon knew he had bottles under there, too. He could hear them clanking in the dark, the gurgle when his father lifted the blanket and tipped one back.

It was the pattern. And if the drinking went longer and deeper than usual, Gideon didn't blame him. They both had reason to hate, and Gideon, too, knew the ache of failure. He didn't pull the trigger, and that made him as weak as his father. So he tolerated the drunkenness and long stares, the time his father stumbled to the bathroom and vomited until the sun rose. And when the nurses asked Gideon about the mess, he'd said it was him; that the painkillers made him sick.

After that they gave him Tylenol and let him hurt.

He didn't mind.

The room was kept dark, and in the gloom he saw his mother's face, not as a photograph—flat and faded—but as it must have been when she was alive, the color of it, the animation of her smile. The memory couldn't be real, but he played it like a favorite movie, over and over and bright in the dark. The confession caught him by surprise.

"She died because of me."

Gideon started because he didn't know his father was in the room. He hadn't been for hours, but now he was by the bed, his fingers hooked on the rail, a look on his face of desperation and shame.

"Please, don't hate me. Please, don't die."

Gideon wasn't going to die. The doctors had said as much, but his father's breakdown was complete: red eyes and swollen face, the smell from his mouth like something pickled. "Where have you been? When did you get here?"

"You don't know how it is, son. You don't see how it piles up—the things we do, the consequence when we love and trust and let others inside. You're just a boy. How could you know anything about betrayal or hurt or what a man can do if he's pushed?"

Gideon sat up straighter; felt stitches pull in his chest. "What are you talking about? No one died because of you."

"Your mother."

"What about her?"

Robert Strange pulled once on the rail, then rocked onto his knees as a bottle clattered from a coat pocket and slid across the floor. "It was just an argument, that's all. Okay, wait. No. That's a lie, and I promised no more lies. I hit her, yes, three times. But just the three, three times and done. I did that, but apologized. I swore to her son. I told her she didn't need to leave me or go to the church. She'd done a bad thing. Yes, okay. But, I'd already forgiven her, so there was no sin to pray for, no need for God or the cross or reason to pray for me, either. All she had to do was stay with us, and I would forgive every bad thing she'd ever done, the lies and distortions and the secrets of her heart. Tell me you see it, son. So many years I've watched it eat you alive, to be motherless and stuck with me, alone. Tell me you forgive me, and I think maybe I could sleep without dreams. Tell me I did what any husband would do."

"I don't understand. You hit her?"

"It wasn't like I planned it or enjoyed it." Robert pulled at his hair and left it spiked. "The bad part happened so fast, my fists . . . that was twenty seconds, and maybe less. I never meant it. I didn't want her to leave, didn't think she'd die over twenty seconds. Just like that, one, two, three . . ."

He was moving his fingers—counting—and Gideon blinked as it all soaked in. "She went to the church because of you?"

"Her killer must have found her there."

"She died because of you?"

The question was hard, and the father grew still, his head tilting so light caught in his eyes. "You still think she's some kind of saint, don't you, some perfect thing? I understand that, I do. A boy should feel that way about his mother. But she left you in that crib, son. I was angry, yes, and maybe I broke up the kitchen and smashed some things, and maybe I lied to the cops about what really happened. But she's the one who left."

"Only because you hurt her."

"Not just because of that." He slumped to the floor and hugged the bottle to his chest. "Because she loved Adrian Wall more than she loved me."

Gideon struggled with it all: the man on the floor, the revelation. His mother loved Adrian Wall. What did that mean? Did he kill her or not?

Gideon looked again at his father. He sat with his arms around his knees, his face buried. There'd been no abduction. His mother met her killer at the church or some other place. Not in his kitchen. Not as he'd watched from the crib.

Was it Adrian?

How could Gideon know? Could she possibly love him? That question was too big. It was massive, incomprehensible.

There'd been no abduction . . .

The boy closed his eyes because the larger questions were coming hard and fast.

*Was she leaving for good?*

*Was she leaving him?*

She couldn't be that flawed, that . . . wrong.

"She was a good woman, son, warm-spirited and loving, but as conflicted as the rest of us."

"Reverend. Black?"

"I didn't mean to eavesdrop, Gideon. It seemed like an important moment, and I didn't want to interrupt, either."

"You startled me. I barely recognize you."

"It's the beard, or the lack of it. Then there're the clothes. I don't always wear black, you know." The preacher stood in the gloom at the edge of a green curtain. He smiled and stepped all the way inside. "Hello, Robert. I'm sorry to see you in such a state. Let me help you." He extended a hand and drew Gideon's father to his feet. "Difficult times, I'm sure. We must strive to rise above them."

"Reverend."

Robert dipped his head and tried to tuck the bottle out of sight. Reverend Black smiled. "Weakness is not a sin, Robert. God built us all with special flaws and left us the challenge of addressing them. Facing the things that hurt us most is the real test. If you came to church with your son, you might understand the difference."

"I know. I'm sorry."

"Next Sunday, perhaps."

"Thank you, Reverend."

"What are you drinking?"

"Uh . . ." Robert scrubbed a forearm across his face and cleared his throat. "It's just bourbon. I'm sorry . . . uh. What I said about Julia. Hitting her, I mean. I guess you heard that?"

"It's not my place to judge you, Robert."

"But, do you think I got her killed, somehow? She ran from me, and then she died. Do you understand how it could be like that?" Robert was teary-eyed, still breaking. "I've carried that secret for so long. Please tell me she didn't die because of me."

"I'll tell you what." The reverend put an arm around Robert's shoulders and took the bottle, holding it up to find it almost full. "Why don't you find someplace quiet?" The reverend walked him past the bed, toward the door. "Not home. A place close by. Take this with you, and have a nice quiet drink. Spend some time with your thoughts."

Robert took the bottle. "I don't understand."

"The garden, perhaps, or the parking garage. I don't really care."

"But . . ."

"No one knows more than I about the depths of human frailty.

Your own. Those of your wife. I'd like to help your son understand, if I can. In the meantime, enjoy the bottle. I give you permission." Reverend Black pushed him into the hall and closed the door down to a crack. "Tomorrow is soon enough to contemplate the multitude of your sins."

He closed the door the rest of the way and stood for a long time in the silence. To Gideon, he looked different, and it wasn't just the clothes or missing beard. He seemed stiffer, narrower. When he spoke, he sounded less forgiving, too. "Your father is a weak man."

"I know."

"A man with no will for necessary things."

The reverend turned from the door, and his face was all dark eyes and angles. They'd spoken often of necessary things. Sundays after church. Long prayers on difficult nights. And the prayers weren't like Sunday sermons. The reverend had explained it more than once, but Gideon didn't pretend to understand it all: the Old Testament versus the New, an eye for an eye as opposed to a turned cheek. What Gideon did understand was the concept of *necessary things*. Those were the things you felt in your heart that no one else would do for you. They were difficult things, things you kept to yourself until it was time to act. The acting is where he'd failed. "About Adrian Wall . . ."

"Shhh." The reverend held up a hand, then pulled a chair beside the bed. "You did nothing wrong."

"I didn't pull the trigger."

"All I ever said was to follow your heart and be unafraid to act. Adrian Wall's fate was always in larger hands than your own."

Gideon frowned because that's not how he remembered it. The reverend's talk of necessary things had not been so much about *following* as about *acting*. Always the acting.

*This is the time they let prisoners out.*

*This is the place they go.*

*The best place for you to hide.*

It seemed wrong coming from the reverend, but sometimes

Gideon misunderstood the big concepts. God *did* drown the world. He *did* turn Lot's wife to a pillar of salt. It all made sense when the reverend explained it. Cleansings. Punishment. Creative destruction. "I thought you'd be angry with me."

"Of course not, Gideon. You're a child and wounded by fate. You should also understand that necessary things are rarely *easy* things. If they were, then there'd be no distinction between men of will and those of low character. I've always believed you to be the former, and no imagined failing could dissuade me of that conviction. You've always had an eager soul. Your mother can see that, you know." The reverend touched Gideon's hand. "The question now is, if you're still willing to help me."

"Of course. Always."

"Good boy. Good. This may hurt a little." The reverend stood and stripped the needle from Gideon's arm.

"Ow."

"I want you to get dressed and come with me."

"But the doctor . . ."

"Who do you trust more, the doctor or me?"

The preacher's eyebrow went up, and the stare between them held, one of them unflinching and hard, the other unusually frightened. "My clothes are in the closet."

The preacher crossed the room and found the clothing. At the bed, he offered the first real smile Gideon had seen. "Come along now. Quickly."

"Yes, sir."

Gideon climbed shakily from the bed. He was weak. His chest hurt. He got one leg in his pants, then the other. When he straightened, he saw the preacher's blood. "Your neck is bleeding." He pointed at the preacher's neck, and when the old man touched it, his fingers came back red. Gideon saw then that the collar was bloody, too, and that a purple bruise was spreading along the side of his neck. It all felt wrong: the preacher in red flannel and bleeding, the way he'd stripped out the needle and sent Gideon's father off to get drunk.

"How did you hurt yourself?"

"It's like I told you, son." The preacher tossed a shirt at the boy. "The necessary things are rarely the easy ones."

After that nothing felt exactly right. The way he looked Gideon up and down, how he checked the hall and spoke too quietly. "Balance okay? You can walk?"

"Yes, sir."

"Then walk normally. If someone speaks to you, let me respond."

Gideon followed him out and kept his head down. He knew it wasn't right, what they were doing. The doctor had been clear: *A week at least. Those are delicate stitches in your chest. We don't want to knock them loose.*

"I think I'm bleeding."

They were alone in the elevator, Reverend Black watching floors tick down. "That's normal."

"Is it a lot?"

"It's fine." But, he didn't even look. They went from the fifth floor to the second, where the elevator stopped and a nurse got on. She looked at Gideon, then at the gash on the preacher's neck. She opened her mouth, but Reverend Black cut her off. "What are you looking at?"

The nurse shut her mouth; faced front.

Out of the elevator other people stared, too, but no one stopped them. They went through the ER and out the glass door. In the parking lot, Gideon struggled as they moved faster through the crowded lot. He felt weak. The sun was too bright.

"This is not your car."

"It runs."

Gideon hesitated. He'd been in the preacher's car before, a minivan with immaculate paint and a cross on the plates. This one was small and dirty and, in places, rusted through.

"Let's get you situated." Reverend Black pushed Gideon into the car, then strapped him down and slid behind the wheel.

Gideon wrinkled his nose. "It smells funny in here."

"How about some quiet while we drive?"

The reverend turned the key and drove them through town and out to the poor side of things. Air whistled through his teeth as the car moved, and Gideon thought at first they were going to the old, white church on its skinny lot. The thought comforted him because he'd always felt safe in the church. He liked the hymns and the candles, the cushions and wood and velvet hassocks. The church was little, but Gideon felt the warmth of it, too. The preacher had a deep voice, and his wife was like the perfect grandmother. Elizabeth would often drive him to Sunday service. She wouldn't go in, but was always waiting for him when he came out, and that, too, was special. But they passed the turn for the church. He watched it fade as the preacher drove instead to the hillside road that dropped into the dim, cool shade that seemed to lie so often on Gideon's house. "We're going to my house?"

"I need a special favor. Will you do that, son? Grant me a special favor?"

"Yes, sir."

"I never doubted you. Not once."

The reverend pulled to a stop near the porch and got the front door open. His movements seemed hurried and erratic. Tripping once on the stairs. Darting eyes and color in his face. Inside, the air was stuffy, all the curtains were drawn. He got Gideon onto the sofa and sat him down.

"This favor. You need to be smart and do it right." The reverend pushed a phone into Gideon's hands. "Call her. Tell her you want to see her."

Gideon felt the wrongness piling up: the eagerness and dry lips, the sudden, fierce intensity. "I don't understand. Call who?"

"Elizabeth." The preacher took the phone from Gideon's fingers and dialed a number. "Tell her you need to see her. Tell her to come here."

"Why?"

"Tell her that you miss her."

Gideon kept his eyes on Reverend Black and waited for Elizabeth to answer the phone. It took five rings, then Gideon said what he'd been asked to say. There was a silence after his words; in the hesitation, he said, "I just miss you is all."

He listened for ten more seconds, and when she hung up, it felt like part of the wrongness. Why he was home. Why he was calling her.

"What'd she say?"

Eager fingers took the phone, and Gideon felt a strange regret. "She said I shouldn't be out of the hospital."

"What about the rest of it?"

"She's coming."

"Now?"

"Yes, sir."

The preacher got up and paced the room twice. He took Gideon's arm and led him to the bathroom. "The next thing is really important."

"What?"

He squared up the boy and put heavy hands on his shoulders. "Don't scream."

Gideon didn't know the girl in the tub. Silver tape covered her mouth and was wrapped around her head two or three times. Her wrists were taped, too; but Gideon stared mostly at the swollen eyes. She was chained to the radiator, wrapped in a tarp. "Reverend . . . ?"

The preacher put him on the toilet seat and knelt as the girl struggled. "You don't want to do that."

Gideon, watching, knew he'd never seen anyone so frightened in all his life. The girl was wide-eyed and grew still. He tried to understand, but it felt as if the world had changed while he slept, as if the sun had set one day and come up dark the next. "Reverend?"

"Stay here. Stay quiet."

"I'm not sure I can do that."

"Do you trust me, son? Do you believe I know what's right and what's wrong?"

"Yes, sir." But he really didn't. The door closed, and Gideon sat still. The girl was watching him, and that made it worse. "Does it hurt?" he whispered.

She moved her head up and down, slowly.

"I'm sorry for the reverend," Gideon said. "I don't understand what's happening."

# 34

Elizabeth drove because she had no other choice. She couldn't stay at the house, couldn't leave the county.

So she drove.

She drove so the warden wouldn't find her, and not the cops, either. She stuck to the gravel roads and the dirt, to the narrow lanes that led to forgotten places. The movement was all she had left, just that and worry and the fear her courage would break. Elizabeth dreaded prison with the kind of fear born bloody from knowledge of what happens when helplessness becomes the final rule. Prison was powerlessness and subjugation, the antithesis of everything she'd fought to be since she'd first known the bitter taste of fallen pine. She'd denied that for a long time, but all she had to do was look at Adrian to know the truth of it. So she drove as she had as a kid, wind-struck and wild and untouched. Yet with every intersection came a choice, and every choice took her west. She didn't even notice until she hit the county line, then she turned east because the children were east, and those were the bars of her cage—Channing and the boy, the county map with its unforgiving lines.

The call, when it came, was a tortured blessing.

Gideon sounded bad.

Something was wrong.

It took time to work her way back into town, and for the first time in her life she regretted the old Mustang. Cops knew it. It stood out. Turning at the shuttered plant near the tracks, she worked farther east and then down, passing the same chalk-yellow house and bending right at the creek. It was dim in the draw, and she drove as fast as she could, the hillside piling up on her right, old millhouses looking down.

The car at Gideon's house was rusted and battered and unfamiliar. She didn't think twice about it until she saw blood on the paint.

"I hit a whitetail out on one fifty."

Her father stepped onto the porch. His face was crooked, the eyes somehow dull and impenetrable. Elizabeth straightened from the car, ran her fingers over the metal. "No dents."

"He was already gut-shot when I hit him. Not much of an impact, really. Just bumped the car and slid off. I suspect he's dead by now, lost in some field or another."

She touched the blood. It was dry, but still sticky. "What are you doing here, Dad? Whose car is this?"

"It's a parishioner's car. I'm here for the boy."

"And your neck?"

"I was doing some work around the parsonage. A bucket fell off the ladder. What's with all the questions?"

"You know how I feel about this."

She meant the boy, and her father knew it. Gideon liked church for good reason, but Elizabeth had her own demons, and the rules had grown clear over time. Church was for Sundays. The rest of the week her father stayed away.

"How do you feel about his private room? Or the money we've raised for his medical bills? You don't think his father has that kind of cash, do you? That's the church at work, your mother and all the people you no longer see fit to value."

Elizabeth shrugged off the guilt; it was nothing new. "Did you ask Gideon to call me?"

"Things have taken a turn." He shrugged. "Complications. Timing."

"I don't know what any of that means."

"It's all wrapped up together, childhood and innocence and trust." He opened the door and held it for her. "Come on inside." The dirt was as she remembered it, the greasy rags and bits of engine. "He's in the bathroom."

"I'll wait."

"It's not like that." He indicated she should walk with him. "Not in the shower or anything. The boy felt unwell and wanted to be in there just in case. He knows you're coming." Her father gestured again and let her move in front. He was to the left, one hand reaching for the knob as she settled into the hollow place between his arm and the door. "There's such love in a child," he said. "And that's the thing I tell myself. Everything that happens. The road that leads from here." His hand touched the knob. "It's all about the innocence."

"Are we still speaking of Gideon?"

"Gideon. Family. The next hour of your life."

Her father opened the door, and Elizabeth saw it like a blur: Gideon and an injured girl, blood and skin and bright, silver tape. She saw it all and, in the span of a heartbeat, felt the world collapse to something inexplicable and cold. She didn't know what was happening; couldn't possibly. But the battered eyes were Channing's, and that meant nothing in the world was as she'd thought. She moved on instinct to duck and turn, to find space to figure this out. But he was behind her and ready. He drove her into the doorframe with one hand and used the other to push something hard and slick against her neck. She got a foot on the frame, but knew even then she was too late. Energy ripped into her neck, and he followed her to the floor, keeping the charge against her skin as she twitched and drummed and felt a scream that never left her throat. Her body was burning, on fire. She smelled the charge and through the bathroom door saw Gideon, openmouthed, and Channing, the girl, whose own scream was every bit as trapped as hers.

*The preacher stood, breathing hard. He felt old, but the feeling would pass. What he'd told Elizabeth was true. It really was about the love—what he'd done, what he was doing—and nothing was stronger than a father's love for his daughter.*

*Not God's love.*

*Not his wife's.*

*He'd cherished his daughter more than all of those things combined, more than breath or faith or life itself. She'd been the world entire, the warm, bright center.*

*Of course, this wasn't his daughter.*

*Not the one he loved.*

*He nudged her with a foot and heard the same voices in the dark of his mind, the lot of them disharmonic and thin, saying, "Stop now, turn away, come back to God." But he'd learned years ago that the voices were but pale remnants of cast-off morality, mere ghosts that knew nothing of loss or grief or betrayal's lancinating pain. He'd been a young father with a wife and his own church. His daughter had loved, respected, and trusted him. They were as God meant them to be. The family. The child. The father.*

*Why did she turn away from that?*

*Why did she kill her unborn child?*

*Those were the cornerstones of the great betrayal, and he confronted them every time he tried to sleep: the lowered eyes and false acquiescence, the secrets and lies and the blood on his porch. She was supposed to be in bed, yet he'd found her there, half dead and womb-stripped and unrepentant. His hands bore the stain even now, the red in the cracks only he could see. His daughter's blood. His grandchild's. She'd defied her own father, and God had let it happen, the same God who'd allowed the butchery in the first place and delivered her heart, in time, to Adrian Wall. The betrayals were so large they drove even light from the world. What room remained for the father who'd first held her? For the man who'd raised and taught her, and whose own heart, even now, was broken?*

*No room, he thought.*

*None at all.*

*So he did what he had to do. He took the gun, then bound her hands and feet and watched her eyes in case she woke. He didn't care to explain or debate. He wanted her, at last, on the altar of her youth. There, she'd trusted him most, and there he'd find her if he could. Deep in the eyes. All the way down.*

*He looked at the children in the bath and felt the first and only remorse. Would they die, in the end? He didn't know. Maybe Elizabeth would. Maybe it would be him. He only knew the clamor would cease. No more longing or despair, no voices in his head or plaintive cries from those he'd tried to love and buried, instead, beneath the church. He lifted the pistol and wondered. Would it quiet the voices if he put it in his mouth? Would it reveal God's true face, at last? Such contemplations weren't the first, but these were more immediate. He would find his daughter or not. And should he not—should she die in the search—did it not make sense for him to die as well? Would there not be closure in such a thing, a conjoining at last?*

*He tilted the gun and put it in his coat pocket.*

"Stand up, son." He gestured for Gideon, who rose as if on a string. "Come here." The boy did as he was told, wide-eyed and washed out. "Necessary things. You remember our discussions?" The boy nodded. "Purpose. Clarity. Do you believe I possess such things, and that what may seem cruel is, in fact, a kindness?"

"Is she hurt?"

"Just sleeping."

"And the girl?"

"Necessary things, Gideon. We've had the discussion many times. All I ask now is that you trust in my purpose, even if you can't understand it." He watched the boy blink and swallow, a windup toy waiting for the spring to tighten. "Do you understand?"

"I don't know."

"Can you try?"

"Yes, sir."

"Come with me, then." He led Gideon to the front door and opened it with care. Nothing moved on the street. An old lady stood in the yard three houses down, shading her eyes in a housecoat and no shoes. "Open the car, Gideon. The back door. The hatch."

"Reverend . . ."

"Don't argue, son. The hatch." Gideon opened the hatch and stood immobile as the reverend put Elizabeth in, still loose. The girl followed, but was struggling in the tarp. Up the street, the old woman was watching, but he wasn't worried. Things were moving too fast. "Get in the car, Gideon."

The boy got in, and the preacher did, too. He would go to the church because his daughter had been baptized there and loved her father there. The good years between them were as baked into that church as the mortar itself, and that made the decision simple. Daughter or not, failure or success, it would end as it began, the father and the child and only honesty between them.

Gideon was smart enough to know that everything happening now was wrong. Liz shouldn't be hurt like that, and not the girl, either. They shouldn't be in a car that smelled like pee, and the reverend shouldn't be so scary. He had never been before. He'd been firm and, at times, judgmental. But those were the little things, and Gideon never worried much about the little things. The bigger things mattered more, such as how the reverend was calm and quiet and seemed to know so much, the way he spoke of life and how it should be lived, and how he made every day seem solemn and purposeful. Gideon had always wanted a life that felt as if the minutes and hours had weight of their own. A life like that wouldn't dry up and blow away. A life like that mattered.

The reverend whistled as he drove. The flat, shapeless tune

raised the hair on Gideon's arms. It felt as wrong as fingernails on a blackboard. But that could be the car, the blood, the way he looked at Gideon when the road got straight. "Do you know what a sand tiger shark is?"

His voice was quiet, but Gideon twitched because they were the first words the reverend had said in ten long minutes. They were beyond the edge of town. The girl had stopped struggling. "No, sir. Not unless you mean regular tiger sharks."

"Sand tiger sharks have embryos that fight and die in the mother's womb. Once they're large enough, they go at each other right there in the tightness and the black. They tear each other apart until only one is left alive; and that's the one that's eventually born. Everyone else is eaten or left to rot. Brothers. Sisters. Even the eggs, if any are left." He drove for another mile. "Does that sound like God to you? That savagery?"

"No, sir."

"Does it sound like me?"

Gideon didn't answer because it was clear he was not supposed to. The reverend was driving with his eyes down to slits, and muscles rolling in his jaw. Gideon risked a look behind him and saw the girl watching. She was sucking hard through her nose. Trying to breathe. She shook her head, and Gideon felt the same fear.

*Crazy.*

*Full-on, batshit crazy.*

Two minutes later he saw the church. The reverend drove past it twice, studying it, craning his neck. He stopped at the drive, watching the road through the glass, the rearview mirror. "Do you see anything?"

"Like what?"

"Police. Other people."

"No, sir."

"You sure?"

Gideon kept quiet, and after a moment's silence the preacher pulled up the twisting drive and parked.

"Stay in the car."

He opened his door, and wind carried the smell of every summer Gideon had ever known. For a moment, he thought of better times; then the hatch opened, and Liz started fighting, the thrashing so violent and loud and hard to watch that Gideon was screaming by the time she flopped onto the dirt, and the same horrible, crackling sound made her go as limp as if dead. He wanted to help her. But, the reverend nailed him with those dull eyes and crushed whatever part of him thought there would be an explanation. He'd imagined it mere seconds ago. The car would stop. The preacher would wink and laugh, and suddenly everyone else would be laughing, too. *Joke's on me,* he'd realize.

But, it was no joke.

The preacher had his daughter on a shoulder. He was tearing down tape, leaning into a wooden door that opened with a lurch and swallowed them up. Suddenly, Gideon was alone with the girl. "Please, don't cry. He's just sick, I think. Or confused."

But the girl fought when the preacher reappeared. She screamed behind the tape and fought as Liz had fought, so red-faced and desperate that Gideon got out of the car and pulled at the preacher's arm as he dragged the girl out.

"Reverend, please! She's just a girl. She's scared."

"What did I say about the car?"

"Let's just go back to town, okay? This doesn't have to be real. None of it has to be real."

It was like a nightmare, and he was begging to wake up. But the sun was too hot for it to be a dream, the church too solid and tall. He tried again to stop what was happening, but the preacher shoved him away, hard enough to make something tear deep in Gideon's chest. He fell hard on the ground and felt heat on his skin as the bandages soaked through. The preacher had the girl under an arm. Gideon caught his belt; tried to pull himself up.

"Let go, son."

"Reverend, please . . ."

"I said let go."

But Gideon refused. "This is not right, Reverend, and it's not you.

Please stop!" He pulled harder, his feet dragging in the dirt. "Please!" He tried a final time before the stun gun touched his chest, and the Reverend Black—without looking twice—pulled the trigger and put him down.

Elizabeth woke to movement and shadow, the church gathering around her as if conjured. She was being carried past tumbled pews and colored glass, and for that instant it felt as if childhood, too, had been conjured. She knew every beam above her head, and every creak the old floor made.

"Father . . ."

After a moment's peace memory began its aching return, the pieces, as dull and scattered as crushed glass. *Silver tape. Pain.* None of it made sense.

"Dad?"

"Patience," he said. "We're almost there."

She blinked, and more of it came, the kids and the back of a car and the burn that took her down a second time. Was it real? She couldn't believe it, but her vision was blurred, and she hurt as if the most vital nerves had been stripped from her body.

He was looking down and smiling, but no reason was in his eyes. "We'll be together soon," he said; and the rest of it crashed down: the struggle and the silence, a blue tarp and movement and the heat of Channing's skin. She fought then, so he dropped her and put metal prongs against her skin. When she woke again, she was naked on the altar. "Don't cry," he said; but she couldn't help it. Tears burned her face. She was hurt and terrified and choking. This was not her father, not her life. She strained to sit, saw Channing on the floor, and cried for her, too, that she also was in this place.

"Why are you doing this?"

"Don't be embarrassed." He turned away, and she fought the ropes. "There's no need for that here, not between us."

He said it softly, removing his jacket and putting it on a pew.

Beside the coat was a package. When he opened it, Elizabeth saw white linen, neatly folded. He shook it free, and that's when the enormity of his sins took root and blossomed like some terrible flower.

*His church . . .*

*Such horrible things . . .*

"All those women."

"Hush now."

"This can't be happening." Her head rocked side to side. He put a hand on her forehead. "You don't have to do this," she said. "Whatever's happening here, whatever you think this is, you don't have to do it."

"Actually, I do."

He shook the linen again and spread it with care across her body, folding it beneath her chin until the top edge lay just above her breasts. He adjusted it at the bottom and sides, smoothed the wrinkles until it was just so. All the while colored light hung on his face, the light of her childhood that, as a girl, she'd thought to be the light of God himself.

"Dad, please . . ." She was breaking; she felt it. Her father. The church. "So many women."

"They died as children. Stripped of sin."

"What does that mean?"

"Hush now."

"Gideon's mother? God. Allison Wilson?" She choked again, but it was more like a sob. "You killed them all?"

"Yes."

"Why?"

He stood by her side, both hands on the altar. "Does it truly matter?"

"Yes. God. Of course. Dad . . ." Her voice failed.

He nodded as if understanding her deeper need. "Gideon's mother was the first," he said. "I didn't plan it that way, didn't plan any of it. But I saw it in her eyes, right here: the pain and loss and hints of the child beneath. It began as simple consolation. She was distraught and confessed all that troubled her, the failed marriage and abuse and infidelity. It was an old story, yet as she wept, I came back to her eyes. They were so deep and unguarded and such a color as yours. When she leaned into me, I touched her cheek, her throat. After that it happened as if I were a passenger on some unstoppable vessel. Yet even at that remove I felt the presence of profounder truth, how we passed from the sway of time and mere things. I saw her, then. Truly *saw* her. That's when I knew."

"What?"

"Innocence. The path."

"And the others?" Elizabeth asked. "Ramona Morgan? Lauren Lester?"

"All of them, yes. Children, at the end."

"Even Adrian's wife?"

"She was different. I would take that one back."

"Why, for God's sake? Why any of this?" Elizabeth was grasping, desperate. He leaned above her, his face scraped clean, the eyes deep and dark. He smoothed her hair, and she felt revulsion more profound than anything from the basement or the quarry. The sickness was too close. His eyes, like her eyes. The same eyes. Her father.

"Catherine Wall was a mistake. I was angry at her husband. He took you from me, so I took his wife and his house. I admit the sin of it and am ashamed. Her death served no purpose. The house should not have burned. Both acts were born of weakness and spite, and that's not my purpose."

"What possible purpose?"

"I told you before." He smoothed her hair again. "It's all about the love."

"Let Channing go." She was begging. "If you love me at all . . ."

"But, I don't. How could I do that and still honor the child you were?"

"I don't understand."

"Let me show you."

His hands settled on her neck, and she felt the pressure build. It was gentle at first, an even force that mounted as he leaned closer and the world began to fade. In the distance, she heard Channing kicking at pews, trying to scream. The world ended for a time, and when Elizabeth came back, the transition was from soft to hard: his fingers on her throat, the altar beneath her head. He waited for her to focus, then choked her again, but even slower, the pressure building with a smoothness made terrible by the knowledge of what was to come: the last seconds of light, the way his eyes bored into hers and his lips drew gently back.

"Where are you?" His voice was tender. Her mouth opened, but she couldn't answer. She saw tears on his face, colored light, and then nothing. She came back coughing, with the taste of copper in her mouth. The third time was even worse. He brought her to the edge of blackness and held her there.

"Elizabeth. Please."

After the tenth time, she lost count. Minutes. Hours. She had no idea. The world was his face and his breath and the hot, hard fingers that pushed her down again and again. He never lost his patience, and each time his stare went deeper, as if he could touch the soft place she guarded like a secret. She felt him there, the brush of a finger.

When she came back from that place, he was teary-eyed and nodding. "I see you." He covered his mouth to stifle a sob. "My baby . . ."

"I'm not your baby."

"You are, of course you are. You're my lovely girl."

He pressed his lips against her face, kissing her cheeks, her eyes. He was weeping joyfully even as Elizabeth choked and coughed and tasted her own bitter tears.

"No."

"Don't be silly. It's Daddy. I'm here."

"Get away from me."

"Don't say that."

"You're not my father. I don't even know you."

She closed her eyes and turned her head away.

It was all she had.

All she could do.

"No." His voice rose, tears spilling onto her face as he choked her hard and fast and ugly. "Come back!" He leaned into it. "Elizabeth! Please!" He squeezed Elizabeth's throat until her eyes filled with blood, and she went deep in the black. After that, even when she returned, she was barely there. She sensed his anguish, and the light that dimmed in the church. Everything else was vague. His hands. The pain. "Please let me see her." Elizabeth's head lolled; he caught and held it. "Why are you keeping her from me? Do you hate me so very much?"

Elizabeth forced a whisper. "You're sick. Let me help you."

"I'm not sick."

She blinked.

"Don't you know this place? Can't you feel it? The place where we spoke of life and the future, of God's plans and all that we meant to each other? I was your father, here. You loved me."

"I did." The barest whisper. "I did love you."

"And now?"

"Now I think you're sick."

"Don't say that."

But in all her life she'd only lied to him once, so she held his eyes and let him see the truth. That he was a killer. That she could never love him as she once had.

"Elizabeth—"

"Let me go. Let Channing go."

He tightened his grip; her eyes fluttered. "I want the daughter I knew before the abortion and the lies. You took her from me when all you had to do was listen and do as I said. Our family would have survived, our church." He let her breathe.

Elizabeth choked out a rasping sound. "I didn't take her. You killed her."

"I would never."

"Here. At this altar." He didn't understand, and maybe he

couldn't. It wasn't the rape or the abortion that destroyed the girl she'd been. It was him, right here. His betrayal. That was the irony. He'd killed the child he loved, then murdered a dozen women trying to get her back.

"Are you laughing?"

She was. She was dying, and she was. Maybe her brain was starved of oxygen. Maybe, at the end, this is what she proved to be, helpless even before herself. It didn't matter. His face was perfect: the disbelief and wounded pride, the impotence before a dying daughter's last, imperfect act.

"Don't laugh at me."

She laughed harder.

"Don't," he said. "But it was beyond her, now. "Elizabeth, please—"

She sucked deep and pushed it out, a high wheeze that sounded nothing like joy. But it was what she had, and she rode it even as his hands came down, and he rose again to his toes. The laughter ended with her breath, but she felt it inside, bright for a spell, then dim and dying, as was she.

# 35

Gideon woke to the sound of wind and the warmth of a blood-soaked shirt. He felt weak, but the truth was all around him.

This was real.

It was happening.

He tried to sit, but something didn't work right, so he lay back down. The next time he went slower, and when the church stopped spinning, he looked at the yellow tape the preacher had torn down. There'd been bodies here. He could remember some of the names from what he'd seen on TV.

Ramona Morgan.

Lauren something.

Then, there were the ones beneath. Nine more women, they said. Nine more ghosts. The thought made him afraid, but his mother died here, too, and if there were ghosts, maybe she would be among them. She'd been a good person, so maybe the others had been, as well. Maybe they would see into his heart and offer no reason to fear. But, Gideon was a spiritual boy. He believed in God and angels and the bad things, too.

Did that include the preacher?

It shouldn't, but he thought it must. Why else was he here with Liz and the other girl? Why were they tied and taped and terrified? It was too much, too big. But the truth of what he had to do was simple. He had to go inside and see. So he pulled himself up the stairs and at the top looked down at how the valley rolled out, soft and narrow and long. It was pretty, he thought, then opened the door and went looking for the ugly. It wasn't hard to find. The altar was lit, and Liz was on it. Her father was hurting her, and the sight made Gideon weak. Ten steps later the weakness was worse, and he thought of such things as blood loss and shock and the doctor's talk of a stitched artery.

The shirt was heavy.

His eyelids, too.

Holding on to a pew, he waited for the faintness to pass, but it didn't. If anything, he felt worse. Numb legs. Dry mouth. He stumbled and went down on a knee, smelling the carpet, the rotted wood. The girl was screaming, but all he could see was Liz on the altar, how she twitched and jerked, and how ropes cut her ankles. Veins bulged in her neck; her mouth was open. Gideon dragged himself up, thinking, *This is how my mother died. Just here. Just like that.* The gap in his logic didn't close until he was close enough to see the blood that filled Liz's eyes.

She was dying as he watched. Not being hurt. Being killed.

Gideon swayed again, seeing his mother's death, as it must have been.

This place.

This man.

How could that be possible? He'd loved the preacher more than his own father. Trusted him. Adored him. A day ago he'd have died for the Reverend Black.

"Hmmm! Hmm!"

The girl was at his feet, shoved half beneath the pew. Her noises grew frantic as she tried to gesture with her entire body. The preacher's coat was on the pew ten feet away. The girl dipped her head twice, and Gideon saw the stun gun beside the coat. He'd never seen one before today, but it looked simple. Metal points. Yellow trigger. He reached for it, then saw the real gun sticking out of a coat pocket. It was black and hard. He touched it once, but didn't want to kill anyone.

It was still the reverend.

*Right?*

He wasn't thinking straight, and his hands were tingling, too. The whole thing felt wrong, but life often felt that way. Mistakes happened. Things that seemed clear weren't. He didn't want to make a mistake now, but was so dizzy.

Was it really happening?

He bent for the stun gun and fell against the pew. New heat spread on his chest, and his fingers didn't want to obey. They were far away, fumbling at the grip. His knees touched carpet, and blood from his shirt smeared the wooden seat. He turned his eyes to the girl beside him, saw the shiny eyes and yellow hair, the way she struggled and pleaded and screamed behind the tape as if to remind him that a woman was dying, and that it was Liz, who'd always loved him.

Gideon couldn't allow that, so he pushed with all he had; he pushed and bled and found his feet beneath a vaulted ceiling and a wall of colored glass. The stun gun filled his hand, and shallow stairs led to the place Liz was dying. He asked his mother to help if she could. "I'm scared," he whispered, and it was as if a dozen women kissed his face and lifted him. The pain in his chest went away. His head cleared, and he moved as light as any ghost across the carpet and up the steps to where pink light spilled down and motes hung in the air above the preacher's head. Beyond the altar was Mary, in the glass, and in her arms an infant son. They wore halos and were smiling, but Gideon was angry and afraid and beyond such gentle things. He looked once at Liz's bloody eyes, then put metal in the reverend's back and lit the bastard up.

Channing watched it happen and felt a surge when the preacher went down. Above him, Elizabeth was unmoving. Maybe she was breathing, and maybe not. The boy, beside her, looked half dead with his bloody shirt and translucent skin. He wobbled where he stood and looked as if he, too, could drop at any second. She needed out of the tape before that happened.

"Hmmmm! Hmmmm!"

She tried to scream, but the boy seemed oblivious. He stared at the preacher and touched the man with a shoe. Beyond him, Elizabeth was open-eyed and paler even than the boy.

She wasn't moving.

Was she breathing?

Channing screamed behind the tape, tasting it. The boy sat and looked at the face of the fallen man. He watched him stir, and even Channing saw the eyes flicker. He would wake and take the boy out. It would begin all over. Elizabeth would die, and so would she. They'd go back to the silo, or he'd kill them here. Who could stop it? The boy was glass-eyed and frozen. Liz couldn't do it. Could Channing? She struggled against the tape, but it wasn't going to happen. The man was moving for real, and the boy watched it happen. He waited for the eyes to open, then moved as deliberately as anything Channing had ever seen. He rolled to his knees, said something she missed, then put metal against the preacher's skin and kept the trigger down until the battery died.


When it was over, Gideon looked down on Liz, then stumbled to the pew and used his teeth to work the tape off the girl's wrists. Weak as he was, it took a long time; when it was done, he slumped to the floor and watched her do the rest.

She lost hair and skin, but the tape came off. "Is she alive?" That was her first question, and he blinked once. Channing stripped the last tape from her ankles. "Thank you, thank you so much. Are you okay?"

"I honestly don't know."

"Here, lie down, and try not to move. You've lost a lot of blood." She made a pillow of the tarp and got him stretched out on the floor. He felt her hands, but from a distance. "What did you say to him? You waited for him to wake up. I saw it. What did you say?"

"Nothing you'd understand."

"Tell me anyway."

He blinked again and kept his eyes on her face. She seemed nice. He wanted to make her happy. "I said, 'You killed my mother. I hope this hurts.'"

Channing told him again to lie still, then went to Liz, who was alive, but in terrible shape. Her neck was swollen and black, her breath the barest thread. "Liz?" Channing touched her face. "Can you hear me?"

Nothing.

The eyes were blank, unseeing.

Channing worked at the knots that held Liz down, but her struggles had tightened them, and it took a long time. When she finished, Liz was with her, if only just. Her lips moved.

"What?" Channing leaned closer.

"Tie him."

Channing didn't know if the preacher was alive or dead, but it sounded like a good idea. She tied him as tightly as she could.

"What do I do now?" Channing touched Elizabeth's face. "Liz, please. I don't know what to do."

Elizabeth was crushed in the bottom of a deep hole. She thought maybe the hole was a grave. It had hard edges, the right shape, the darkness. The walls were ragged and black, the opening so small above she could barely see it. Her father was somewhere close, but she couldn't think about hurt that big or betrayal so vast. Shadows and black wind and sharp-edged stone. It was the place she couldn't go: her father and childhood and his face as he'd tried to kill her. She wanted to collapse the hole, instead, to pull down earth and rock and all the things that made her feel.

Maybe she wanted to die. That didn't feel like her, but what else did? The blood in her vision? The utter despair?

The hole darkened and deepened.

Her father was above it. Beyond him was a question.

Elizabeth drew a breath that burned all the way down. Something troubled her about the question. Not the question. The answer. People called the police when they were in danger. That was the problem. They called the police.

*Why was that wrong?*

She had the answer, but it slipped away in the dark. She found it again and felt it stick. Channing needed to understand the danger. She wouldn't see it coming.

"Channing . . ."

She felt her lips move, but knew the girl hadn't heard. Her face was in the world above, a slash of color, a kite.

"No police . . ." It was the smallest sound.

The girl leaned closer. "Did you say no police?"

Elizabeth tried to move her head, but could not. "Beckett . . ." She was in the grave, and hurting.

"Call Beckett."


When Elizabeth woke, the light was dim but she sensed Beckett in the church. It was his size, the way he loomed. "Charlie?"

"It's good to have you back. I was worried."

"There was a grave . . ."

"No. No grave."

"My father . . ."

"Shhh. He's alive. He's not going anywhere."

Beckett moved to where she could see him. Same face and suit. Same worried eyes.

"Channing told you?"

"Let's talk about you, first." He put hands on her shoulders to keep her down. "Just breathe for a minute. You're hurting. You're in shock. I feel your heart running like a train."

She felt it, too, the thunder and noise. "I'm going to be sick."

"You'll be fine. Just breathe."

"No, I'm not." Panic was a fist in her chest. "Jesus. God. I'm not." She felt slippery and cold. Her hands were shaking.

"He can't hurt you, Liz. He can't hurt anybody."

She risked a glance and saw him on the floor. He was tied and handcuffed, still unconscious, still her father. She lost it then, the rush of bile and the hard, hot vomit. She rolled left, and it spilled out of her like belief and warmth and life. She curled into a frozen ball, and Beckett was still touching her: his hands, the press of his cheek. His voice was there, too, but like the sound of surf. She thought of Channing and Gideon; wanted to move, but absolutely could not. The grave was all around her; she was choking.

"Breathe . . ." Beckett's voice was an ocean beyond the horizon. "Please, Liz. I need you to breathe."

But, the pressure in her chest crushed everything. The world built and pushed her down, and when it dragged her back, Beckett was still there.

He lifted her so she could sit. "Liz, look at me."

She blinked, and the rough edges filled in. She saw his face, his hands.

"Are you okay?"

"I'm fine."

"Can you stand?"

"Give me a minute."

Elizabeth touched her throat, felt swollen flesh and ridges from her father's fingers. She squinted around the church, saw the kids and her father and no one else. "Where is everybody?" She meant cops, paramedics. "There should be people here."

"You're still wanted on charges. Did you forget that?"

She nodded, but everything was fuzzy. She was dressed again, which must have been Channing's doing, or Charlie's. "Give me some space. Okay?"

"You sure?"

She raised a hand, and he backed off. Whatever happened next, she needed to do it on her own, to know she could. She swung her legs over the edge, coughing hard enough to choke all over again.

"Liz!"

Elizabeth pushed out with the same hand, keeping him back. She touched her chest and focused on taking careful, shallow breaths. He moved closer. "Don't. Just . . . don't touch me."

She slipped off the altar, stumbled, but stayed on her feet. Her father was on the floor. She hugged her ribs.

"Channing told me everything. I'm sorry, Liz. I honestly don't know what to say."

"I don't either."

"You'll deal with it. Time, maybe. Maybe therapy."

"My father tried to kill me, Charlie. How could I possibly deal with it?"

He had no response. How could he?

"Channing? Are you okay?"

"I'm all right."

"And Gideon?"

"He's bleeding. I don't know. Your friend won't let me call an ambulance."

Elizabeth moved to the bottom step. Gideon lay on the floor by Channing. He opened his eyes, but looked bled out and rough. Elizabeth glanced the length of the church and understood, at last, that something was very wrong. It was too quiet after so much time. Channing was wide-eyed and frightened and shaking her head in a small way. Elizabeth knew the look; she felt it. "Where are the people, Charlie?"

He turned his palms. "I told you . . ."

"You told me why there are no cops. Where are the paramedics? The boy is hurt. Channing is hurt. There should be paramedics. You could have made that happen, kept it quiet."

She moved toward the kids, but Beckett stepped between them. He was still palms up and smiling, but the lie was in his eyes. "We need to talk, first." She stopped after the bottom step. "Come on, Liz. Don't look at me like that." He forced a smile that failed.

Elizabeth had never been good at hiding the way she felt, and it was all in her face now, the distrust and doubt and anger. "Goddamn, Liz. I'm here to help you. The girl called and I came. Who else would do that? No questions. No doubt."

"What's going on, Charlie?"

"This whole week, who has been by your side, your friend? I've been that friend. Just me. Now, I need you to be mine."

She gauged the way he stood. Chin down, feet spread. His hands were out as if he'd grab her if she ran. Whatever was happening, he was serious about it. "Are you really standing between me and those children?"

"We just need to talk. Two minutes. We'll talk and call the ambulance, and this will all be over."

Her eyes fell to the gun in his belt. He was good with it. Plus he weighed 250. Whatever this was, she couldn't take him.

"Why don't you sit down."

She stepped sideways. Her father groaned.

"Please, Liz. Sit."

Elizabeth kept moving. She had no intention of sitting, and Beckett saw it. He nodded and sighed, and something artificial fell away. "Do you know where Adrian is?"

It was the last thing she expected.

"Adrian Wall. I need a location."

"What does Adrian have to do with any of this?"

"It's for everyone's good. You. The kids. I'm asking you to trust me."

"Not without an explanation."

"Just tell me."

"No."

"Goddamn it, Liz! Just tell me where he is!"

"Yes, please tell him."

The voice came from the back of the church, loud and familiar. Elizabeth registered the sudden desperation on Beckett's face, then saw the warden with Olivet and Jacks and Woods. They stood in the open door, four in a line and the sky behind them burning.

"Gideon. Channing."

She called the children to her, and they obeyed, Channing on her feet, the boy stumbling. They moved past Beckett, but he didn't try to stop them. His head was down. His shoulders slumped. Elizabeth got the children behind her as the world slowed, and everything came into sharp focus: the scrape of air in her throat, Beckett's sweat and fear and sudden despair. "You should have told me," he said, and though she heard the words, she wasn't listening. The warden led his men down the aisle, and Liz paid attention to the things that mattered. Two autoloaders. Two revolvers. Olivet looked scared.

"Please give him what he wants."

"Shut up, Charlie."

"Please, Liz. You don't know this man."

"Actually, I do."

The warden was close, now, fifteen feet, then ten. Elizabeth spoke when he reached the final pew. "I guess you two know each other better than I thought."

"Of course," the warden said. "Detective Beckett and I go back many years. How many is it, Charlie? Fifteen? Sixteen?"

"Don't pretend we're friends."

Beckett spat the words, and the warden tilted the pistol in his hand. "Friends. Acquaintances."

The arrogance was more obvious, now, the smile lazier and slow. It made Elizabeth's stomach turn. The warden wore a summer suit. His men, behind him, were in plainclothes. She kept her eyes on the warden. "Does he know what you did to Adrian?" She pitched her voice to carry. "The torture and abuse? Does he know your men tried to kill him?" She backed closer to the altar, and the children moved with her, up two steps, then three.

The warden and his men moved forward, too. "I like Vegas," the warden said. "It's the motto, I think." He waved a circle with the gun; held up both hands as if framing a marquee. "'What happens in Vegas stays in Vegas.' My prison is like that."

*His prison.*

He could call it that, and who would contradict him? Guards? Prisoners? Not if he was hard enough, malicious enough.

"Did you know?" she asked Beckett. "Did you know they tortured Adrian? That they killed his cellmate?"

"It doesn't matter what I know."

"How can you say that?"

"Desperate men," the warden interrupted. "I thank God for them every day."

"There is no money," she told the warden. "No pot at the end of your sad, little rainbow."

"I've explained once that we're beyond that. This is about William Preston, who was dear to me. It's about payback and endings and the natural order of things. Prisoners don't touch my guards. Inside the walls, beyond them. It doesn't happen." The barrel of his gun came up. "Detective Beckett, would you step away from them, please."

"You were supposed to wait outside." Beckett stood sideways to the warden, his chin down. "You wait outside. I come in. That was the deal."

"I'm an impatient man. It's a weakness."

"I gave you my word."

"Yet I have no reason to trust you."

"You have every reason! You know you do!" Beckett was begging. Elizabeth had never seen him beg. "I can get what you want. Please. Just leave them alone. Give me two minutes. I'll find out where he is. No one has to get hurt. No one has to die."

"You think I would kill someone?"

"I didn't mean it that way. Please . . ."

"Is that man alive?"

The warden pointed his gun at Reverend Black, bound on the floor. Elizabeth opened her mouth to speak, but before she could, the warden shot her father in the heart. The bullet went in small and came out big. The body barely moved.

"That was to get your attention."

Elizabeth stared at her father.

Channing threw up.

"I want Adrian Wall." The gun was a .45, cocked. He pointed it at Gideon. "He seems like a nice boy."

"No!"

Elizabeth leapt in front of the gun, her fingers spread. She was bent at the waist, desperate and small, and begging, too.

"Goddamn it!" Beckett yelled. "This was not our fucking deal!"

"Our deal's off." The warden shot Beckett in the gut. For a second the big man stood, then crumpled.

"Charlie!" Elizabeth dropped beside him. "Oh, Jesus Christ. Charlie."

She put a hand on the bullet wound in his stomach, then felt the exit wound in his back. It was large and ragged, and beneath it was a pistol. Pain swam in Beckett's eyes, but he mouthed a single word.

*Don't . . .*

She looked at the warden and his men. Guns were up and level. "You bastard."

"Stomach wounds are extremely painful," he said. "Yet, people recover."

"Why . . . ?"

"The violence? This?" He waved an arm across the dead and dying. "So, you would take me seriously, and give me what I want."

"Charlie. Oh, God . . ."

His blood pooled against her knees. His fingers twined into hers. "It wasn't supposed to be like this." She felt him fading. "Liz, I'm sorry . . ."

She touched his throat when his eyes closed. He was in a bad way, but breathing. "What do you have on him?" Her voice cut, and she rose, fearless. "He wouldn't have done this without a reason."

"Brought me here? No. But I was with him when the little girl called." The warden made another circle with the barrel of his gun. "He was trying to protect you. He told me he could get what I want. Obviously, he could not. Now, here we are."

"He needs medical care."

"Like William Preston needed medical care?" The warden held the stare; she had no words. "It's a funny thing, really." The warden sat on a pew, speaking conversationally. "When we first met, I felt as if I knew you. What you value. The person you really are." He lit a cigarette and pointed the gun at Gideon's chest. "Where is Adrian Wall?"

"Don't."

He swung his aim to the girl. "You see how this works." The gun moved back and forth. The boy. The girl. "I want you to call him. Tell him to come here. Tell him he has an hour before I start killing children."

"He's farther away than that."

"I'm an impatient man, but not beyond reason. We'll call it ninety minutes."

Elizabeth held the stare. The warden smiled.

At their feet, Beckett lay dying.

# 36

Adrian was at the window when the phone rang. Only Liz knew he was here, so he answered, "Liz?"

"Adrian, thank God." She was curt, her voice strained. "Listen to me, and listen carefully. I don't have much time. You remember my father's church? The old one?"

Of course, he remembered. He'd joined the church a month after finding Elizabeth at the quarry. He'd hoped to marry Julia there and start a new life. It had, for a time, embodied dreams of better days.

"What's going on, Liz?"

"I need you at the church, and I need you soon."

"Why?"

"Just come, please. It's important."

"Are you in some kind of trouble?"

"Do you remember the last thing I said to you? Our last phone call?"

"Yes. Of course."

"I mean it now more than ever."

Adrian wanted to know more. He had questions.

The phone went dead.

The warden took the phone from Elizabeth's fingers and slipped it into his pocket. The conversation had been on speakerphone. His insistence. "Were you being clever, just now?"

"No."

He leaned close enough to smell his skin, the gel in his hair. He was closely shaven, his eyes too soft and brown for the man he was. Elizabeth averted her gaze, but he touched her hair with a finger, tapped the gun against her knee.

"What was the last thing you said to him?"

"You wanted him here. I said what I had to say to make sure he'd come."

"I find that answer unsatisfactory."

She glanced at the children, then at Beckett. His eyes were open; he was watching. "The last thing I said was that I loved him. He'll come because of that."

The warden measured her words, her face. "Are you lying to me?"

"All I want is for the children to live."

"Eighty-nine minutes."

*Stay away from this place. Stay away from me.*

Those were the last words she'd said to him. Did she really want him to stay away? He doubted it. Else why call him at all? Something had changed, and it wasn't something good.

Cops, maybe?

That was equally doubtful.

The warden?

That was the best bet, but it didn't really matter. Liz would not have called unless she needed him. The beautiful part was that he had clarity at last, knew what to do and when to do it. He heard Eli as if he were in the room.

*It's only worth so much, boy* .

Six million dollars, he thought.

Liz was worth more.


In the church, it was hot and still. Beckett was alive, but as close to dead as Elizabeth had ever seen a man. She asked the same question for the seventh time. "Please, may I help him?"

Gideon and Channing sat on either side of her, the three of them herded onto the step at the bottom of the altar and held at gunpoint. Olivet was at the door. The warden stood gazing at stained glass.

"He's dying," she said.

"Two minutes left." The warden tapped his watch. "I hope he makes it in time."

"I've done what you asked. No one else needs to die."

She said it as if she meant it, but deep down she knew the truth. If the warden had his way, no one would get out alive. Witnesses. Risks. He would accept neither, not with one man dead and another dying, not once he had Adrian.

"Talk to me," she said. "Let's work this out."

"Stop talking."

"I'm serious. There must be something—"

"Bring her here." The warden gestured, and one of the guards hauled Elizabeth to her feet. "Put her down there. Cuff her to the pew."

"Why are you doing this?"

"So I have a clear shot at the children."

She jerked an arm free, but the guard pushed her down, pulled her hands behind her back, and cuffed her to the leg of the pew. "You wouldn't."

"Actually, I'd rather not." The warden stooped beside her. "Can't you feel it, though?" He traced the line of her cheek. "The suspense." He was speaking of Adrian, and confidence underlay it all. "Sixty seconds."

"Don't pretend you'll let us live."

"Not even for the children?"

The smile seemed shockingly real, but the eyes said it all. He'd shot one man in the heart, and put a bullet in a cop's stomach. It could only end one way. He knew it, and she did, too.

"Movement." That was Olivet at the open door. Beyond him, it was dusk. Purple sky. Cicadas in the grass. "Car's turning in. Some kind of green wagon."

The warden looked at his watch and, before he stood, gave a wink Elizabeth would never forget. Craning her neck, she saw three men at the door, one watching the children. Elizabeth caught Channing's eye, and the guard—seeing it—put his gun to Channing's head. "Everybody just stay calm," he said.

But, that was not possible.

It was not even close.

When the church appeared on the hill, it was more to Adrian than glass and stone and iron. It was the past, his youth, his undying regret. He'd hoped to be married there, and to start a life with the woman he should have married all along. The building was old, and solid. He'd liked the feel of it and the permanence, the reverend's message of birth and hope and forgiveness. He'd thought of it often as his marriage failed. At times he'd driven to the church and simply watched it on the hill, thinking, *If I am honest at last . . .*

Instead, he'd gone to trial for Julia's murder and never spoken of regret or redemption. He spent thirteen years dreaming of the life he'd lost, and when the church rose tall in those dreams, he saw Julia die alone and pleading; and it wasn't God she called for, or her husband. The name on her lips was his, night after night. She was afraid and dying, yet he was never there but in the dreams. When next the nightmares came, would he see his wife, as well? Or Liz? The thought was unbearable so he made a promise as the road fell away and gravel shifted beneath the tires.

*Whatever it takes.*

*Never again.*

Cresting the hill, he saw men in the door and parked cars. He stopped twenty feet from the granite steps. The warden stood outside the door with Olivet and Jacks. Woods would be there, too, probably with Liz. Adrian killed the engine and put the key in his pocket. The air outside was warm.

"You should have run and kept running."

The warden stepped out, his shoes scraping granite. The trees above his head were dark and heavy.

"Maybe I should have killed you. First day out. First night."

"You don't have the balls."

"Maybe you underestimate me. Maybe you always have."

"That implies you had secrets to keep, and that you kept them. I find that hard to believe."

Adrian fished a gold coin from his pocket and tossed it so it rang on the steps. The warden kept an eye on Adrian and picked it up, tilting it. "You could buy the same in any pawnshop."

Adrian flung another dozen coins.

"So, it's true." The warden didn't stoop that time. He smoothed a thumb across the coin; showed it to Jacks. "How many?"

"Five thousand. They're yours if you let her go."

The warden studied Adrian with new eyes. Respect was there, and even a little fear. All that time, unbroken. All that pain. "There's still the matter of William Preston."

"It's six million dollars," Adrian said. And that was the only truth that mattered. He saw it in the warden's face, and in the way Jacks shifted his feet. Friendship was fine, but the money came first.

"Do you have it with you?"

"I'm not stupid."

"How do you propose to do this?"

"If Liz is okay, I'll take you to the gold. She stays behind."

"If I say no?"

"You can torture me again, for all the good it'll do."

"Maybe I'll torture her, instead."

"Death is death," Adrian said. "We all win or none of us do."

The warden rubbed his chin, thinking. "And when she tells her story about what happened here?"

"Do you love your wife?"

"Not so much."

"It's six million dollars. Untraceable. You can put it in the trunk and go anywhere. Tomorrow morning you start a whole new life."

The warden smiled, and it made Adrian nervous. "I don't think Detective Black would accept the idea of her torture as lightly as you."

"She wouldn't have called me unless she'd thought it through."

"Perhaps, she thought you'd come in, guns blazing."

"I'm nobody's hero. She knows that."

The warden ran the same thumb across the coin. "Jacks is going to pat you down." He gestured, and Jacks took the stairs.

The pat-down was rough and thorough. "He's clean."

"All right, then." The warden picked up the other coins, bounced them in his palm so they rattled and clinked. "Let's go inside and talk this thing out."

Adrian followed the warden and felt Olivet and Jacks close up behind. He had no confidence his plan would work, but it was all he had: gold and men's greed and his own readiness to die. He knew the warden, though. He was pushing sixty, tired of his job. Six million was a lot of money. Adrian thought the plan had a shot.

That disappeared when he saw the kids.

Before that moment, it was all or nothing. The plan worked or it did not. If Elizabeth died, he'd die with her. There'd been acceptance in that, and a kind of difficult peace. Liz made her choices. He made his.

That had nothing to do with the kids.

They huddled beneath the altar, not just frightened, but wounded. He knew Gideon, of course, who was as close as anything alive to the woman Adrian had loved with all his heart. The girl would be the one from the papers, Channing. A man was dead on the floor. Elizabeth's father, he thought. The other man was Beckett, who was dead or close to it. Elizabeth was secured to a pew on the front row. "I want her free. Right now."

"Adrian—"

"Hang on, now." The warden cut her off. "This is still my show, so let's try this again." He drew his pistol and put the barrel against Elizabeth's knee. "Where did you hide it?"

"I'll take you to it."

"I know you will."

"The five of us in a car," Adrian said. "We drive east on back roads. No cops. No witnesses. Two hours later, you're rich."

"My leverage is here."

"It's the smart move. Six million dollars."

"Bring me the boy."

"No!" Elizabeth fought the cuffs. "You son of a bitch! You bastard!" She kicked the warden once.

He struck her on the head, knocking her bloody. "The boy. Now."

Gideon tried to fight, but the guard was too strong. He dragged the boy down the steps and across the rotted carpet. He left him at the warden's feet, screaming as a foot pushed on his throat and the barrel of a gun dug into the place he'd been shot. "You see how this works?" The warden leaned on the gun and twisted. "No one around. Lots of time."

"Stop it," Adrian said.

"Where's Eli's gold? Come on, Adrian." The barrel twisted again. An edge of smile carved the warden's face. "You remember how we do this."

Adrian tore his eyes from the boy. Three guards. Three guns.

"Girl's next," the warden said. "Then, Liz."

He pushed harder, and Gideon screamed again, his voice as high and clear as that of any choirboy who'd ever sung in the ancient church.

———

Beckett was in all kinds of hurt, but alert enough to know how badly he'd messed up. The warden. Liz. The reverend . . .

He saw the dead man, the open eyes.

He found Liz, then blinked and thought of Carol.

*My beautiful lady . . .*

They were his life, the both of them, his partner and his wife. He loved them each, but the choice had never been in doubt.

His wife.

It would always be his wife.

*But this . . .*

Death and children and the way Liz looked at him. He'd never had a choice, but goddamn it was bad. The kids. The hole in his gut. He was dying; had to be. There were words he couldn't understand, a musty smell and movement like a spill of color. He was fading, nearly gone.

But there was also the pain.

*God . . .*

He blinked, and it chewed through him, dragged him in and out, and broke him like a bottle on a rock. Right now he was lucid, if only just. The boy was screaming; the guards were focused on Adrian.

That left Channing.

Beckett tried to speak, but couldn't; tried to move, but his legs didn't work. One arm was trapped beneath him, but the other was clear. He could barely move it—just his fingers—but he got fabric in his grip and worked the jacket up, an inch, then five. When the gun at his back was exposed, he tried to say her name, but came up empty. It hurt. Every bit of it hurt like hell. But this was his fault, so he asked God to take pity on a stupid, fucked-up, dying man. He prayed for strength, then drew air into his lungs and said her name again. It came out a croak, the barest whisper. But she heard it and saw the gun.

The girl, who was bending above him.

Channing, who could shoot like a dream.

Olivet saw it first, a slip of girl with a gun too large for such tiny hands. He wasn't worried. She could barely stand, and thirty feet of carpet stretched between them. His instinct was to hold out an open hand and say, *Careful, little girl.* Instead, he said, "Warden."

The warden looked up from the bright-eyed, bled-out little boy. The girl staggered right, as if the gun were pulling her down. Her eyes were barely open. She was basically falling.

"Somebody shoot that little bitch," the warden said, and Olivet's first thought was *Damn.* His own daughter was not much smaller and this one was kind of cute, trying to be brave and all. He'd rather just take the gun and sit her back down.

But nobody crossed the warden.

He took his aim off Adrian, but Jacks was faster, gun dropping low, then swinging up and going level. Olivet saw the little girl go still when the gun started coming her way. For a microsecond she seemed to slump; but it was not a slump. She dropped into a perfect stance and snapped off three shots as crisp and clean as anything Olivet had ever seen. Jacks's head sprayed blood, as did Woods's and the warden's. Two seconds. Three shots. Olivet's gun was on her, but he hesitated. She was fast and sure, and so like his own little girl. His last thought was to be impressed with whatever daddy taught her to shoot like that, then bright light appeared at the end of her barrel, and the world, entire, went dark.


When it was done, Adrian stood in disbelief. The warden's head had been a bare foot above Gideon's, and one of the guards had stood directly behind Adrian, so close that Adrian felt the bullet split air as it passed his ear. Now they were gone, all of them, and the church was graveyard still, the girl quietly crying. Adrian's first instinct was to check the bodies, then see to Liz and the boy. Yet, he did none of those things, choosing instead to pick his way through the bodies until the girl appeared, small, beneath him. He took the gun from her fingers and placed it on the altar.

"I killed them," she said.

"I know."

"What's wrong with me?"

There were no words beyond the obvious, so Adrian said them: "You saved our lives," he said, then spread his arms and wrapped her up as she fell.


It took time, after that, to know what to do. Liz was out when he uncuffed her, and when she woke, they argued. "Charlie needs immediate medical attention," she said. "So does Gideon."

"I'm not arguing that."

"I won't leave until they're safe."

Even in the carnage, she was fiercely protective and certain of what was right. Channing wanted to come with them, and Adrian thought that was just fine. But, Liz would not leave until an ambulance was at the church.

"I can't be here when the cops come," Adrian said. "Neither can you. It means prison for both of us. Murder. Accessory to murder. The warrants haven't gone away."

"Beckett's shot through the spine," Elizabeth said. "We can't move him."

"I know, yes. And the boy may be bleeding inside. But, you and I can go. So can the girl."

Elizabeth turned to Channing, who was so small and rolled inward she looked no more than ten. Liz took her hand and knelt. "No one will blame you for what you did, sweetheart. You're the victim. You can stay."

She shook her head. "No."

"This is your home—"

"Why would I stay?" Emptiness thinned the girl's voice. "To be pointed at for life? To be the freak who was raped for a day and half, the dangerous, fucked-in-the-head little girl who killed two men and then four more?" She broke, and the sight dissolved every hard edge in Adrian's soul. "I want to stay with you. You're my friend. You understand."

"What about your parents?"

"I'm eighteen. I'm not a child."

Adrian saw Liz accept it, the way she leaned in and placed her forehead against the girl's. "How do we handle it?" he asked.

Liz told them what she wanted to do. When it was agreed and understood, she stood one last time above her father's body. Adrian had no idea what she was thinking, but she didn't linger or touch her father or say a single word. Instead, she called 911 and said the words that would make everything happen: "Officer down," she said, then knelt by Beckett and touched his forehead. "I don't understand, and I'm not sure I ever will. But I hope you're alive when they get here, and that one day you can explain."

Maybe Beckett heard her, and maybe he didn't. His eyes were closed, his breathing shallow.

"Liz."

"I know," she said. "Clock's ticking."

But Gideon was harder. He wanted to go, too. He begged. "Please, Liz. Please don't leave me."

"You need a doctor."

"But I want to go with you! Please don't leave me! Please!"

"Just tell the truth about what happened. You've done nothing wrong." She kissed his face, and kissed it hard. "I'll come back for you. I promise."

They left him calling her name; and Adrian realized then that he might never have a hard edge again.

So much love.

Such heartbreak.

Outside, in the dusk, the sirens were drawing near. "They'll be okay," Liz said, but nobody answered. She was talking to herself.

"We need to move."

She nodded to tell Adrian he was right and she knew it. "Will you drive?"

"Of course."

She put Channing in the back and took the front seat for herself. "We'll be okay," she said, and no one responded to that, either.

Adrian kept the lights off as he felt his way down the drive. "Wait here," Liz said; and they waited until lights crested a far hill, and they were certain. Ambulances. Cop cars. Gideon would be okay, and even Beckett might make it. "Okay," she said. "We can go now."

Adrian turned the car away from the sirens and the lights. When they were clear, he clicked on his headlights. "Where are we going?"

"West," Elizabeth said. "Very west."

Adrian nodded, and so did the girl.

"We have to make one stop," he said; and when the first chance came, he turned the car east.

# EPILOGUE

## Seven Months Later

The view from the desert hilltop was extraordinary. Mountains rose all around, as brown and splintered as old bone. The house was the same color, ninety-year-old adobe that blended like a tortoise into the saguaro and eucalyptus and paloverde. The walls were two feet thick, the floors Spanish tile. In back was a walled courtyard with a swimming pool. The front was all about the covered porch and long views and morning coffee. Elizabeth was on her second cup when Adrian stepped through the door to join her. He wore no shoes, and jeans that were faded nearly white. The scars were white against the tan, but so were his teeth. "Where's Channing?"

He took the second rocking chair as Elizabeth pointed. Channing was a smudge on the valley floor, the horse beneath her dapple gray. They were picking their way along the arroyo that flooded when rains fell in the mountains to the north. Liz couldn't see her face, but guessed she was smiling. That was the thing about the gray.

"How's she doing?" Adrian asked.

"She's strong."

"That's not really an answer."

"The therapy helps."

Adrian glanced at the truck that sat, dusty, in the drive. Twice a week Elizabeth and Channing took it into town. They never discussed particulars with Adrian, but they both thought the therapist there was good. They were looser when they came back; the smiles came easier.

"You should go sometime," Elizabeth said. "It helps to talk to someone."

"I do that, already."

"Eli doesn't count."

He smiled and sipped the coffee. She was wrong about Eli, but he didn't expect her to understand. "And, how are you?" he asked.

"Same answer," she said, but he knew better. She woke screaming at times, and he often found her outside at three in the morning. He never bothered her, but watched to make sure she was safe from coyote or mountain lion or the dreams that came with such fierce predictability. She'd find her way to the same place at the edge of the arroyo, a flat, narrow stone that held the heat of the day. She'd stand straight in a thin gown or under a blanket, and always she looked at the stars, thinking of her mother or Gideon or the horrors inflicted by her father. Adrian didn't know and never asked. His job was to be there on the porch, to nod quietly as she returned to the house and trailed a finger across his shoulder as if to say thanks.

"Is today still the day?" he asked.

"I think it's time. Don't you?"

"Only if you're ready."

"I am."

They sat in easy silence after that, the moment made comfortable by all the ones that had passed before it. They were good together in that easy way. Nobody pushed. Nobody took. But, something had changed in the past few weeks, and both of them felt it. An energy was there where none had been before, a spark if one's skin brushed the other's. They didn't talk about it, yet—it was too small and fragile—but the time was coming and they both knew it.

She was healing.

They all were.

"Are you sure you won't change your mind?" He waited until she looked his way. She was as tanned as he, her face leaner, the lines at her eyes a little deeper. "I can come with you."

"Too dangerous, I think." She brushed his hand. The lightest touch. "I'll make sure we get back safe and sound."

Her fingers moved away, but the charge lingered. "When will you leave?"

She kept her eyes on the girl. "When I finish this cup of coffee."

She sipped slowly, and Adrian watched her as she rocked in the old chair that had come with the house. She wore peacefulness as if it were a blanket she'd decided to wrap around her shoulders. Even now that couldn't be easy, not with her father a monster and the story out there for everyone to see. Both had followed the news as events played out after the church. Dyer used two bloody fingerprints found on the dash of the old car to tie Reverend Black to the murdered women. They were Ramona Morgan's prints, and reporters speculated she'd left them there after tearing skin trying to claw her way out of some dark and lonely place. Nothing yet tied him to the other victims, but there was little doubt, official or otherwise. Liz lost sleep, at times, thinking she should go back and fill in the blanks. But, nights like that were growing less frequent. What further insight could she offer? The victims would be just as gone. Their families would have the same person to blame.

Besides, her father was dead.

The story of the warden and his corrupt guards was the one that lingered. The fury over why they were dead in the church soon gave way to larger questions. What were they doing there? Why did they die? An old man came forward a few days later, an ex-con with an almost unbelievable story of how he'd been tortured, once, and how others had died hard deaths in the warden's care.

He was not the most credible person, though, and the story almost ended with him. But, two more convicts came forward, then a guard who'd seen things he should have talked about sooner. That was the crack that blew the story wide open.

Torture. Murder.

The attorney general had ordered a full review.

Charges still stood against Adrian, and he'd go down if the authorities ever found him. They stood against Liz, too, but no one was looking for her, and she had no plans to make a life anywhere but the desert. She liked the heat of it, she said, its emptiness and unchanging nature. Plus, Channing and Adrian were in the desert. No one said it out loud, but the words hung like a shimmer far out on the valley floor.

*Family.*

*Future.*

Adrian stood and leaned against the rail. He wanted her to see his face, so she'd think about it as she drove. "Will you be okay if he says no?"

"Gideon?" The look in her eyes was gentle, the smile easy and slow. "I don't think it'll be a problem."

Elizabeth took the truck and drove ten-hour stretches. Sunglasses covered her eyes. A white Stetson rode her head. She stayed in inexpensive motels, though money was not a problem. On the eighth hour of the third day, she crossed the county line and was back. Nothing had changed, but an ill wind pressed against her as if she were somehow different and every living creature in the county sensed it.

She drove the side streets, then went to her mother's house, stopping first at the boarded-up church. The clapboards were dirty and peeling. Windows were broken, and someone had used black paint on the walls, spelling words such as *killer* and *sinner* and *devil*. Circling to the back, she found the parsonage little different than the church. Shattered glass. The same paint.

The door was locked, but she took the tire iron from the truck and forced it. Inside, she found bare floors and dust and difficult memories. She stood for a while at the kitchen window, thinking of the last time she'd had a drink there with her mother. Had she known, then, the depth of her husband's evil? Had she ever sensed it? Elizabeth wanted an answer and found it on the mantelpiece above the small fireplace in the empty living room. The envelope was yellowed and dry. The name *Elizabeth* was written in her mother's hand.

> *Liz, my darling girl. I can't imagine a daughter's pain in learning such darkness dwelled in her father's heart, or in knowing the death and suffering he'd caused so many for so many years. Please know I share your bewilderment. Your letters have been so helpful—life-affirming, actually—and it pains me that you live in some secret place to which I can neither respond, nor seek you out. I've never doubted your assurances, the promise that we would once again be together. But I can no longer live in this place. The hatred of your father overwhelms me, and I find myself bereft. I leave this letter in hopes you'll discover it when you deem it safe, at last, to return. I've gone to stay with my old friend in the north. You've met her, the one from college. I won't leave her name or address for obvious reasons, but trust you will seek me out, in time. I miss you so much, my lovely child. Please do not let this path lead you to self-doubt or your own dark place. Be strong and of good heart. I wait for you in patience and in love, your friend and trusting ally, your mother for all time.*

Elizabeth read the note twice, then folded it with care. She'd ached for her mother, but in a way was relieved. As much as they loved each other, how could the horrors her father had wrought not thrive in whatever place they shared? Too many shared looks and memories, childhood and holidays, and a thousand different nights. They both needed to find their way first, some manner in which to meet each other's eyes without drowning in the guilt of their long and mutual ignorance. The time would come, Elizabeth knew, but not soon and not easily. In the meantime, she'd write again and let her mother know she'd found the letter, and that time, at least, remained their friend.

Beckett came next, and the meeting would be hard. She'd spent long nights concocting theories of why he'd done the things he'd done. She had one or two, but theories weren't answers, and she needed to understand so many things.

Parking near his house, she saw him on the porch in a wheelchair. He couldn't walk anymore and wasn't a cop. He taught criminology at the community college, and in the pictures she'd found online, he seemed well enough, though sad. She watched him for a long time, realizing as she did that, in spite of everything, she'd missed him. They'd been partners for four years, and he'd saved her life more than once. Was the wheelchair a large enough price for whatever mistakes he'd made? She didn't know, yet, but planned to find out.

He didn't move when he saw her. He didn't smile, either. "Every day." He nodded when he said it. "Every day I've waited for you to come." His eyes were dark and troubled, his legs wasted beneath a quilt.

Elizabeth stepped onto the porch. "I've tried very hard not to hate you."

"There's that, at least."

"Why'd you do it, Charlie?"

"I never thought anyone would die." His eyes filled as he said it. "Please believe me when I say that."

"I do. Now, help me understand. What did he have on you?"

"Elizabeth . . ."

"I want to know what leverage was so strong you'd put those children and me in danger. No bullshit, either, Charlie. You owe me the truth, at least."

He sighed and watched the street. "If I do this, I'll never repeat it again, not to you or anyone else."

"You understand I can't make the same promise." Elizabeth couldn't hide the way she felt. She was angry and frustrated.

Beckett seemed to accept that. "My wife is an educated woman. College degree. A master's. She didn't always cut hair."

"Okay."

"When she was young, she worked for the county." Beckett smoothed the quilt. "Specifically, she worked for the comptroller."

"She was a bookkeeper?"

"An accountant," Beckett said. "Gideon's father worked for the county, too. He was an assistant county manager, believe it or not. A different man before his wife died. Young, ambitious. He didn't drink. Didn't even smoke."

"I remember he was working with Adrian and Francis."

"A quarter million dollars were missing from the county treasury. He was helping Adrian and Francis figure it out. They were close. Another week and they'd have found her."

Elizabeth saw it, then. "Your wife."

"I couldn't let her go to prison. She had a problem then, but not anymore. Gambling in secret. Stupid stuff that caught her out. She's not a bad person. You know her. You have to believe that."

"She was stealing funds, and Adrian was close to figuring it out."

"I just wanted him distracted. That's it. I thought the beer can would make him look sloppy, make people doubt. It was just a distraction. Liz, please . . ."

But, she had to walk away, down the porch and back. "You planted evidence in a murder case. You implicated another cop."

"I didn't know about the scratches or the DNA match. I didn't think Adrian would go to prison. When the match came back, I thought he was guilty, that I'd actually helped."

"You didn't."

"I know that."

"We could have caught the real killer—"

"I thought we *had* the real killer! Don't you see the horrible truth of it? I thought I'd done this selfish thing and gotten lucky. I thought it was providence."

Elizabeth stared out at the street, feeling the weight of it. The can led to Adrian, then to the blood sample and the DNA match. It led to his conviction, his torture, and all the evil the warden had brought into Elizabeth's life. "Without the can we might have caught my father thirteen years ago. Lauren Lester, Ramona Morgan, Adrian's wife. They might all have lived. Eleven women, Charlie. We could have stopped it."

"Maybe."

"Is that what you tell yourself so you can sleep at night?"

"I'd apologize a thousand times if I thought it would help."

But Elizabeth didn't want to hear his apologies or explanations. It was all so clear. A stupid crime and a simple misdirection, prison and pointless death, ripples on some foreign shore. "Tell me about the warden."

"We were friends before I knew what kind of man he was. I got drunk once and told him what happened. My wife, the beer can. He's held the truth over me ever since."

"What did he want?"

"Adrian's location. He wanted that, and he wanted you to stay clear. That's it. That's all."

"Until he tortured Gideon and killed my father."

"Liz—"

"The innocent people in that motel room."

Beckett looked down. He had no words.

"Does your wife know?"

"None of it. She can't. It would kill her."

Elizabeth leaned against the porch rail, crossed her arms.

"What are you going to do?" Beckett asked.

"About you? That's Adrian's decision."

"Liz, listen . . ."

She didn't plan to listen. The anger was too intense. It was all so stupid and needless and destructive. She felt the love for Charlie down deep, but like a shadow on her heart. Her father should have been stopped years ago. Those women should be alive, and Adrian should never have gone to prison. What excuse was there? What path to forgiveness?

She was about to leave without another word, to turn on her heel and never look back, but she saw Charlie's wife in the open door, Carol, who'd started it all.

"Hello, Liz." She stepped onto the porch, a soft, round woman with warm eyes and a broad, rich smile. "I'm so happy to see you."

"Are you?"

Elizabeth felt the stiffness and the cold, but Carol seemed oblivious. She swept across the porch, wrapped her arms around Elizabeth, and pulled her into all that softness. "You poor thing. What you've suffered, my God. You poor, sweet, unfortunate thing." Elizabeth kept her guard up, but Carol's affection was unstoppable. "Charlie told me you saved his life, that he'd have died without you. Thank you for that, for my husband's life."

She stepped back, and Elizabeth wondered at the lie Charlie had told. There was such love between him and Carol, and maybe that's why he'd done it, so Elizabeth would be part of that, too. She didn't know, and looking at Carol's broad, beaming face, she didn't really care. The past was past, and she was moving on.

"You should know," Elizabeth said, "that Charlie would do anything for you." She held Carol's eyes. "Anything at all. That's how much he loves you."

Carol beamed even more, and that was Elizabeth's final gift, not of forgiveness but silence, the chance for one good thing to remain when she left.

"Good-bye, Charlie." She stepped off the porch and left them there. "I'm sorry about the wheelchair."

"Liz—"

"Take care of each other."

"Liz, wait."

But Elizabeth didn't wait. She walked away and took a final look from the truck. Beckett was in the chair and unmoving, his hands spread on the quilt as his wife leaned close and smiled and kissed his cheek. What would Adrian do with what she'd learned about Beckett's betrayal and Carol's original sin? She didn't know for sure, but a stillness had been in Adrian these last weeks, a keenness to lift his arm and let life break like a current around him. Like her, he cared more for the future than the past, more for hope than anger.

She thought Charlie would be okay.

Starting the truck, she worked it past the abandoned plants, and down the long hill on the bad side of town. She followed the creek and found Gideon's home as abandoned and broken as the one she'd left behind the clapboarded church. A foreclosure notice was nailed to the frame, but it seemed the bank didn't care too much for the house. The door stood open. Dead leaves stirred on the threshold. Elizabeth sat for a long time and worried for the boy. Without her, the house was all he had: the sad, small house and the sad, small father. Turning across the broken road, she went to the fourth place on her list and found Faircloth on the front porch of his grand old home. He was draped in blankets and safeguarded by a round-faced nurse with a sunny disposition. "Are you here to see Mr. Jones? How lovely." She bustled across the porch and met Elizabeth at the top step. "He gets so few visitors."

Elizabeth followed her to Faircloth's side. His mouth and left eye drooped. At his right hand was a table with pen and paper, and an old-fashioned with a straw that was curved and damp and as red as the cherry in the bottom of the glass. "He can't speak," the nurse said, "but he's in there all the same."

Elizabeth took a seat and studied the old man. He was thinner and older, but the eyes were still bright. His hand shook as he wrote. "So happy."

"I'm happy, too, Faircloth. So very happy to see you."

"But dangerous," he wrote.

She took his curled left hand and held it in both of hers.

"I'm being careful. I promise. Our mutual friend is fine, too. He's far away and safe. Channing is with us."

Faircloth began to rock minutely. Tears brightened the seams of his face. "Give love," he wrote.

"That's why I'm here. We have room for you, too. We have space and time and money for nurses. Come back with me." His head moved as if he were shaking it. "It would be no inconvenience. We've talked about it for months."

He looked at the pad. His hand moved. "Lived here. Die here."

"There's no need for you to be alone."

He wrote again. "Pretty nurse. Soft hands." Elizabeth looked up from the pad and saw the smile in his eyes. "Belvedere?" he wrote.

"Faircloth . . ."

"I'll get it." The nurse stood. "He asks me all the time, this time of day. But I'm not much for alcohol or forward men."

Faircloth wrote, "Tease." The nurse kissed his forehead, then went inside to fix Elizabeth's drink. When she was gone, he wrote, "Gideon?"

"That's part of the reason I'm here."

He wrote an address, then, "Foster."

"Foster parents."

"Not good." The light left his eyes.

Elizabeth squeezed again. "I'll find him. I'll make it right."

The nurse returned and handed Elizabeth the drink. "I'm going to start dinner. Will you sit with him for a while?"

"There's nothing I'd rather do." She waited for the nurse to leave, then lifted the old-fashioned so Faircloth could take a sip.

"You and Adrian?" he wrote.

"He's a strong man, and healing. I think we're doing well."

"How well?"

She saw the twinkle that time and took the question exactly as Faircloth meant it. "The next man I kiss will be forever. Adrian knows that."

"So kiss him."

"Soon, I think." She lifted her glass and sat beside the old man. "Happy," he wrote. "Will die happy."

Elizabeth found Gideon in a neighborhood park three houses down from the one his foster parents owned. He was alone on a swing, and she watched from beneath the brim of her hat. None of the other kids called out or looked at him. He sat still on the plastic seat, his sneakers scuffing in the dirt. She watched for a long time as if her own heart beat in the emptiness of that park.

He never looked up.

He barely moved.

Even when her shadow stretched across his feet, his interest was perfunctory. That changed when he looked up and the hat came off.

"Hello, Gideon."

He didn't say a word, but came off the swing in a tangle of limbs. His face was hard and hot as he squeezed her.

She felt tears through her shirt. "Are you okay?"

He squeezed harder, and Elizabeth checked the park for parents or cops. No one looked at them twice. "Let's take a walk." She caught his hand, and he fell in beside her. "You've grown." He smeared a forearm across his face, and she knew he was embarrassed. "Are they feeding you well?"

"I guess."

It was a start. She squeezed his hand. "How's your father?"

"Homeless. Still drunk."

"I'm sorry, Gideon. I would fix him if I could."

"It's been seven months." He pulled his hand free. "You said you would come for me."

"I know. I'm sorry. I wanted you to have a chance."

"To do what?"

"Decide." She sat on a bench. She wanted his hands again, but they were shoved deep in his pockets. "I'm here, now."

His eyes were bloodshot and bright, but different, too. Older.

More guarded. Behind him, the sun was setting. "Decide what?"

"If you wanted to stay here or come with me. It's a big decision. I wanted you to be ready for it."

He looked down the street. "I was in the hospital for three weeks."

"I know."

"Everyone I had was dead or gone. My father only visited once." Anger. Shiny eyes.

"People were looking for us. Police. FBI. They may still be looking."

He weighed her words, and she hated the distance between them.

"Do you like your foster parents?"

"Your father is the one that did it." He wiped his nose again, intent. "In the church. He killed my mother."

"I know, sweetheart."

"What if I'd killed Mr. Wall?"

"You didn't."

The boy looked down the street, and Elizabeth realized he was looking at his foster parents' house. "He lives with you now, doesn't he?"

"He does, yes."

"Does he hate me?"

"Of course not."

"Is he nice?"

"Yes, he's nice. He's also smart and patient and knows everything about horses and cattle and the desert. He loved your mother very much. I think he'll love you, too."

"If I come?"

"If you come, yes." He stared at the dirt. "That's my truck." She pointed. "It's a three-day drive. Just you and me."

He looked at the truck. It was dusty and travel-streaked. "What about my stuff? You know . . . ?"

"I'll let your foster parents know you're safe. Your father, too, if you like. People might look for you, but we can handle that, if need be. As for your stuff, we'll get new stuff. Clothes. Toys. A new name if you want it. Channing is with us, too. She hopes you'll come."

He looked at the house again, and at the near-empty park. "Is it nice where you live?"

"Very."

He tried to be tough, to be grown up about it. But, his face crumpled as she watched. "I've really missed you." He leaned into her.

She hugged him until it was time to stop. "Are you ready?"

He nodded.

"Can you tell me which way is west?"

He pointed at the yellow sky.

"Are you hungry?"

"Yes, ma'am," he said. "Very."

The drive back was slower, gentler; and they talked a lot as she drove, about cactus and tarantulas and a dapple-gray mare with a brother for sale two valleys south. The days were warm for March, and long; and the boy stared often through the window. Elizabeth wondered at his thoughts and guessed they were of a father he might never see, and of a girl who might just make a sister. He grew quieter as the green fell away, and rivers dwindled. But, there was nothing wrong with silence, and he was wise to know as much so young. So, she left him to the fullness of his thoughts and led him into the desert. It was another day, another life, and family waited beyond the mountain.

In the best books, the ending often comes as a shock.
Not just because of that one last twist in the tale,
but because you have been so absorbed in their world,
that coming back to the harsh light of reality is a jolt.

If that describes you now, then perhaps you should track down
some new leads, and find new suspense in other worlds.

Join us at www.hodder.co.uk, or follow us on
Twitter @hodderbooks, and you can tap in to a
community of fellow thrill-seekers.

Whether you want to find out more about this book,
or a particular author, watch trailers and interviews, have
the chance to win early limited editions, or simply browse
our expert readers' selection of the very best books,
we think you'll find what you're looking for.

And if you don't, that's the place to tell us what's missing.

**We love what we do, and we'd love you to be part of it.**

www.hodder.co.uk

 @hodderbooks

HodderBooks

 HodderBooks